The Ravanmark Saga
Book Three

I0639285

Trials

of the

Redeemer

Sandra Miller

Trials

of the

Redeemer

Trials of the Redeemer

Published by Onda Mountain Books

Cover Art

© Kriscole | Dreamstime.com

© Mega11 | Dreamstime.com

© Photowitch | Dreamstime.com

© Chorazin3d | Dreamstime.com

Cover Design

By Karri Klawiter, www.artbykarri.com

Discover other titles by Sandra Miller at

www.sandra-miller.com

Sandra Miller

Chapter One

DAHLIA

"Okay," Alannys said, rubbing at her temples, sitting on the edge of the bed in her wagon, "so that was unexpected." She figured that was probably the understatement of the year—she'd left the Great Palace on a mission to help the king, but also to run from the hopeless fact that she loved him more than anything, and he was engaged to the Princess of Cadenda. And after all this time traveling with the Singari, growing closer to them—to Chen—this strange, belligerent woman showed up and announced her betrothal to Chen? It was beyond unexpected—it was more like a giant slap in the face from fate. "Engaged?"

Chen flopped into the chair by her writing desk. He had marched her straight back to her wagon without a word, at a pace that precluded any conversation.

Naturally, the woman had followed them. She had barged right into the wagon as though she belonged there, and hovered now by the door, a thundercloud ready to rain all over whatever parade Chen was planning.

Chen sighed, and flashed a look in the woman's direction that clearly wished she was just about anywhere else. "Look, Alannys, it really isn't like that."

"It is so!" the woman piped up.

Chen shook his head. "My parents arranged that marriage when I was sixteen. Without any input from me, I could add. And Dahlia has been gone for two years. It isn't fair at this point to hold me to—"

The woman at the door exploded into a fury of Singari words spoken so quickly Alannys couldn't make out a single one.

"Wait," Alannys said. "You are Dahlia?"

The woman balled her fists and drew a deep breath, forcing herself under control. For just a moment, she seemed to sway where she stood, and reached out to the doorframe for support. "Yes. What of it?"

"Nothing. I—I've heard of you." Alannys was thoroughly torn. Dahlia obviously didn't care for her, just as obviously because Chen did. And yet, Alannys still remembered the story Dorramon had told her, and she was inclined to regard her as a friend. This woman had saved him, at a time when it would have been easiest and safest to go about her business. Alannys had to admire that, and she felt some measure of gratitude towards this fiery woman.

Dahlia quirked an eyebrow at her, but didn't seem inclined to pursue it. "I don't understand. You say that Chen is not *markortha*. And he and I have been betrothed for years. Yet he," she jerked her chin in his direction, "acts as though I have intruded on something."

Chen ran a hand through his hair. "You have to know that no Singari would honor a betrothal when their betrothed has been gone from the tribe for two years. Tradition gives me—"

"Gone to look for her!" Dahlia protested shrilly, pointing at Alannys. "You can't pretend not to know what happened. You yourself were present when I prophesied the coming of the Redeemer. You were there when the *zhotha* gave me the mission to go and seek her out. You knew where I was and why, and now you want to hold it against me?" She shook her head. "Tradition! What has Chen ever cared for tradition?"

"You're right," he said. "I don't care to bow to tradition just because it is tradition. And arranged marriage is one tradition I have no use for."

Dahlia looked stricken. Her face looked unnaturally pale and waxy in the low light—except her cheeks, which burned a brighter red than seemed possible from just anger or embarrassment. "But Chen, surely—"

"Alannys is right," he cut her off, standing. "I am not *markortha,* regardless of what the tribe may think. She has not accepted me. But I mean to keep trying, Dahlia. The day that Alannys accepts my suit is the day I marry. No other."

"I see." Her voice was brittle, splintering in Alannys's ears. "And the king? Does he know of this?"

Alannys could feel the color drain from her face under Dahlia's shrewd gaze, but Chen just shook his head. "The king has his own betrothal to contend with, and little choice. His fate is set."

"As is yours! You do not have the right to do this. You do not have the *choice* to do this."

Chen turned from her. "It is late, and I think we have kept Alannys from her sleep long enough. Perhaps you should go to your wagon now. Your mother will want to see you."

"Yes," Dahlia said bitterly, "she will want to hear how you are trying to break what your parents arranged between us." She turned on her heel and left, slamming the door behind her.

Chen sank back into the chair. He looked completely exhausted.

"You can't put her off forever," Alannys said quietly.

"She'll take it to the council."

"Let her," Chen said. He sounded completely exhausted, too. "I will not be forced. What would you have me do, Alannys? Do you really want me to marry somebody I don't love and never have, just so that you won't have to bear the burden of my presence anymore?"

She looked away. "No, of course not. No one should be forced to marry. And you are not a burden, Chen. You've saved me, over and over. If anyone here has borne a burden, it's you."

"Then may I bear that burden forever," he said. He leaned over and kissed her forehead, then let himself quietly out of the wagon.

♫

It all felt very unreal in the morning. Alannys vividly remembered the fear, though, and the helplessness she had felt when that cloaked figure dropped out of the trees right in front of her. So she got up before the sun, strapped on her belt with Songstrike in its sheath, and went out into the forest to find herself a clearing.

The slight, familiar sound of the blade clearing the scabbard seemed comforting somehow, almost welcoming. She crouched into Ready posture, hefting Songstrike in front of her, relishing its balanced weight in her grasp. Her feelings surprised her. Why had she come here? For practice?

Or punishment?

It didn't matter. She progressed through the various defense postures, and then the attack postures, moving slowly, stretching, giving herself time to warm up.

Her stretches finished, she fell back to Ready posture, imagining a faceless, sword-bearing opponent across the clearing, mirroring her posture back at her, ready to fight.

Her eyes narrowed, studying her shadowy opponent, waiting for him to make the first move. Even in practice, she would not strike first. She was not looking for a fight.

"Aren't you, though?" Her opponent's voice sounded breathy and faint in her mind, but if he'd had a clear face it would have been smug. "Don't kid yourself. You aren't here because you're frightened—you're here because you're *jealous*."

The voice only existed in her mind—the *person* only existed in her mind—but the words hit her like a slap in the face. For a moment she considered jamming Songstrike back into its sheath and going back to camp.

But if the words carried a sting, it was only the sting of truth. Finding out about Chen's engagement *had* upset her, and it shouldn't have. She knew these accusations came from some part of her own mind, and if she didn't do something about it, she'd hear this kind of bitterness constantly, in her own thoughts.

"Poor little girl," the shadowy apparition said, with venom in its voice, "every man she gets close to is already engaged. Just destined to be the other woman, aren't you?"

Alannys flexed her fingers, and tightened them around Songstrike's grip. She could already feel her muscles shaking, and she hadn't even really started practicing yet. Just how far out of shape was she? "Chen doesn't acknowledge that engagement."

Great, now she had gone right past hearing voices to *talking back*.

With a wordless shriek, her opponent charged her, sword high. Alannys raised Songstrike to block.

The impact was imaginary, just like the rest of the battle, but Alannys swore she could feel its jolt in her arms and shoulders, could feel the weight of her opponent pressing into her blade, trying to force it aside. For the first time, she seriously wondered what was going on here. She grunted, pushing back.

"Only because of you!" Abruptly her opponent's form

was Dahlia's form, the angry eyes that glared at her were Dahlia's eyes, and the venom in its tone became Dahlia's venom. "If you weren't here, Chen would honor his engagement, have a wife and a family. You're ruining his life!"

Alannys dug her boots into the earth, braced herself, and flung Dahlia backwards. She charged in with a low attack, goaded by guilt. "That's not true! He just doesn't want to marry you."

"Which never happened until you came." Dahlia turned sideways, neatly dodging, and spun to face her again in a guarded Ready position. "What about Dorramon, the one you claim to love oh-so-much?"

"Shut up." Alannys's voice was a snarl in her own ears. They were both fighting with all they had, but only she was out of breath. It was easy—too easy—to forget that this opponent was imaginary. She should have been able to turn and walk away—but she found herself afraid that, if she did, she would be run through. "I do love Dorramon, more than anything. I'm doing all of this for him—I've given up everything for him. I love him more than life!"

"Then let Chen go!" Dahlia howled, launching a vicious middle attack.

Alannys danced out of the way—narrowly. She swore she could hear the hiss of the blade skimming across the cloth of her shirt. "I'm not holding him!" She wrenched Songstrike back around to Ready position. "I don't have any claim on him—I don't even have any right to try!"

Dahlia's eyes narrowed, surveying her shaky stance and sweaty, matted hair. When she spoke, it was in a hiss so low Alannys had to strain to hear the words, but hate and contempt dripped from each syllable. "Then *stop leading him on!*"

Alannys stood stunned, frozen in place as doubt and

fear washed over her in waves. Chen was her friend. She valued that friendship, treasured it, but...

Was Dahlia right?

A sharp, predatory smile split Dahlia's face, and her blade streaked forward. Before Alannys could even begin to raise Songstrike to guard, the blade pierced cleanly through her chest.

♫

Songstrike slid from Alannys's limp grasp, and she sagged to the cold, damp forest floor. She knew she couldn't really be hurt—and yet she lacked the energy to keep herself upright. Had she really driven herself this far, punished herself this hard, battling her inner demons?

A guilty conscience, she thought, cannot be vanquished with a sword.

Grass pressed against her face, wet and uncomfortable. It would have been nice to get up off the ground, to go rest her tired body in her own bed.

It would have been nice to fly, too. One was about as likely as the other. She'd been sick and injured too many times—her reserves were too low, and she wasn't going to be able to move until she'd rested, one way or another. She fought it, but she didn't even have the strength to keep her eyes open. Sprawled out on her face in the foggy forest clearing, Alannys fell unwillingly asleep.

It was dark, suddenly, disorientingly dark, and where she lay huddled on the ground, gasping, unable to move, she could hear trees rustling and frantic shouts. She knew things were bad, and she knew it was her fault, and she knew she was about to pay for it. She couldn't move, and the calls of her friends were still much too far away to save her from the doom that hovered over her now.

Her skin prickled, and the hair stood up on the back of her neck, and she knew without even looking that she was being watched through a painting. If she could turn to look behind her, she would see the telltale gray formless blur of the opening the painter had created.

Of course, if she could turn to look behind her, she wouldn't waste time looking. If she was capable of any movement at all, she would be out of there, running for everything she was worth.

But she couldn't, so she laid there, her body as useless as an empty shell, until rough hands grabbed her from behind and hauled her through the void behind the gray blur, into the painting and away from all her friends and anyone who could possibly help her.

"Alannys—Alannys!"

The voice was Chen's, she knew that. But it seemed so far away. Sleep weighed on her like a physical force, and it was easier just to drift back down under it.

"Dammit, Alannys!" A sharp, quick pain stung one side of her face, then the other.

She dragged her eyes open. "Did—did you just slap me?" Her words were slurred and indistinct, heavy with sleep.

Chen was kneeling beside her in the grass, clutching her against him. His hands tightened convulsively on her, but it took him a moment to answer her. "Yes. Yes, I did. Muses, Alannys, I came out here looking for you and found you face down in the grass with your sword by your hand—you felt cold—I couldn't wake you—I thought you were dead!"

Even in her muddled state, she could hear the anguish in his voice. It did nothing for her guilt, and she struggled to lighten the mood, putting on a weak smile. "I wonder how I would have died, out here all alone with no injuries?"

He stood up and dragged her to her feet, sighing. "How would I know? When you start dealing with Talent, anything is possible." He peered worriedly into her face. "What in the Seven Hells were you doing out here by yourself, this far from camp?"

She stretched and turned from side to side, testing her balance. Her heavy nap had left her feeling dazed and off kilter, but she did seem recovered from her exhaustion. "Practicing. I haven't had a good practice with Songstrike in a while now." It wasn't exactly a lie, but it *was* a half-truth, and the look on his face said he knew it. "I can't get too rusty. I can't always rely on others to protect me."

He folded his arms and regarded her crossly. "Not if you insist on running off by yourself, you can't. Did it ever occur to you to ask someone to come with you? Did it ever occur to you that maybe it was dangerous for you to be out here alone?"

"No," she said honestly. "But I wouldn't have asked even if I had thought of it. You need to stop taking risks for me, Chen."

"Not going to happen. So you came out here to practice. Fine. Why did I find you unconscious on the ground? What happened?"

She could feel her face burn. "I wasn't unconscious—I was asleep. I overdid it a little, I guess—I was so tired when I finished I couldn't even stand up, much less walk back to camp. So I took a nap." She could hear the hollowness in her words—it wasn't a convincing story, even to her own ears.

Chen buried his face in the palm of his hand. "You overdid it. Yes. You came out into the wilderness in a strange place and worked until you collapsed, all alone." He leaned over and picked up Songstrike, and handed her the blade with a sigh. "I know you don't want to rely on us too much, Alannys. But please think about what you're doing before you take this kind of unnecessary risk. This whole world is depending on you, whether they realize it or not. They need their Redeemer. If you go and get yourself killed, where will they all be?"

She slid Songstrike back into its sheath, trying not to notice the slight tremor in her hands. "Appealing to my sense of civic duty, Chen? That isn't like you."

"It's the only thing I think might get through to you. You obviously don't want to hear how I feel. Maybe the rest of the world will have better luck." His voice sounded tight and controlled, but she could see the strain on his face. "But...Alannys, if you have the slightest feeling for me at all, you will not wander off alone again."

She couldn't look at him, and since there was nothing else in the clearing to look at, it made for a very awkward situation. She couldn't give him the promise she felt he was asking for, but she couldn't bring herself to say that.

Chen sighed. He seemed to sigh an awful lot lately, and the thought made her sad. He had been such a happy, carefree person when they met—it seemed she had dragged him farther down the longer she had known him. "I was looking for you because the Council of Elders have called a meeting this morning. They felt you should be there."

"Good enough for me," she said. "Lead the way."

"Sure," Chen snorted. "After the way I found you, it makes perfect sense for you to just skip back to camp on your own."

"Chen, I—"

"No. You gave me a scare once today; you're not doing it again." He took her arm and tucked it around his own, and started back towards camp.

Alannys forced herself not to sigh. She really *had* shaken him—even now his grip on her arm was tighter than it needed to be, as though he feared she might slip away. And if she was honest, she was leaning on him perhaps a little more than she strictly had to. Neither of them spoke, as he pushed aside his pain and she pushed aside her reservations, so that they could stay together a while longer. Neither of them said what they really felt. It almost wasn't necessary; the way they walked together said it all. And she couldn't help but wonder — how much longer could he take this?

How much longer could either of them take this?

♪

One of the young guards held open the *zhothamol* door, and Alannys nodded to him as she passed, still clinging to Chen's arm.

She had not been in the wagon since the proceedings where Brutagar had been exiled. It was amazing how much the same everything was in there. The same simple furnishings, the same threadbare rug on the floor, the same wooden chairs — but one was now empty. It was the first meeting of the *zhotha* since Legara had died, and her replacement on the council had not yet been appointed. That empty chair pulled at Alannys's conscience. If she had never come to these people, would Legara still live?

She had no answer for that. Unappeasable guilt assailed her, though, and she had no defense. She allowed Chen to escort her a chair on the right side of the room, suddenly not much in the mood for idle conversation with anyone there.

Dahlia sat on the left side of the room, regarding Alannys through narrowed, suspicious eyes. Alannys wasn't much in the mood for that conversation, either — she had her own suspicions about the reasons for that look.

Chen pulled up a chair right next to Alannys and sat down without glancing at anyone else in the room.

"Let's get started," Bayred said. "Dahlia, the *zhotha* would like to hear about your time away from the Singari."

"As you wish." Dahlia stood and moved to the center of the room. She had a proud, almost regal bearing — Princess Delline herself could not have crossed that room with more dignity. "As you know, almost two years ago I was dispatched on a mission to find and protect the Redeemer, and to bring her back to the Singari."

Chira nodded. "Yes, child. Can you report on the success of this mission?"

"Considering that she lives among us now as *kortha*, I would report the mission as a success."

Chen snorted.

"Ballocks," Bayred said. "Alannys found us on her own, and we convinced her to be *kortha* — you weren't anywhere around. Just what have you been doing since you left?"

Dahlia swayed on her feet. She grabbed the back of a chair to steady herself, then favored Bayred with a venomous glare. "My prophecy indicated that the Redeemer would be found in Glennayre. More specifically — "

"Yes, yes," Bayred cut her off. *"Brought into the land by Lord Malrec's hand*...we all know. Getting down to brass tacks, then, you went to Glennayre?"

"I did." Dahlia's irritation was evident, though it seemed to Alannys that she was working hard to contain it. "I spent quite some time in the town of Glennayre, living among the people, making connections. But by the time I heard of her arrival, Alannys had already been at Castle Glennayre for two days. Lord Malrec was very deliberately keeping that quiet. I made my plans to go to the castle the next morning. I had even arranged for quick transportation out of the holding if it became necessary. But during that night, Prince Dorramon and Arch-Prince Raman broke into the tower and rescued her. By the time I heard of it the next morning, they were well on their way to the Great Palace with her."

Chen glanced at Alannys sidelong; this was apparently a part of her story he had not heard before. Everyone in

Ravanmark knew she was involved with the king—very few, it seemed, knew how that had happened. She blushed, remembering. It all felt like another lifetime now.

Dahlia looked at Chen looking at Alannys, and a positively unholy smile spread across her face. "I stuck to my duty and followed them. I knew I was on the right trail when I discovered their campsite. I wasn't sure it was theirs at first, to be quite honest with you—I knew they had three travelers, but I could only find evidence of two tents. Of course, they only had two horses—they were used to sharing. But after the Tibadoan assassin attack we've all heard about, I found that they had three horses—but they still slept in those *same two tents.*"

Alannys's head flew up from her melancholy contemplation of her hands in her lap, her cheeks burning with anger and embarrassment. Dahlia was misrepresenting everything, and the gloating smile on her face said she knew it.

"By the time I reached the Great Palace," Dahlia continued, "the prince and the arch-prince had already returned to the keep, taking Alannys with them, of course. As you know, I am not permitted into the keep, so I spent that night in the Outer Ward, collecting what information I could. The palace servants are always a rich source. Through them I heard that Alannys had a cold reception from the king and queen, and that Prince Dorramon supported her with a passionate outburst and dared to leave their presence unexcused. He even—he even *went back to her room with her!* It all sounded so romantic," she said with a wink at Alannys, "I was sorry I couldn't have been there."

Alannys felt her hands ball into fists in her lap. She glared at Dahlia with everything she had, but she knew she was blushing to her ears.

Bayred frowned. "You are dwelling on details. The

palace was a waste of your time, Dahlia. Lady Alannys was already very well looked after."

Dahlia laughed cruelly. "Indeed she was."

"You've been warned," Chira said, "and I suggest you stop. I don't see what reason you could possibly claim for doing this."

Dahlia did not respond, but Alannys looked at the way Chen's shoulders slumped, and thought that she could see the reason easily enough.

"Is that all you've done?" Bayred demanded. "Follow her?"

Dahlia shrugged, trying to look unconcerned, but her face was hard. "It is true that I have spent a good deal of time following after her, always ending up a day or two behind. I miscalculated in Brookeshire Holding. I went on into Grissom, when apparently she had met up with you and turned south to Pinevale. By the time I figured that out and went that way, you had moved on."

Bayred regarded her severely. "I see. Is there anything you can tell us, then, that we don't already know? Or was your mission a complete failure—just a jumble of wasted travel and useless gossip?"

Dahlia bristled. Alannys took a vicious pleasure in seeing her get some of her own back. "Don't think I have been idly resting these past two years. I have risked life and limb and suffered much hardship to collect information that will be useful to us all."

"Yes, yes." Bayred rolled his eyes. "Such as?"

"King Caleb was murdered."

♫

A sudden silence gripped the *zhothamol*. No one moved, no one spoke. It felt as though the entire world had suddenly stopped spinning as Alannys tried to make sense of what she had just heard. She finally released a breath she hadn't been aware of holding. "How do you know this? King Caleb died of rye fever."

Dahlia's mouth quirked up in a hard smile. "Indeed. But don't you think it was odd there was no big outbreak? Just a handful of cases, all within the palace staff. No one died but the king."

"But how can you know it was deliberate?" Alannys pressed. This changed everything...everyone at the Great Palace had assured her Lord Malrec could gain no foothold there. But if King Caleb's death had been an assassination...

...then everything that had happened since had been deliberately planned, from the fiasco at the coronation, to the preparations for civil war. Just the thought made her stomach cold.

Alannys clenched her fists even tighter in her lap, feeling the bite of her own nails digging into her palms. Surely Dahlia was reaching. She must have been relying on the curious circumstance of the small outbreak to decide it was an intentional murder, to try to save her reputation with the *zhotha*. Anything else was unthinkable.

"I had it from the man himself," Dahlia said. "The one who brought the contaminated rye into the kitchen, who made sure the bulk of it was used in King Caleb's meal, and the rest sprinkled into some other random meals. He had a bit too much to drink one night at the Oaken Shield and told me all about it."

Alannys stared at her. She could hear the ragged panting of her own breath, the labored, irregular thumping of her heart in her ears. This—couldn't be true. Her hands felt cold. "Who is this man? What is his name?"

Dahlia regarded her curiously. "His name was Romas, not that it matters now. The man is dead. He was found murdered in his home two days after the king died."

"Murdered? And nothing was done?"

She shrugged lightly. "You have had a privileged life in Ravanmark, Alannys. Among royalty and nobility, such

21

a thing would be scandalous. But the kitchen servant was a peasant. No one will notice or care about one peasant more or less."

Her attitude seemed heartless, but Alannys knew where it came from. Substitute "Singari" for "peasant", and you had a pretty good summation of the way the world regarded the tribes. Even the peasants considered themselves above the Singari.

Alannys sat back heavily in her chair, weak with sudden despair. She couldn't find a hole in Dahlia's story, couldn't find anything on which to hang an argument that it was untrue. She rested her elbows on her knees and buried her face in her hands.

"So." Bayred sounded displeased. "We still must decide the outcome of Dahlia's mission. I vote failure. She didn't find the Redeemer, or even *help* the Redeemer—not even once. And the death of the king is hardly information worth the effort."

"I disagree," Chira said. "I vote that the mission is successful, for even if what you say is true, you cannot fault her intent. Dahlia has worked hard, for a long time, separated from her people. That has to count for something."

Bayred grunted. "One failure, one success."

"This has never happened before." Chira frowned. "A two-person council is unfortunately prone to splits. Lady Alannys, as *kortha*, you will cast the deciding vote."

"Success," Alannys said, without lifting her face. She felt Chen's sympathetic hand fall on her shoulder, but she didn't move. "Dahlia has fought hard and suffered much, and uncovered things no one else could have. She is a hero."

"Then it is settled," Chira said. "Dahlia's mission has been found a success. We will go make the announcement. Dahlia, come with us, please."

The elders filed out of the wagon, and Dahlia followed.

Alannys could almost hear her mind spin in the heavy silence they left behind, struggling to figure out all the ramifications of what she had just heard. It seemed too big for comprehension. Every possible consequence of this that she could think of was negative. Her pained sigh sounded like it came from someone else.

"Alannys?" Chen sounded hesitant. He squeezed her shoulder. "Are you all right?"

She sat up reluctantly. It was amazing, really, how the world could keep on looking the same when everything in it had just changed. "Yes. No. I think my whole life just cracked."

"I understand it was unexpected news," he said, even more hesitantly than before, "but is it really that shocking? I mean, it doesn't really affect you."

"Doesn't really affect me? Are you kidding me?" She stood up out of her chair, suddenly unable to sit still. "Everything we did, everything we planned, was based on the assumption that Lord Malrec didn't have any influence inside the Great Palace. I argued with them—I *told* them, but they wouldn't believe me. And now—this changes everything. Just everything."

She slammed out of the *zhothamol*, stomping off toward her own wagon in a sudden aggravated fit of motion. Chen followed her, hurrying to keep up. "What are you doing?"

She threw open the door to her wagon and stomped inside. She unfastened her sword belt and laid it and Songstrike carefully across the writing desk, then flopped down on the edge of her bed. "I need to talk to Dorramon. This changes *everything*. He has to know." She glanced sharply at him standing in the doorway. "And I'd like to be alone."

Chen looked uncertainly back over his shoulder, then at her glowering on the bed, but he made no move to leave. "I'm not sure I want to know what this mindlink communication between you two is like," he said slowly. He came into the room, and sat down in the chair by the desk. "But I'm not leaving you alone, not like this. Whatever it is you have to do, you're going to have to do it with me here. I promise to stay out of your way."

She regarded him balefully a moment, hoping he would cave in and leave. The mindlink was the most personal thing she had, and it made her very self-conscious to think of deliberately using it in front of Chen. Still, she knew it didn't matter; she had to speak to Dorramon. Immediately. She just wished she didn't have to do it with an audience.

"If you think I like this any more than you do, you're out of your mind," he told her flatly. "I would rather do just about anything else than sit here while you commune with my rival. But you aren't yourself right now, you have to see that. You've been acting weird all day, and I am not leaving you alone like this."

She kicked around the idea of leaving the wagon herself, but she couldn't think of anywhere else to go where she would be guaranteed any kind of privacy at all. At least here she only had to deal with Chen—nobody else was going to come wandering into her wagon.

Fine, then. She ignored him, leaning forward and burying her face into her hands, resting her elbows on her knees. She hadn't used the mindlink in so long it felt strange to open it. That upset her—how had she slipped so far from Dorramon?

Dorramon? Your Highness, can you hear me? It was like shouting into a long, dark tunnel, and she was certain no one could hear her.

Alannys? Alannys, is that you?

Yes, she told him, though privately she wondered who else he expected to hear talking to him in his mind. He must have been feeling much the same as her. *I need to talk to you.*

Hold that thought, he told her. *Let me make my excuses and get out of here — I can't concentrate with all this drama going on.*

Busy day at court?

She could hear his wry laugh in her head. For some odd reason, it drove home the distance between them, and that made her sad. *Aren't they all? Ambassador Thell can't come to my court, but lately he's conceived of the very clever notion of sending lackeys in his place. It looks like I'm going to have to ban all emissaries from Cadenda as well, to keep any peace at all around here.*

Alannys hesitated. *Ambassador Thell is still banned from court?*

Yes, why?

Well...aren't you engaged to the Princess of Cadenda?

Last time I checked, yes. His tone was dry.

She tried to word her thoughts carefully; Dorramon seemed sensitive on the issue and she didn't want to provoke him. *Then does it make sense to ban Cadenda's emissaries? I mean, you are going to have to talk to them eventually, if there is going to be a wedding, right?*

If there is going to be a wedding, he said, *yes. Hold on, let me get Raman out here to cover for me.*

Alannys sat for a moment in confused silence. She didn't pretend to understand all the complexities of being a king, but she didn't see what this oddly antagonistic approach to Cadenda was getting him. Maybe it was a bargaining strategy that aided him in their negotiations over how exactly the royal marriage would be handled. Or something. She couldn't really even guess. It was plain Dorramon did not wish to discuss it, however.

I'm back, sorry, Dorramon said suddenly. *I wasn't*

expecting to hear from you.

She wasn't sure what he meant by that, but it made her uncomfortable. *Well...this is important. Someone just returned to camp with news I think you need to know now.*

You sound upset. What news is this?

Alannys took a deep, steadying breath. *She tells me that King Caleb's death was no accident, Dorramon. She says your father was murdered.*

There was a short, shocked silence. *This could be meaningless rumor,* he said, and she could hear the strain in his voice, could hear him struggling to remain calm and objective.

I wouldn't have bothered you with a meaningless rumor.

Of course not, Alannys. I'm not trying to fault you at all. Like I said, I can hear that you're upset. I know this is important. I just want to be sure I understand the whole situation. Who gave you this information?

Dahlia.

Dahlia? Larric's sister Dahlia? Even in her mind, his surprise was clear.

Yes. She has apparently been away from camp for nearly two years, and she's spent a lot of that time recently following me around. She just got back last night.

Dorramon swore. *If Dahlia is your source, I'm more inclined to believe it. Did she have any specifics about this?*

She told me that she heard the story from Romas, the man who delivered the contaminated rye into the king's meal and several others, one night when he had hit the ale a bit too hard. She says that Romas himself was murdered shortly after King Caleb died.

If Romas indeed worked in the palace kitchen, and is now dead, I can confirm that easily enough, Dorramon said slowly. *But I don't see any reason to doubt her story. This is distressing news.*

Distressing? Distressing? Distressing doesn't begin to describe it! Dorramon, don't you see what this means?

Everything we have done has been done on the assumption that Lord Malrec has no foothold in the Great Palace. I left to draw the threat away from you. But what if that is what Lord Malrec intended all along? What if instead of drawing the threat away from you, all I have done is left you unprotected? What if everything I have done, my entire mission, has been wrong from the beginning?

Calm down, Dorramon said soothingly. *I'm not unprotected — you know that. And Lord Malrec isn't going to attack me directly, not yet.*

Why not? She made an earnest effort to be calm, but she could still hear the fear in her voice.

Because he doesn't have you. You are the biggest force in this war, Alannys, and he has known that since he brought you here. He isn't going to make any direct play for the throne unless and until he has you.

She swallowed hard. *I don't like the sound of that.*

I don't either. But now that we know about this — there are precautions that Raman and I can take here at home to help guard against this type of sneak attack. Short of a full-on physical assault, Lord Malrec isn't going to be rid of me.

I don't like the sound of a full-on physical assault either, to be honest with you. I don't like where you are sitting right now, Dorramon. It's too dangerous.

Dorramon laughed gently. *Wherever a king sits is dangerous. That never changes.*

She could feel a hard lump in her throat. It was a good thing they weren't face to face after all; she would never have been able to speak. His courage humbled her. *Just — just be careful, okay?*

His tone grew serious. *I am here in my castle, surrounded by loyal forces. But you — you are out there alone. I know the Singari would do their best to defend you, but they have never faced anything like what is coming. I'm worried about you, Alannys.*

She could feel his genuine concern, like a warmth

enveloping her. *I know. Time is running out, I can feel it.*

Promise me you'll finish your work as quickly as you can and come home safely.

Dorramon, I don't know if I can make that promise. Things are moving fast, and Lord Malrec has sworn to kill me if I refuse him in the end. I may not —

Don't talk like that! I want your promise, Alannys. It's the only way I'll be able to sleep at night.

She had a fleeting but clear impression of dark nights spent tossing and turning in the royal bedchamber, an impression she was sure he had not meant to let slip. Dorramon was losing sleep at night — over her? *I promise. I promise you, Dorramon, I will finish out here and I will come back to the palace, just as soon as I can. Don't waste any time worrying about me, okay? You have enough to deal with right now without making it worse.*

She could hear him sigh. *Thank you, Alannys. And thank you for bringing me this news. You be careful out there. Listen, I know I shouldn't be saying this to you, but I love you. No matter what happens, please don't ever forget that.*

She could feel her eyes burn with sudden tears. She wondered if she could keep them out of her mental voice. *I love you, too, Dorramon.*

They closed the connection between them, but she didn't move from her huddled position on the bed. If she didn't move, she wouldn't have to talk to Chen. And right now, she just wanted to be alone with this aching pain, this gaping hole inside her that she didn't know how to close. She wasn't ready to share, or worse, to act like nothing of any significance had just happened.

It worked, for a few moments. But before long her tears seeped through her fingers and splashed to the floor between her feet, and she felt the bed give under the weight of someone sitting next to her, felt a hand fall gently on her back.

"Alannys? Are you all right?"

"Yes." Her voice was muffled in her hands—even so, it sounded anything but all right.

"What happened? Is the king angry?"

"No, no, nothing like that." She sat up, wiping tears from her face with her fingers, and hauled a handkerchief out of her pocket. "I don't really want to talk about it. It won't make anything better. He's just—he's just so far away."

Against her will, she began to cry in earnest. Speaking to Dorramon had opened a huge, jagged wound in her soul, a wound she managed to keep covered most of the time. But it was open now, and her tears would not be held back. She pressed her handkerchief against her face and sobbed.

"Oh, no," Chen said, reaching for her. "No, no, no. Come here." He pulled her into a warm hug, rocking her side to side. "It's all right."

She didn't feel all right. Nothing felt like it would ever be all right again. She leaned into his chest and cried and cried. He never rushed her, never pushed her, just held her close and waited for her tears to subside.

And eventually they did. Little by little she pulled herself back together, until she finally stood up from the bed and dug out a clean handkerchief to dry her face.

Chen regarded her somberly. "Better?"

"I am, thank you." She turned away from him and strapped on Songstrike, then slung her leather cloak around her shoulders and fastened it.

"Hey, wait—what are you doing?"

"I'm going into Shadowkeep. We need to know what the town is like, find out if there's anything we can use there."

Chen stood up, staring at her in surprise. "Are you sure you want to do that right now?"

"I have to. I'll go crazy if I sit around in this wagon all

day." She threw open the wagon door and hopped down the steps, untying Quicksilver from the hitch. "A ride will do me good."

"A ride it is," Chen said, and whistled for Nightfire. "Slow down, Alannys. Why are you moving so fast? Are you trying to outrun me?"

"No," she said, and forced herself to slow down. She was moving so fast, so erratically, that she hadn't yet managed to undo the knot in Quicksilver's lead rope. She made herself move slower, and prepared Quicksilver for the ride. Chen didn't demand any further explanation, so she didn't offer any. No, she wasn't trying to outrun Chen.

She was trying to outrun something much more painful than that.

♫

"So tell me," Chen said, "how do you know Dahlia?"

The sound of his voice was sudden and jarring in the heavy quiet of Orinthal. They had been riding without speaking since they left the camp. If it had been left to Alannys, they would have ridden all the way to Shadowkeep without exchanging a word. She knew she was lousy company, but what could she do?

"I wouldn't say I know her," she said slowly. "I believe I said I had heard of her, which is more accurate. Dorramon told me about her."

"He did, did he?" Chen laughed. "I have to admit I had kind of forgotten that story. I'm surprised he told you, really. It doesn't put him in the best light, sneaking off and hunting up trouble."

For some reason this assessment bothered her. "No, I suppose not. Still, at least Dorramon owns up to his mistakes. It's not like we don't all make them."

Chen held up his hands in surrender. "Of course, of course. I didn't mean anything. Not everybody would be as forthcoming. You sure wouldn't get that story out of Dahlia."

"Really?" Alannys frowned, considering it. "I would have figured she'd be proud that she saved the Crown Prince."

Chen laughed again. She didn't know if he really found everything amusing today, or if he was just trying to raise her spirits. "I don't know about that. But she sure did get in some trouble for it. Unmarried people don't dance, for one thing. But that's how Dahlia is, nobody ever talks sense into her when there's something she's decided she wants to do. And then kissing him?" He shook his head. "The council had a special hearing about it. She was severely reprimanded."

"How did she take that?"

"I could tell you, but I wouldn't use words like that in front of a lady. You know, I wouldn't be surprised if that was a big part of the reason her request to go on this crazy mission to find the Redeemer was granted. I think the *zhotha* were relieved just to get rid of her for awhile, to tell you the truth. She does have a tendency to stir up trouble."

Alannys looked at him sidelong. "And you are engaged to her?"

"*Was* engaged, Alannys, was engaged. You've got to remember I had no say in that. I had no desire to marry her then, and I still don't. My parents were very ill, for a very long time. I was only about sixteen. They were worried about what would happen to me when they were gone. They arranged the engagement to obligate Dahlia's parents to take care of me." He shook his head again. "And that didn't even work. It made them feel better, but I was always capable of taking care of myself. They worried about me because I am not really the responsible type...but I am nowhere near as hotheaded and reckless as Dahlia is. I do well enough for myself. Dahlia's mother has never had to lift a finger for me."

Alannys nodded and said nothing, not really eager to explore the subtleties of Chen's relationship with Dahlia. The atmosphere around them was heavy and oppressive. Gray light filtered from the dark clouds over them, and off in the distance she could see flashes of lightning. It felt like there was always lightning flashing somewhere in Orinthal. On their ride they had passed only one house, and it had been burned to the ground.

"Alannys, please..." Chen's voice sounded strained. "If there is any chance for us at all, don't turn your back on it because of Dahlia. She's a grown woman who is perfectly able to take care of herself. I will not be held to anyone else's idea of what I should do with my life. I know you care for the king, but I know you care for me, too, even if you aren't ready to admit it."

Her face burned. "Chen, it isn't possible to love two people at the same time. Not like that."

He didn't look at her. "It is," he said, and his voice was low. "You don't see it yet, but everyone around you can. Don't count me out just yet."

She didn't have an answer for that. She rode in a silence that suddenly felt demanding, trying to imagine what she could possibly say to him now.

Quicksilver suddenly stopped short, dancing sideways and snorting when Alannys tried to urge him forward. He had been acting oddly the last few minutes — tossing his head and hesitating in his steps. His ears had swiveled and twitched, and he'd seemed jumpy.

Now, though, he refused to move on at all, turning back hard the way they had come.

Alannys gave up. "I can't hold him," she said, dismounting. She led him off the path into the trees, staking him in the center of a thick patch of grass. Quicksilver had been a Tibadoan warhorse. He bore more battle scars than she could count, and he had the stoutest heart of any horse she had ever seen. What could make him carry on this way?

Chen slid off of Nightfire next to her. "Looks like we're on two feet for the rest of this ride." He patted Nightfire's head and spoke quietly to him. The horse settled in grazing next to Quicksilver, seeming content.

Alannys shook her head. "I don't know how you do that."

Chen shrugged. "It isn't me. Nightfire is an exceptional horse."

They walked back out to the path into town. Quicksilver's behavior had put them both on guard, and Alannys found herself paying closer attention to their surroundings than she had before. The destroyed house they had passed seemed an ill omen.

They had only walked a few minutes when she stopped suddenly, sniffing the air. "Do you smell that? I swear I smell smoke."

Chen frowned. "No, I don't smell anything. Are you all right?"

She was turning in slow circles, staring hard as far as she could see in each direction. She didn't see any rising smoke, though, or anything else out of the ordinary. She sighed. "Yes, I'm fine. I guess Quicksilver just spooked me a little."

Chen grinned at her. "You'll be fine. You have a big, scary Singari bodyguard." He took her hand in his, and they continued walking.

They came to the top of a little ridge, and there, hunkering at the bottom, was the town of Shadowkeep.

The town looked like it had been through a war. Everywhere Alannys looked her eyes met with evidence of recent devastation. Houses stood empty, doors gone and glassless windows staring like vacant eyes. The houses that were occupied were locked up tight, with windows boarded over or hung from the inside with heavy cloths and blankets to block the light and keep the inhabitants hidden. A few dogs and cats roamed the streets, once pets, now feral. There were starved people, their lean, desiccated bodies left in the streets. The few crops left around were brown and withered, and no one could be seen tending them.

"This place is a nightmare," Alannys murmured. They'd shambled down the hill towards the corpse of Shadowkeep in a shell-shocked, disbelieving haze. But as soon as she set foot in the town, all she wanted to do was leave. "What happened here?"

"I don't know," Chen said, frowning, gazing around him as though he couldn't credit the evidence of his eyes. "This—this is unreal—last time we were through here, it wasn't anything like this. Orinthal has gone downhill in a big hurry. Whatever happened here, happened fast."

Was it her imagination, or did she see a twitch of movement in the cloth covering that window? And that one? Was she going crazy with paranoia, or were there behind some of those shuttered windows those who watched?

She pulled her hand out of Chen's, checking Songstrike in its scabbard. The feel of the solid grip under her fingers was reassuring. She leaned closer to Chen and spoke softly. "How are you with a blade?"

"I carry a knife," Chen said, "but I've never needed to use it."

"I'm not sure whether that is reassuring or not. Is it because you never encountered trouble, or because you are so good at dealing with trouble you never even needed the knife?"

Chen laughed dryly. "I'll leave that to your imagination."

She shook her head, but kept walking up the main

street. "I don't know, I'm getting a pretty bad feeling about this place. If we weren't so bad off ourselves I wouldn't set foot in this town. But surely there's an inn — a tavern — *something* where they can tell us what happened here and where we might find supplies."

"Surely," Chen echoed, walking beside her. She didn't think he sounded convinced.

They wandered the town for some minutes in wary silence. The further in they got, the more hollowed-out buildings they found; just burn-marked, roofless shells. Signs of civilization, or habitation at all, became fewer and fewer. A haze of acrid smoke hung over the middle of town, stinging their eyes and making them water.

"That's it," Alannys said, pulling the collar of her shirt up over her nose and mouth. "We are leaving. We'll just have to make do until we find another town."

"Wait," Chen said. His voice was muffled; she turned to find he had covered his face with the crook of his elbow. "Look down there. I can see a sign."

He was right. A splintered sign hung in front of a two-story building down a small side street, creaking in the slight breeze. *The Last Abode*, it said in careful hand-lettering, next to a painted picture of a bed. The little street was a dead-end. A shiver skittered down her back.

"I don't know," she said doubtfully. "I think we had better just go."

"Come on," he said, grabbing her hand and pulling her down the street. "We have to try. That's what we came here for, right?"

She didn't answer, but she allowed him to drag her along with him. *Just a quick detour,* she told herself, *and we are out of here.* This place was seriously giving her the creeps.

As soon as they reached the inn, they could see the effort had been futile. The inn had been burnt, gutted by fire. The entire second story had burned to nothing, leaving the blackened, ragged edges of the first-story boards reaching up into the emptiness like skeletal, splintered fingers. Jagged bits of thick, cloudy glass hung in the window frames like old teeth, and the remnants of a door hung crooked from one broken hinge in the doorway.

Alannys stared up at the wrecked building in horror. She remembered well enough Ibira's sobering descriptions of the terrible state of Orinthal in general, but somehow that had not prepared her for the level of deliberate, lawless destruction she was witnessing in this town. Was the entire holding like this? She was suddenly, fervently thankful that Baroness Lae and her twin baby girls were safe at the Great Palace, far away from this horrible place.

"Well, Chen," she sighed, "this was a wasted effort." She frowned. When had he let go of her hand?

"Not at all, luv," said a strange voice from behind her, "not at all. We ain't had strangers in town for ages."

Alannys froze, and turned around in slow, dull terror. While she had been staring at the ruined inn, three of the ugliest, meanest-looking men she had ever seen had descended on them. Two of them stood a few paces away, holding Chen with his arms wrenched up behind his back. One of them had stuffed a dirty rag in his mouth as a makeshift gag.

Closer to her was the third man, bigger than the other two, watching Chen's predicament with evident pleasure. His hair clung to his head in dirty mats, and in his unpleasant grin she could see several missing teeth, and several more that were black.

"You b'lieve our luck, boys?" the big man called. "The Singari's come to town! I tell you, I was bored somethin' fierce, and I just *love* the way they dance."

The other two snickered. The sound reminded Alannys

of rats rummaging in loose garbage, and it made her skin crawl.

"Whaddya say, boys," the big one continued, drawing a long, pitted sword from somewhere in his layers of filthy clothes. "Wanna make the Singari boy dance?"

"Naw, Ralep," replied the skinny, pale man on Chen's left. He had a reedy, thin voice, and he continued to snigger even while he spoke. "We ain't had fresh meat in ages. Let's eat him."

"*Eat* him?" echoed the man on Chen's other side. "Are you serious?"

The skinny man shrugged. "He's only Singari. And I'm right hungry."

The big man laughed as though this was the best joke he had heard in days. "Always thinking with yer stomach, you. There's time for eating later. Dancin' first." He stepped forward, raising the sword.

Alannys felt suddenly cold, even under her heavy cloak. "That's enough!" she said, her voice ringing with command. "Let him go. Let him go right now and I may let you live."

Chen looked at her, his eyes wide with fear, and shook his head. She stared at him in pole-axed shock. Was he honestly telling her she shouldn't have spoken? Was that why he had kept so quiet, to give her a chance to run?

She couldn't believe it. There was no way she was leaving him like this.

The three men goggled at her. She didn't know if they hadn't noticed she was there, or if they just hadn't expected her to speak up.

The big man—had they called him Ralep?—reached out and caught her arm in one meaty hand, pulling her right up against him. She could smell the rancid reek of him, feel his sour breath waft across her face when he spoke. "Well, look, the Singari boy has a lady-friend! Don't worry, darlin', we'll make you dance, too—but later. Women shouldn't dance in the streets, you know, but in our beds. Ain't that right, boys?"

There was a peal of nasty laughter from the other two. Chen struggled against them, and she could hear him trying to shout around the gag in his mouth.

Before she could frame a response to that, Ralep gave her a shove that sent her flying into the rubble at the end of the street.

Alannys pushed herself up on her hands and knees, her brain churning frantically. She desperately wanted a peaceful way out of this. This place was crawling with danger, and not just from these three. Given the condition of the town, it was infested with bullying, sadistic scum like these. The odds were sorely against her. She couldn't afford to draw any more attention to them, effectively sending up a signal flare calling trouble to them.

"Jealous, are you?" Ralep took a step closer to Chen. It made Chen look small somehow, and helpless, held there in front of that hulking giant of a man. Chen glanced at her, and drew himself up as straight as he could against his captors. "Don't worry, my little Singari friend. We ain't forgotten you. I expect we'll have all kinds of fun together."

His size was deceptive. The man moved like a striking snake and thrust the sword deep into Chen's side.

Alannys couldn't move. She wanted to scream, wanted to shriek from the bottom of her soul, but she couldn't force herself to move, couldn't even breathe. The entire world seemed to stop turning, and everything she felt, everything she was, narrowed to the sight of that piece of metal, sinking inch by inch into the abdomen of a man who had ever been her friend.

Chen stiffened, jerking against the men holding him, and the sheer animal howl that came from him chilled

Alannys's blood. She knew in that frozen moment that she would carry the echo of that sound to her grave.

How had this happened? How had she failed him so utterly?

She came up off of the ground with Songstrike in her hand, just as Ralep pulled the sword out of Chen. "You are going to regret that."

With a speed that seemed impossible given his bulk, Ralep turned to face her, his bloody sword held in front of him. "Look, boys, the Singari's woman wants to play!"

She and the big man circled each other warily. Neither wanted to strike first, and give the other an opening. Alannys could feel time pressing her like a physical force. She needed to get Chen out of there, and now.

The other two looked on uncertainly. "You want us to help you?" She didn't know which one had spoken; the two were interchangeable to her.

"No, you thimbleskulls," he retorted. "I want you to hang on to the Singari boy. You think I can't take care of an uppity bitch waving around her boyfriend's sword?" He laughed unpleasantly, eyeing her stance for weak spots. "This won't take but a minute. And she'll still be good for later, you watch."

Alannys didn't like the way Chen slumped against the two thugs that held him. She had to hurry this up. She reached out with a middle feint, hoping to draw her opponent into giving her an opening, but he didn't bite.

He swung his blade wide. By the time she realized he was feinting, she had already moved to block. It put her within arm's reach of him, and his hand shot out and grabbed her arm, yanking her closer. She just had time to see his giant fist rushing towards her face before she was knocked back onto the packed dirt road.

She had never fought someone like that—his rough-and-tumble techniques had caught her completely off guard. He slashed wildly at her with his sword as she fell, and ripped the shoulder of her shirt open.

Alannys pushed herself back up onto her feet, shaking her head to clear it. Her face was bloody and her shoulder burned, but she didn't have time to worry about that right now. As soon as Ralep saw her get back up, he closed in again.

"Look," he said, "she wants to play some more! I like a woman with spunk. We're going to be good friends, you and me. You just got to learn who's your better."

He stepped in toward her, and Songstrike flared blue in her hands. Finally! She couldn't figure what had taken so long—maybe she had been confident on her own until that sucker-punch had landed her on her backside.

Ralep froze. "Seven Hells! What's that sword doing? What's that mean?"

"It means," she said with a cruel smile and a good deal more confidence than she actually felt, "that you are about to meet your doom."

Before Ralep regained his wits and attacked her, she started to sing.

"Songstrike glows blue,
with the power of the Muses
to punish those who do wrong..."

"Ag! The bitch can sing!" Ralep dropped his sword and clapped his hands over his ears. "Run, boys! We got to tell Ethal about this one. He'll fix her!"

Before she even finished the three lines, the thugs had scattered, disappearing like rats into openings in and between the derelict buildings, openings that she couldn't even see.

Chen crumpled limply to the ground, like a marionette whose strings had been cut. Blood soaked his white shirt in a wet, scarlet circle, still expanding.

Alannys ran to him, falling on her knees at his side. "Chen!" She pulled the rag from his mouth, and frantically grabbed his hand. It scared her to find it cool, and pale.

"Alannys." His eyes fluttered open, and focused on her. "Alannys, you're hurt."

She shook her head. "How can you even worry about that right now?" She grabbed her sleeve where it had been cut and ripped it from her shirt. Balled up and pressed into Chen's side, it seemed to help stem the bleeding. She yanked off her belt, slid Songstrike's scabbard off of it, and buckled it around him to hold her makeshift bandage in place.

He didn't make a sound while she did all this, but his lips were pressed into a thin, tight line. "I'm sorry," he breathed. "That bastard...Alannys, you should have run."

"No." She blinked back tears. "If you say that again I'll hit you myself." She looked frantically around for something, anything, to help her move him. "We have to get you back to camp."

"Nightfire," he rasped.

She shook her head. "I'll never get you to him, not in the shape you're in."

"Call him."

"You really think he'll come?" She hated questioning him—he sounded as though every word was a monumental effort. But Nightfire came when Chen whistled. She couldn't see any reason to believe he would come for her, and she couldn't go hunt him down herself.

Chen's pale lips quirked up in a small, painful grin. "I love you. That's enough for him. You'll see."

He sighed and closed his eyes, and she felt black, dizzying panic swirling up like a maelstrom in her mind, ready to swallow her whole. What if he died here? What would she do? She almost blacked out until she saw his chest rising and falling and realized he was still breathing.

She had no other options, and time was running out. She stood up and turned her face to the sky, cupped her hands around her mouth and shouted to the heavens. "Nightfire! *Nightfire!*"

Time seemed to crawl by. She knew the horses were outside of town, but still, it seemed to her to be taking too long. The whole idea was crazy anyway — how could Nightfire even have heard her? How would he find her, if he had? She couldn't blame Chen for the idea — he had lost a lot of blood and wasn't thinking clearly. But how could she have believed it? How could she have thought help would come?

No, this was going to be entirely up to her. She had to get him back to camp, and come back for the horses later. Hopefully no one in this godforsaken town would find them before she came back — they would probably eat them.

She stood up, scanning the burnt-out husks that used to be buildings for anything she could use. She couldn't carry him, and he couldn't walk, or even hold himself upright. Maybe she could make some sort of stretcher, and drag him back...? It sounded awful, but what else could she do? They were both dead if they stayed here.

She heard a sound from the main road and spun around, grabbing Songstrike up off the ground. What new trouble was this?

Alannys had never truly understood the meaning of not believing one's eyes — not until she looked down the road and saw Nightfire trotting towards her, shaking his mane, with Quicksilver close behind. Quicksilver was dragging his lead rope, stake still attached, with roots and dirt stuck to it.

"I don't believe it," she breathed. "Chen was right."

She never was quite sure how she managed after that.

The next clear memory she had was riding hell-for-leather out of town on Quicksilver, Chen slumped unconscious in front of her. Nightfire stayed right with them. She never saw a soul as they left Shadowkeep. That was fine with her.

She had all she could handle worrying about the fast-fading soul she held in front of her.

♪

Quicksilver didn't slow down until he stood in front of Alannys's wagon. Silently, she thanked him — she'd had her hands too full with Chen to guide the horse.

Chen had not fared well on the ride. His lips were pale and blue-tinged, his breathing shallow and erratic. He felt alarmingly cool, even though he had been pressed up against her for the entire ride. She was afraid to think about how much blood he must have lost. She hauled him out of the saddle and attempted to wrangle him up the few steps and in the door.

It wasn't easy.

"You!" The voice behind her was bitter, and shrill, and unmistakably Dahlia. "It's about time you showed up, I have been looking everywhere for — "

She came up next to them and stopped short, staring. "Merciful Muses," she gasped, and turned on Alannys like an avenging angel. "What have you done to him? How did you let this happen?"

Alannys shook her head. She could understand Dahlia's concern, but couldn't the woman see this was no time for explanations? "Help me...get him...inside." It was all she could do to get the words out; somehow Chen was much heavier going uphill.

"Are you daft? *Your* wagon? In case you have forgotten, Chen is *my* betrothed. I don't know what you were thinking, running around with him all day, but I'll not allow — "

"Lady Alannys, is there a problem here?" The quiet,

dignified voice came from Alannys's other side, and it cut cleanly across Dahlia's tirade. She felt Chen's weight on her lighten as someone helped lift him.

"Drigo! Oh, thank heaven — Drigo, Chen is wounded. Badly. Help me get him inside."

"Of course, my Lady. Dahlia, if you would please stand aside..."

And in his polite, cultured way, Drigo shouldered Dahlia out of the way and carried Chen inside the wagon.

"Put him in the bed," Alannys told him, following him inside.

"This is an outrage!" Dahlia fumed, following Alannys. Her face was red and damp, and she held the door frame for support. "*Your* bed? You can't seriously intend to keep him here!"

Nashara appeared in the doorway. "Pardon me, but it looked like I was needed here."

"Please," Alannys said. "Do everything you can for him." She stepped back from the bed.

Nashara clucked over her patient, carefully removing Alannys's jury-rigged bandage and probing the wound with her fingers.

"That's how you brought him back here?" Dahlia's accusing tone was really beginning to grate. "A leather belt and the sleeve of a dirty shirt? Muses, it's a wonder he's alive at all!"

"Hush," Nashara said severely. She looked at Alannys, and her eyes were sympathetic. "You did well, child. You saved his life."

"Saved his life?" Dahlia snorted. "She's the only reason he's in this condition at all!"

"OUT!" Alannys hadn't realized she was going to explode until she shouted. "I want everybody out of this wagon right now except Nashara!"

Dahlia put her hands on her hips and didn't move. "I

don't think so. You aren't going to—"

Alannys grabbed her by the arms and forced her bodily out the door and down the stairs. Drigo followed them without comment, closing the door softly behind himself.

Dahlia seemed too furious for coherent speech. "I—you —you *dare*—"

"Shut up," Alannys told her flatly. "Listen to me, and listen good, because I am only going through this once. You are not coming in that wagon. Not today, not tomorrow, not until and unless Chen asks for you."

Dahlia stared at her in speechless shock.

"Your engagement is your own problem. I can tell you that Chen does not recognize it, but you already know that. I don't care. That man is wounded—he is in there fighting for his life and you are bitching and moaning about where he is and who is taking care of him. I don't know what's wrong with you and I don't care. He deserves better than that." She pointed with her finger right in Dahlia's face, forcing her to step back. "You—are —not—coming—in—there. Nobody tends to Chen but *me*."

Nashara came quietly out of the wagon carrying her leather bag, wiping her hands on her apron. She looked over at Alannys and nodded slightly.

"I'm sorry," Alannys told her. "I don't mean to slight you, Nashara, but I'm serious. I have to do this. Nobody tends him but me. I would be forever in your debt if you will help me to do that."

"Of course," Nashara said mildly.

"Drigo, please make sure we aren't disturbed with anything unnecessary. I'm counting on your help."

Drigo inclined his head. "Of course, my Lady."

Her patience was gone. With one last warning glance at Dahlia, Alannys went back inside her wagon, and slammed the door.

♪

The faint pink light of dawn began to scatter through the Singari camp at the foot of the Cloudytops, but Alannys never noticed. A single lantern burned low in the corner of the dark wagon, as it had burned all night. Her eyes were raw and red-rimmed, her face was dirty, and her shoulder was caked with blood where Ralep's sword had clipped her when he cut open her shirt. She didn't notice any of these things.

She sat in a plain wooden chair drawn up to the side of her bed, as she had sat all night. She held Chen's hand in both of her own, and she sang, as she had sung all night.

It reminded her, in the back of her preoccupied mind, of another time, another place, when she had sung all night for another man who had been grievously wounded accompanying her on this journey. That was where the similarities ended though—she had been able to tend to Raman immediately. Chen had gone much longer without proper treatment—while she fought the thugs in Shadowkeep, while they waited for the horses, while she brought him back to camp. These things mattered, these things made a huge difference when you were considering a person's chances with such a severe wound in a place where the medical care was so primitive, at least by her standards.

She knew all of that, and it scared her.

But what choice did she have? Alannys was no doctor —and even if she had been, there was precious little that could be done here, with no access to the tools and drugs modern medicine had provided her all her life.

So Alannys did what she could do, which was sing. Sometime during the night Chen had spiked a fever. He had spent the night sweating and shaking, never regaining consciousness. Alannys held his hand, sponged his forehead, and listened to his agonized breathing, worried that every breath he drew would be his last. And she sang.

Just after daybreak, the door opened, and Drigo backed in, carrying a clay bowl and a waxed paper packet. He pulled the door shut, and turned around to face her.

"Lady Alannys," he said, stopping short, "have you been sitting there singing all night?"

She nodded, still singing.

Drigo turned to the writing desk and set down the bowl and packet. "Look, you can't keep at this. You have got to take a rest."

"I can't." Her grip on Chen's hand tightened convulsively. "Don't you see? He's getting worse. How can I rest while he's suffering like this? What if — what if he dies, Drigo? What if he *dies*, because I couldn't save him in Shadowkeep, while I am sleeping? I couldn't live with that. I just couldn't."

Drigo stood behind her, a sympathetic hand on her shoulder. "I understand," he said, looking sadly at his best friend. "I do. But Chen would not want you to push yourself like this."

That remark sounded too much like past tense for comfort — it stoked her fear, and a shiver ran down her back. She shook her head.

Drigo came around and knelt next to her chair. "What if I sit here with him? I cannot sing, but I can tend him. You could go rest..."

"No. I'm not leaving him."

Drigo sighed. "What if I bring Dahlia, then? You could be sure he would have attentive care — "

"Attentive?" She saw him recoil and realized she was shouting, but she couldn't seem to help it. "Attentive? You have to be kidding me. After the way she carried on when we brought him in? She griped and complained about everything from where he was to who was taking care of him, without ever stopping to look at him at all. I don't know whether her first concern is for Chen, or for pushing this engagement he doesn't want to hear about."

Drigo sat back on his heels. "Are you sure that's your only reason? Dahlia didn't handle that the way she should have, I can't fault your feelings there. But, Alannys — seen from a certain angle, what you have done is basically barred her from seeing her betrothed — at least in her eyes — while he needs care. Why is that, do you think? Don't you think there could be more to it than just her behavior?"

Alannys stared at him, shocked. "I'm sure I don't know what you're talking about."

"Don't you? Look at it from where I stand. The two of you are bickering like a pair of jealous girlfriends. That seems odd, considering only one of you was ever actually his girlfriend. I think you would not do this without a stronger motivation than what you have said."

"You sound like Chen. He always tells me that I have feelings for him I won't admit even to myself. It's rubbish, do you hear me? I'm not going to discuss this with you." She sat back in the chair, ignoring the flare of pain in her stiff back, and crossed her arms. "And I am not leaving him, Drigo."

Drigo stood up, shaking his head. "All right. You aren't leaving." He sighed. "I'll be back later — I will bring some extra pillows and blankets, so you can make yourself a bed here. Maybe you will rest if you are still in here and I sit up with him."

She stared stubbornly at Chen.

Drigo quietly let himself out. Alannys felt bad — he was only trying to help, she knew that. Maybe she was over-tired, but she couldn't seem to be reasonable. All she knew was that this mess was her fault, and she had to fix it. Anything else — any other 'motivation' — was just over-active imaginations at work. She'd be crazy to waste any more time on it.

She pushed herself out of the chair, and stretched her back to audible pops and snaps. Drigo had left her a bowl of lukewarm broth with a spoon, and some dried fruit and cheese wrapped in waxed paper.

Alannys carried the bowl back over to the bedside. She had a notion the soup might be good for Chen, if she could get him to eat any of it. She sat down in her chair, pushed his sweaty hair back from his forehead, and started spooning him the soup.

It didn't work—Chen didn't respond, didn't even swallow what she gave him. She dropped the spoon back into the bowl, gripped with a sudden fear of drowning him. Wasn't there *anything* she could do to help him? How could someone so supposedly powerful be so utterly useless? She had failed him in Shadowkeep, and now she was failing him here.

Frustration and anxiety washed over her in a wave, and before she realized what she was going to do, the bowl of soup crashed into her front door. Broth splattered the door, and bits of broken pottery littered the entrance.

For a moment, all Alannys could do was stare at the mess she had made. How had she lost it so completely? Drigo was right—she was pushing herself to exhaustion.

It didn't matter. She couldn't quit, she couldn't give up. She tried to imagine walking away from this spot, making herself a bed somewhere and sleeping as if Chen wasn't lying here fighting infection and heaven-only-knew what else. Her frustration bottomed out and all at once she collapsed against Chen's chest, sobbing.

"Don't die, please don't die—I couldn't bear it. You were right, Chen. All along you were right. I love you. Muses forgive me, I love you, and I can't do anything about it. If you knew what was good for you you'd get up this instant and leave this wagon and go marry Dahlia. I won't stop you, I won't even complain. Just—just *please* don't die."

Her position was impossible, she knew that. She couldn't turn her back on the king; she loved him more than anything—more than everything. She had promised him she would return, and she meant to keep that promise, no matter what. As long as Dorramon loved her, she would do anything he asked of her. And she had to admit that she couldn't stay away from him, not forever.

But Chen—Chen had all the freedom Dorramon did not. He was selfless, and kind, and he loved her, and like it or not she loved him back. And it didn't matter, it didn't change a damned thing, because she couldn't stay here.

She cried and cried, holding onto Chen with one hand, and clinging to the Seeing Stone with the other.

♫

The slow minutes crept into hours, then the hours blended into days. How long had Alannys sat singing by the bed, while Chen burned with fever? She didn't know. Or care. The days ran together like hues in a watercolor painting.

Fleeting impressions occasionally broke the haze. Nashara came in from time to time to change Chen's bandages, and apply pastes and compresses to the wound. Drigo brought pillows and blankets and made her a bed on the floor in the back of the wagon, but she never used it.

Once, in the silence of the wagon, she could hear a confrontation, right outside her door. In a different time, she might have gone outside, but in her current state she just sat staring at Chen's pale face, the angry words washing over her like waves over uncaring rock.

"You can't be serious. Chen is my betrothed, and that woman has kept him locked up in there for days—"

"You can't imagine how serious we are, Dahlia." The voice was Drigo's. "Chen would not want you in there, you know that."

"That's what *she* said. But what gives her the right to —"

"She is the *kortha*." Drigo's tone brooked no opposition. "And you know well enough the *zhotha* have upheld her decision. They don't recognize this engagement any more than Chen does."

"I won't stand for it!" Dahlia shrieked. Her words sounded slurred. "I'll break down the door! I'll take apart this *mol* with my bare hands! I'll—"

"You'll get thrown in the *prathamol* with Trago if you don't watch yourself." That was unmistakably Grald. "That what you want? You're raving."

Trago. The name meant something. It buzzed around the edges of her mind, demanding notice. She gave it none, and it faded away.

It wasn't important right now anyway. Chen still burned with fever, still had not regained consciousness. That was all she had time to worry about. She shook her head, and continued singing quietly. Days blended into nights, Drigo brought meals and took them away uneaten, and still she sang. Her voice became cracked and hoarse, her body rebelled against the lack of sleep, and her mind seemed to slip, but still she sang.

Was she doing any good? She couldn't say. She couldn't see any change in Chen, and Nashara stayed uniformly grim while she carried out her duties, never indicating one way or the other what she thought about her patient's progress or lack thereof.

It didn't matter. There was nothing else she could do. Singing was all she could offer Chen, and so she sang.

Until the day when the words stopped coming, the notes stopped flowing, and she slid limply from her chair to the floor.

♫

The sun was setting as Larric pushed open the stablehouse door. It had been a long day, and it wasn't nearly over. Lord Malrec and Princess Delline had recently returned from an evening ride in the carriage, and Larric needed to tend to the horses and put them up for the evening. It was nothing out of the ordinary. But an uneasiness had settled over him since Kalyn had left, and it gripped him especially hard tonight. He wished his Second Sight was more reliable—he might have known exactly what he was uneasy about.

Ah, well, he thought, stepping into his room in the stablehouse, nothing to be d—

Lord Malrec was standing in the little room.

Larric's heart nearly jumped out of his chest. He didn't need Second Sight to know that this was bad—really bad. He could imagine only one reason for Malrec to be here, now—and it didn't bode well at all. The revelation took his breath away for a moment, and his heartbeat pounded heavy in his ears.

Lord Malrec regarded him calmly. "Good evening, Larric."

"Good evening, my Lord. What—what brings you to the stablehouse this fine night?" He tried his best to sound conversational, but he knew it didn't matter.

"The princess and I have just returned," Lord Malrec said mildly. "As I believe you already know. We discussed some interviews we have had, seeking a replacement for Kalyn."

"Oh." Larric had known the conversation would turn this way. Still, he had to do what he could to turn it away. If things weren't handled just right... "Did you have any luck?"

"No. Can you believe it? Not a single person willing to come to work in Castle Glennayre." He shook his head and turned away from Larric, idly inspecting the row of leather cloaks and riding crops hanging on the wall. "Have you heard anything from Kalyn, Larric?"

"H — heard anything, my Lord?"

"Well, yes. You were her friend, correct? Inasmuch as Kalyn had friends. She really only knew you and I. And I certainly have not heard a word from her."

Larric didn't say anything. What could he say?

"Odd, that," Lord Malrec continued. His heavy velvet cloak moved with him, enveloped him like a shroud, as he wandered the room aimlessly, stopping here and there for a closer look at some object or another. "Don't you think? All those years here — she grew up with us — and then she leaves without a word. In the middle of the night. I wouldn't have thought she had that in her, would you?"

The silence stretched until it was awkward. Larric realized he would have to answer this question, somehow. "Well," he began slowly, "I — "

Lord Malrec turned slowly around to face him. He was idly twirling something heavy at the end of a ribbon in his hand.

To his utter horror, Larric recognized his royal medallion. All at once, he understood what it was that had worried him since Kalyn left — and it was every bit as bad as he had feared. He tried to smother his reaction. Involuntarily, his eyes flashed to the nightstand by his bed, the nightstand with the secret compartment where that medal had lain hidden for years, ready to secure him fast transport out of the holding, should he need it.

He suspected he rather needed it now.

"Yes," Malrec said, flicking the medal into the air and catching it, "it is a peculiar trinket for a stableboy, don't you think?"

There was nothing to say, so Larric said nothing.

"And do you know what else?" Lord Malrec sounded for all the word as though he were discussing nothing of much importance. "I found burlap in the burn barrel, and twine. I wonder how a man might ride into town with an incapacitated servant girl, put her in a carriage to the Great Palace, and make it look as though only one horse left that night?" He turned away, carefully hanging the royal medallion on a hook next to the riding crops.

Larric swallowed hard. "My Lord," he said, "I—"

Lord Malrec whirled back around, whipping his sword from under his cloak, and jammed it into Larric's gut with a force that buried it to the hilt.

Larric couldn't move, couldn't make a sound. Malrec yanked his sword back, and Larric stumbled to his knees, aware of the warmth spilling down his front, and his back.

"I am not your lord, you mongrel! For fifteen years you have worked here. Fifteen years, living under my roof, tending my horses—and serving another!"

Larric reached out and put his hands on the floor to keep from falling onto his face. His arms felt curiously heavy, but then, so did the face they were protecting. "Yes."

"At least you do not deny it! The Great Palace shall learn no more of my secrets from you!"

Larric heard a horrified gasp, somewhere above him. "Larric! Oh, Muses...Larric..."

He raised his head to regard Princess Delline, surprised by the effort it required. The pain had gone, replaced by a cold numbness, creeping outward from his wounded abdomen. "Your...Highness," he gasped. "I...am sorry."

Her face was streaked with tears and ghostly pale, as pale as his dying hands on the dirt floor in front of him. "No...no..."

"I hope...your brother can...forgive me..."

Lord Malrec stepped in front of him, his cloak spreading behind him like the wings of the Angel of Death. "You have bigger worries than your precious king, you filthy spy!"

The blood-slicked sword came down on Larric's neck,

and he knew no more.

♫

Princess Delline stared at the gore on the stablehouse floor in unseeing horror. "Lord Malrec — what have you done? How could you do such a thing — such cruelty — so unnecessary? How?"

Lord Malrec turned on her, the bloodstained sword still in his hand, hearing his own furious pulse pounding in his ears. "Unnecessary? That man was a spy! A spy for the Great Palace, living in my castle! And you — you knew that. All this time, I harbored a spy and *you never said a word*. Why? Your loyalties cannot possibly lie with me if you let a spy live unreported among us."

He could see her throat work in agitation. "That's not fair," she protested, and backed away from him, pushing herself against the wall. "Look at what happened to him! I've known Larric since I was a child. How could I bring that on him in good conscience?"

Quicker than thought, the point of Malrec's sword was at her throat. "Your tender conscience will have a good deal more than that to deal with if we are to reach our goals," he told her, and his voice was low. "This is it, Princess, last chance — are you with me or against me?"

He could see her trembling, but she held her head high and didn't give in. "How can you ask me for honest answers when you are holding me at swordpoint? Are you interested in my genuine feelings, or only in getting the answers you wish to hear?"

He threw the dirty sword down in the dirt and stepped in close to her, putting his hands against the wall she leaned on, one arm on each side of her. "You aren't leaving this place until you answer me, your Highness."

Unshed tears glistened bright in her eyes. "How can you even ask that of me? I've given up my home for you, turned my back on my family for you — I didn't even attend my own father's funeral!"

Lord Malrec regarded her evenly.

"You have everything I can give you," Delline said brokenly. "You have my heart, you have my hand. You have my undying love, my everlasting loyalty. I would give you my very soul if it would help you achieve your ends. Is that enough for you?"

Lord Malrec pulled his arms back and turned away from her, rubbing at the bridge of his nose. "You are right. I may seem foolish to question you. And yet..." He gestured at Larric's remains on the floor. "This is no small thing. My trust has been shaken, and I am unsure how to restore it."

Delline did not follow his gesture, keeping her eyes carefully averted as she stepped closer to Lord Malrec. "I am sorry. I think if you reflect upon it, you will understand my position. But still—I believe I have a way to prove my loyalty, and restore your trust in me."

Malrec raised an eyebrow. "Indeed?"

She swallowed hard and nodded. "Yes, my Lord. Forgive me, but—when Kalyn left, she took your focus statue with her, did she not?"

"Hmph." Malrec glanced disdainfully at the carnage on the floor. "Yes."

"Well, then. It seems to me that you are in need of a new focus. If...if I were to volunteer for the focus-bond..."

"Indeed. Indeed..." Lord Malrec took her hand, his eyes alight with something fearsome as he led her from the room.

♫

Alannys woke with a start, emerging suddenly from the thorny grip of the tangled, hellish dreams of Muse's Fever. She found herself wrapped in sweaty, unfamiliar blankets. It hurt to open her gritty eyes; her neck made grinding noises when she turned her head to look around her.

"M'lady!" Grald sat next to her on the floor. "You're

awake! We weren't expecting you back so soon."

Alannys realized she was in the makeshift bed Drigo had prepared in her own wagon. She was on the floor; everything looked strange. "How long was I out?" Her voice grated in her throat, rusty from disuse.

"Two days. After everything you did, we were afraid it'd be a whole lot longer."

He was right. She wasn't even sure how many days she had sung — it could easily have killed her. Two days was a bargain.

But still, two days — two entire days and nights, flat on her back and useless while Chen suffered — anything could have happened!

"And Chen?" she demanded with sudden urgency, pushing herself from the pillows to sit up, ignoring her protesting muscles. "How is he? What happened?"

"Is that Alannys I hear? Is she awake?" The voice was faint, strained, like a pale echo of its usual self. But it was *Chen's*, and hearing it made her heart stop. Grald offered a hand to help her up, and she made her way stiffly to the bedside.

Chen grinned up at her. He looked pretty rough, but he was alive and he was awake, which was better than he had been a couple of days ago.

Alannys sank down heavily into her usual chair. She was bone-tired; just walking those few steps had exhausted her. "You're alive," she gasped.

Chen reached for her hand and drew it solemnly to his lips. "Only because you saved me."

Alannys blushed a deep, vivid red, and pulled her hand back. She could still remember her breakdown, the agonizing confession the frustration and anxiety had wrung from her. But she also knew that no one else had witnessed her complete loss of control; no one else knew anything of the feelings she had expressed that day.

And she intended to keep it that way. Her heart was still Dorramon's, first, foremost, always. She could not give it to Chen, and she would not tear it in two. The only option, then, was to bury these feelings deeper than they had ever been buried before, and reveal herself to no one.

The silence had become awkward. Chen regarded her oddly. "Alannys," he said carefully, "are you —"

A shrill keening wail from outside the wagon cut him off, a sound like a heart rending in two. It sounded like something dying.

Alannys pushed herself from the chair and hurried outside into the evening air. She froze at the bottom of the steps, her befuddled brain trying to make sense of what she saw.

Drigo stood near the bottom of the steps, aghast. He didn't even seem to notice Alannys coming out of the wagon right next to him.

A few steps away, Dahlia huddled on her knees in the muddy grass, clawing at the sides of her head and screaming. A tureen lay on its side, spilling a heavy stew onto the ground in front of her.

"What have you done now, woman?" The cutting voice came from Drigo's other side, and Alannys stiffened at its sneering tone even before she recognized it as Pesia's. "She was just named a hero by the *zhotha* — can you leave nothing alone?"

"I didn't do this," Alannys snapped. "Drigo, what happened here?"

Drigo shook his head, looking pale and stunned. "I swear before the Muses I don't know. She said she was going to bring some soup for Chen. Then when she got here — this."

"It's your doing, somehow," Pesia insisted. "You've had it out for her ever since she returned to camp with glory and a claim on Chen."

Alannys ground her teeth together, forcing herself not to respond.

"You've even robbed my son of his chance to lead!" Lack of response did not seem to deter Pesia. "Why, with you and Chen both dead, Drigo would—"

"That's enough!" Drigo erupted into a fiery explosion of temper, like nothing Alannys had ever seen from him before. "I don't want to hear another *word!* You've gone mental—I've never wanted to lead, where I am now is as close as I ever want to be to *kortha.* The last thing I want in the world is to see anything happen to Alannys or Chen. Now you're throwing this mad fit while Dahlia is suffering, and I won't take any more of this! You're no longer welcome around me—leave!"

Pesia staggered away, stricken. Alannys turned her back and hurried to kneel beside Dahlia, who was still screaming like a wounded animal. "Dahlia? Dahlia, can you hear me?"

"Is she all right?" Chen stood in the doorway of the wagon, looking rather slanted, leaning heavily on the door frame. Alannys stared at him in surprise, wondering how much he had heard.

"She will be." Alannys glanced back at Dahlia, trying to believe her own words. "Go back to bed, Chen. We'll take care of her."

He nodded and staggered back inside, leaning on Grald.

Dahlia stopped screaming. She lay silent on the ground, quivering in the grass. Her eyes were wide and staring, but completely blank.

Alannys shook her head, passing her hand in front of Dahlia's unblinking eyes. "We've got to get her home, Drigo. She needs bed rest."

Drigo nodded, scooping Dahlia up off the ground. She hung there in his arms, limp and unresponsive. "I'll take her home."

"I'll bring Nashara," Alannys said, and headed towards the healer's wagon. She wanted to run, but she found that even a brisk walk made her vision go black around the edges.

The walk wasn't long at all, but her breathing was ragged and uneven when she got there. She leaned against the wagon, trying to catch her breath.

The door opened suddenly, and Nashara hurried out. "Alannys!" she said, surprised. "I was just on my way to check on you and Chen."

"I'm fine," she gasped. "Chen's fine. But Dahlia..."

Her lungs wrenched in a painful spasm and she couldn't say any more.

"Oh dear," Nashara murmured. "I had better go see her."

She hurried away. Alannys tried to follow her, but she soon fell behind. Luckily it wasn't too far, and she could see where the healer was headed. The wagon was neatly whitewashed, with tidy flowerboxes under the windows. Another matching but slightly smaller wagon sat behind it, attached by a short tether. A few goats milled around outside, grateful for the rest stop and the thick grass.

Nashara had gone to the smaller wagon, so Alannys followed.

Inside, Nashara leaned over a bed, checking Dahlia's eyes and the temperature of her forehead. A few steps back, an unfamiliar woman stood with her arms folded around herself, talking to Drigo.

"...just don't know what to do," she said fretfully, shaking her head. "She just hasn't been herself since she came back to camp."

"Now Deia, you must admit Dahlia was never what you'd call quiet," Drigo said, as neutrally as he could.

"Well, no. She's always been a bit spirited. But since

her return, she's been so shrill, and she seems feverish, all the time. She sways and stumbles—and that's not to mention her obsession with this silly engagement..."

"I believe it is generally agreed that the betrothal is no longer binding."

"Of course!" Deia sounded frustrated. "Any reasonable person should see that. Dahlia should have expected as much when she left, and to be honest, I thought she did. But the *zhotha* have had to adjudicate the matter, because she just won't let it go! I realize she has always been fond of the boy, but—"

"A light in the darkness, once bright, now gone." The voice was Dahlia's, but it was strange. Her words were stilted, as if the act of forming them hurt. She scanned the room with eyes that were wild and unseeing.

Alannys stood next to Nashara, noticing for the first time the rhythmic way Dahlia clenched and unclenched her fists. "Is she all right?"

Nashara shook her head, frowning.

"Cold," Dahlia continued. "The cold hand, the cold ground, the cold blood."

"She's raving," her mother whispered in quiet horror.

"The decision, once made, cannot be unmade." Dahlia spoke these words as though they were of great importance. Alannys had to agree she wasn't making a lot of sense. "Fate has turned. Fate has turned! The change, now made, cannot be unmade! *Larric is dead!*"

The words knocked the wind out of Alannys. As she watched, Dahlia began to quiver, then to shake, then suddenly she was in the throes of back-arching convulsions.

"A spoon," Nashara demanded, trying to keep her patient on the bed. "Bring me a wooden spoon!"

Alannys had no idea how Deia managed to lay hand to a spoon so quickly. Nashara wedged it between Dahlia's teeth, preventing her from biting off her own tongue.

"Is there anything we can do?" Alannys asked in dull horror. Dahlia seemed to be foaming at the mouth.

Nashara shook her head. "The fit will pass on its own. All we can do is wait."

Deia wrapped her arms tightly around herself. "What ails her?"

"Brain fever." Nashara pushed her gray hair out of her eyes.

"Brain fever?" Deia gasped. "But how? Why?"

"I don't know. We have not seen this in the camp. She must have picked it up from the outsiders."

"No." Tears welled up in Deia's eyes. "No, it can't be. It's too horrible!" She turned and ran from the wagon.

Nashara shook her head. "Drigo, stay with Dahlia. Come get me if she gets worse. I'll go fetch Deia back — we will need her to help keep watch over her daughter." She gave Alannys a sharp look. "And you need to be getting back to bed. It is not wise to push so hard, so soon after Muse's Fever."

"But Nashara...what she said — do you think..."

The healer waved a wrinkled, dismissive hand. "Don't think too much about it, Alannys. The ravings of brain fever are meaningless."

Nashara hurried out of the wagon. Alannys waved to Drigo, and let herself out.

She walked slowly back to her own wagon, trying to get her head around what had just happened. Most of Dahlia's metaphorical riddle-speak had gone right over her head.

Larric is dead.

Except for that. It seemed pretty clear, and if it was true, she couldn't even begin to calculate all the horrible ways their situation had just changed.

But what could she do about it? No one else took

Dahlia seriously, and she had to admit she could understand why. If, out of half a dozen nonsensical comments, one appeared to make sense, how much confidence could she really have that it was true? With the screaming and the convulsions, it was pretty clear that Dahlia was not in any kind of control.

It was, she had to admit, entirely possible that Dahlia's statement had been a random product of the brain fever, and completely meaningless.

The problem was that she didn't have any way to verify it either way. Even if she contacted the king, he would have no way to check on Larric without ruining his cover, and then he really would be dead. If she did contact Dorramon, she would only be upsetting him with information that was most likely not true.

If only she could verify it...

She shrugged, pushing open the door to her wagon. There was nothing she could do about this. She didn't like it, but she was going to have to accept it. She headed for her temporary bed in the back, moving quietly so she wouldn't wake Chen, trying hard to put the whole thing out of her mind.

♫

Nashara examined Chen's eyes, checked the temperature of his forehead, and listened carefully to his breathing. "You'll live," she pronounced. "Now get out of here."

Chen whooped, grabbing Nashara and Alannys into a bear hug.

"Now don't get stupid," Nashara admonished, as Chen's whoop dissolved into a groan of pain. "You're still wounded, young man. I said you'll live, not that you're healed."

"I understand, Nashara. Thank you." Chen kissed the old healer on the cheek and let himself out of the wagon.

"He seemed happy," Alannys commented with a grin.

Chen's good cheer was contagious.

Nashara made a non-committal sound, more acknowledging that she had heard than indicating agreement. "Alannys, I wonder if I could talk to you for a minute."

"Sure," Alannys said, surprised. "What's on your mind?"

"Trago. I wonder if you might go see him."

"What?" Alannys sat down heavily in her desk chair.

"He seems better. So much better I am thinking about advising the council to lift the sentence of *pratha*."

"That's terrific," Alannys said. "I had no idea. I haven't seen him since Chen got hurt."

"I know." Nashara hesitated. "I really think you helped him more by staying away than you did by visiting him every day."

"Then why in the world do you want me to go see him?"

Nashara sighed. "That's what worries me, actually. He seems well recovered. But what if he still has problems around you? You were the trigger for his last breakdown. What if it happened again?"

Alannys felt suddenly cold.

"Let me be very clear. I would like you to go talk to Trago. I don't want you to go inside the *prathamol*. Not for any reason. No matter what. You understand?"

"Nashara, I..." Alannys hesitated. "I'm just not sure this is a very good idea."

"Me, either," Nashara said grimly. "But his *pratha* was meant to be temporary, Alannys—if it's decided that it wasn't a temporary condition after all, he'll be executed."

"*Executed?* Isn't that a little drastic?"

"It's as drastic as it has to be. *Pratha* is dangerous—you've seen that better than anyone. If he can't recover, he'll be removed. I don't want to see that happen, so I'm under some pressure to get him released. But he'll be a danger to himself and to others if he's released when he isn't really ready. I don't want that to happen, either."

"And that's where I come in," Alannys muttered. "I see your point, I do, but—isn't there another way? Do I have to go alone?"

Nashara's expression was dark. "I hate asking you to do this. But taking anyone else would defeat the purpose. It has to be you, alone. Only then will I be sure he's really recovered."

Alannys nodded. She still felt kind of numb—it was hard to believe Nashara was asking her to visit Trago specifically because it might provoke him. She still saw his enraged face, felt his vicious blows, in her nightmares.

Nashara didn't wait around for Alannys to change her mind. She hurried to the door. She paused there, and turned back to Alannys. "I'm serious about what I said— do not go inside the *prathamol*. I don't want to patch you up again. Don't forget."

She gave Alannys one last, hard look, then turned back to the door and disappeared.

♫

Fierce wind whipped Alannys's clothes around her as she made her way to the *prathamol*. She hadn't grabbed her cloak for the walk across camp, and she was beginning to regret it. The wind was chilly, with an edge that promised rain.

The *prathamol* looked the same as ever, its plain dark sides drawing no undue attention, giving no hint of the drastic changes that had supposedly taken place within. All in all it looked the same as it had last time she'd been here, when Trago had spat in her face.

That, she thought, did not bode well.

Trago was not at the window. Either he hadn't heard her approach, or he just didn't want to talk to her. Alannys thought about the way the wind was roaring in her own ears, and decided to give him the benefit of the doubt.

Rain began to spatter against her face as she stepped up to the little barred window. "Trago?"

"Alannys." His voice was low and flat, with no inflection that might have given a hint to his emotional state. "Nashara said you might come here."

The rain picked up. With the driving, capricious wind behind it, Alannys found it was soaking her pretty quickly. And it was cold. She was beginning to wish she had begged off of this particular duty. But she knew that had never really been an option. She owed Nashara too much.

"Yes," she said, "she thought I should visit." Alannys shifted uncomfortably, transferring her weight from one foot to the other. Her words had sounded stilted and forced; she could hear it herself.

Trago said nothing, regarding her through the iron bars.

The silence stretched out until it was awkward. Then it stretched out some more. The sky opened up and the rain fell with brutal intensity, stinging like needles where it struck bare skin.

"You're soaked," Trago observed dispassionately. "You should come inside."

"No. I can't."

"Then go home."

Alannys shook her head. She couldn't leave yet; she hadn't done her job. Her teeth were starting to chatter though; she hoped this wouldn't take much longer.

"Stubborn, aren't you? Have it your way, then. No matter to me—I'm not the thimbleskull standing in the rain."

He had a point. She gritted her teeth and tried to think of something to say to him. How was she supposed to assess the likelihood he would attack her, anyway? She hadn't done so well with that before, when he had nearly killed her.

That line of thought didn't bring her any closer to something to say that would hold up her end of the conversation. She cleared her throat and shifted her weight back to the original foot.

A hailstone bounced off of her arm and landed near her feet. Alannys thought for a moment that Trago had thrown something at her, and before she had worked out what was happening, two more hailstones the size of plums landed near her. She threw her arms up over her head and huddled next to the wagon—she couldn't imagine what it would feel like to get hit by one of those, and she didn't want to find out.

"That's it," Trago said, and he sounded harsh. "Come in or go home, but don't just stand there. You'll be killed if you stay out in that."

He was right. The hail fell faster now—she didn't think she could even make it back to her wagon. Alannys edged around to the front of the wagon, trying to stay under the narrow eave, and unbarred the door.

Nashara would kill her, she knew that. But if she didn't get under some shelter, she would be dead before Nashara ever got to her.

Alannys hurried up the few steps inside the wagon. She stopped short, shivering in her wet clothes, and stared around the little room in disbelief.

She had already known that the *prathamol* was smaller than any other wagon in camp. What she had not realized was how barren it was inside, lacking all of the charm and the furnishings of wagons like her own. There was a pile of threadbare, moth-eaten blankets next to the back wall that apparently served as a bed, and a chamberpot in the corner. Beyond that, the room was completely empty, just weathered wood and iron bars.

"This is where they've kept you all this time?" Her voice sounded faint.

Trago shrugged. "You're supposed to spend your time in here thinking. It wouldn't work if there were distractions." He leaned back against the wall, regarding her over folded arms. "A person really has to let go of their anger to find any kind of peace in here."

Her teeth chattered. There was nothing in the room she was comfortable looking at—not the nest-like tangle of blankets, not the chamberpot, and certainly not him. "So did you? Find peace?"

"Almost." There was something about his lopsided grin that made her back up a step; it looked more mean than amused. He stepped closer to her, like a predatory animal moving in. "I heard the *markortha* almost died. You almost got what you deserved. We were almost even. And I almost had peace."

Alannys gaped at him, shivering, while his words washed over her colder than the hailstones falling outside. She thought of Chen, and the abuse he had taken trying to secure her a chance to flee. She thought of his fevers, and sweats, and the countless hours she had spent singing, not knowing if he would live or die.

Anger exploded in her chest and before she knew what was going to happen, Trago was pinned against the wall, her left hand clamped around his throat. Almost of its own volition, her right arm drew back for the biggest blow she had ever delivered to anyone in her life, the blow that would cave his face in.

Trago laughed. It was a tired, hoarse laugh, more than a little insane.

The sound of it stopped her for just a split-second, made her pause just long enough to realize what she was doing. She froze, suddenly understanding the terrible precipice on which she stood. Trago laughed, waiting for her to jump off that precipice, waiting for her to beat him senseless.

It never happened. She lowered her arm, and took her hand away from him stiffly, as though it was someone else's fingers she was prying loose from his throat.

Alannys stepped back, unable to look at him, appalled at what she had become. "I'm sorry," she said, rubbing her hands roughly over her face. "I'm tired — I've been sick, and worried — and I'm just not myself. I'm sorry, Trago." She stumbled toward the door, ready to face the rain, the hail — whatever it took to get away from there.

"Damn it, Alannys!" Trago grabbed her shoulder and turned her back around. "Why won't you just hit me? I know you feel like it, you know I deserve it."

"No. If I started hitting you, I'm afraid I'd never stop. And that's not the kind of release either of us need."

"Maybe I do," he said darkly. "Maybe I would be better off as the man a woman beat to death than as the man who nearly beat a woman to death."

"No." She took a deep, shaky breath. "I know it must be a hard thing to live with, but you're going to have to find a way. The Singari still need you."

Trago threw up his hands in frustration. "Where is your anger, woman? You of all people must condemn me for what I did!"

Alannys thought about it. "I condemn what you did. I do not condemn you." She turned away to regard the rain falling outside the little window. "I can't explain it. But Dorramon is in constant, terrible danger, and I can't do anything about it. And watching them attack Chen, and how he fell ill, how he suffered..." She shook her head. "It gives me a tiny, pinhole view into what you went through, Trago. A tiny glimmer of understanding of what it must have been like. I can't judge you for how you handled it, especially knowing that I'm the one who caused it."

The sigh that came from Trago then sounded like a soul collapsing under a weight too heavy to bear. "You didn't cause it. I will never like you, Alannys, but I can't keep laying that on you. Mirenne believed what she believed, and she acted on her own." His voice broke. "It wasn't your fault she died."

Alannys turned around in shock. Trago wept, big tears tracking through the dirt and stubble on his face.

She understood. That was an admission she had never expected to hear him make. The blame he had cast on her for Mirenne's death—and the subsequent rage—had shielded him from the crushing grief that now threatened to consume him.

She could have tried to comfort him. But he didn't like her and he never had, and she was sure that any move she made would be unwelcome.

"I'm sorry," she whispered, and bolted out of the wagon, barring the door behind her.

The rain had faded to a heavy mist. Alannys barreled through it, head down, intent on getting back to her own wagon.

"How was he?" The voice was Nashara's, from somewhere to her right. "Do you think he should be released?"

Alannys nodded sharply and kept moving. She didn't trust herself to speak just then.

♫

It didn't seem like very much later when Chen came bounding into the wagon. If you didn't know better, Alannys thought, you would never guess that his ribs were still tied up tight underneath his shirt, that the deep wound in his side was packed but not healed. He seemed paler than usual, but his eyes danced, and the smile on his face when he greeted her was genuine.

"I need you," he said, and stopped suddenly in the middle of the sentence, frowning at her.

"We knew that," she said. She tried to laugh, but it came out sounding weak. "What do you need?"

Chen watched her, chewing on his lip. "What happened?"

"Nothing."

She could see him thinking it over, probably considering pushing her. Finally he shrugged and let it go, and she sat back in her chair, relieved.

"I need you to come with me to see Dahlia."

"I have to admit," she said, "I didn't expect to hear that. Doesn't that seem a little...odd?"

"Maybe. She would certainly think so." Chen looked away. "But no matter how she's been acting lately, Dahlia is my friend. And she's sick. I have to go see her."

"True. But why do you need me?"

"I need you *because* of the way she's been acting lately! If I go by myself, she's going to get the wrong idea."

"Hmm. You're right." Alannys pushed her chair away from the writing desk, and stood up. "That's fine. I was wondering how she was doing anyway. It looked pretty serious when I saw her last."

Chen nodded solemnly, holding the door for her. "It sounds like it was. I've heard that was the worst of it, though, and she's recovering."

"I hope so. I don't see how it could get much worse."

The whitewashed wagon was as she remembered it. Dahlia sat up in her bed, eating soup and talking to her mother. Deia had a chair pulled up to the bedside, but she left it when Chen and Alannys came in.

"Chen! And Alannys — I'm so glad you two could come." She grabbed Chen up in a motherly hug. "She's much better. I think you'll have a nice visit." She glanced over her shoulder at her daughter, patted Chen on the shoulder, and let herself out of the wagon.

"Well, that was sudden," said Alannys, looking after

her.

"Like mother, like daughter," Chen laughed. He grabbed her hand and pulled her over to the bedside, keeping her close to him. "Hello, Dahlia."

"Chen! I'm so glad you came." Dahlia glanced down at his hand holding Alannys's, then looked back at her soup. "I hope you two won't mind if I keep eating. I know it's rude, but I'm half-starved."

Alannys pulled her hand out of Chen's and used it to make fluttering dismissive gestures. "No, no, that's fine with us. You need to get your strength back."

Dahlia shot her a look that might or might not have been grateful, and spooned out some of the thick soup in her bowl. "How was Trago today?"

Alannys thought the stunned look on Chen's face probably matched her own. Chen hadn't known she went to see Trago; she hadn't known Dahlia knew about it. "News doesn't take long to reach you," she observed, lowering herself into Deia's chair. "Trago is well. Or rather, he will be. He faced some difficult truths today. I think he will be released soon."

"That's good. It's disgraceful—the Baron-Apparent of Orinthal locked in the *prathamol*."

"Baron-Apparent?" Alannys spluttered in considerable surprise. "What are you talking about?"

Dahlia looked at her as though she had made a rude noise. "Are you serious? Trago is the Baron of Orinthal's son. His only son. From his first marriage, before Baroness Lae."

Alannys sat back in the chair, gobsmacked. She just didn't have any words. Prubard's son? That certainly explained why she didn't get along with him.

Dahlia was still watching Alannys. "You really didn't know that? I know his status doesn't mean much here, but it caused quite a scandal in the outside world when the baron's only son ran away at sixteen to serve indenture to the Singari. Prubard cast out his wife over it." She looked at Alannys speculatively. "Did he really attack you?"

"Muses, Dahlia, what kind of question is that?" Chen flared out in anger before Alannys could even open her mouth. "Of course it really happened. He's lucky the *prathamol* is all he got. If it had been up to me, things would have gone a lot worse for him."

Dahlia stared at him. She couldn't hold his fiery gaze, though, and looked back down at her soup. "I don't doubt it. You've become quite violent since I left."

"Violent?" Chen seemed honestly surprised. "What are you talking about?"

Dahlia laughed. "Wasn't it you holding a dagger to my throat the night I came back to camp?"

"Not fair," Chen protested. "We thought you were Lord Malrec's cloaked swordsman."

"What? What's this about?" Dahlia frowned, suddenly serious. "A cloaked swordsman? Not the same one who infiltrated the Great Palace?"

"The very same," Alannys said. "He's been following me ever since. But how did you know about that?"

"You'd be surprised how fast news can travel, if you know where to listen for it." She shook her head. "But Alannys, that swordsman isn't working for Lord Malrec."

"What?" Alannys couldn't seem to get her brain to accept that. "I don't understand — who else would send an assassin after me? And how is he finding me, how is he keeping up, if he isn't using paintings to get here?"

Dahlia chewed on her lip. "I don't know how he is doing it — perhaps he is simply very good at his job. But I know what Lord Malrec is doing, and sending assassins does not figure into it."

Alannys gaped at her in stunned silence. It was Chen who finally spoke. "How could you know what Lord

Malrec is doing? Does he post notices in the Glennayre town square?"

"Ha, ha," Dahlia said. Her tone was sour, but she seemed uncomfortable and she wouldn't look at him. "Anyone will tell you anything with the proper incentive. Lord Malrec is very powerful, but even he can't do everything alone."

Chen's eyes bulged. "Incentive? You mean, you slept with him?"

Dahlia's face turned red, but she held her head high. "Lord Malrec? Of course not! I can't believe you would suggest that."

"Look at her face," Chen said, dropping a hand on Alannys's shoulder. "She slept with someone, all right."

"As luck would have it," Dahlia said stiffly, "there is a taxidermist in Glennayre, who was essential to Lord Malrec's current project. I spent a night there, and heard of it from the man himself."

"Told you," Chen said.

"Mock me if you like. Information is my job. The more valuable the information, the more extreme the measures you have to be willing to take to get it."

"Leave her alone, Chen," Alannys said.

Dahlia inclined her head. "Malrec's current project is something the taxidermist had never heard of before — a collar that would prevent a person from singing. Honestly, the taxidermist didn't believe it could be done."

Chen's hand tightened on Alannys's shoulder. "What do you think, Dahlia?"

"Malrec is not the kind to waste time on foolish pursuits. Still, this collar..." She shook her head. "I have a hard time believing something like that could actually exist."

"It's real," Alannys said flatly. "If anybody would know about a thing like that, it's Princess Delline. And she's on his side now. But what does this have to do with the cloaked swordsman?"

"According to the taxidermist, the collar is a big project. Bigger even than painting. Lord Malrec has already spent weeks in its preparation, and it's taken him a lot of effort to get all of the things he needs and have them put together properly. A collar like that could only have one real target, don't you agree?"

Alannys nodded, swallowing a lump in her throat. She knew only too well that Lord Malrec had never abandoned his ideas of using her as a weapon. He had been forced to release her only because he lacked a means to control her voice—a problem for which this collar sounded like a perfect solution.

Dahlia leaned back against her pillows. "Then it seems pretty obvious to me he is not the one behind these attacks. Why would a man like Lord Malrec spend so much time and money on a tool to aid in recapturing you, only to have you assassinated before it was complete?"

"He wouldn't," Alannys said, struck by the truth of it. "Lord Malrec is too logical, too methodical. I can't imagine how furious he would be if he put all this effort into a collar only to have somebody else off me before he ever got to use it."

Chen squeezed her shoulder. "Don't talk like that."

Alannys shrugged.

"Still," Dahlia said thoughtfully, "that doesn't tell us who actually is sending this man. Maybe one of the other rulers? I have heard that Baron Prubard and Lord Diabon have no love for you."

Alannys shook her head. "No, I don't think so. They are working for Malrec these days. They know his wish is to capture me, not kill me. I can't imagine they would take such an action against his will."

"You're right. I'm afraid I just don't have any answers

for that question." Dahlia didn't sound happy about it.

"Dahlia," Alannys said hesitantly, taking advantage of the lull in the conversation to broach the subject she could not leave without discussing, "about your brother..." She couldn't find any good way to word her question.

Dahlia sighed. It was a heavy, weary sigh. "My brother." She paused, staring blankly into her soup. Alannys could feel dread weighing on her like a physical force. She had to know. But she wasn't sure if she could handle the knowing. "I'm sorry, but I really am very tired," Dahlia said flatly. "Do you think you two could excuse me?" She leaned back into her pillows and closed her eyes.

Alannys sighed. What could she do? She followed Chen out of the wagon, making as little noise as possible, and shut the door behind herself. "That was odd," she remarked.

Chen shrugged. "I wouldn't read too much into that. She's not feeling well. And her brother is a bit of a taboo subject anyway."

"What? I always had the impression she loved Larric."

"Oh, without question. It's just—complicated."

"Complicated." Alannys considered it. "Because he was born out of wedlock, you mean? With an outsider?"

"Not so much that..." Chen held open the door to her wagon, glancing around as though he didn't want anyone overhearing them. "I think I once told you that the Talents usually flow through the maternal line."

Alannys flopped down on her bed, more tired than seemed reasonable from the short walk. "I remember."

"Usually, but not always. And the Second Sight is a bit different from the Talents. It's exclusively a female power."

"I don't understand. Didn't Larric have the Sight?"

"Yes," Chen said, "and that is why he is taboo here.

Seers are always Singari. There is no question that he got his power from his father, which is odd to begin with. But a male Seer..." He shook his head. "A male Seer is an abomination. It isn't his fault, and it's nothing against him personally. But the tribe won't speak of him, or acknowledge him. He would certainly never be accepted here, not even by his father."

"But Dahlia loves him," Alannys said reflectively.

"You can see where that would put her in a tricky position. It's not really surprising she isn't comfortable talking about him, at least not while she is here."

An abomination. Alannys could remember several times that same word had been used to describe her. It seemed she and Larric had more in common than she had ever realized.

It would be a shame, she thought, if she was only discovering their common ground after he was dead.

♫

That afternoon, Alannys gave another music lesson to her Singari students. This time, almost twice as many people showed up for the lesson. It gave her chills, hearing them sing together in their instinctive harmony. She knew she was going to have to get them singing together for a purpose soon, and it scared her to think of that much raw power converging on any single point. Perhaps it was fortunate after all that the Singari so rarely agreed on anything.

That night she gave the command to move out. Before daylight the next morning, she and Chen, Drigo and Grald, made the rounds of the camp, supervising the pack-up. Her urgency seemed contagious, afflicting first Chen and his deputies, then the rest of the Singari, and they were ready to move in record time.

Alannys felt better than she had in days, riding Quicksilver out in front of the wagon train, knowing that Shadowkeep and every one of its wretched inhabitants was receding into the growing distance behind them. Maybe Ibira was right; maybe they never should have come here. Unfortunately they were here now, and going back the way they had come was out of the question. Alannys doubted any of them would ever enter Eversnow Pass of their own will again.

She knew she wouldn't.

So there was nothing for it but to move on and get through Orinthal, and she intended to do just that, as fast as humanly possible. She couldn't help but wonder, though, if she might not be rushing headlong into worse danger than what she was leaving behind. She needed to get some answers, and she could think of only one person who could give them to her. She started to guide Quicksilver over to the side, and let the wagon train pass her by.

Nightfire stepped closer to Quicksilver, and Chen leaned over to catch the reins in his hand, forcing her to stay where she was, at the front of the wagon train. "Where do you think you are going?"

"Looking for Trago. I thought I might ride with him for a bit."

Chen frowned. "Suicidal now? Is my company that bad?"

"That's not funny." She pulled Quicksilver's reins back out of his hands. "I was more of a danger to him than he was to me, last time I saw him."

Chen snorted. "No more than he deserved, if you ask me. You didn't even hit him."

"Whatever. I'm going to find him. I want to talk to him."

"Talk to him all you want, Alannys. But we'll bring him up here to do it. I don't think you should be alone with him yet, not on his first day out of the *prathamol*. I'm not as big as he is, but I can damn well stop him from killing you."

Alannys gave up. "All right. If it will keep you happy, we can bring him up here."

Chen nodded at Drigo, who turned sharply and disappeared into the wagon train.

They rode in relative quiet for a few moments, listening to the hoofbeats of the horses, the creaking of leather saddles and rolling wagons, and the noises of the various livestock that followed along with them as they traveled. Chen was being overcautious as usual, but she found she could appreciate it. Her place was at the front, and she always felt like she was abdicating her responsibilities if she rode anywhere else. She wasn't about to thank him for it, though. Chen was difficult enough to deal with—given any encouragement, she feared he would become incorrigible.

"Have you spoken any more to the king?" Chen was studiously looking straight ahead, but she could hear the tension in his voice.

"No." She remembered the last time she had used the mindlink; forever ago, it seemed now, before the ill-fated trip into Shadowkeep. Before Chen got hurt, before her Muse's Fever...now that was an uncomfortable thought. She had completely forgotten her Muse's Fever. Who knew what thoughts she had been sending to Dorramon, burning up with fever and half out of her mind with worry over Chen? She struggled to push the possibilities out of her mind. "I need to, though. He was going to check into what Dahlia told us about Romas, find out if he could corroborate any of it."

"Why?" Chen sounded surprised. "Do you doubt her?"

"No. And I don't think Dorramon does either, not really. It's just very hard for him to conceive of that level of treachery, inside the very keep of the Great Palace...and I can't blame him, really. The idea terrifies me, too."

Chen darted a glance her direction, then looked straight ahead again. "Well, if you believe her, and he believes her...then there really isn't any need to contact him, is there?"

Abruptly she remembered something else about the last time she had used the mindlink—her breakdown afterward. "Chen, I'm sorry if that upset you, last time. Honestly, that wasn't my intent. I did try to get you to leave."

Chen shook his head. "Not your fault. I know that. I just..." He gazed off into the distance, collecting his thoughts. "I've heard the rumors; everybody has. But I'm afraid I underestimated your connection to him, even so. Alannys, I never imagined anything like that."

She stared down at her saddlehorn. "I tried to tell you, Chen. I tried to warn you that you were wasting your time."

"Now, stop right there—I never said that. I don't agree with that. I underestimated your relationship with the king. I admit that. But that doesn't mean a single minute I have spent with you has been wasted. And it doesn't mean there is no hope. You know that."

She didn't have an answer for that. In truth, she had to admit he was right. As long as she was with the Singari, with Chen, there was a possibility she could change her mind. No matter what she said, until she actually left them and went back to the Great Palace, her choice was not really made. It wasn't really final.

"I hear that I've been summoned." The voice was loud and sarcastic, and she identified it as Trago's in the same moment he rode up next to her, falling into place on her right. He looked perhaps a bit gaunt, but the madness and anger were gone from his eyes.

"Summoned may be a bit strong," she said. "I just wanted to talk to you. But thank you for coming."

"As if I really had a choice," Trago said. "Your deputies are very effective."

"They had better be," she replied. "They have to be ready to take over for me when I am gone."

"Don't talk like that," Chen said sharply, from her left.

Alannys shrugged.

"It seems a very reasonable outlook to me," Trago said. "No *kortha* can lead forever. What did you want to talk to me about?"

"I understand you are the son of Baron Prubard."

Trago glanced at her. "Yes. I have heard rumors that my father has taken a liking to you."

Alannys frowned. "It is true that he made some foul propositions to the king regarding me. Your father is a vile, disgusting man."

Trago laughed out loud. "You and I can agree on that much, at least, Alannys."

"You know what they say," Chen grumbled, "about the apple and the tree."

Alannys shook her head. "Say what you like, but Prubard is a genuinely horrible person. Trago isn't perfect. He's failed. But Prubard is nothing but one long string of failures. He's a failure as a human being."

"She's right," Trago said. "Why do you think this holding is such a mess? It reflects the man who rules it. He wasn't always that way — when my mother married him, when he first became baron, Prubard was a good man, or seemed to be. By the time she had me three years later, though, he had degenerated into a querulous, lecherous, selfish bastard."

"Sounds charming," Chen muttered.

"Oh, you can't imagine, if you haven't met him. My mother no longer had any love for him, and as I grew, neither did I. I adored her, and he made her miserable. As soon as I could walk I started venturing outside of House

Orinthal, seeking solace in the towns below. The bigger I got, the farther I went, and the farther I went, the fewer people knew me on sight. I found happiness out there, among common people who did not have my father's twisted appetites, nor the leisure to indulge their darker sides. That's how I first met the Singari, and Mirenne. They were only in town for two weeks, but it was long enough for me to know where I wanted to spend the rest of my life—I could not go back to House Orinthal and spend my life upholding my father's corrupt regime. So when the Singari left, I went with them, starting a seven-year indenture to Mirenne's uncle."

"I have heard that didn't go over so well," Alannys said, as diplomatically as she could.

Trago laughed darkly. "You might say that. Prubard cast my mother out in disgrace. But I think that was destined to happen anyway. He was no longer satisfied with my mother, and had not been for many years. The only difference was that with her gone, he didn't even have to try to hide his activities. A string of women went into House Orinthal, and back out again—sometimes within a week. Young, old, peasants and nobles, some little more than girls—all of them made whores by my father and his complete inability to care about anything but his own wants."

"I take exception to that," Alannys said stiffly. "Lae is no whore."

Trago shook his head sadly. "The baroness is a good woman, a true lady. Her only flaw is her husband. I am genuinely sorry she got caught up with him. He wasn't kidding, Alannys, when he proposed to the king to bring you into House Orinthal and put her out, and her babies with her."

Alannys shuddered. "Such a vile man."

"He said that?" Chen said incredulously. "He said he

meant to take you for that purpose? To King Dorramon? And did the king beat some sense into him?"

Alannys laughed. "I believe court protocol would prohibit that. He did look like he might have enjoyed the chance, though."

Chen leaned over and patted her arm. "Sometimes it's hard to be king."

"You got that right." Alannys took a deep breath, steeling herself for the main point of this conversation. "Tell me, Trago, have you ever heard of a man called Ethal?"

Trago's jaw tightened. "That is a name not often spoken. Coming from a lady like you—it sounds like swearing. Where did you hear that name?"

In a flat voice, like the whole thing had happened to people she didn't even know, Alannys told Trago about the ill-fated trip into Shadowkeep.

"Great Muses," Trago breathed. "Do either of you have any idea how lucky you were?"

"She should have run." Chen stared straight ahead, but his voice was strained. "If those men had gotten hold of her..."

"Stop. You're talking crazy. There isn't any way I could have left you there to die." Her voice cracked on the word.

"Of course not." Trago's tone was surprisingly gentle. "But Chen is right to worry. Those men—well, they sound like the kind of people who will naturally cause trouble in the absence of anyone to stop them, and Orinthal has been in that situation for a while now. But if they are working for Ethal..." He shook his head.

"Who is he?" Alannys was surprised by the darkness she heard in her own voice.

"No." Chen cut cleanly across any reply Trago might have had in mind with surprising firmness. "Thank you, Trago, but that's enough. I don't think it would be wise to pursue this conversation any further."

Trago said nothing, chewing thoughtfully on his lip.

Alannys looked back and forth between them in confusion. "What? But...why?"

Chen wouldn't even look at her. The set of Trago's face looked grim, but he held his silence.

She hoped her sigh didn't sound as impatient as she felt—and then she thought it might be all right if it did. "Come on, this is important. You can't just tell me not to talk about it."

Chen just shook his head.

"I don't think you can win this one, Alannys," Trago said. "There's an old Singari superstition—"

"It's *not* a superstition," Chen said hotly. "You shouldn't talk about bad things like this. You'll bring them to you."

"I...see," Alannys said, stalling for time to consider this. "But you must see that doesn't make sense, Chen. Ethal is looking for me already, we can be pretty sure of that. How can understanding the threat make things worse?"

Chen pressed his lips into a thin, stubborn, silent line.

"Talk to me, Trago," Alannys said. "What kind of man am I dealing with here?"

"He's a monster," Trago said shortly. "My father's own, personal monster. In any other holding, Ethal would have been executed years ago. But Prubard saw a use for him—Ethal lives to kill those with Talent."

"What?" Alannys gasped.

"My father was not Talented himself. And he was always aware of how easily the power he valued could be taken away from him by someone who was. Having a man around who specialized in destroying those people seemed like a good idea to him."

"How? How does he do that?"

Trago shook his head. "I don't know, Alannys.

Something isn't right about it, though. My father never told me much about Ethal, but...but I think what he does to those Talented people is worse than just killing them, somehow. He seems to use them to make himself stronger. And I don't have any earthly idea how such a thing can be done, but it sounds unnatural, and...and *wrong*."

"That's the most horrible thing I think I have ever heard." Chen sounded shaken.

"It isn't just that though — Ethal just likes to murder in general. My father is a morally barren man, but he is nothing next to Ethal. My father has defiled many women, to be sure, and will undoubtedly defile many more. But Ethal — Ethal captures women, and holds them, torments them and tortures them. Prubard uses them and sends them on their way. If a women escapes Ethal at all, she is disfigured and worse, a hollow shell of the person she used to be."

"I told you, you should have run." Chen's voice was rough.

Alannys swallowed hard, but said nothing. She understood his sentiment, but she could not agree with it.

"Orinthal is one of the Seven Hells, Alannys," Trago said evenly. "Always has been. Always will be."

Now that, she could agree with.

♫

The conversation with Trago only increased Alannys's resolve to get out of Orinthal as quickly as possible. She kept the Singari riding longer than she probably should have; it was dark outside by the time she finally called a halt.

They set up camp, and started a fire out in the clearing. She could smell the woodsmoke and the cooking meat, but it held no attraction for her. She was too dead-tired to care about food. She tied Quicksilver to the wagon and fell into her bed, beyond caring about sleeping in her clothes.

Her sleep was fitful and restless. Thankfully she didn't

have the same dream about the painting, but her talk with Trago had unnerved her too much for real sleep.

Alannys rolled over onto her back, and stared at the wooden ceiling. She wondered how she would be fit to lead the wagon train tomorrow if she didn't rest any better than this. She kicked around the idea of finding herself something to eat, but she couldn't seem to get excited about it. Her appetite had disappeared along with her ability to sleep, and she suspected the cause was the same for both.

A soft melody from plucked strings crept into the wagon and wrapped itself around her, gradually pulling her attention away from her thoughts. She didn't think she had ever heard anything quite so beautiful—haunting and melodic, aching with sadness, the gentle song was a call she could not refuse. As if she had no will of her own, Alannys left her bed and stepped outside.

There was a wooden chair, tipped back against the wagon so that the two front legs weren't even touching the ground. Kicked back in the chair was Chen, and he was playing the ancient lute. His head bowed low over the instrument, and he didn't even seem to be aware of her standing there. She didn't have to wonder if this was a traditional song—it was plain that this particular tune came directly from his heart.

Left to herself, Alannys would have sneaked right back into her wagon. She didn't want to intrude on this private moment, but she had no choice. The music compelled her —maybe if she hadn't been so tired, she would have been better able to resist it. One haunting phrase pulled her closer, and a delicate, sad, embellishment drew her hand to his shoulder.

Chen jumped, startled, and stopped playing. Her hand fell to her side, and she could feel her control return along with it. Her breathing was shallow, uneven, as though she had exerted herself more than the few steps she had taken would indicate. "Alannys! Are you all right? I thought you were sleeping."

"No. But even if I was—I would have come anyway." She pointed with a shaking hand at the lute. "I didn't have any choice."

Chen glanced down at the instrument in his lap. "Oh. Oh! Alannys, I'm so sorry—I didn't realize—I wasn't trying to...I didn't mean to disturb you."

"Please don't apologize. It was worth it to hear that song. Could you—do you think you could play more of it?"

He looked surprised, but he dipped his head toward her. "For you, anything." His fingers found their places, and he picked up the melody that already sounded familiar to her. "I don't understand. How could I...call you...when I didn't mean to?"

Alannys didn't want to speak, to interrupt the spell the song created. It was almost as if it had been written for the express purpose of capturing her heart. "You meant to. Maybe not consciously, but on some level, the intent was there. Music doesn't care about politeness or complications—music expresses what you feel." She sat down on the steps of her wagon. "I wish I had my violin. I would play along."

"Sing," he suggested.

"No! No, I—I can't imagine singing along with that, Chen. The words, they would be so...so sad." Tears burned the back of her eyes just thinking about how those lyrics might go.

He smiled at her, but it looked like it hurt.

Alannys thought she might cry if she didn't change the subject, and fast. "What are you doing out here? Shouldn't you be sleeping?" She didn't know how long she had been trying to sleep, but the campfire was smoldering ashes now, and there was not a person in sight.

Chen shook his head, adding a little ornamental trill to a phrase that had not been there before. "I wouldn't be able to sleep anyway."

"You too? What are you worrying about?"

"You," he said simply. "You heard Trago today. That man is out there somewhere. He knows that you're here. And thanks to Ralep and his friends, he knows that you have Talent."

"You have Talent, too," she said gently. "It isn't only me we should be worried about."

"It's not the same, Alannys. You know it's not. I can't close my eyes without seeing it, all the horrible things that could happen to you..." The melody faltered as he missed a note, and he stopped playing.

"Chen..."

"I'm not leaving here. I can't. If anyone wants you, they are going to have to go through me to get to you."

"Come here." The stairway was narrow, but she scooted over to one side and made room for both of them to sit.

Chen let the chair down, and moved to sit beside her, still carrying the lute. He looked as tired as she felt. "I'm sorry. I don't mean to be pushy."

"Pushy." The sound she made was somewhere between a laugh and a snort. "There aren't words to tell you how lucky I am to have you, Chen."

"There are. You just won't say them, is all."

She couldn't answer that. She put her arm through his and they sat side by side in the quiet, listening to the sounds of the night.

"Would it bother you if I play?" he said finally. "I think it makes me feel better."

"Not at all," she said. She understood. All of the emotion in that song had to come from somewhere, and expressing it somehow could only be good for him. It wasn't easy to listen to, though — at least not for her. The haunting, lilting melody cried out the words he was begging for from her, the words he did not know she had already given him.

She had to close her eyes against the wave of emotion the song washed over her when Chen began to play again. No wonder he wanted to play — nobody could possibly hold all of that in. Alannys listened for a moment to the now-familiar tune, and without consciously meaning to, she began to hum a harmony line.

They sat under the stars, speaking no words but expressing everything just the same, singing and strumming the tune that had drawn her from her wagon. The song came finally to a natural end, their last note ringing in the air around them, quiet and perfect and inexpressibly sad.

"Chen, I — "

He turned towards her, as though he wanted to hear her better, and before she knew what was happening his lips were warm against hers and his arms were tight around her and his hands were tangled in her hair. She didn't know what to do — she knew she couldn't have Dorramon, but she wasn't willing to entertain the idea of replacing him, either. She stiffened, and reached up to push Chen away.

Alannys?

The single, questioning word was as clear as though someone right next to her had spoken, but it was in her mind. She gasped and jerked back from Chen, jumping to her feet, flushing with the sudden, shameful realization of what had just happened.

"Alannys?" Chen sounded as shaky and uncertain as she felt. "Are you all right?"

She shook her head, pressing her fingers to her

temples, trying to keep herself together until she could give a coherent answer to the king. "It's—it's Dorramon. I have to talk to him."

"His timing is fabulous." He reached for her shoulders. "You don't have to talk to him right now. Let me—"

She jerked away from the touch. "No. No, I have to go. This was a mistake, Chen—I'm sorry."

His face was a picture of shock and hurt. "Alannys?"

"I'm sorry, Chen." She reached out toward him, but let her hand fall back to her side before touching him. "I am so, so sorry."

"Alannys, wait. Please don't—"

She pushed past him and ran back inside the wagon. She threw herself down on the bed, trying to squelch the tears that threatened her.

Alannys? Is this a bad time?

No. She sat up, leaning against the wall, scrubbing at her eyes with the heels of her hands. *No, it's fine. I'm sorry. I was — talking to someone.*

This late? He sounded surprised. *Is everything all right?*

Yes, and no. We just learned some troubling things about some dangerous people in the area. Nothing for you to worry about, though – we're going to be fine.

Are you sure? I don't like the sound of that.

Well, to be honest, neither do I. Her nervous laugh sounded hollow. *But it isn't as bad as it sounds.*

If you say so. He didn't sound convinced, but thankfully didn't push it. *I just found out that Dahlia's story is true. A man named Romas did work in the palace kitchen. He was murdered two days after my father died.*

A tight knot of fear constricted around her heart. *Dorramon, I have to come back. Right now.*

Have you finished, then? You're satisfied with what you've done?

No. No, I still have a ways to go. But I can't stay out here while you're in danger. And I can't—I can't—I just have to come back. Now.

There was a pause. *You sound frantic, Alannys. Are you all right?*

Yes. No. She felt like crying. But she couldn't tell him everything that was driving her. *I just — you're so far away, Dorramon. And I'm scared. For both of us.*

I know. His tone was comforting. *I am too. I wish more than anything that I could just leave everything here behind and ride out there to you.*

I wish you would, she replied petulantly.

But I can't, because too many people are depending on me. And you are in the same spot, Alannys. You have so many people depending on you right now — and you just told me you are in a dangerous place. How would they get through it without you?

She wanted to remind him that the Singari had been a self-sufficient people long before she came along. But she knew that wasn't the point. She took a deep, steadying breath. *You're right. I know that.*

I will be here when you get back, Alannys. No matter what. Just make sure that you come back.

I will, she told him. *No matter what.*

Alannys sat in the silence in her wagon long after the conversation had ended, staring at nothing and wondering how everything had gotten to be such a mess. Things had seemed so clear to her when she first left the Great Palace. Now everything was a giant muddle, and she couldn't see what she was supposed to do. Tears ran unheeded off her face. Her lips still felt tingly and strange from Chen's kisses. She held the Seeing Stone tightly in her two hands and thought about it.

After a while, she could hear the haunting melody start up again outside. She rolled over towards the wall and clenched her eyes shut, ignoring the burning of fresh tears.

♪

The next day was a grueling one. There was a tension

between Alannys and Chen that seemed to trickle through the entire tribe. Neither of them knew how to address what had happened between them, or put things right again—but neither of them could stop thinking about it, either. As an uneasy compromise they spoke to each other only when they had to, and kept their conversation only to what had to be said. It set them on edge, and it seemed to put everyone else on edge, too.

Trago rode with them, between them, buffering them from each other and easing the friction. Alannys wasn't sure why he did it, but she was grateful for his presence. It helped her deal with Chen, but Trago also knew more about Orinthal than anyone else in the tribe. She was glad to have his support, riding through the most hostile land they had been through.

They stopped early for dinner, planning to ride on for a few more hours before stopping for the night. The stop highlighted the trouble they were facing. Dinnertime was usually a fun affair, and it was the time of day when Alannys and Chen were at their best—light-hearted, funny, and the banter between them was a high point in their day. Not on this day though; on this day dinner was rushed and stilted, and the little talk that did happen was formal and uneasy.

After dinner, they got back on the road. It seemed the entire group shared a growing desire to get Orinthal behind them; the sooner, the better.

"You know," Trago said conversationally, which instantly put Alannys on guard, "I could have sworn I heard the lute playing last night. Was that you, Chen?"

Alannys was very careful to keep her eyes straight ahead, but it seemed like she could feel Chen stiffen up on the other side of Trago. "Yes. I did have the lute out last night."

"I thought it was you. You really play that lute better

than anyone else, Chen. I didn't recognize that tune, though."

"It was just something I made up." Chen didn't sound like he wanted to talk about it.

Trago didn't seem to notice, though. "Really? It was very pretty. What do you call it?"

The silence stretched until it seemed like Chen would not answer. When he finally spoke, his voice was low. "The Last Kiss."

"Oh — that seems rather — poignant."

A sound like a strangled sob escaped from Alannys's throat, though she was trying very hard to make no sound at all. Trago glanced at her in apparent surprise.

"Oh. Oh! I'm sorry, I didn't mean to pry."

Alannys shook her head, trying to get control of herself. She expected either she or Chen or both would tell him it was fine, but before anyone could get a word out, they heard the sound of hoofbeats approaching behind them. She craned around in her saddle, using the opportunity to wipe her eyes with her glove.

Dahlia rode up to them, on a cream-colored pony. She glanced at Alannys, and at Chen. "I hope I'm not intruding on anything."

Trago laughed, but it sounded uncomfortable. "Don't worry, Dahlia, if there was anything to intrude on, I have already barged in and stomped it to dust."

"Dahlia," Alannys interrupted, eager to leave that line of conversation, "are you sure you're feeling up to riding?"

Dahlia shrugged. "Three days stuck in my wagon is plenty enough for me. Since we'll only be riding a few more hours, it seemed like a good chance to get some air. Besides," she continued, and her tone turned dark, "I think you'll be needing me this evening."

Alannys wasn't sure how to take that, and she wasn't

sure she wanted to push any farther to find out. She hadn't had a single exchange of comfortable conversation all day, and she was ready to just quit talking.

It seemed that her companions agreed. Now four instead of three, they rode together out in front of the wagon train, in a silence that stifled everything that needed to be said.

♫

The dying sunlight finally gave way to darkness as they rode, but still they pressed on, by the light of a single waning moon.

"Muses, Alannys, what are you doing to that horse?" Dahlia sounded annoyed. Alannys figured Quicksilver's antics were hindering everyone's attempt to ignore each other.

"Not a thing," Alannys replied shortly, fighting to stay in the saddle of her side-stepping, shuddering mount. "Quicksilver was a warhorse before I got him. He's usually unshakeable. Something's got him spooked now, though, and that can't be good."

Dahlia frowned. "You're right." She looked around them, peering into the surroundings they could only indistinctly see, and her frown grew deeper and more unpleasant. "Stay here, everyone. I'm going to ride ahead and have a look around."

Alannys gave up wrestling with Quicksilver and slid off, looking around them for anything that might have set him off. It just wasn't like him to act like this for no reason — heck, last time he had done this had been on the ride into Shadowkeep, and they still hadn't recovered completely from that. The time before that had been Eversnow Pass, when the cloaked swordsman nearly killed her and she got trapped in the avalanche...

Remembering all that made this situation seem suddenly much worse. "Dahlia, wait," Alannys called. "I don't think you should go off alone." She spoke too late;

Dahlia was already riding away from them.

Alannys had a sudden vision, a quick sharp impression of noise and flames and Dahlia, dead by the roadside. Her Second Sight didn't kick in often, but when it did, it took her breath away. "Dahlia! Dahlia, STOP!"

Alannys ran after Dahlia on foot. Chen and Trago stared after her in confusion, not sure whether they should follow, or stay where they were, or even what was going on.

"Dahlia! Damn it, Dahlia, listen to me!" Alannys was running for all she was worth, but she could see it was no good; she would never catch her in time.

"Stay back!" Dahlia's words barely reached back to her, but they sounded determined. "Get back with the others, while you still have time."

Suddenly Alannys sensed a painting opening. She resisted the urge to swear, searching frantically around her for the tell-tale gray blur. It was so hard to see anything clearly in the weak moonlight. There—off in the heavy brush by the side of the road up ahead, closer to Dahlia than to her. No sooner did she find the blur than it winked out of existence. Her senses confirmed it; the painting had been suddenly, abruptly closed.

Why would anyone go to the trouble of painting, only to—

A sudden, bright light ripped through Alannys like a physical force, knocking her effortlessly into the air and plowing her into the thick, spiny brush. Blistering heat rolled over her, intense and mercifully quick, punctuated with smaller, sharper pains. She couldn't say for sure how badly she was hurt, but she knew that it was bad enough. She felt certain she would die there, tossed into the brush like a rag doll.

In the aftermath, the entire countryside seemed to share a moment of quiet horror. No sound moved through the wreckage—and then, all at once, flurries of activity erupted all around. She could hear Chen's voice, raised in concern, and Trago's. But she couldn't see anything.

It was dark, suddenly, disorientingly dark, and where she lay huddled on the ground, gasping, unable to move, she could hear trees rustling and frantic shouts. She knew things were bad, and she knew it was her fault, and she knew she was about to pay for it. She couldn't move, and the calls of her friends were still much too far away to save her from the doom that hovered over her now.

Her skin prickled, and the hair stood up on the back of her neck, and she knew without even looking that she was being watched through a painting. If she could turn to look behind her, she would see the telltale gray formless blur of the opening the painter had created.

Of course, if she could turn to look behind her, she wouldn't waste time looking. If she was capable of any movement at all, she would be out of there, running for everything she was worth.

But she couldn't, so she laid there, her body as useless as an empty shell, until rough hands grabbed her from behind and hauled her through the void behind the gray blur, into the painting and away from all her friends and anyone who could possibly help her.

Chapter Two

RAVAN'S LIGHT

"Get the rope. Bind her hands." The voice was hard and male.

"But Driach! She is grievously injured! We must tend to her." The woman sounded outraged.

"And so we will, but not until we are sure we are safe. Lord Malrec has gone to considerable lengths for this one, Nyrin. She may be a very powerful ally."

"Or a very powerful enemy. He may have been trying to destroy her. You shouldn't make assumptions."

The man sighed. "I don't think Malrec would miscalculate that badly. If he had wanted her dead, she would be dead. He wanted her exactly as she is—incapacitated. Now do as I say. You are wasting time."

Alannys could hear them clearly, but she still couldn't see very well—her vision was a dark, blotchy black, with spots of lights and fragments of shapes starting to break through. What could have happened to her? At least her vision appeared to be returning, albeit slowly, so that was encouraging. A temporary blindness then, like flash blindness. She did remember an enormously bright light, painful in the darkness.

A bright light, a deafening sound, a wave of heat and stabbing pain—had she been in an explosion?

Had the unseen painter been transferring a *bomb*? A black powder bomb, here in Ravanmark, where gunpowder had only ever been used to propel decorative fireworks? It was utterly unthinkable.

And yet—the faceless Driach had clearly said that Lord Malrec was responsible for this. Lord Malrec, who had spent far longer than she ever realized observing her culture. It made sense, in a sickening sort of way. It was the only explanation she could accept for the stomach-wrenching, violent devastation she had just witnessed.

Hands pushed back her riding cloak, probably seeking her hands so that she could be bound. She felt the leather fall away from her hip, and heard the sudden intake of air from the woman whose face she could only half see.

"Driach!" Nyrin gasped. "Driach, it's Songstrike!"

"What?" Heavy footsteps hurried over, and another half-visible face knelt down beside her.

"This is no ally of Malrec's, Driach. This is..."

"Alannys," Alannys croaked. It was somewhat surprising to find that her voice still worked at all, given the way she felt. "Good to meet you. What just happened?"

♫

Apparently no one wanted to tackle the question of what had just happened while Alannys was lying injured on the cold floor. In a span of time that was to her a vague blur, she was tended, and somehow during the activity she fell asleep—or passed out.

She woke up in a strange bed, in a dark room lit only by an olive oil lantern, wearing a linen robe that was not hers. A cool, greasy ointment coated her arms, neck and face, and she had bandages on her forearms.

"Lady Alannys, I am glad to see you awake." The voice from the bedside startled her; Alannys had not realized anyone else was there. She recognized the voice as the lady called Nyrin in the same instant she turned and saw her there, in a wooden chair.

"Thank you." Alannys looked back down at her hands. Even in the poor light, she could see their color was wrong. Burned, most likely, from the explosion—and probably on her face and neck as well. And the bandages...she must have been cut. Shrapnel.

Lord Malrec. Damn him.

"Where am I?" Alannys looked around the unfamiliar room for some clue, but saw nothing that helped her.

Nyrin smiled. She had a pleasant face, lined but plump, with curls of steel gray hair falling around it from under the shawl she wore over her head. "This is the harborage of Ravan's Light. Others might call it a cave. This particular cave has many small recesses and a few larger rooms that suit it well for a living space."

That certainly explained why it seemed so dark. "Ravan's Light? What is that?"

"Not what, dear, but who. I and my husband and a few others live here in these caves. That is the name we choose for ourselves. You might call us a resistance."

"Resistance," Alannys echoed. "What is it that you resist?"

"Do not answer that question." The voice was cold and commanding, and Alannys knew before she looked that it must have belonged to Driach. He swept in like a chill wind, bringing a hard edge of tension and anger with him. "I must admit I am surprised to find you talking with her so congenially. How do you know you can trust her?"

"Driach..." Nyrin sounded tired, like they had been over this before—maybe more than once. "She is the Redeemer. If we can't trust her, we can trust no one."

"How do you know she's the Redeemer?" Driach demanded. "I think you are relying too much on the happenstance of her carrying Songstrike."

Only, Alannys suddenly realized, she wasn't. Songstrike and her dagger were both gone. She didn't even have the Seeing Stone. "What have you done with my things?"

Driach crossed his arms. The look her gave her wasn't exactly a glare, but it was close. "I'll ask the questions here, young lady. I know my wife trusts you, but quite frankly I do not. I know who you want me to believe you are. I want some proof that's who you really are."

"Proof?" Alannys echoed dumbly.

"Driach, please," Nyrin said. "She's been through enough. We should—"

"Hush, woman," Driach cut her off. "You know too well the horrors in our past, Nyrin. Would you bring them upon all who live here, as well?"

Nyrin sighed and looked down at her hands, folded in her lap.

"Look," Alannys said, "I'm a woman wearing men's clothes, traveling the country and carrying Songstrike. If that doesn't convince you, I don't know what will."

Driach snorted. "You're hardly the only person in the world to wear riding clothes. And anybody who overpowered the Redeemer could take the sword. It could even be a forged replica. I want something that will prove to me you are the Redeemer, something only the woman our king dispatched from the Great Palace would know."

"But..." Alannys gestured at her robe. "You've already seen everything I have."

Driach's eyebrows twitched, and he turned suddenly away. "My wife changed you. I've seen nothing," he said brusquely.

A tiny smile played around the corners of Nyrin's mouth, and Alannys wondered, had she—had she embarrassed him?

It made her opponent seem more human somehow.

She found she could be grateful for that much at least, as she pursed her lips and tried to think of a way to fulfill the impossible demand he'd laid on her. "I see. So, then...something only the Redeemer would know...tell me, Driach—I trust you've heard of my time in Garrant? How I sang to turn back a tidal wave?"

Driach inclined his head almost grudgingly. "Of course —everyone has heard about that. But I hope you don't think to satisfy me with a story everybody knows."

"No. What I'm about to show you, only a very few people in the world know about—one of them is the king, as you will see."

Driach raised a skeptical eyebrow, but said nothing.

"After my success in Garrant, I spent over a week in the Healing House. While I was there, the king sent a rider with a message of congratulations."

"I *know* that."

"Yes, but you don't know this. The messenger left me with more than just the king's thanks. King Dorramon also sent me this." Alannys held out her arm, and pulled back the sleeve of her robe.

Driach crossed the room in two steps, taking hold of her wrist and examining the royal bracelet. She heard his gasp, and she couldn't blame him. Even in the low light of the oil lantern, the bracelet was breathtaking; the gold glimmered richly and the enamel shone as if it was wet.

"I hope this settles the question," Alannys said.

Slowly, Driach began to nod. "Something like this...making it—or wearing it—without permission is treason. There can be no doubt that you are who you claim to be." He released her and stepped back. "I do apologize —a man in my position cannot afford to trust lightly. There is more than just myself to worry about here." He paused. "You asked what we do here."

"I asked what you resist, yes."

"I believe you will find it to be the same thing that you resist, Lady Alannys." His voice, without the hard edge of anger and tension, was soothing, like balm for her ears. "We resist the darkness, in all its forms, which is spreading across Ravanmark."

"Darkness." Alannys thought about it. "Like Lord Malrec, and the Dark Alliance. And Ethal."

Nyrin stiffened, pulling her shawl down tighter over the top of her head. "Indeed."

"But—why have you brought me here? What happened to my friends?"

"Friends?" Driach frowned. "You were quite alone when we found you."

Alannys shook her head. "I was riding with three others—Singari. The rest of the tribe was somewhere behind us. I think," she said, and her voice wavered, "that one of my friends did not survive the explosion. But the other two—I know they were out there. I could hear them looking for me, but I couldn't call out to them."

Driach's frown deepened. "I did not know this. I assure you, our intent was only to rescue you from Lord Malrec—not to separate you from your friends."

"I don't understand," Alannys said.

"Nor do I," Nyrin said. "What happened there? The painting we had was a pretty countryside, with greenery and trees. But when we opened the painting, what we found was black and burnt, and some fires were still burning. Was this your doing?"

"No!" Alannys said defensively. She saw Driach shaking his head; evidently he had already figured that out. "I'll tell you my side of the story, and you can tell me yours, and maybe we will all have a better understanding of what is going on here."

No one spoke. Driach pulled another chair up to her bedside and sat down.

"I believe what you saw when you opened your painting was the aftermath of a bomb — something that has never existed in Ravanmark before. They are destructive, explosive devices whose only purpose is to cause devastation, injury, and death. I believe Lord Malrec discovered these things in my home world before he brought me here, and that he is the one using them now. That explosion..." She shook her head. "We rode right into it. None of us had any idea an attack like that was even possible."

"Nor we." Driach sounded reflective, and Alannys couldn't imagine what he was thinking. "As you know, we opened a painting — apparently immediately after this explosion — and we found you there and pulled you through. Lord Malrec would have taken you if we had not."

Her scalp prickled. "What do you mean?"

He regarded her evenly. "The way the painting was done...and the way this explosive device was positioned...when the painting was opened, you were right in front of it. This is no coincidence. Lord Malrec planned to reach through and take you."

"But how can you know that?"

"Because my painting is an exact copy of his."

Alannys stared at him, trying to wrap her mind around this idea. "How — how is that possible?"

Driach smiled. "I am his ghost. You see, Alannys, I went to work for Lord Malrec many years ago, when Glennayre was first founded, before the burning of Archford. I worked as his household servant for many years — until about a year ago, as a matter of fact."

Alannys tried to fit this fact in with what she knew. "Then you knew Kalyn. And Larric."

"Yes. I taught her how to run the affairs of the castle. And I helped Larric, more than once, to cover up his true activities. You see, I went to work for Lord Malrec for one reason: because he is a painter. I also have that gift. But I did not know how to use it. It was my hope that working in Lord Malrec's house, I could surreptitiously learn some of his techniques."

"I see."

Driach shook his head. "But I made one mistake. I became focus-bonded to Lord Malrec."

"That would be a mistake," Alannys said dryly.

"Yes. I had no choice, really—it was a condition of my continued employment. So the focus-bond was forged, and I continued to work for Lord Malrec."

"Until a year ago," she said. "What happened then?"

"I had always suspected that Malrec had designs on the throne. Over my years at Castle Glennayre I saw those suspicions confirmed. But some of the things that happened more recently—the obsession he had with you and your culture, with kidnapping you as a weapon, the way he spoke of our Prince Dorramon, with such bitterness and personal hatred—I could no longer stay there and see these things progress. Our current monarchy may not be without flaws, but a King Malrec is not what this country needs. Our king is descended from Ravan herself, and that line should be preserved."

"Ravan's Light," Alannys mused.

"Long may it shine." Driach smiled, but it faded quickly. "So at the first opportunity that presented itself, I stole the focal statue, grabbed my things, and fled Castle Glennayre. I have never gone back there."

"I don't understand. How can your painting be a copy of his, if you've never seen his?"

Driach sighed. "I knew one should never enter a focus-bond with another painter, Alannys, but I never knew why. I shattered the statue. If I were a normal person, that would be the end of the focus-bond. But I'm not. I am a painter, too, and some remnant of that connection survives. When Lord Malrec paints, I can paint along with him. Whatever he paints, I paint as well."

She stared at him. "That works?"

"It's the most effective manner of spying on a painter I have ever seen. It works. And I was terrified that he would be coming to eliminate me. I kept running until I made it here to Orinthal, and even then I looked over my shoulder for months. But it seems that he can't tell that I am ghosting him — the connection is one-way."

"And Lord Malrec has no idea it exists?" She asked the question, but she supposed she already knew the answer. If Lord Malrec had any idea this ghosting existed, he would have destroyed Driach immediately.

"No. No, Malrec never knew I could paint at all. He would have no reason to suspect anything."

Alannys sat back against the pillows. So Lord Malrec had done this, as she had suspected. The first painting she had sensed — that had been him, transferring the bomb. He closed the painting right away so he wouldn't get caught in the blast himself. And he had done it deliberately — planned it so that the blast would throw her toward his other painting, where he could snatch her up before her friends could get to her.

The collar Dahlia told her about must be finished, then. And Malrec was on the warpath in a big way.

"I'll never be safe again," she said, suddenly feeling the truth of it. "He can paint a way to me anytime he fancies. I can't hide from him."

"I forbid you to give up." Nyrin's voice was stern. "You have not come this far for nothing. A painter stalks you...that is a problem, but I believe I can show you some things that will help you."

"You are in no shape for that yet, though," Driach interjected. "You need to rest, to heal. I would not worry much about Lord Malrec right now. He had to use the Herb of Sight to prepare these paintings. He will need a few days to recover from that before he will be able to paint again."

Alannys sighed. "You are right. Thank you, both of you. I don't know where I'd be without you."

Actually, she could imagine, only too well, and that was the scariest thing of all.

♫

After Driach and Nyrin left, Alannys turned over in her bed and tried to sleep. Driach was right; she did need rest. And it was the middle of the night. Still, though, she laid awake for what felt like hours.

"This is ridiculous," she muttered, turning over for the umpteenth time.

"Ah, Lady Alannys. I thought I might find you like this."

The voice from the cavern bedroom's entrance was quiet, but it startled Alannys nearly out of her skin. She shot bolt upright in bed to see Nyrin, heading for the chair at the bedside. "Nyrin! I—didn't expect to see you."

"No, I imagine not." Nyrin's smile was gentle. "I had a notion you might want to talk."

"Did you? I can't imagine why—I've got nothing to talk about." Alannys deliberately swallowed everything she would have liked to say—she hadn't quite gotten over being required to prove her identity. Of course, they had later loosened up, and Driach had told her far more than he'd had to, but still—the sting of distrust was hard to get over. She couldn't decide if it was in her best interest to tell these people anything.

"Well, perhaps you're right." Nyrin's smile never faltered. "Perhaps the one who really wanted to talk was me."

"You?" Alannys didn't know what kind of response she had expected, but that wasn't it.

"Indeed. I wanted to apologize again—we did not intend to separate you from your companions. We really did think you were alone."

"Oh." Alannys propped her pillow behind her and leaned back against it. She didn't know what else to say.

"I hope you don't doubt me? It was never our intention to harm you, only to keep you from Lord Malrec."

"No, I don't doubt you, but...why do you think you've harmed me? The only harm I can see came from Malrec's bomb."

"Well, I suppose that is true, if you're talking only about physical harm. You seemed very upset about your friends, though."

"Yes." There was a grim pause while Alannys thought about all the things she'd been avoiding—the real reasons she couldn't sleep. "Dahlia died in that explosion. I'm certain of it."

"I'm very sorry. Dahlia, she was a friend of yours?"

"It's...complicated. I don't think she liked me much, and we were often at cross-purposes, but she was a smart, outspoken person who didn't deserve to die that way."

"I see," Nyrin said.

Alannys had to wonder how Nyrin had done it—this was a lot of gut-spilling for someone who had said she didn't want to talk. The problem was, now that she'd started, she couldn't seem to stop. "She didn't deserve to die. But Lord Malrec was willing to kill her, just to get to me. How am I worth that? How can I fight against that level of obsession—of evil?"

"The same way you always have, I should think," Nyrin said. "I am sorry, but I don't have any magic words for you."

There was something odd about the way Nyrin's eyes slid from hers, but she couldn't stop to think about it. "And what about the others? I was riding ahead with a few people, but the entire Singari tribe was following us. I was leading them, Nyrin—they were relying on me. And then I just disappeared after that explosion—what must they have thought?"

"Oh, dear." Nyrin sounded honestly shocked, as though every thing Alannys mentioned was a possibility that had never occurred to her before.

"They need to leave. They need to get out of here—Ethal knows I am in Orinthal, traveling with Singari, and he is hunting me. Every minute they stay here puts them in more danger. But Chen won't..." Her voice broke and she swallowed hard. "He won't let them leave. If he thinks there's even the slightest possibility they might find me, he'll make them stay and search. No matter how unsafe it is."

"Alannys—"

"And what if they *do* leave?" Alannys pressed on, driven by the guilt and anxiety. "What if I never see any of them again? What if the last day I ever spend with Chen is *this* day—the day I wasted refusing to talk to him? What if —what if he lives out the rest of his life thinking I never cared anything for him at all?"

Nyrin seemed too stricken now to even reply, but Alannys was too worked up to notice, or care. "The cynic in me says it would be for the best. But that can't be true, can it? I've spent more time with him than anyone else in Ravanmark. He means more to me than almost anybody. Feelings are important—I believe that. But what good are they if they stay trapped inside? Feelings only matter if they're expressed—otherwise you might as well not have them at all." She laughed, a harsh, bitter sound. "But that doesn't make me feel any better, somehow..."

Nyrin stared at her for a long moment, shaking her head. "Alannys...my Lady...I don't know what to say to you. Honestly, we didn't mean to cause this. Our only intent was to help—and to stymie Lord Malrec."

"I know." Alannys heaved a colossal sigh and fell back against her pillows. "I can't complain, though—you saved me. There is no way my friends could have reached me in time. I'm just worried, I guess, about what happens now."

"You rest." Nyrin sounded sterner than before. "That is what must happen now. Those wounds are not trivial. If you don't rest, they can't heal."

"I know. It's just hard to stop my mind running in circles."

"Just close your eyes, and you'll be asleep before you know it."

Alannys frowned. "What, sleep with you sitting there?"

"Yes." Nyrin smiled her gentle smile again. "I will make sure you are not disturbed. Go on—close your eyes."

"If you...if you say so." Feeling extremely self-conscious, Alannys closed her eyes.

A soft, soothing tune washed over her mind, like a lullaby, lilting and gentle. A sweet voice, female and warm, sang words she couldn't quite make out.

She struggled to open her eyes, to sit up and tell Nyrin to stop, this wasn't necessary. But she was dead tired, and the song was strong. A cool hand enfolded her own hand in its grasp, and the singing grew closer. Alannys fought against it a moment longer, but the music settled into her brain like a fog, and pushed her under the murky surface of sleep.

♫

Alannys couldn't even guess how long she slept, but she woke up feeling worlds better. She hadn't woken at all during the night, hadn't even dreamed. Her entire recollection was of Nyrin's song, winding through her consciousness, soothing her wounds and resting her mind.

Alannys stood up out of bed, frowning. Her brain felt muddy. Had that really happened? Or had she dreamed the singer and the song? It had certainly seemed real.

But then, the room was certainly empty now.

She didn't know what to think. All she knew for sure was that she was ready to venture outside this little room and see what waited there. But the shapeless linen robe she was in didn't fit her very well, and it wasn't what she would call comfortable. It reminded her of a hospital gown.

Her own clothes were nowhere to be found, though. Her clothes and cloak, Songstrike, even the dagger Raman gave her—all missing. The little room only had the bed, the small table that held the lantern and a couple of chairs, so there wasn't much place to hide anything.

It didn't matter. Her memories were fuzzy and indistinct, but she didn't think that her wounds had been tended in this room. Her things were probably in another room, wherever she had first arrived here. So for now, she either sat in bed alone all day, or she wandered out into the cave, barefoot in an ill-fitting robe.

Not her idea of a good time, either way.

Alannys left the little cavern-room, moving slowly through the narrow cave on the other side of the arch-shaped entrance. The walls were lumpy and uneven, and occasionally the ceiling dipped so low she had to stoop to walk under it. Considering it was a cave, though, she thought it could have been a lot worse.

The narrow passage opened into a wider, roundish cavern. This was an entrance to the cave, if the sunlight flooding in was any indication. That light looked too bright to be real, spreading across the packed earth floor, painfully bright.

Alannys stepped outside, and found that it was indeed painfully bright. She shaded her eyes with her hand and did her best to ignore their watering.

Outside of the cave was a grassy area enclosed by high

rock walls. A stone well stood in one corner, complete with bucket and crank handle. A few large shade trees cast their shadows across a chicken coop, and one whole side of the grassy clearing had been cultivated into a garden. She could see lots of plants, and some fruit trees.

Kneeling in between the rows of vegetable plants, working with a spade to pull weeds, was a teenaged boy. He looked up when Alannys walked out, sat back on his heels and waved. "Good morning!"

The chickens clucked at the sudden disturbance and eyed Alannys suspiciously. She walked over toward the garden, surprised to see vegetables on the plants, and fruit on some of the trees.

The boy stood up, dusted off the knees of his heavy pants, and reached out to pick a fruit off of a nearby tree. "You're up late," he said. "I'll bet you're hungry." He tossed the yellow-skinned, smallish fruit to her.

Alannys caught it and turned it over in her hands, surprised by its weight and the solid sound it made slapping into her palm. "I'm surprised you still have fruit this far into the winter. What is this?"

"It's a winter plum. Not so sweet as the summer plums, but denser, more filling. Good for breakfast, anyway, even at lunchtime." He grinned at her.

"Thank you." Alannys bit into the plum, and looked around the yard again. It seemed to be empty, except for this boy and the chickens. "Do you know where Nyrin is today?"

"Usually, she'd be out here helping me tend the gardens. I'm Josak, by the way." He stuck his hand out and shook hers enthusiastically. "So usually, you'd be in the right place. Today, though..." He shrugged. "She's in her room. Muse's Fever."

"Muse's Fever...so that wasn't a dream. Nyrin did sing last night."

"She did. And why wouldn't she? From what I heard, you were pretty rough last night. Nyrin ain't the type that can just walk away from that."

Alannys flushed, and took another bite from the yellow plum. "No, of course not. You know her well, then?"

Josak grinned. "About as well as I know anybody, I suppose. She's the closest thing to a mother I've ever had."

"Really? How did you meet her, if you don't mind me asking?"

There was a long silence. Alannys glanced up from her plum to find Josak staring off into the distance, scratching awkwardly at the back of his neck. "I'm sorry," Alannys said, "I don't mean to pry."

"No, it ain't that," he said, but he still didn't look at her. "This here's quite a pickle. I don't mind telling you, and Nyrin said we was to make you welcome. But Driach —he said not to tell you nothing unnecessary. He'd have me head."

"Unnecessary," she echoed. It did sound like Driach. It saddened her—she'd begun to think they trusted her after all. "So I'm to know nothing about where I am, or who is keeping me here."

Josak winced. "No—no, that ain't what he means, I'm sure." She turned away, and he took a deep breath. "Look. I never knew me parents. I grew up in me aunt and uncle's house. I don't know what happened to me parents—no one would ever talk about it. I didn't know I could paint, then, either. But one day they found me working on a charcoal sketch, and—well, I was just lucky not to be turned out into the street, or worse."

Alannys turned back to face him, grimacing. She'd heard this kind of story before.

"But from then on, any time someone's livestock died, or their crop didn't produce, or someone took ill of a sudden, folks looked me way. Proving you did something is easy, but proving you didn't do something—now that can be a trick."

"Fear and prejudice don't listen to reason very well," Alannys said.

"Exactly. And then two newborn babies died within a week...and you can imagine how far reason got me then. They had me backed up against the wall of the barn, throwing stones, when Driach and Nyrin arrived. They would have killed me otherwise. I still have the scars on me arms and legs."

"That's horrible!"

Josak nodded. He knelt back down among the plants and resumed weeding. "Sure enough. Being here at the harborage, though—it's like a whole different world. Driach and Nyrin have taken care of me as good as any parents. And I'm Driach's apprentice, now, so I actually am learning how to use me Talent, not hiding it out of fear."

"That's quite a story," Alannys said, looking around the yard again. "This is an amazing place."

"It is that."

"It has to be because of the amazing people running it," she said. It seemed like a good time to dig for more information, if she could keep Josak talking. "I heard Driach's story last night. But you know, he never mentioned having Nyrin with him during all of that. Did she find him later?"

Josak froze in his weeding, looking, Alannys thought, cornered. "Nyrin was the first person Driach met in Orinthal," he said carefully, "before he even found this cave. She's been with him ever since."

Alannys watched the chickens scratch, considering that. It was plain there was a story there. It was equally plain that Josak either would not or could not tell it. Perhaps he had divulged all he felt he could. She took another bite of her plum, and turned back to face him. He was putting away his gardening tools. "Finished already?"

He shook his head. "Well, no. But the rest will have to wait until tomorrow, at least. Driach's given me a mission."

She could hear the pride in the young man's voice. "That sounds important."

"Oh, it is. I'm riding out this morning to begin the search for your Singari friends."

"I'm coming with you." The words were out before she knew she was going to speak.

Josak looked at her in frank surprise. "No, you can't. I mean, you must realize you ain't in no shape to ride."

"But—"

"I'm sorry, miss, but I got to insist. Driach'd *really* have me head. You're in no way to travel. Don't you worry. I'll find them, if they can be found."

He disappeared into the cave in quick, hopping steps, glancing back once to make sure she didn't follow him.

She didn't. He was right, even she could see that. Still, it bothered her to sit idle while other people worked on her behalf.

She stood regarding the yard a moment: the well, the orchard, the chickens and their suspicious eyes. How could she be of any use here?

Finally she picked up Josak's tools, and knelt in the moist dirt of the garden, tending the winter plants.

♫

Mindless, repetitive labor suited Alannys well that day. It kept her hands busy, and numbed her mind until it quit running in circles of stress and worry.

And the garden looked like it really needed the attention. With so much else to attend to, Josak and Nyrin were only able to do the very minimum that needed doing each day. Alannys didn't know how long she worked in the garden that day, but she began to suspect she would run out of sunlight long before she ran out of garden.

A deep ringing tone sounded through the yard. Alannys knew it had to be coming from the cave, but it seemed to emanate from everywhere at once. Just a single, musical note—but that note was laced with command. Wherever Nyrin was, she had to be responsible for it; she was the only other musician here. Alannys had little choice but to lay down her tools and follow that sound.

The ringing seemed to hang on the air unnaturally long, leading her in the cave and down a long, uneven corridor she had not been through before.

At the end of the corridor she found the biggest room she had yet seen in the complex. It was large and open, and looked like they probably used it for many purposes. Right now, several tables had been placed around the room, with chairs around them. A long counter built against the back wall held a few large serving platters and bowls, and that was where everyone seemed to be, moving in a quiet line past the food and collecting what they wanted onto plates before going to sit at the tables.

That compelling sound had been—a dinner bell?

"Lady Alannys!"

Alannys turned to face the call—it came from the kitchen area to her left, where a girl who looked a bit younger than herself was wiping her hands roughly with a dishtowel. She had coppery brown hair and brown eyes and the friendliest smile Alannys had seen in a while. She hurried over to Alannys, tossing the towel over her shoulder. "I'm so glad you made it in."

"Thank you," Alannys said. "Is there somewhere I can wash up? I've been in the garden."

"Oh, my." The girl looked surprised. "Have you been out there all afternoon? We all assumed you were resting in your room! You really should have been, you know—it isn't wise to push too hard after an experience like yours.

You need your rest to recover."

"I know. I just...there wasn't a lot to do in bed. Josak had to leave early on his search, so I thought I could pick up some of the slack in the garden."

"Oh, I'm not criticizing! I'm very thankful for your help —with Josak gone, like you said, and Nyrin down today, we are really falling behind. I'm Cenda," she said. "Follow me, I have a basin over here where you can wash."

Alannys washed her hands and face as well as she could manage in the large bowl, and dried with the dishtowel Cenda offered.

"The food's over there," Cenda said, gesturing at the counter Alannys had seen before. "Just grab a plate and take whatever you want. I should warn you, Nyrin usually handles the cooking. I'm filling in, and I am not half the cook she is. I hope it won't be too terrible."

"It smells wonderful," Alannys said truthfully. She took a plate from the stack at the near end of the counter and worked her way down the line. She found fried potatoes, crusty warm bread, a thick brown soup, and dried, salted fish. Maybe it was because she was on the mend, or maybe it was because she had spent all day working in the garden, but she was ravenous.

She took a table by herself, over on the far side of the room. There were only a few other people in the room— Driach and Nyrin sat together at a table, eating and conversing quietly. Nyrin looked pale and a bit unsteady, but she was up and eating, which was a definite plus.

At another table sat a large hulking man, all by himself. He huddled over his plate, staring down at the table as though he might have liked to hide under it. He was muscular and bald, with a neatly trimmed beard.

Cenda filled a plate of her own and came to sit with Alannys. "You don't mind, do you?" she asked, hesitating next to the chair she had pulled out for herself. "I mean,

I'll understand if you'd rather be alone."

"Oh, no, you're fine. Please, sit down."

"Thank you!" Cenda seated herself and scooted the chair in, leaning over the table toward Alannys. "I've been dying to talk to you. Is it true what they say? That you're the Redeemer?"

Alannys pushed her potatoes around in the puddle of soup on her plate—it was thick and delicious, and made good gravy. "That's the question, isn't it? If you had asked me that when I first came to Ravanmark, I probably would have laughed at you. But now, after everything I've done...I've got to tell you, I have to wonder myself." She hesitated, not really eager to continue that line of conversation. "And what about you? Ravan's Light is made up of Talented people, right? What's yours? Do you sing, or paint?"

Cenda laughed. "Neither, actually. I am a scribe."

Alannys goggled. "A writer? I didn't think there were any around anymore."

"Well, there aren't very many. And they aren't likely to shout what they are to the world, you know? But yes, I can write—and make magic with it."

"Wow." Alannys leaned over the table toward Cenda, suddenly not interested in eating. "How does that work?"

"Hmm...it's hard to explain." Cenda took a bite of her dinner and thought about it. "Well, first you have to write down what it is you want to happen. But you have to be very careful how you do it—you have to specify exactly, and you have to limit it as closely as you can. Because when you work this kind of magic, you're changing what has happened, you know? You're wrestling against streams of reality, rivers of time...and each little change you make now can have profound effects later on in that river. All of the energy to make those changes comes from you. You could make a small change here that has enormous effects later, and the energy required to pay for those enormous effects could kill you. It's very risky."

Alannys stared at her. "You can write...changes to reality?"

"Well sure, the same way you can sing to change things. Writing can be powerful, and dangerous. I could try to bring back a dead person, for instance. But it would kill me to do it — my life for theirs. All of my energy would be transferred to them. And then there would be no energy left to handle the changes caused by that person now living, instead of dying. Probably," she mused, "we would both end up dead."

"How do you know, when you're writing, how much energy will be required?"

"You don't. You do your best to frame small, manageable changes, and you hope for the best when you invoke the pages."

"Invoke the pages? So the writing itself isn't the magic?"

"Oh, no. Well, sort of, I suppose. Anything that's written down properly has the potential to be invoked. But until it is actually invoked, potential is all it is — and precious few people know how to invoke pages anymore."

Alannys sat back in her chair, considering. "So it's kind of like written music — it doesn't actually do anything until it is performed."

"Kind of. Written music can be performed over and over again. Written pages are destroyed when they are invoked."

The big man finished eating, and stood up from his table. He carried his dishes over to the counter and placed them in a washtub. As Alannys watched, he approached their table, his head still down, moving as silently as a shadow.

"Cenda, thank you for the meal." His voice was a

reflection of himself; big and deep, and if he had spoken loudly it would have easily filled the room. But his tone was barely above a whisper, and he never looked at either of them.

Before Cenda could respond, he turned and walked quietly out of the room.

Alannys watched him leave, frowning. Talent usually instilled some level of confidence, and he did not look like the shrinking violet type.

"That's Saukar," Cenda said, as if that explained everything. "He's very shy." She leaned forward and lowered her voice. "Something bad happened to him, but nobody knows what."

"Something bad. That seems to be a theme here. How did you end up with Ravan's Light, Cenda?"

"Something bad happened," she said, and she laughed, but it was a hollow laugh, without much humor. "My husband walked in on me when I was preparing to invoke some pages I had just finished. He stopped me. He was horrified. The spell would have killed me, but he didn't know that—he was just horrified that I was a scribe. He put me out."

"Put you out, just like that? How could he—I mean, didn't he—didn't he—"

"Love me? Oh, I think he did. Love can only tolerate so much, you know, and then the only thing to do is walk away."

Alannys stared at her, amazed at the calm with which she had uttered those words. "But that's not right! When you love someone, you're supposed to love them forever, no matter what. Especially if you *marry* them! I mean, I can see it if you did something like murder somebody— something really awful—but for something you can't even control, like having Talent?"

"Being Talented *is* awful." Cenda's knuckles were

white and strained on the tabletop. She was still smiling, but it felt sharp somehow — it made Alannys wonder if she'd been wise to push back on this at all. "Are you suggesting that he shouldn't have put me out? That it would have been better for him to consign himself to a lifetime of the danger of living with Talent, a lifetime of stillborn babies because Talented people aren't meant to reproduce?"

The blunt, matter-of-fact way Cenda said that seemed to knock the wind out of Alannys, and she just stared in silent shock.

Cenda apparently took her silence for acquiescence. Her smile became gentle. "I'm sorry, where was I?"

"You — you said what you wrote would have killed you. If you don't mind me asking, what was it?"

Cenda sighed. "I had just delivered our first baby. A girl. Stillborn."

"I'm so sorry," Alannys said.

She shook her head. "Thank you. The pages would have brought her back. I would have died, whether the spell had worked or not, but to me it was worth it. But I never even got to try. My mother supported him in casting me out, and I wandered for weeks searching for Ravan's Light. It was the only place I might have a chance. I don't know if it was from the birth, or from the destruction of the pages, but I have been sickly ever since that day."

Alannys shook her head, overwhelmed. Talent was a great gift, and granted great power, she knew that. What she had never realized before was how it seemed to attract tragedy. Talented people seemed to have disproportionately sad stories. Even her own was no picnic.

And the real kicker was, it wasn't really the Talent causing all the heartache. No, it was the stigma attached to it that was making everyone miserable. Little by little, she could feel that beginning to change around her, but the process was so slow!

"Thank you," Alannys said, standing and gathering her dirty dishes. "Dinner was great, and so was the company."

Cenda inclined her head. "Anytime, Lady Alannys."

Alannys deposited her dishes in the washtub, and walked over to Driach and Nyrin's table, where it looked like the couple was just finishing up. They looked up at her in surprise.

"Good evening, Lady Alannys," Driach said. "And how does this night find you?"

"Well, thank you," she said. "Much better because of your efforts, and Nyrin's. That is why I bothered you, actually—I wanted to stop and thank you both for everything you have done for me."

"No thanks are necessary, you know that." Nyrin said. "It was nothing."

"Muse's Fever is a bit more than nothing," Alannys said wryly. "I am sorry that you went through it for my sake. But I am grateful all the same."

Nyrin smiled broadly. "Thank you, Alannys. I hope you realize that you are welcome here as long as you wish to stay. Who knows, you may find that life here suits you better than roaming across the country."

"Who knows," echoed Alannys. She didn't have the heart to let them down.

The truth was that while it was tranquil here, and life in this little community left her peaceful and fulfilled, she couldn't imagine staying. One day in the garden was a welcome change, but she suspected that it wouldn't take much time at all before she began to find the simple life here confining. The Singari relied on her; she didn't know if she had it in her to walk away from them before she had to.

But it didn't even matter, because in the end it wasn't

her choice to make. She had a duty to Ravanmark to finish what she had started — the stories she had heard here were very effective reminders of exactly why her mission here was so important. And when that was done, she had made a promise to the king — a promise she intended with all her being to keep, even if it broke her heart.

And it was looking more and more certain, from where she stood, that it would.

♫

The next morning, Alannys went out to the yard as soon as she woke up. It was only shortly after sunrise, and everything outside had that fresh clean look that only happens in the early morning.

She found Nyrin by the well, having some trouble getting the large wooden bucket pulled back up. She hurried over and helped turn the crank.

"Thank you," Nyrin said, a little short of breath. "This is usually not such an ordeal for me — I must not be quite back to normal yet."

Alannys never saw Saukar approach; she just saw Nyrin step back, glanced up, and there he was. He never spoke a word, just grasped the crank handle in one meaty hand, gently sliding her hands out of the way with the other. Before she had gotten her mind around what had just happened, he had pulled up the water and set the sloshing bucket at their feet.

Then he was gone.

Alannys hefted the bucket for Nyrin. "Does he do that often?"

"Quite often," Nyrin said.

"Does he ever talk to you?"

"Never. Saukar is a good man and a great help, but not much of a conversationalist."

Alannys followed Nyrin back to the kitchen, hauling the water bucket. 'Not much of a conversationalist' seemed a bit of an understatement to her. He always looked so sad when she saw him. How could this silent, lonely existence be helping him?

She helped Nyrin wash up the dishes that morning after breakfast. She spent the morning tending the orchard with Cenda.

When they finished, Cenda went back inside to rest. She tired easily, Alannys noticed, and wondered if that was part of the sickness she had mentioned the day before.

But for herself, she couldn't tolerate the thought of rest. It felt as though she had been resting every moment since she came to this place. She was beginning to get antsy.

Alannys fed the chickens and wandered back inside the cave. At this hour most of the corridors were dark—not many people were inside.

One of the smaller corridors branching off of the left side of the main entrance was the exception. She could see warm light flickering down that way.

Alannys followed the light to the end of the corridor, which turned out to be not as long as she had imagined. The room she found at the end was almost completely filled by a large weaving loom. A small cot was squeezed in between the loom and the wall.

Seated at the loom was Saukar. His big hands, with fingers like overstuffed sausages, worked the loom with grace and precision that astounded her. How could those hands be so nimble?

The work fascinated her, and the gentle, repetitive sounds of the loom soothed her. It was several minutes before she realized that he was watching her.

As soon as her eyes met his, he looked away. "Perhaps," he said, "you should leave." His voice was low and faint, scarcely more than a breath in the quiet room. And yet it held something of the size, something of the commanding aura, of the man behind it. It made Alannys want very much to do as he said.

Instead, she fidgeted. "I'm sorry I haven't properly introduced myself. My name is Alannys."

"I know who you are."

"They tell me you are Saukar?" He really was intimidating—it took a conscious effort of will to keep standing there, keep talking to him.

"That is my name."

Silence stretched out between them, broken only by the quiet noises of the weaving loom.

"I'm sorry," Alannys said finally. "I don't mean to intrude, but...do you mind if I sit with you for a while?"

Saukar studied her for a long moment with no emotion she could identify, his hands working all the while. "Do as you wish. I won't stop you."

Well, he certainly hadn't invited her in, but he hadn't told her to get lost, either. She decided to assume the best and grabbed a wooden chair from against the wall by the door. She wasn't even sure what he kept it for—maybe to prop his feet in? She pulled the chair over near him and sat down.

Saukar seemed to have no reaction to this development at all.

"You are very good with that loom," she said. "You must have been weaving a long time."

Silence.

"You know, when I heard that everyone here is Talented, I assumed everyone either painted or sang. I never imagined there could be scribes here, or weavers. I really thought those Talents were lost."

Saukar looked at her sidelong.

"It's great that they're not, you know? I have this dream, of a place where people with Talent can go to learn how to use it. Wouldn't it be great if they could learn writing and weaving there?"

No response.

"Well, that is quite a bit down the road, that is true." This one-sided conversation was getting a bit difficult to maintain. Alannys was reaching pretty hard for things to say, and she knew it. But she figured if she kept talking for long enough, Saukar was bound to talk back, if only to tell her to go away. "That is a really beautiful tapestry, Saukar. This is the backside, right?"

His head dipped in what may have been an almost imperceptible nod.

"I can't imagine how pretty the front must be, if the back looks this good. Tapestries are kind of rare where I come from, you know? I remember that was one thing that hit me right away about my rooms at the Great Palace. There was this enormous tapestry in the sitting room—it was the biggest one I had ever seen. It showed the royal family, and it was so detailed—I don't think a portrait could have been any more accurate. I can't imagine how much time and skill must have gone into it. It kind of annoyed me at the time, because I felt like I couldn't escape from it, you know? But I sure would love to see it now."

She was rambling, she knew that. Her eyes had misted over, and she was talking more to herself than to the man next to her. Maybe this hadn't been such a good idea after all.

"It's enchanted." The words were soft, barely even audible, and for a moment she couldn't believe they had come from Saukar.

"What?" She was so shocked that he'd actually spoken to her that she had to think back over his words to figure out what he had said. "I didn't think anybody knew how to do that anymore."

Saukar laughed darkly. "Well, now, that's just what we'd want you to think. No weaver worth a single strand of the thread he uses would let on. But that tapestry you talked about—I'd stake my life that it was enchanted."

Alannys sat back in her chair, considering. "What does an enchanted tapestry do?" An awful thought struck her; suppose an enchanted tapestry could be used to spy? Suppose every one of her sarcastic comments, every one of her petty fits, had been transmitted clearly to King Caleb and Queen Farrine? It would certainly explain their dislike for her.

"Communication," Saukar said, and Alannys could feel her heart begin to beat double-time. "That is, later on. While the subject of a tapestry is alive, the tapestry is as you said; just a portrait. But after they are dead, with the proper procedure, a the tapestry can be used to talk with their spirit."

"Seriously? Can anyone do it, or only the weaver who made the tapestry?"

"Oh, anyone could, if they knew how. The weaver is the only one who can create the enchantment, but after that, anybody could invoke it."

"Wow. I had no idea such magic existed."

"No one does, anymore, except people who can use it." A small smile played around Saukar's mouth, then faded. "Even my wife did not know. She used to sit with me at the loom too, you know."

"I didn't know that." Alannys wasn't sure what to say. He spoke of his wife in the past tense, and judging by everyone else here, the story couldn't be good. "I didn't know you were married, Saukar."

He nodded. He kept his focus so tight on the loom it might have seemed he didn't even know she was there. "Wife, three kids. All gone."

It hit her like a physical blow. "What? How?"

"You know, Alannys, I wish I knew. Some of the villagers, they set fire to my house one night. My family, they—they never made it out. I know that the fire was meant for me. But the funny thing was, I had slept out in the barn that night — we had a horse in foal, and she was having a difficult time of it. What I'll never know is what made them come after me. I can't for the life of me figure out how they knew. Even my wife, even she never knew."

"I'm sorry," Alannys said, aware of the inadequacy of the sentiment. "I'm so, so sorry."

For the first time since she had been there, Saukar's hands faltered in their work. "That's why you must succeed, Alannys. So there will be no more...no more..."

She could see tears welling up in his eyes. He couldn't seem to finish the sentence. Alannys supposed that was all right.

She already knew what he meant.

♪

The stories Alannys had heard rattled around in her head all the next day. Every story at the harborage of Ravan's Light increased the pressure she felt. All of these people bore such deep hurts, and all of them counted on her to heal them. What if she failed? What if, in the end, it turned out that she was never the Redeemer at all, but just some extra-Talented freak from another world?

The silent weight of the expectations of so many people was unbearable. She couldn't stand to be alone with her thoughts, but she couldn't handle the company of others. The strain leeched her appetite, and she dumped her dinner dishes in the washtub with a sense of relief, eager to leave the common room behind and wallow in solitude for a while.

"Lady Alannys?" The quiet voice behind her stopped her in her tracks. "I'm sorry to bother you, but I wonder if I might talk to you."

Alannys turned around. "Of course, Nyrin. Anytime."

"Come with me." The older lady led her out of the common room and down an unfamiliar corridor, into a bedroom. The paintings around the room told her that this had to be the room Nyrin and Driach shared. "I am sorry to bother you; I know you must be ready to rest. But I must discuss something with you, something of utmost importance—something it would be just as well if the others did not hear."

Nyrin gestured to a chair, and Alannys seated herself. She had to admit her curiosity was piqued. What could this be about?

"You have said," Nyrin said, "that Ethal hunts you." She lowered herself into a chair across from Alannys gingerly, as though speaking the name had aged her. Looking at her now, Alannys realized that Nyrin was not nearly as old as she had first assumed—her haggard face and prematurely gray hair gave a false impression of advanced age.

Hearing it put so bluntly gave her a chill, but Alannys could not deny the truth of it. She nodded. "It's pretty scary, honestly."

Nyrin sighed heavily, not quite looking at her. "Not half as scary as it would be if you understood what you're up against, I'm afraid. The man is a monster."

Alannys stood up suddenly out of her chair. "You know, I promised Cenda I'd help clean up. I should really —"

"Sit down, Alannys." Nyrin's voice was firm, filling the room, brooking no opposition—like a mother speaking to a disobedient child. There wasn't a trace of musical command in the words, but Alannys sat down anyway. "Just a moment ago, you had plenty of time. Why do you wish to run from this?"

Alannys squirmed uncomfortably in her chair. "A friend of mine once told me that to talk about something is to draw it to you. I dismissed it, but—maybe after everything that's happened, I'm not so confident now. If it's all the same to you, I'd rather not draw this to me."

Nyrin finally smiled, but it was a thin, strained smile. "This must have been your Singari friend. Charming, primitive people — but unfortunately prone to superstitions. Your friend sounds caring, but not very wise. Nothing you could do will keep Ethal from you now."

Alannys bit back an impolite response to her remarks about the Singari. "Forgive me if I'm prying, but you sound as though you have experience with this man."

"Experience." The word was dark when Nyrin said it, unpleasant. "Alannys, let me tell you a story. There once was a family, not all that far from here, who thought they were quite special, because they had more money than most of the families around them. This family had a daughter, only one, and of course because they were so special, it wouldn't do for her to marry just anyone. Because they were so special, the only reasonable thing they could do was find another special family who had a son, and arrange that their daughter should marry him."

Alannys sat still and said nothing. Arranged marriages never seemed to lead to anything good — although she supposed that could be her own bias talking. Certainly King Caleb and Queen Farrine had lived out their lives without murdering each other, and Lord Arik and Lady Marin seemed to genuinely care about each other. But Nyrin's sour tone made her think that was not the direction this story would go. "Was this special family yours, Nyrin?"

"Yes. And I did not blame this young man for all the silliness that led to our engagement. He was a wonderful man, kind and generous, and we had been friends for years before. It is true that our families were of some influence in our rather small town, but not enough influence to catch Baron Prubard's notice, which was all for the better.

"So my young man and I were looking forward to a wedding a few months in the future. And then his mother fell dreadfully, horribly ill. The healers did all they could, then they told us there was nothing left but to make her as comfortable as we could for the time she had left.

"I hated to hear that; I liked her. And my young man was utterly distraught. I asked permission to sit with her for a while." Nyrin paused, remembering.

"And you sang," Alannys guessed.

"Yes. For several hours I did nothing but sing. We were a small sort of town, and I think that our healers must not have been the best. If things had truly been as bad as they said, all of my efforts should have made no difference. But she lived."

"Well, that's wonderful!" Alannys said, trying to figure out where Nyrin's tone was coming from. So far, it sounded like everything was working out fine. "Your betrothed must have been thrilled."

"He was. About his mother, anyway. But...he had walked in on me while I sang. He said nothing at the time; he didn't stop me, just turned and left. After it was all over and his mother was recovered, he told me that he was dissolving our engagement. He said he appreciated what I had done, he loved me, and he would always keep my secret, but he refused to marry Talent into his family.

"My life in that small town was ruined. He was true to his word and never breathed a word about my Talent. But in the absence of any other reason, everyone in town assumed that I had been unfaithful. From then on I was shunned in the town, except for one really disturbing man who followed me relentlessly, showering me with lewd propositions. I guess he felt it was justified by what everyone knew I had done."

"How horrible!" Another life ruined, not by Talent, but by society's inability to accept that Talent.

"It was. But the worst was yet to come. You see, I had no idea how horrible that man really was. I found myself unable to sleep late one night, and went for a walk alone. It wasn't something any respectable girl would do, but then, I didn't have to worry about that, did I?" The sarcasm in Nyrin's voice was sharp, cutting. "I could feel the painting open, could see him swagger out of it, confident and cold, as if no power in the world could stop him. I screamed, I fought, but all to no avail, and he hauled me back through the painting with him. I will never know whether nobody in that town actually heard me, or whether they honestly felt I wasn't worth saving."

Alannys stared at her, shocked. Was it really possible that these people, people Nyrin had grown up with and around, could have left her to that fate? People she had *saved*? Just because she was Talented?

Alannys shook her head. Who was she kidding? Of course it was possible; she had heard stories like it far too often to pretend otherwise. And yet, they never quite seemed to lose the ability to shock her, every time. "So," she said slowly, "this...man...was Ethal?"

"Indeed he was. I spent the most horrific week of my life in his company, after he abducted me that night. The painting led to a cavern, with natural light trickling in from somewhere up high, and a deep pond surrounded by fruit-bearing bushes. It should have been beautiful—it *sounds* beautiful, to hear it described like that—but it wasn't. The place had been desecrated too many times, used for too many horrible profane rituals. The rocky walls and the ground seemed to bear permanent blood stains, and the air felt heavy and oppressive, as though it did you more harm than good to breathe there. The pond was dark and murky, and the water seemed thick. The fruit on the little bushes was bitter and twisted. Everything in that place seemed to bear the scars of living in close proximity to the horror that was Ethal. I don't know how to explain it, but just being there seemed to — to *drain* me, somehow."

"I don't understand," Alannys said. "How could a person defile a place that way? I mean, he's just a man, after all."

Nyrin shook her head. "He was once, I have no doubt. But whatever Ethal is now, he is not just a man any longer. The things he has done have changed him. I speak not of what he did to me, although that was horrible enough. Suffice it to say that there are reasons why Driach and I have no children. No healer can overcome the damage Ethal wrought, with his sick appetites and twisted tools. Even that was not the worst.

"The worst came on my second day in captivity. Ethal was gone most of that day, and I thought that was a good thing.

"I was wrong."

Alannys shivered. The room just kept getting colder and colder — or maybe it was her. She wasn't sure she wanted to hear all of this — in fact she was pretty sure she *didn't* — but Nyrin was right. If there was any chance she was going to have to face this man, she needed to know everything she could. And the more she heard about his obsession with Talent, the more certain she was that she would be facing him, eventually.

"Now understand, Alannys, that Ethal had no idea I could sing. He took me because he thought I was pretty and he had a grudge against me for dismissing his proposals. It never occurred to him that I might have other uses as well. I had heard the whispers — everyone had — about Talented people disappearing, about the murders, but I never really understood until that day.

"Ethal came back to the cavern with Sari, the woman who was to have been my law-mother; the woman whose life I had saved."

"Wait." Alannys knew she shouldn't interrupt. She had not intended to interrupt. Her surprise blocked everything else, even common decency, and her confusion demanded immediate answers. "Your mother-in-law. Your fiance's mother. Ethal had the mother of the man you were going to marry. Is that right?"

Nyrin nodded, her face closed and expressionless.

"Why?" Frustration welled up in Alannys, blinding her to her own discourtesy. She had thought, through everything she had heard, that she was finally beginning to form a concrete understanding of this man called Ethal, of how he worked, of what he wanted. This revelation threatened that entire understanding. "I don't understand. What did he want with her?"

"Sari could sing," Nyrin said shortly, as if she didn't trust herself to speak further.

Alannys gaped at her. "Wait, wait," she said again, waving her hands in front of herself. "Hold on. You are telling me that Sari—the mother of the man who broke your engagement because of your Talent—was Talented? And she let your betrothal dissolve, and never said a word?"

Nyrin lifted her shoulders in a stiff shrug. "Yes, and yes. If you are wanting me to excuse her actions, I am afraid you will be disappointed. I think I can explain it though, by reminding you what happened to me when my Talent was known, even to only a few. Sari had concealed her Talent her entire life; it was the only reason she had her position, her influence, her family. She could not support me without bringing scrutiny upon herself, and possibly losing everything she valued if the truth became known. Of course I had known she could sing from the first time I heard her speak—and she had known the same of me. But I would not reveal her, any more than she would reveal me."

"Her Talent was secret. Okay. But Ethal is not a musician, right? Then how could he know she would be any use to him?"

"I think every Talented person keeps that Talent a secret," Nyrin said philosophically, "as long as they can. But we all have a limit, Lady Alannys — we all have a point where the price of secrecy becomes too high. For Sari, that limit was her son. My former betrothed took a bad fall from a horse. His condition was quite serious; his recovery was doubtful. Sari sang to save him.

"But things went wrong. Ethal found her. She didn't even accomplish her goal — she wasn't able to save her son. He died the day before Ethal brought her back to the cavern. She had lost everything.

"But she was about to lose much more."

Alannys shivered in a sudden, ominous chill. "I've heard Ethal is a notorious murderer," she said, hoping it might forestall any grim details she could do without.

"Ah, Alannys but there is murder, and there is murder." Nyrin's gaze nailed her to the spot. "A murderer would have murdered Sari, and she would have been dead, and that would have been that.

"Ethal murdered Sari, and she took three days to die."

Alannys couldn't seem to move, couldn't seem to breathe. She felt her mouth moving as if of its own accord, forming the words *three days*, but no sound came from her. She was shocked to her core. How many different kinds of evil were there? The Dark Alliance had evil intentions for all of Ravanmark, and each of its members were evil in their own personal jurisdictions, in ways that contributed to the frightening whole. But their darkness spread over masses of people, and compared to what she heard now it seemed almost diluted by that fact. Ethal took the evil that Lord Malrec or Baron Prubard might have applied to an entire holding, and concentrated it on a single individual. Didn't that make him worse, then, that he destroyed a handful of people so utterly? Or were Lord Malrec and his ilk really the greater evil, because they afflicted so *many?*

Alannys wasn't sure. And honestly she didn't want to examine the question too closely. She didn't have the heart. How many types of evil were there? It sounded like the setup for a bad joke, and she didn't want to hear the punch line. The truth was she just didn't even want to know. Too many, that was all, and she had run across more of them during her tour of Ravanmark than she wanted to think about.

Nyrin saw her mouth form the silent words and nodded grimly. "This is no ordinary man, Alannys, and he intends you no ordinary malice."

"That...seems clear." Alannys stumbled over the words, still trying to come to grips with what she was hearing. "I don't understand. Why on earth does he do that—is he that senselessly cruel?"

"Yes," Nyrin said without hesitation. "But he actually has reasons for it in this case."

"Reasons?" Alannys spluttered. "What possible reason could there be?"

"These inhuman rituals," Nyrin said, "are the means by which Ethal strips his victim's Talent and transfers it to himself."

Alannys stared at her.

"I do not know what he did to Sari before he brought her to the cavern. I only know that she was limp, helpless —unable to stand or resist. I feared at first that she was dead.

"I will not recount what he did to her after bringing her to the cavern—I do not think I could handle it. I will simply say that in retrospect, it would have been better for her if she had been dead.

"The rituals exhausted Ethal, though, and he slept for at least a day afterward. During that time I was able to break free. The cavern had drained me so completely I probably should not have been able to move, but my fear and horror drove me harder than I could have imagined. I was able to climb out and escape the cavern. Driach found me wandering in the wild shortly after, and I have never seen Ethal again. Muses willing, I never will."

Alannys didn't speak. There was nothing she could say.

♫

The silence yawned between Alannys and Nyrin, deep and impenetrable, seeming bigger than the cave itself. It felt as though it might continue forever, implacable, insatiable, swallowing them both.

"I can't imagine it," Alannys said finally. "I don't know how you survived it. I don't know how you manage from day to day, even now."

Nyrin's hand tightened convulsively on the ends of the shawl hanging over her head. "It isn't easy. But I am not as strong as you must think. This makes it easier." With obvious effort and shaking hands, Nyrin lifted the shawl from her head and laid it across her lap.

"Your...shawl makes it easier?" Alannys could hear the confusion in her own voice.

Nyrin smiled gently. "I know that your friends at the Great Palace have helped you as much as they could. And doubtless you learned much at Castle Glennayre, whether Lord Malrec willed it or not, and you can hardly have helped acquiring yet more knowledge in your travels. But even so I would remind you that there are yet things hidden in Ravanmark that are known only to a few."

"So your shawl is...enchanted?"

"Yes. When I use this shawl, I cannot be seen in paintings."

Alannys could feel her brain lurch sideways. "Wait.

You're telling me you can *hide* from *paintings*?"

"It may surprise you to learn that the Talents—and the Talented people who wield them—have not always been...friendly. Historically they have been prone to work for each other's destruction, for no better reason than that they viewed each other as competition. Until Soth, I don't believe any one person ever possessed more than one Talent. It's still terribly rare—I don't think I've ever met a multi-Talented person, or even heard of one.

"But the Talents have their own type of balance, and this may be the only reason they all survived. Much of the knowledge is now lost, but the rule remains—where there is a Talent, there is a way to defend against that Talent."

"Painters can spy," Alannys said slowly. "Their power is sight—seeing places where they should not be able to see. And you defend against that by hiding."

"Put simply, yes. This magic protects you from being seen in a painting. And a painter cannot pull from a painting that which he cannot see."

"I see," Alannys said. "It makes sense. More than sense—it's ingenious."

"Yes."

"Does it have to be a shawl?"

Nyrin seemed to be caught off guard by the question. For a moment, Alannys had the feeling she had interrupted whatever the older woman had planned to say. "No. You could enchant anything, I suppose; anything that you kept on your person always. You never can predict when you might need it. But Saukar made this shawl for me, and he is one of only a few who know the necessary procedures to place the enchantment. Perhaps the only one who remains."

Alannys's mind raced, trying to process the implications of what she had heard, trying to understand this new idea from every angle. She had a million questions; she had never dreamed such things were possible and it felt like the entire world had just shifted under her.

But before she could put words to a single one of her questions, Nyrin leaned forward and placed the black shawl reverently in her lap.

Alannys stared down at it, then looked over at Nyrin. "I don't understand."

"It is my dearest possession, as you have probably guessed. But I feel that you need it more than I. I would like for you to have it."

"No." Alannys scooped the shawl up off her lap, holding it out away from herself as though she thought it might bite. "No, I can't take this from you."

"My dear," Nyrin smiled, "you must."

"But that isn't fair!" Alannys protested. "Every person here has suffered. Everyone here is in danger — why should I be special?"

"All of us have suffered, yes, but none of us have faced what lies ahead for you. You will not survive on your own — you must learn to accept aid from those around you." She reached out and gently closed Alannys's fingers around the flowing black material. "Take the shawl, Alannys."

"But can't we ask Saukar to make another?"

Nyrin shook her head. "It is kind of you to consider, but there simply isn't time. The weaving and the rituals take months. Lord Malrec moves against you even as we speak — and perhaps others do as well. You must accept this, now, and I must begin instructing you immediately on its use. You must never allow it away from your person, not ever, for even a short time." She met Alannys's gaze bleakly. "I feel the peril surrounding you, Alannys, and I feel that time grows desperately short."

Alannys shivered, but she couldn't argue.

She felt the same way.

♫

Lord Malrec swept into the castle library, practically dancing in his excitement. "Did you see? Did you see how it worked? Do you see how everything has changed?" His voice rang with joy—for the first time in perhaps his entire life, Malrec was thrilled with everything around him. First Delline's unexpected gift, and now...this...

She turned from her stacks of books and beamed at him. "See what?"

His shoulders slumped. She was merely pleased to see him, then—she had no idea what he had come to gloat about. "The bomb, my dear, the *bomb!* Did you see how perfectly it worked? Our tests had shown us as much, of course, but to actually see it operate!"

She crossed her arms. "I don't know that I would call it perfect, my Lord. If everything went so perfectly, where is the music mage now? How did she escape this miracle weapon?"

For just a moment, that stung. Alannys's unexplained disappearance had been the only thing in the whole plan that had gone awry—and he still had no satisfactory explanation for it.

But no matter. Princess Delline was clearly missing the bigger picture here. "It doesn't matter!" Malrec crowed. "Don't you see? We don't need her now. With my explosive devices, we can attack the king directly, and with no risk to ourselves. We can end this war, before it even starts. *Instantly!*"

"What?" Her face was pale, but her cheeks burned red. "Attack the Great Palace directly—attack the very King of Ravanmark himself—with a device as dreadful and dishonorable as that? No. No, I won't stand for it. I absolutely forbid it!"

"You?" Malrec sneered. "You forbid it? And tell me, my dear wife, what do you intend to do about it?"

"Do about it?" She sounded almost surprised. Malrec thought unkindly that she must not have thought her position through very well.

"Yes." He stepped toward her threateningly. "Let us say I have decided this device, used within the Great Palace, directly against the king himself, will end this war before it begins. It will allow me to ascend to the throne almost immediately, with little risk to myself. And let us say I have therefore decided to use it."

"You—" she began.

He cut her off with a single finger laid against her lips. "Let us further say that you have made your objections on the matter abundantly clear. Let us therefore say— hypothetically, of course—that I have you locked and guarded in the tower room. I take my action, and the entire country believes I have taken it with your consent. I am King of Ravanmark, and you are locked in the tower bedroom. What then, my dear Lady of Glennayre, would you do?"

He had pushed too far, he could see it before she even spoke. Delline had been playing very nice lately, attempting to patch up the cracks she could see in their relationship, but he had crossed a line she seemed determined to hold. "What would I do, my *Lord*? First of all, I would leave this place. I would escape this castle by any possible means. If I had to, I would jump to my death from the window. I suppose my mangled corpse outside your castle might give the lie to my 'consent.'"

Lord Malrec felt the blood drain from his face, but said nothing.

"You cannot honestly hope to keep me here. And once I am free, I will stop at nothing to oppose you. Do you believe your mage is the only one capable of talking directly to the people, of stirring them to action? I am still the Princess of Ravanmark, and without my support you are nothing but a common usurper, a Lord of the Holdings who decided his title wasn't good enough for him. Do you imagine achieving the throne by such terrible means would endear you to the public? I would *personally* lead the revolt against you, my Lord, and I would *personally* hoist your head on a pike above the drawbridge of the Great Palace."

Malrec took an instinctive step backward. He cursed himself for the weakness it showed, but he couldn't help it. He could see her vividly in that moment, holding that pike—could see her chestnut hair blowing in the wind, the frozen expression of horror on his own dead face. All this time, he had really believed that Delline was cowed, that she was his, that she would never stand against him. Had he really miscalculated so badly? "You are impertinent, my dear. Is this how you show your allegiance to the one you have married, whose very title you have taken as your own?"

It was the wrong approach. Delline was past punishment now, past any sharp reminders of her place. She was incandescent in her anger, glowing like a tower of righteous flame. "Your title means to me precisely what it means to you, Malrec—nothing! The only title that matters to me is the title I was born into, and it comes with a responsibility, a grave duty to the people of this land. Do you think I have forgotten that?"

He eyed her, uncertain how to proceed. "Is—is your love as fickle as that?"

She stared at him evenly, her blue eyes suddenly as hard as flints, as cold as ice. "Love has nothing to do with it, as you should know very well. I love you till the death, Malrec. But when it comes to the throne, I will only support you so long as you remain the best man for the job. This sort of craven, cowardly attack would make you necessarily *not* the best man. And if I change my mind, if I remove my support from you — if, Muses forbid, I lend that support to my brother instead — what do you have?"

He clenched his hands into white-knuckled fists, pressed his lips into a painful thin line, trying desperately not to show the shaking that was threatening to undo him. "I have the throne. If I detonate these devices in the Great Palace, I will have the throne, uncontested. By the time you rouse your peasant rebellion, I will already be king."

"And how long do you imagine you will *remain* king?" Her tone boiled over with anger and condescension. "A wise ruler does not attempt to gain or hold power with tactics like these, Lord Malrec. By detonating those devices you will lose not only my support, but the support of the people you seek to rule. You need to ascend the throne with them cheering you on, not plotting your demise behind your back. My brother and I may not see eye to eye, but if you defeat him in this underhanded, cowardly way, I will avenge him. And I will not be alone."

He whirled away from her, staring unseeing out of the window, gripping the stone windowsill as if he wished to crush it under his hands. He counted a slow ten in his mind, forcing himself to calm down.

Because she was right. He couldn't deny it. He *needed* her, whether it was convenient or not. And he needed to do this thing the right way, if his victory was to last.

"Thank you, my dear." His voice amazed him, calm and even, betraying none of the anger and betrayal coursing like a drug through his veins. He hated being humbled this way, *hated* it, and he hated her for doing it to him. He turned to face her, keeping his expression carefully passive. "Of course you are right. I don't know what came over me. If your dear brother falls to me, Princess, he shall be honestly bested in fair combat. Does that settle your concerns?"

She smiled, but it did not reach her eyes. "Of course,

my Lord. It would be most upsetting, should I hear of any such attack on the Great Hall or the keep. I assure you that I would not relish being the instrument of your downfall. I shall be pleased to support you." She leaned forward and brushed her lips against his cheek. "Good day, my Lord."

A swirl of gown, a whiff of roses and clover, and she was gone.

"Damn!" Malrec turned back to the window, slamming his fists ineffectually onto the stone sill. His easiest, most expedient option of dealing with King Dorramon was barred to him. It crippled his plans.

But arrogant as she was, her points had been true. He did not take it as given that she could escape from him — although he privately admitted that, had he not been warned, her chances would have been good — but even if he kept her imprisoned forever, it would not save him. The very people who should love him as a liberator would despise him for a horrific attack of that nature on the Great Palace they idolized.

So he would not use his bombs, not on her precious brother. But Malrec was clever, and he was resourceful. He would get where he was going. He would just have to take the long way, that was all.

But in the end, the king would fall to him.

And his death would be anything but honorable.

♫

"Alannys? Are you awake?"

The voice charged into her sleep, slicing through her dreams with all the softness and subtlety of a speeding arrow finding center-target. She wasn't ready for it, and she awoke confused and completely disoriented.

"Yes," she lied, her voice thick with sleep. "Yes, of course." Where was she? What was going on? She was in a room with lumpy, uneven stone walls that seemed utterly unfamiliar, lit by a dim lantern that was burning low. The flickering flame cast dark shadows that jumped and danced like wild things in the corners of the room.

"I am sorry to wake you so early." The deep voice sounded sincerely apologetic. She rolled over and sat up in the bed. A tall man stood in the entrance to the room, holding a lantern of his own and regarding her somberly. Even in the low light she could see that his complexion was unnaturally pale, almost sickly.

She knew this man, she just couldn't seem to wake up enough to put a name to him. But even in her state, she knew she had never seen him look like that.

"I'm sorry," he repeated. He seemed to understand that she had not yet found her bearings. "I know that you were up very late working with Nyrin. But I had to speak with you at once—it's very important."

Nyrin. At the name, the heavy fog in her brain lifted, and she remembered. She had spent most of the night with Nyrin, learning how to use the black, finely woven shawl. That was why she was so ungodly tired.

And this man in front of her—this was Driach, of course. She was ashamed of her momentary lapse of memory; perhaps the recent stress was too much for her. Or maybe after so many weeks of rapidly moving from one place to another through the country, her lack of immediate recognition was to be expected. She had only been here a couple of days, after all.

"Of course, Driach," she said, raking her fingers through her hair in an attempt to look less bedraggled. "It's perfectly fine. What did you need?"

Driach sighed. Now that it came to it, he didn't seem eager to talk. "I hope you will forgive me if I sit," he said, and dropped his tall frame into a chair as if he could not bear supporting it any longer.

"Of course," she repeated, baffled. "If you don't mind my saying so, you don't look like you are feeling very well. What happened?"

"Lord Malrec," he said shortly. "He paints."

"What?" Her fingers clenched in the bedclothes; she had to restrain herself from snatching at the shawl neatly folded on the chair next to her.

Driach held up a calming hand, but it shook too much for the motion to have any impact. "His paintings cannot reach in here. But he has painted the garden outside — it is plain he is searching for you."

"Can't reach in here?" Alannys felt like her mind was racing in too many directions at once, tearing her thoughts apart in the middle. "I don't understand. With the Herb of Sight, he can paint anywhere, right?"

"Almost. You have probably seen that we have preserved some knowledge here that was thought lost." He slumped against the back of his chair and gestured weakly at the shawl. "Part of that knowledge was how to prevent the use of Talent in a room."

Alannys frowned; his words nagged at her memory. "Lord Malrec said something like that once — I remember him saying the tower room I stayed in had been Talent-proofed."

Driach smiled with little humor. "Interesting you should mention Lord Malrec. That is exactly where I learned how to prepare the Talent-proofing solution. Part of his preparation for bringing you to Ravanmark was to give me the recipe for the solution, with orders to prepare it and treat the tower bedroom. I copied down the recipe for my own use, and brought it with me when I fled Glennayre. Many of the rooms in this complex have been Talent-proofed — including this one, now. We treated it yesterday, while you were out in the garden. Even the Herb of Sight cannot thwart this. Your room is closer to the outside than to other open rooms, so that is what he sees. But he will never see this room in any painting."

Alannys tried to think that through. "So he is looking

for me...but he is finding a garden full of things that are not me."

Driach nodded. "I do not believe he knows of the precautions we have taken here. He must assume that you are near the location he has painted."

"But he can't be sure," Alannys pointed out. "He can't know for sure how far away I am, or where he might have to look, or what he might encounter on the way."

"Exactly. I do not think he will lightly risk stepping into that unknown situation, especially so soon after the Herb of Sight. For now, he will be content to wait. You must stay inside, my Lady—away from the garden, and away from my room."

Alannys shivered, suddenly understanding why it had been so important to catch her early. She had been to both of those places yesterday. If she had not known, and had gone back out to work in the garden...or back to see Nyrin to ask some question...

She shivered again. "That won't work for long."

"No," Driach conceded. "Lord Malrec is not known for his patience. He will decide to investigate—or to send someone better armed to search for you."

"I'm going to have to leave."

Driach did not dispute it. He faced her directly, with eyes that were bleak and haunted. "I am not eager to see you go, Alannys. I think this is the best place for you in all of Ravanmark. But Lord Malrec knows you are here. We may be able to protect you at first, but we will not be able to defend against everything he can send through that painting."

She nodded. "When did he paint this?"

She knew it was an odd question, but if Driach thought so, he gave no visible indication of it. "Fifteen minutes ago, maybe twenty? I came here as soon as I could, but you were slow to awaken."

"So...do you think it's safe for me to go out to the well for a drink? I'm parched. I should be able to tell if he opens the painting."

Driach frowned, and slowly nodded. "I would imagine he is sleeping off the effects of the Herb of Sight right now. This is probably the only safe time we are likely to see. I'll go with you. I do think you should take your shawl, just in case."

Alannys wondered exactly what Nyrin had told him about the shawl. She rolled out of bed, her clothes moving with her stiffly and uncomfortably. She had been wearing the same linen robe since she got here, and it was well past needing to be cleaned. And now she was stuck inside...she wondered if she could manage to wash the thing herself in her room, if she could talk someone into bringing in some water for her.

She grabbed the shawl and pulled it over her head. It didn't matter anyway — she had bigger worries than her dirty clothes. She had to plan her escape from this place — without a horse — without any idea how far away she was from the place she had last seen her friends — without any clue where her friends were now.

She couldn't even begin to get her head around it. A drink of water might not have been the answer to her problems, but at that moment it sure seemed like a step in the right direction.

A soul-curdling scream rang through the rocky corridor, freezing Alannys in her tracks. "Nyrin?" she gasped. Her brain refused to make sense of it. "But it isn't even light yet! Why would she be outside this early?"

Driach ran toward the garden. "Same as you — she was thirsty. She didn't sleep well without her shawl close to hand."

Alannys chased after him, struggling against a wave of sudden guilt. Driach's heavy cloak flapped behind him like angry wings, and she realized with a shock that he was wearing a sword underneath it. The sight drove it home to her in a way his words had not—he really was expecting trouble.

But neither of them were prepared for what waited in the garden. Nyrin lay frighteningly still on the cold ground, a slick red stain covering the middle of her heavy gown.

Standing over her was a barrel-chested, meaty brute of a man, with dark, ragged hair receding from his thin face. He tossed a bloodied sword from hand to hand as if it was hot, regarding them with a sharp grin over uneven teeth that gave Alannys the unsettling impression of facing down a hatchet.

"Ethal." Alannys didn't know how she could be so certain. She'd never met the man, and Nyrin had never described him physically. But she knew, knew as certain as she was standing there, that this grinning abomination facing her now was Ethal. "You monster."

Her words were barely more than a murmur, but those soulless eyes regarded her keenly, with a predatory gleam. She understood in that lightning-flash moment that Lord Malrec had not been the only one painting that night, that she had brought this doom to the people of Ravan's Light. Whatever he said, whatever he did, Ethal was here for only one reason.

Alannys.

"You monster!" The voice came from Driach, but the sound was hardly recognizable, a wail of pure agony. It was the sound a soul makes, cloven in two. "What have you done?"

Nyrin made a weak sound—part moan, part whimper —a wet gurgle she hadn't the strength to complete.

Ethal laughed, a sound like dry twigs crunching under hard-soled boots. "Something I should have done a long time ago. She deserved it. She ran away. I didn't come here for this one, but it's always nice to tie up a loose end." He took two lumbering steps toward them, stepping over Nyrin, dragging the tip of his sword through her throat almost casually, like an afterthought.

Alannys took an instinctive step backward, every nerve ending alert. What kind of man murdered someone like that, as though he wasn't even paying attention? Nothing she had seen in her travels of Ravanmark had led her to believe there were people like this in it.

Driach took a bold step forward, blocking Ethal from the cave entrance, drawing his sword as he moved and falling into a wary Ready position. He was no cloaked swordsman, but he handled the weapon with a grim familiarity that bespoke competence. By comparison, Ethal was obviously less skilled, but swung his blade with a ferocity and a raw power that made him dangerous.

Driach gave Alannys a healthy shove backwards into the cave. "Get inside! Rally the others — hide yourself!"

"Save yourself the trouble," Ethal growled, "and surrender now. I'll be coming for you anyway, as soon as I dispose of this nuisance." And he swung a savage blow at Driach, coming so quickly from stillness to violent motion that the taller man barely managed to sidestep.

"Alannys," he gasped, "run!"

She turned and dove inside the cave, stumbling on the slick stone, clumsy in her haste. She heard anxious voices approaching, and found herself facing Saukar and Cenda.

"What happened?" Saukar demanded. "We heard a scream, and — merciful Muses!" he interrupted himself, catching his first good glimpse of her face. "What is it? Out with it!"

"E — Ethal," she stammered. "In the garden. He's murdered Nyrin. Driach is fighting him now."

For a fraction of a section, the horrible words seemed to

freeze the big man. Then his fleshy face twisted, screwed up into something unrecognizable and frightening, and he pushed past her with a sudden agility that she would hardly have credited, given his size. "Driach shall not fight this monster alone," he declared, and he was gone.

Alannys turned to follow him, eager to strike a blow in defense of her new friends, but Cenda caught her arm in a surprisingly strong grip. "Come with me."

"But—"

Cenda cut off her half-formed protest with a cry that sounded perilously close to becoming a shriek. "You must come with me, Alannys. You must!"

Alannys stared at her in dumb shock. She couldn't imagine what could make her presence so important to Cenda, and she offered no resistance when the other woman turned back into the cave and dragged her along.

"You must tell me everything that happened," Cenda said, in her newfound tone of command. "Everything. Omit no detail."

This request mystified Alannys—what possible difference could the details make to Cenda now?—but she wasn't willing to agitate her any further. She spoke hurriedly as they walked, trying her best to give Cenda a complete picture of what had passed after she and Driach left her room.

Cenda walked into her own room with Alannys close behind, and stopped by a wooden desk, closing her eyes. "I see," she said. "You heard the scream, same as we did, and went with Driach, and that's how you found Nyrin." She didn't open her eyes. "Tell me, Alannys, what was she doing in the garden?"

Alannys couldn't see what possible difference that could make. "Driach said she was thirsty. She was by the well when we found her; I suppose she was drawing water?"

Cenda nodded, still standing with her eyes closed. "And you said Ethal murdered her." Her face remained placid, but a single tear rolled down it. "Tell me about that."

Alannys couldn't help stealing a glance behind her, out into the dark hallway. Why were they wasting time discussing this, when they could be helping Saukar and Driach? "He—he slit her throat when he approached us. But he had already wounded her, it looked like she had been run through with the sword. She couldn't get up, and I think she would have died anyway, I think it was already too late."

Cenda nodded again. Alannys didn't see how she was keeping her composure. "So Ethal came here after her? And Driach fights to avenge her death?"

"No. I mean, that's part of why Driach is fighting of course, but he's also defending us. Ethal did not come here for Nyrin, he said so very plainly. I don't think he even knew she was here till after he came. Ethal came here for me."

Cenda's eyes popped open. "I see." She dug frantically through the few drawers of the desk, pulling out a stack of thick paper, and a handful of charcoal pencils. "Then it is possible this might work."

Her impossible calm unnerved Alannys. Past her worries about wasting time, she began to realize that something was very wrong. "Cenda, what are you doing?"

Her eyes were unnaturally bright. She took up a pencil and began writing, quickly but very neatly; long, even lines spread across the page with a speed that Alannys found hard to believe. "The only thing I can do." The pencil never faltered, but her voice shook. "We can't let her die, Alannys. We just can't. And I'm the only one who can do something about that."

Alannys stared at the papers with newfound horror.

"Cenda, wait. Tell me you aren't—"

The pencil never paused. "Please don't argue with me. You won't change my mind, and if you distract me, I may miss some detail and this whole thing will fail."

"What?"

"I have to cover every person who was involved in this. I have to rewrite everything so that what they remember makes sense to them, and makes sense taken together with everyone else's memories. It's a lot to remember at once, but if I mess it up, the magic will fail. And it will consume me."

"But—"

"I know, that will happen anyway. But I'm prepared to make that sacrifice. She can't die, Alannys. She's been like a mother to me. A real mother. To go through everything she has, only to have Ethal win in the end—I won't bear it. Besides, you are going to need her. Painting won't save us now, Alannys, not while Driach fights with swords and his brushes sit useless in his room. Tapestry-weaving, writing—these are all useless against Ethal now. The only thing that has a chance of helping us now is singing. I can't sing, but Nyrin can. She can help you."

Alannys just stared, unsure how to shake such resolution. "Cenda, please..."

She might not have spoken for all the difference it made. Cenda ignored her entirely, gathering her papers and tamping them into a neat stack. She put the stack into a polished silver chafing dish, which looked out of place on the rustic desk. Without a glance at Alannys, she cupped her hands around the sides of the dish, bowed her head and began to chant rapidly.

"With this flame, as sharp as the sword which is Justice, as bright as the beacon which is Hope, I consecrate this writing unto you, the Muses holy and fair, with the earnest prayer that you will take its words unto your hearts and hold them, as everlasting as yourselves."

Sometime between the moment that Alannys glanced over her shoulder in worry and impatience, and the moment she turned back to the desk, the stack of papers burst into bright, biting flame. Her time in Ravanmark had taught her to expect the unexpected, but she couldn't suppress a gasp. She moved instinctively to find something, anything to put the fire out.

Cenda held out a restraining hand. "No! We must not interfere with the flame. It must burn completely out, all on its own."

"What? Why?" Alannys risked another glance behind her.

"I was told it symbolizes our submission to the divine will of the Muses."

Alannys looked back at Cenda. "You symbolize your submission to the Muses, in a ceremony of magic meant to thwart them?"

"I didn't create the ritual, Alannys, I'm just telling you what I was told. Personally, I think it serves a more practical purpose—I think every word that was written must be burned. The only way to make sure that happens is to let every scrap of paper burn."

Alannys looked at the little fire; already it had consumed the pages, more thoroughly than she would have thought possible. The little flame sputtered, and went out completely. "This is madness. Come on, Cenda, we need to go help—"

"Put your hand on my arm." Cenda's tone was firm. It made her voice sound unfamiliar and vaguely threatening, and Alannys found that she had complied before she even had time to make a considered decision to do so. Cenda took up the chafing dish, cradling it in the arm Alannys held. "Don't let go, no matter what you see. When I do this, no one else will remember what happened. But you will. You can save Nyrin, get her to sing with you."

With hardly a pause, Cenda reached into the dish and threw the ashes up over their heads. "I give this sanctified writing unto you, oh Muses all-knowing, ever-lasting, and most-wise, and beseech unto you that all that these consecrated words proclaim may come now to pass, for once and for evermore."

Alannys tipped her head forward a little, instinctively turning her face from the falling ash, waiting unconsciously for the light touch of it settling onto her hair and skin.

But it never came. As Cenda spoke, the air in the room began to circle around them, carrying the ashes with it into a whirlpool that gathered speed amazingly fast.

"Don't let go," Cenda reminded her, calm and resolute in the center of the chaos, raising her voice to carry over the howling wind. "Don't...let go..."

As if she had turned to sand, Cenda became suddenly dissolute, disintegrating into the whirlwind around her.

And Alannys stood, alone and horrified, in the vortex of whipping wind, the air around her as heavy with black ash as her heart was heavy with grief and fear.

♫

The wind settled as quickly as it had risen, and fine black ash settled over everything in the room, except the circle where the two women had stood. For a moment Alannys stood there, horrified by what she had just witnessed. For the first time, she wondered if magic in Ravanmark was worth the cost it extracted. She had thought Muse's Fever was bad, but this—this was beyond anything she could accept or justify. How could anything be worth that?

Cenda had obviously felt it was worth it, she reminded herself. Cenda had known better than anyone what her writing could do and how much it would cost her, and she had done it anyway. For weal or for woe, the deed had been done. The intentions behind it had been the best.

It was up to her to honor those intentions now.

Alannys ran out of the little room, cursing her linen robe, which hindered her movements and slowed her down. It would have been so much easier if she'd had her own things. For that matter, where was Songstrike? She couldn't imagine facing this without her blade.

There wasn't time. She had no idea where they had put her things, there was no one to ask, and there was no time to search. She was just going to have to do the best she could with what she had — herself.

She didn't know what to expect as she approached the cave entrance. She heard people outside, and Driach's unmistakable voice rumbled, "Protect Alannys."

She wasn't prepared to see Nyrin run into the cave, skidding to a halt in front of her. "Lady Alannys! Ethal attacks — we must make ready to defend ourselves." She glanced down the hall behind Alannys. "Where is Cenda?"

Alannys shook her head. "She's gone," she said, and her throat closed in on itself.

Nyrin looked at her strangely, but said nothing. Alannys followed her back into the big common room, where she apparently planned to make their final stand.

"We have but one hope," Nyrin said, "and that is to sing."

"It would be better if I had Songstrike."

Nyrin looked surprised. "Of course — I forgot. It's in — "

She never got to finish. Ethal swaggered into the room, breathing hard, swinging a bloodied sword in wide arcs as though he was looking for something to stab with it.

His eyes lit on the two of them, and it was evident he had found it.

Time seemed to move too slow and too fast, all at once. Alannys followed the swinging of the blade with her eyes, and wondered idly if Nyrin's blood was still there, or if the temporal shift had taken care of that. It didn't matter. The look in the big man's eyes promised that there would soon be more, and that Alannys's would join it.

"We'll see about that," Alannys muttered. She heard Nyrin beside her drawing a deep breath, and they both began to sing.

Alannys couldn't have said what she was singing, even as she sang it. She and Nyrin both sang as powerfully as they could, with the result that neither of them was intelligible.

But it didn't seem to matter. As soon as they started to sing, Ethal stopped, eyeing them warily. This was encouraging, and Alannys really opened up, singing the most aggressive, attacking song she had ever sung.

Ethal fell to his knees, curling over, leaning heavily on his sword. He could paint, but he had no defense against song, and it was plain that he was suffering. His head drooped low, and his body trembled. The muscles in his shoulders tensed and knotted spastically. Alannys began to realize that this was going to work; they were going to make it. Cenda's sacrifice would not be meaningless—if Nyrin was saved she would achieve her purpose. Alannys took a step forward, singing with renewed vigor and purpose, determined to succeed. Beside her, she could hear Nyrin's voice swell with the same resolution.

All at once Ethal unfolded, springing to his feet the same way a jack pops out of the box. He flung his arms out wide, threw his head back and wailed—a sound that seemed to come from the bottom of his being, a shout that was more like a roar. The air in front of him seemed to waver, to shimmer, rushing forward like a wave of pure malevolence, and all of the sudden Alannys couldn't stand up anymore.

For a moment all was pain; white-hot pain filled her

consciousness, as though electricity had flooded every nerve in her body. She couldn't move, she couldn't even twitch. In the flash-fire midst of that intense pain, she forgot what it had even meant to move, what it had been like to exist without pain.

The electricity finally receded, leaving flaming tendrils of agony in more places than Alannys had even known she possessed. She felt utterly spent, unnaturally bone-tired. Even singing, even Muse's Fever, even being buried under an avalanche had never left her like this. She couldn't seem to muster sufficient strength to turn her head to check on Nyrin, sprawled on the ground beside her. She heard a shuddering, gasping breath, and figured that Nyrin was doing about as well as she was herself.

What on earth *was* that? How had they lost the upper hand here, just when it seemed they were gaining ground? Had Driach and the others fallen to that strange, unnatural power as well?

Ethal appeared beside her, his sword hanging forgotten from his hand, staring down at her. His eyes seemed lit from within, burning with the unholy light of insanity. "The almighty Talented are not so powerful when their own music bounces back at them, are they?"

"Please," she gasped, and coughed. Flames of pain shot through her throat, and she couldn't seem to get out another word.

"Do you plan to beg for your life? Your freedom?" Ethal asked, regarding her with sudden interest.

Alannys tried to shake her head in vigorous offense, and managed a barely perceptible twitch.

"Pity," Ethal said. "That would have been entertaining. What is your pathetic mewling for, then?"

"Spare her," Alannys croaked. "Please. I won't fight."

Ethal laughed his dry, raspy laugh. "Oh, I don't doubt that. You seem to me to be overestimating your position.

Do you think I don't know how completely incapable you are of anything at all right now? I don't believe that you could stand if your life depended on it. Or hers," he said contemplatively, looking at Nyrin as though just remembering that she was there.

"Wait...please..."

His face clouded. "No, that tears it. What you are failing to grasp is that as of this moment, you, my dear Redeemer, idol of the unwashed masses, savior of all you survey, are *nothing*. You have, for all practical purposes but mine, ceased to exist. You are my thing now, Alannys, to use as I please. You do not get to make demands, you do not even get to beg." He stepped over Nyrin, and before Alannys could even form a protest, he swung his sword in a wide arc up over his shoulder and down into her throat with force sufficient to decapitate her.

Alannys was thankful she couldn't turn her head. Murdered twice, in one day. Everything Cenda had suffered seemed for nothing. Was that the only reason Cenda's magic had even worked? Because Nyrin was not going to live long anyway? She couldn't bear to consider it.

Her own situation was not looking much better. Having summarily disposed of every other living being in the harborage of Ravan's Light, Ethal jammed his sword back into its scabbard, scooped Alannys up, and tossed her carelessly over his shoulder. She bounced and jostled uncomfortably out of the caves, too weak to move, too shell-shocked to cry, as she passed the mangled and lifeless bodies of her former comrades.

Ethal walked with a cheery bounce in his step as he carried his prize into the formless gray blur hovering in the far corner of the garden.

♬

Alannys felt all her hope leeched from her in the bitter cold of the colorless, timeless void that swallowed them up before Ethal's painting released them. Who could possibly help her now? Who could even *find* her? A painting had brought her from Earth to Ravanmark in a journey not perceptibly different from the one they had just taken. There was no way she could calculate, no way she could even estimate the distance from Ravan's Light to wherever she was now. There was no way anyone could track her to this place from there. Ethal had been right. For all practical purposes, to everyone else she might as well not exist.

Ethal dumped her unceremoniously onto the ground, knocking the wind out of her. Even if she'd had the strength to get up, the blow she sustained crashing to the ground would have made it impossible. He turned from her immediately, pulling fistfuls of powder out of his pockets and tossing it behind her.

This strange ritual completed, he turned back and looked down at her, with a grin she could only describe as nasty. "You've been an awful lot of trouble, my dear Redeemer. But I suppose you'll be worth it in the end." He stood up straight and leaned backward, pressing his hands into his lower back. "But right now, it's almost dawn, and I'm dead hungry. I doubt you'll be able to get up to much mischief—you probably can't even move yet. Nobody I rebounded ever managed to leave this place. My dear daughter is waiting for me with breakfast. Stay here and be a good girl while I'm gone, won't you?"

She didn't dignify that with a response.

Ethal turned away with a chuckle that matched his grin. She knew he had to be worn out—he'd been fighting battles all morning, and probably painting before that. And that rebounding—she didn't know how he did it, but it must have cost him. Still, she could only dream of having the kind of energy it took him to hoist himself up some rock formations, using hand and foot holds that appeared to be natural, and haul himself out of sight.

She was finally alone. But unfortunately, he was right. She didn't think she could even move yet, let alone follow him on the arduous climb he'd taken. Surely there was some other way out—there had to be something she could do to escape. She wasn't likely to get another chance.

She was in a cavern, with tall, moss-covered rocky sides that arched up into darkness. The whole of the grotto seemed to be lit only by moonlight filtering through openings in the ceiling above her, similar to the one through with her captor had just exited. None of the other openings appeared to be reachable.

Alannys groaned and pushed herself to her feet. It seemed to take every ounce of strength she had, and once she was upright she wobbled and stumbled in a manner that seemed to suggest she wouldn't be that way very long. Ethal's rebounding had really hit her hard. It probably would have been best for her to just rest, but she knew she couldn't afford the time. Ethal knew who she was, and Ethal murdered Talented people. She hadn't a prayer of survival if she didn't get out of there before he came back.

She pressed her hands to the sides of her head in a futile attempt to stop the spinning. She could finally clearly see how she had come into this grotto—as she'd expected, a large painting lurked behind her. She'd never seen a painting treated quite like this—it wasn't even on an easel, but propped haphazardly against the cave's damp, mossy, rock wall.

Alannys stumbled closer, unsteady, listing hard to one side. What kind of person would do that? Talent was rare, and painting was hard work. To treat the fruits of that with such astounding lack of care...she did not like what that said about Ethal, or the regard in which he held his stolen gifts.

The painting itself was a serviceable representation. She could see the garden she had spent so many hours tending, still bearing its harvest for people who would never eat it again.

Alannys brushed her fingers over the surface of the painting, hoping against hope that the gloss was still active, and escape would prove as easy as stepping back through. But the surface was completely dry, and she understood suddenly what Ethal had done after tossing her down—drying powder. He'd closed the portal before she had even formed the idea of going back through it.

Of course there would be no gloss in this cavern—Ethal would have taken it away with him. But even if he hadn't, it would have made little difference—Alannys already knew she had no Talent as a painter. She'd tried before to open a painting, and failed miserably. And yet, right now, she felt differently—as though if she had held a paintbrush in her hand, she wouldn't have even known what to do with it at all. As if she couldn't have carried the simplest tune, couldn't have held a single note. As if she had no Talent, and never had, and couldn't even conceive of what the word might mean.

No Talent...

Alannys staggered around in a circle, as quickly as she could manage, inspecting every direction around her. There was no mistake—there were only two ways out of this place. Through the ceiling she couldn't reach, and through the painting she lacked the Talent to open.

Lack of Talent. It was a profoundly disturbing thought. She cleared her throat and tried to sing.

Nothing happened.

Alannys felt a jolt of fear that surpassed anything she'd felt so far—it seemed to stab into her very soul. She just physically could not sing; she strained her throat until her face turned red, and blood pounded in her ears, but she could not produce a single sound. She could speak, but not sing.

Such a thing shouldn't even be possible. What had happened to her? Was this some sort of after-effect of Ethal's strange attack, or some horrible ability of the grotto itself? She should be feeling better, she knew that; she should be starting to recover. And yet she felt just as drained as when she had arrived. Was it possible the place sapped her energy?

Was it possible it sapped even more than that?

The mindlink. What about her mindlink with King Dorramon? Mindlinking was a form of Talent, just like singing and painting. But to her, it was integral to her definition of herself, to what she'd become since arriving in Ravanmark. She remembered once thinking that losing the mindlink would be like losing a part of herself.

In a fit of panic, she tried with every fiber of her being to contact the king.

Dorramon? Dorramon, can you hear me? Please, please — you have to hear me! Dorramon! DORRAMON!

She was screaming, but only in her own mind. Her frantic cries would never be heard by another soul, she knew that — she could feel it. There was nowhere for them to go. Her mind was completely cut off, isolated unto itself.

She thought she might go mad. The sudden, sickening realization of the loss of something irreplaceable washed through her. She was going to die here. She would never see Dorramon, or Chen, or Raman, or any of her other friends again. She would fail in her promises to the king. She would never be able to put things right with Chen — their last argument would be his last memory of her, forever. She would breathe her last in this terrible place, a tortured death at Ethal's hand, and everything she had fought for would come to naught.

Desperation prodded her into frantic action, filled her with a ferocious energy and a burning need to be free of that horrible cavern. She launched herself at the tall, rocky formations, clawing at the hand-holds and fumbling her way up. She could see the opening she needed.

But it was no good. Her last, desperate surge of adrenaline was no match for the mysterious sapping force the cave itself exuded. Helpless against a sudden, bone-deep weariness, she could only cling weakly to the rock as she slid back down to the ground, scratched and bruised and no closer to escape than before.

Bitter tears burned her eyes, and she scrubbed at them with her dirty hands. What good were tears to her now? She had left only whatever time Ethal decided to allow her, and only this — this *place* in which to spend it.

Now that the sun was up, the light trickling in from outside was stronger, and she had a better idea of what exactly this place was. She was trapped inside a natural cavern, large in terms of caverns in general, but quite small when one faced spending the rest of one's unfortunately short life there.

The cavern housed a pond, fed by the water that worked its way in through the openings above. Some of that water had carved the rock formations she had tried so unsuccessfully to climb. The pond was surrounded by thick bushes that somehow managed to thrive in the perpetual twilight of the grotto. A quiet cave, with a pond, and fruit-bearing bushes — Nyrin had been right. The place should have been beautiful. But it wasn't. The closer Alannys looked at her surroundings, the more disturbing it all became.

There was something off about the pond. It didn't reflect the light bouncing onto its surface the way it should have — it gleamed wetly in the low light, thick and dark, like something unspeakable that had congealed. Ponds and lakes always seemed to be in motion—this one crouched there in the center of the cave, still as death, as though it was waiting to drown someone. The water, when something forced it to move, didn't drip or ripple as she would have expected—it sloshed heavily. No matter how close she got to the pond, Alannys could not see into the water. Indeed, she doubted it *was* water. She didn't know what exactly was in the pond, but she wouldn't have touched it with a barge pole.

The bushes didn't fare well on close inspection either. The leaves were a sickly mottled gray, and the fruit looked shriveled and unappealing. The edges of the leaves looked jagged, like perhaps they were sharp, but she wasn't willing to get close enough to find out.

Jutting up out of the bushes was a stone structure. She tried to avoid the word, but there was just nothing to call it but an altar. Everything about it, from the size of the concave table—long and narrow, like a military cot—to its height, obviously meant to hold its contents at waist level to a person standing behind it, made its purpose plain. The table wasn't level; she could see that it was tipped slightly toward the pond. Ominously, the edge of the table on the pond side formed a curved lip, a sort of spout, that hung out over a carved stone bowl.

She didn't even want to speculate about the purpose of that. Everything about the place filled her with horror, and she wanted more than anything in the world to find a way out.

All too soon she heard the scuffling of feet on the rocks above her, and Ethal lowered himself back into the cavern. He grinned obscenely at her. "Ah, I can smell despair on the air. Did you have fun while I was gone then, my dear Redeemer? Have you quite accepted your fate?"

Alannys didn't answer. She had found herself a seat on the floor near the wall where the painting rested, as far away from the pond as she could get. She had hoped sitting quietly might help her recover, but unfortunately she could feel her strength continue to ebb away from her, lost to whatever unholy magic the place possessed.

"Bit of a pity, really," Ethal mused, as if to himself. "I was looking forward to breaking your spirit, myself. And Venym was dead certain you'd put up more of a fight. Practically had to tie her up to keep her home. Rabid to meet you, that girl was. Even more excited than when she brought home her new red-headed friend."

Alannys thought that only a monster like Ethal would name his daughter Venym. And her new red-headed friend — could he mean Elossa? But Cruthers had told her Elossa was with *she who commands us all* — how could that possibly mean Venym? She was desperate to know. But she refused to give Ethal the satisfaction of speaking to him, and shifted herself around so that she was turned as far away from him as she could get, leaning against the cold, mossy wall of the cavern.

Ethal looked downright feral. "Now, now, this is no time to pout. Today is a very exciting day! Big things are going to happen today, and you are going to be at the very center of it. Perhaps you should feel honored. You are going to make me the strongest man alive, Alannys — perhaps the strongest man who ever lived." He knelt by the pond, scooped up a double handful of the thick water, and drank it. It clung to his hands and face, dark red and foul.

Alannys made a noise of revulsion and turned away.

"What, does this bother you? Oh, if only you knew! This is very powerful water, made so by the rituals which have been practiced here. It sustains me, it restores me, it makes my powers what they are. I've been up all night, painting and fighting, but in a few minutes this water will have rejuvenated me completely. It's amazing, isn't it?"

She could feel the corners of her mouth twist down. "It looks disgusting."

"Ah, now, that is all a matter of perception. This water is rich with the blood of the Talented who have died here. My rituals have made their Talent my own—drinking this water keeps it so."

"You—you *do* steal Talent? That's not possible—that was just a story!"

Ethal grinned again, revealing unsettling red stains around his gums and teeth. "Almost anything is possible, Alannys, if you approach it properly. For my part, I did not invent these rituals. I am not the first to use this cavern, you see. I discovered ancient journals here, journals belonging to Soth himself, which detailed how the ritual should be performed. This cavern was already imbued with its dark magic when I found it. The Cavern of the Damned. You feel it, don't you? The way it consumes your very strength?"

Alannys looked down at her feet. "I do."

"That is because you are naturally Talented. That is the only purpose this place has ever known—to destroy people like you."

"It doesn't seem to bother you, though." Alannys saw a glimmer of hope in their conversation: the longer she could keep him talking, the longer she would stay alive.

Ethal laughed out loud. "Of course not! I had no Talent of my own, you see—everything I have is stolen. It's why you can't even *sense* your Talent here, and yet I can use mine. My Talent, such as it is, is bound up in the magic of this place. It sustains me, even as it feeds from you." He regarded her contemplatively.

"What are you going to do to me?" His silence alarmed her; she blurted out the first question she could think of to keep him talking.

He chuckled, a peculiar, twisted sound that make her

skin crawl. "How obliging of you to ask! I want you to know, you see — the more you understand, the more fearful you will be. I prefer that you are frightened. It makes the transfer more effective. Besides, I just enjoy it more that way."

Alannys shuddered. On second thought, maybe it would be better if he stopped talking.

All at once he scooped her up. Sick with the draining influence of the place, Alannys didn't have the strength to fight him — until she saw that he was carrying her toward the horrible stone altar.

Her struggle was intense but brief, like a match flaring bright in the darkness and burning out.

Ethal laughed. "Good, good! Fear is important, my dear Redeemer. Don't worry, we are in no hurry. In fact, the slower the better, really. Slow and scary, that's the secret to a good transfer of Talent." He dumped her into the concave top of the altar, and all she could do was lie there and pant for breath. He leaned over her, his rough face filling her vision. "And you, my dear, are going to be the best transfer of Talent ever."

The sour reek of blood on his breath twisted her stomach, and she turned her head away. How many people had died here before her, just like this? She wished fervently for the dagger Raman had given her in the palace market, a million years ago when the world had been a hopeful place — but all of her things were unreachable, somewhere in the caves of Ravan's Light. How many hours had it been since she left those caves? She couldn't even say.

"You may have guessed," Ethal said, rummaging through the bushes around them, "that the most important part of this ritual is blood. To transfer your Talent I require your blood — all of it. Every last drop. That's a bit of a problem, actually, because it would be incredibly difficult to do that by any normal means."

"Normal means," she echoed dully. She knew Ethal was trying to scare her, and she consciously avoided applying any of the concepts he talked about to herself. Still—every last drop? Her heart jumped with panic just thinking the words.

"Fortunately, I have other means." Ethal came back to the altar, tossing a bloated fruit from hand to hand, then holding it up for her inspection. "Do you know what this is, Alannys?"

She wrinkled her nose—seen up close, the fruit was even more disgusting than she had realized. "Should I?"

"It is sacred to the Muses you claim to serve. It is called sun-fruit."

Sun-fruit? She looked again at the nasty, withered, dark red skin of the fruit, pitted and brittle-looking. Who on earth could look at that foul thing and think of the sun?

Ethal nodded, as though he knew what she was thinking. "It grows only in grottoes, with natural ponds— they are also sacred places to the Muses. Of course, they don't usually look like this either."

Abruptly Alannys understood—the place was steeped in corruption. What this thick, bloody water was to a regular pond, that foul fruit was to regular sun-fruit. The whole concept made her feel ill.

"Sun-fruit is usually a glowing golden fruit, sweet and crisp, something like a pear. As I said, it is sacred to the Muses, and it's a particularly healthful fruit for Talented people to consume. *This* sun-fruit, though..."

Ethal gripped the fruit in both hands, and suddenly twisted his hands in opposite directions. The fruit ripped into two pieces. He set one piece to the side and cradled the other in his palm. A bitter, noxious stink rose from the torn fruit. If she'd had the strength to raise her arm, Alannys would have covered her nose.

Inside, the fruit was a sickly mucous-green, runny and slimy where it should have been firm. The seeds were almost black, shiny, and lumpy, like clots of blood floating in the slop. Ethal dipped his index finger into the viscous innards of the fruit, and leaned over her face.

"Now comes the fun part," he breathed.

Chillingly, he seemed to mean it.

With his slime-coated index finger, Ethal drew some sort of symbol on Alannys's face, starting on the cheekbone under her left eye and descending down onto her cheek. She couldn't tell what the symbol was, and after the first second of contact, she quit caring. She had expected the fruit goop to feel sticky, and cold.

But it *burned*.

Everywhere Ethal applied the stuff to her skin, she could feel the burning tracks of it, like acid etching its way into her skin. She wanted to cry out in pain, but she refused to give him the satisfaction.

She couldn't hide her flinch, though. "You feel it, don't you?" he asked, his voice barely above a whisper. "This fruit aids in the ritual. When a cut is made with this fruit on the skin, it will force you to bleed. It will continue the bleeding until there is no more blood."

He said this as if it was a wonderful revelation. Without waiting for any kind of response, he dipped his finger back into the fruit, and drew a matching symbol on his own face.

Slowly, with great care, Ethal drew similar symbols on her right cheek, on both sides of her face near her temples, on the backs of each of her hands, on the top of each of her feet, and at the center of her collarbone. After each symbol was complete, he drew a matching one on himself, in the same location. It took all of Alannys's concentration not to cry out in pain, but Ethal never showed any reaction to it.

Ethal dropped the fruit on the cave floor at his feet,

reached into his dirty, ragged shirt, and withdrew a tiny dagger. The handle was ornately carved bone, and the blade was only about as long as Alannys's smallest finger. She cringed against the stone supporting her. More than anything in the world, she wanted to fight against this, she wanted to run away from this place and never look back. But whatever evil force fed off of her here seemed to be intensified by the fruit—she no longer had the energy to move at all. She couldn't even raise her hands to fend him off as he leaned over her, the polished dagger gleaming in the low light.

Ethal cupped her chin in one hand, holding her head still. He carefully touched the knife to her face, and as gentle as a caress, sliced into the skin of her cheek.

Sheer, white, blistering pain overwhelmed her—being cut through the layer of fruit on her skin was worse than she could have imagined, far worse than a simple, shallow cut with a sharp knife should have been.

Oblivious to her howls of pain, Ethal traced each of the symbols he had made on her skin with the blade of the dagger. After each symbol was complete, he dipped his finger into the blood streaming from her wounds, and used it to trace the same symbol on himself, murmuring reverently under his breath words that she could not understand. But she knew these weren't benedictions, and she doubted they were addressed to the Muses.

Finally he finished his dark work, and stepped back from her. The flaming pain receded as soon as he stopped cutting and she lay there, panting raggedly, hoarse from screaming, too profoundly exhausted to even raise her hand and see how badly she was bleeding.

"Don't worry," Ethal said. "You have some time yet to make peace with your Muses. When the bleeding is finished, I shall burn what remains of you. Your blood and your ashes—of this I shall drink, and your power will be mine. The rest I will deposit into the pond, and so you shall help to sustain me for as long as I live."

"Which won't be very long," came a sarcastic voice from somewhere behind him, "but I can promise you it will be long enough for you to regret this!" The voice sounded like Trago.

Either Alannys was so far gone she was hallucinating, or Chen leaned over her, pale and horrified, but trying his best to smile for her. She could hear the ringing of swords.

Funny, since Chen didn't appear to be sword-fighting.

"Oh, dear Muses," he breathed. "Hold on, Alannys. We're going to get you out of here." He caught her hand up in his, ignoring the blood. "Just hold on."

"Chen..." The sound of her voice was faint even to her own ears. She didn't see how he could possibly hear her. The words seemed to come from far away. "I'm sorry."

Tears welled up in his eyes. "Oh, Alannys. Don't—"

"Chen!" Trago snapped, from somewhere behind Chen, where she couldn't see. "I could use some help here!"

Chen squeezed her hand. "Hold on," he repeated, and released her. She'd never seen him with a sword before, but he drew one now with a savage motion, then turned and charged away.

It took everything she had, but Alannys managed to turn her head. She could see Chen and Trago, fighting with swords against Ethal. Trago was doing well, but Ethal still had the unnatural advantage he'd gained by drinking from the foul pond. Chen, she could see even in her disoriented state, was already flagging as the effects of the place set in and his energy began to drain.

Even with his boost, though, Ethal was not a fair match for a trained swordsman like Trago. Sensing Chen's discomfort, Ethal turned to engage him directly, and before Alannys could process what she was seeing, Ethal was pinned up against the mossy stone wall, with Trago's sword buried in his middle.

"Someone should have done that years ago, you twisted son of a bitch," Trago growled.

Chen staggered up next to the altar, and carefully gathered Alannys into his shaking arms. "Trago! We have to get her out of here. This place...it's evil. She can't stay here in this condition."

Trago looked over at them, and the blood drained from his face. "Seven Hells!" He hurried to the gray blur hovering in front of the far wall, near Ethal's painting, and helped Chen step into it. Alannys didn't know where they were going, and she didn't care.

Leaving the Cavern of the Damned while she was still breathing was enough for her.

♪

"Oh, thank the Muses you found her, I—merciful Muses! What happened to her?"

Alannys recognized the voice as Josak's in the instant before Chen lowered her onto a bed and the young man came running to her side. She tried to smile at him, but she wasn't sure if she succeeded.

"Ethal," Trago spat. "The bastard tried to sacrifice her to steal her Talent."

Josak's eyes widened. He looked unnaturally pale, and Alannys finally remembered he was the only painter in the room. He must have used the Herb of Sight to find her. She tried again to smile.

"Lady Alannys, I'm sorry," he said, and his voice quavered. "I could hear your shrieking, from the painting, but I couldn't see...I didn't know..."

Chen's hand fell heavily on the boy's shoulder. "Josak, do you think you could find us some water? Those wounds need tending."

"Oh! Of—of course! I'll be right back." He scampered out of the room with more energy than Alannys would have credited him with just then.

"You have to forgive him, Alannys," Chen said, pulling a chair up next to the bed. "He feels guilty that he wasn't here when Ethal came."

She understood, but she knew it was for the best. It wouldn't have made any difference, except that there would now be one more lifeless body in the caves of Ravan's Light. She didn't think she had the strength to explain it, though.

Trago stood near the foot of the bed, grimly regarding the painting of the cavern. The muscles of his jaw twitched, as though there were things he would have liked to say. Alannys looked past him and suddenly recognized the place—she was in Driach's room, the room he and Nyrin had woken in that morning, unsuspecting of the sucker-punch fate would soon deal them.

She leaned back into the pillow and sighed. It felt good to be free of the sapping influence of the cavern, but she still felt totally drained. She felt almost like, if she closed her eyes, she might never open them again.

Judging by the anxious way Chen studied her face, he had similar thoughts. He lifted a cup of berry juice to her mouth, watching her as though he expected her to disappear at any moment. She might have reassured him —or teased him—but she was too busy drinking the juice. It was just room-temperature berry juice, but at that moment, it was the best thing she had ever tasted.

"Give me that," Trago said shortly, snatching a cloth from Josak and wringing it in the water. "Apparently Chen's too busy staring to help clean her up."

Chen shot him a guilty look, but he didn't move. He frowned, and chewed on his lip, inspecting her face. She wondered how much he suspected about what had happened to her.

Trago leaned over her from the opposite side of the

bed, and gently swabbed at her cheek with the cloth.

The scream that came from her was blood-curdling. As soon as the water touched her skin, the pain flamed up again, roaring and insatiable, burning her alive.

Chen clutched at her hand. "Trago! Maybe we should leave her alone. She's been through so much already—do we have to hurt her even more?"

Trago looked at her in horror, then looked down at the cloth in his hand. "I don't know, Chen. I don't think we can afford to let this be. Look at this." He touched a finger to the messy cloth and lifted it away, pulling a line of sticky, stringy fruit innards along behind it. "What is this stuff? That's not right—it must be something Ethal did to her, and I don't think we should leave it there. And why is she still bleeding so much? Underneath all that, these are shallow cuts. They should have stopped bleeding by now."

"You're right," Chen sighed. "We don't have any choice. Josak, hand me one of those cloths, please."

"No." Alannys heard the hollow sound of panic in her own words. "No, don't—I can't take anymore. Just leave me alone."

"I'm sorry, Alannys," Chen said. "We have to do this. You've got to stop bleeding—you've already lost too much blood."

"I don't care." She could see real sorrow in Chen's dark eyes, but she was beyond caring about that, either. "I don't care, I just don't want to hurt anymore. I *can't take anymore!*" A couple of minutes ago, she would have sworn she was too exhausted to move, but now she pushed herself up from the pillows, intent on leaving before anybody could do anything to cause her more pain. It wasn't a thinking, reasoned action—she was in a sheer animal panic. No logic could reach her now.

Chen caught her by the shoulders and shoved her back

down on the bed.

"Chen?" Betrayal tore through her, nearly as painful as what she was trying to avoid. "What are you doing? Let me go!"

"I'm sorry, Alannys. I know this is going to hurt." He nodded grimly at Trago, then looked back at her. "Please forgive me."

Alannys didn't have time to forgive him or to curse him before Trago touched the wet cloth to her face again, and white-hot pain consumed her senses. She howled like a dying animal, fighting and bucking with everything she had, clawing at Chen's hands on her shoulders. He never flinched, never relaxed his hold, never said more than "I'm sorry."

In a frighteningly short time, she burned through the burst of energy the juice had given her, and she found herself unable to do more than lie there and pant raggedly, while bitter tears tracked silently down her face. Chen sat down next to her, gripping her hand in his and telling her he was sorry.

It took forever, cleaning and bandaging the wounds. It seemed hours later when she finally lay slumped against the pillows again, utterly spent but no longer bleeding, and in no more pain than would be expected for all the cuts she had received.

Josak brought in Songstrike and her old clothes, from wherever Driach had stored them. She found her shawl, and explained to him that Nyrin had given it to her, and why.

"So it's true," Chen said flatly. "Lord Malrec hunts you."

"It's true," she said. "The explosion was meant to enable him to capture me. It was only thanks to Driach and Ravan's Light that he did not."

"Then the collar Dahlia spoke of must be complete.

Right? Because he wouldn't risk bringing you to Castle Glennayre if it wasn't."

Alannys nodded. She couldn't bring herself to say the words out loud. Old superstition or not, talking about negative things had brought her nothing but trouble lately.

And the one thing she didn't need right now was more trouble.

♬

Alannys? Alannys, are you there? The voice ringing in her mind sounded frantic, and it startled her in the quiet of the cavern.

Dorramon? His voice in her head was the last thing she had expected to hear just then, and yet it was such a relief it brought stinging tears to her eyes. She darted a glance at the entrance—Chen, Trago, and Josak huddled there having a quiet but animated conversation, allowing her to rest.

Thank the Muses! Oh, Alannys, what happened to you? Something felt—wrong, and I couldn't reach you—I thought you were dead!

She tried to laugh, and ignore how close she had come to making that true. *Not dead, fortunately. I was trapped in a cavern for a while, that could apparently drain Talent—including mindlinks. But I'm all right now.*

Draining Talent? How is that even possible? Are you sure you're all right?

Well, I will be. I can't explain it all now—you'd never believe it.

What kind of answer is that? Alannys, you have to tell me what happened to you! I've been sick with worry. And you don't sound right.

She sighed, and closed her eyes. If the others thought she was dozing, maybe they wouldn't disturb her. *Dorramon, have you ever heard of a man called Ethal?*

Ethal? Eth—wait. Please, Alannys, tell me you're not trying to say that monster got hold of you.

Well, yes. But —

WHAT? Alannys, you told me you were all right! He will never let go of you, never! Where are you? I'm coming to get you right now, and I don't care what —

Dorramon! Listen to me! Ethal is dead. Calm down. You don't have to come get me.

Dead? She could hear the tears in his voice. *Oh, Alannys. I can't even imagine what you must have gone through. Tell me where you are. I'm serious, I'm riding out tonight and I'm not stopping until I find you.*

You can't do that! What will happen to the country, when their king rides off in the middle of the night?

Hang the country! I've had enough — I can't take anymore of this. I'm bringing you back, and I'm keeping you safe. Where are you?

She hesitated. *I'm afraid I can't tell you. I don't really know. I was brought here through a painting.*

Damn it! Listen, as soon as you get to a place that you know, as soon as you can tell me where you are, please do.

If it will make you feel better, I will. But Dorramon, I want you to think about this in the meantime. We agreed that I should do this —

That was before Ethal entered the picture!

Okay. But nothing has been done to me that won't heal. I'm fine, Dorramon, and I'm going to continue to be fine. The words tumbled out almost too fast, driven by desperation. She had done it this time, she had broken him just the way she'd sworn not to back in Mirendasith Hall.

Prove it, he demanded.

Look at it this way. You and Raman believe I'm the Redeemer. If that's the case, I can't die yet. The Muses aren't done with me — I haven't finished my job yet.

There was a short pause. Alannys thought maybe her words were sinking in, maybe he was realizing she had a point.

That's the best you can do? That's pretty lousy, Alannys.

I know. But it was an unreasonable request.

The king sighed. *You sound like you are recovering. And I can't come help you when I don't know where you are. But I don't like this.*

I don't, either. This has always been dangerous – nothing has changed. I'm not done out here yet. But I'm getting there. And I will be home soon.

I love you, Alannys. Never forget that. No matter what happens, you say the word, and I will drop everything and come for you.

I love you, too, Dorramon.

She wondered if he could hear her tears as clearly as she could hear his.

♫

When Alannys opened her eyes, she found everyone in the room staring at her.

"Are you all right?" Chen asked.

"Yes," she said, rubbing at the tears on her face. "Better than I've been in hours."

"But you're crying."

"I know, I'm sorry. I just—I just—" She didn't know how to explain; she didn't want to talk about the mindlink in front of Trago and Josak.

"No, don't apologize," Chen said in a rush, waving a hand at her. "We all understand. None of us can imagine what you've been through. I just wanted to be sure you were all right."

She looked at him speculatively, considering his abrupt change in demeanor and wondering just how much he did understand.

Trago looked from her to Chen as though he might be wondering the same thing. "We can't stay here," he said finally. "It isn't safe, and the rest of the tribe is headed this way to join us."

"What about you, Josak?" Chen asked. "Will you come

with us?"

Josak looked around the little room with a heavy sigh. "Might as well, I suppose. There's nothing for me here. I can't live here alone."

"But we can't leave them like this," Alannys said in sudden alarm. "I mean—can't we give them a decent burial? They died protecting me. We can't just walk away and leave them."

"We can," Trago said, "and we'd better, if we want to walk away at all."

"But Trago—"

"No, listen," he cut her off impatiently. "This place is dangerous, and we're all spent. Not a one of us would be worth a damn in a fight if something should happen. We need to get out of here. We don't have time or energy to spend on niceties for the dead, unless we wish to join them."

"You don't understand," she said, and her voice sounded as broken as she felt. "These dead aren't just nameless strangers. They're my friends."

"And me family," Josak said quietly. "I don't like this any more than you do, Alannys. But Trago is right. They gave everything they had to defend you. I don't think they'd be happy to lose you again because you tended to them."

"Just so," Trago said. "At times like this we must do our best to remain practical. Josak, the Singari are low on supplies. Do you think there is anything here that might help us?"

"I'm sure there is, in the kitchen and the pantry. Come with me—I think there are a few other things you should take as well."

Josak led Trago from the room. Alannys had to wonder about his tone, until she remembered Trago's words about being practical and realized he was trying to do just that.

Alannys pushed herself up from the pillows, struggling against the weakness in her limbs.

"Alannys?" Chen looked at her with obvious concern.

"Help me up, Chen. We should go out to the garden. There's more food out there, and livestock."

"Food and livestock." He looked at her evenly. "Sure. And shovels?"

"And shovels."

"I see." He regarded her a moment longer, then silently offered his hand. It took more time than she liked, and a lot of help from Chen, but finally she stood in her own linen workshirt and leather pants, with her riding cloak on her back and Songstrike at her side. If it weren't for the lingering pain, for the uncharacteristic heaviness in limbs and the residual burning in the cuts she'd sustained, she could almost have felt normal.

Chen regarded her dubiously, as if he expected her to topple at any moment. "Are you sure you can do this?"

"No. But I have to try. They rescued me, Chen—they healed me, they fought for me, and they died trying to save me from this. It's the only way I have to honor them."

Chen nodded. He shook the shawl out, and wrapped it carefully over her head, crossing the ends over her chest. After everything she had been through, it seemed like a kind of miracle just to be able to stand with him, to see his handsome, familiar face, and to look into those dark brown eyes that she knew without reservation would do anything for her. She remembered how close she had come to losing that, how close she had come to leaving the recent awkwardness between them as her final legacy to him.

Her gaze fell to her feet. "Chen, I—"

His hand landed on her shoulder, startling her. "I'm with you, Alannys, but now is not the time for us to talk. Later, maybe?"

She smiled in what might have been relief. "It's a date."

Chen took her arm and supported her on the walk out to the garden. "We'll find shovels in the garden shed," she said, and started to lead him in that direction.

"Wait," Chen said, holding her back. "Did you think I brought you out here so you could dig graves? Come on, you know better than that—even on your best day I would argue against that, and this is far from your best day. You'll fall over if you so much as lift a shovel."

"I might," she admitted.

"Of course you would. You sit right here by the entrance, ready to run back inside if a painting opens. I'll dig."

He had no sooner turned away than Trago and Josak emerged from the cave behind her.

"Didn't I tell you we'd find things like this?" Trago grumbled.

"You did." Josak's tone was serious, but she thought she saw a hint of a smile.

"Women are the stubbornest creatures in the Muses's sight, and this one's the stubbornest of all. Sit down, you. This's no work for a lady." Trago complained the whole time, but he and Josak picked up shovels in the shed and followed Chen.

Alannys sat on a large, flat rock near the well and wept while the men handled the digging and refilling of graves. It was hard, exhausting work, but she wished with all her might that she had been able to help.

They met the approaching Singari wagon train as the sun was coming up. They brought the chickens from the garden, and the food from the caves. Josak gave Alannys leather-bound books full of Driach's spidery handwriting, and the remainder of the Talent-proofing solution, safe in a sealed wooden cask.

Alannys was bone-tired and grieving, but standing

next to Chen watching the wagons silhouetted by the first rays of the waking sun, Alannys thought the sunrise was the most hopeful thing she had ever seen. She was battered and bandaged, but she was still *here,* able to stand and feel the morning sun on her face.

She clutched the shawl tighter over her head and hoped that she could keep it that way.

♫

"You told her what?" Raman did not express an opinion on Dorramon's promise to Alannys—he didn't have to. The shock in his voice said it all.

Dorramon sighed. Normally he would not have tolerated being spoken to like that, but since they were in his private rooms he let it slide. "I told her I would ride out immediately, duty be damned. And I would have, if she had been able to tell me where she is. You can't imagine what this whole ordeal has been like, Raman. And then yesterday morning, when the mindlink disappeared—I thought I would go mad. It was like it had never been there at all. I couldn't tell what had happened, whether she lived or died. If she died, out there risking her life for me..."

"I understand how difficult this has been for you," Raman said carefully, "but—"

"No, you don't! When the mindlink opened this morning—it was like a bright light after being trapped in utter darkness. And then, to find out Ethal had her— Ethal!"

Raman and Kalyn exchanged a glance Dorramon couldn't decipher. "But, your Highness," Kalyn said, "didn't you say that Lady Alannys is safe now?"

"She says she is safe. I trust her, but how can I be sure?" Dorramon looked at Raman in frustration. "If that was Kalyn out there, can you honestly say you wouldn't do exactly what I have proposed?"

"Dorramon, that isn't fair!" Raman shot a quick look at

Kalyn on the sofa, as if reminding himself that she was not in any immediate danger. "You know I would do anything for Kalyn. But I'm not the king! I could ride out right now without decapitating the government of Ravanmark!"

"I'm not sure the comparison is sound," Kalyn added. "Lady Alannys is not like me. I could never do what she has done. She's much stronger than I am. But she's also more independent — don't you think? I am afraid it might offend her if anyone rode out to rescue her, at a time when she said she didn't need help."

Dorramon flopped down on the edge of his bed. "You're right. Of course you're right. But what am I to do?"

Raman clapped him on the shoulder. "The only thing you can do, Dorr. Pray to the Muses for her safety, and wait for her return. You have more than enough to keep you busy here. Have you decided to receive Ambassador Thell?"

Dorramon shook Raman's hand off his shoulder. "You know I haven't."

"I've heard that a Cadendan warship has dropped anchor near the ambassador's ship. There are rumors of two more on the way. Cadenda will send a more powerful envoy soon."

"I know that!"

"I am certain Raman would never seek to upset you, your Highness," Kalyn said carefully. "Of course we know how stressful your position is, and we don't want to add to that. I think Raman simply wondered if your Highness has decided yet how to address the new envoy when he arrives?"

"I don't know. I'm not ready to consider marrying that woman, not while Alannys is out and in danger. I can't even think of it. It makes me ill."

Raman folded his arms. "I think you mean that you are

not ready to consider marrying Princess Varilyn ever, under any circumstances, no matter where Alannys is."

Dorramon glowered at him. "I take it you would have me welcome Thell back to court as an old friend, and arrange the wedding as soon as possible?"

Raman held his hands up defensively. "Now don't go putting words in my mouth. I never said anything of the sort! Look, Dorramon, I like her too. You think I can't see the difference in you since Alannys came to Ravanmark? It's obvious to me that if you were anyone else, the two of you would already be married. But you aren't anyone else. You're the King of Ravanmark, and you've been betrothed since birth to Princess Varilyn. You're playing a dangerous game, putting them off like this, and eventually you're going to have to take a stance on the matter, one way or another. I just want you to be aware of all of the consequences of your decision."

"I know, I know," Dorramon muttered, waving him off. "But your constant reminders of the gravity of the situation aren't making anything easier."

Raman shrugged and let himself out of the royal chambers. Kalyn stood to follow him, then suddenly turned and sat down close beside Dorramon, taking his hand in both of her own. He looked at her in surprise.

"Please don't give up," she said simply. "I know Raman is concerned, I know many people are concerned. They don't understand. But I do. Lady Alannys loves you dearly, your Highness. She would do anything for you. She will come back, you'll see, and all of this will work out. I am sure of it."

"I..." Dorramon faltered. He had been putting on a brave face under heavy criticism for so long it seemed like second nature now, and the sudden sound of an honestly sympathetic voice threatened to undo him. "Thank you, Kalyn."

She turned beet red, and jumped up from the bed. "I beg your pardon if I have spoken out of turn. Stay strong, your Majesty." With a hasty curtsey, she turned and hurried after Raman. Dorramon watched her go, wishing he had her certainty. He couldn't believe so easily.

And yet, he would pray every night that what she said would prove true.

♫

Delline squeezed her eyes shut tight, then opened them and tried to force them to focus once again on the page in front of her. She had to check it over one more time — she had to be certain it was all correct.

Her hands ached, her fingers were black from too many hours with the ink and quill, her back was sore, and she had a splitting headache. It would all be wasted though, if there was a single error on this page; none of it would matter.

She could still hear Lord Malrec's angry voice, could still hear the bitterness in his tone the last time he had spoken to her, when he had furiously ordered her out of his chambers. Her cheeks burned just thinking about it. That had been three days ago. He had not spoken a word to her since. She had not passed him in the corridors, or seen him anywhere, even once. She still came down to dinner in the big dining room at the appointed time, but he never joined her there. Their new serving girl made unconvincing excuses about how busy he was, how he took dinner in his chambers so that he could continue to work.

Not that she believed he wasn't busy. She knew that he was — she had no doubt that he was working harder than ever. Delline set her paper carefully to the side and wiped her hands as clean as she could get them, annoyed at the way ink had settled into the lines and wrinkles — lines and wrinkles that had not been there even a week before. Since the completion of the luch-ul collar, Lord Malrec had been working frantically to get everything in order, so that the Dark Alliance could move ahead with their plans, plans she only half understood.

At the same time, her own relationship with Lord Malrec had been going steadily downhill, culminating in their fight three days ago. Since the completion of the collar, there seemed to be little that he needed her for.

The paper she scooped up off of the table now would change all of that, she was certain. Lord Malrec never invited her to sit in on his meetings with the Dark Alliance anymore, but she already knew that their plans were stalled, faced with the impossible requirement of one painter in two places at the same time. Lord Malrec had even taken the unthinkable step of taking an apprentice, but teaching him enough to be useful to the Alliance would take too long, they all knew it. He had not yet managed to learn how to *make* a passable gloss—let alone how to use it. They were well and truly stuck.

Delline had thought of little else in the last three days. If she could offer Lord Malrec a solution to this problem, he would be hers again. She would bask in the warm glow of his approval, and pretend the last three days had never happened.

If she could offer him a solution.

The primary problem they faced was the drying time of the gloss that turned a work of art from painting to portal. The drying time was nothing they could control; it was determined by the chemical composition of the gloss itself.

If, however, there was a *different* composition...another formula, for a longer lasting gloss...

She had worked tirelessly in the hope that something like that could be found. She had not seen her bed for three days, but in all that time in the library she had done the impossible. The paper in her hand held the only existent copy of a new formulation for gloss.

Her footsteps slowed as she approached the study, where Lord Malrec and his cohorts usually holed up to plot and argue. She could hear their voices down the hall, and suddenly felt a lot more reluctant to barge in there.

"...and I'm certainly willing to put aside the problem for now," came Diabon's cutting voice, "although I question the wisdom of that—we need Lord Malrec in two places—possibly three—for the operations to succeed. That is the single biggest problem we face, and we have been spending so much time preparing the music mage's prison we have not been able to work on that problem."

"Diabon, my friend," she heard Lord Malrec begin, in the tone he used when he wanted to sound congenial but really felt like having someone beheaded.

"But," Lord Diabon cut him off loudly, hardly pausing to draw breath, "we still have a second problem, almost as large as the first. These plans can only succeed if the palace forces are divided—if we can separate the king from his army. We are depending on that, but we have no reason to think that they will in fact separate."

"Ah, but we do." Lord Malrec sounded downright magnanimous. Delline supposed he must be furious, but couldn't risk fracturing the alliance at this juncture. Relationships must have been strained all around.

For some reason that did not make her feel better.

"Long have I planned the resolution we are working toward," he continued grandly. "As soon as I realized the young prince seriously entertained the notion that this woman was the Redeemer of prophecy, I also realized that we possess the means to ensure that he leaves the safety of the palace and his army."

"Well, out with it, then!" Diabon demanded. "Don't be coy, Lord Malrec! Don't you think Prubard and I deserve to know every contingency we are working with?"

"Hmm," Lord Malrec said, either considering it or

pretending to do so. "No. I don't. There are parts of our plans that depend upon absolute secrecy...things which will be revealed to our enemies which they must believe they are learning against our will. Any small slip could ruin everything."

"Lord Malrec, I must protest!" That would be Baron Prubard, making himself heard for the first time since Delline had come within earshot. She shuddered; Prubard always made her skin crawl. The way he looked at her, the way he talked about her — she didn't see why Lord Malrec permitted it. "Diabon and I have risked everything to join you. We have invested our holdings, our fortunes, indeed our very lives on the outcome of these plans. How can you decline to trust us?"

"Now, gentlemen, as I have explained, the issue has nothing to do with trust—"

"It has everything to do with trust!" Diabon exploded. "Look around you! We are supposed to be designing these operations together. And yet it seems that you always know things we do not, or have done things you have not told us, or have already worked out details we spend hours agonizing over. And now you withhold a crucial piece of information from us, even when we ask directly! We should not have to ask to be included in our own plans. The issue is not whether you should trust us, but whether we should trust you!"

"I see," Lord Malrec said coldly, and Delline shivered. "In that case I advise you to get yourselves with all possible haste to the Great Palace, and throw yourselves and your holdings on the mercy of the young puppy currently on the throne. Perhaps he will strip you of titles and possessions and imprison you for life. Mayhap he will hang you, or have you drawn and quartered, or burnt alive, or maybe he will *sing* you to death! Whatever end he chooses you may go to it peacefully, knowing that if you stayed here and spoke betrayal to *me,* your palace death would look positively *merciful* by comparison!"

The heavy study door flew open and Lord Malrec stormed out. Delline could almost see the anger radiating from him. His mood was not improved, it seemed, by finding her there.

"You! Great Muses, woman, what do you mean by lurking in corridors?"

She had hoped he might take her arm, but he brushed past her and continued on his way with hardly a look in her direction. She gathered herself up and hurried after him, burying any sting his disdain might have carried. "I had hoped to see you, my Lord—I did wish to speak with you."

Lord Malrec stopped at the foot of the grand staircase, pinching the bridge of his nose between his thumb and forefinger with the attitude of a man greatly put upon. "I trust that you have not come to vex me further with whining about your current accommodations."

"No, my Lord."

"Or the dining arrangements."

"Indeed, no."

"Then you have doubtlessly come to harangue me about my lack of leisure time to fritter away with you, at a time when you can see that I carry inhuman burdens?"

"My Lord! Of course not."

Lord Malrec folded his arms and faced her. "Very well, then. With what gravely important matter have you come to trouble me?"

Delline tried to smile brilliantly, but she could tell she hadn't pulled it off. It felt timid—it seemed she was not as sure of her reception as she wanted to believe. "I have a gift for you, my Lord. A wonderful gift—you can't imagine how wonderful."

"I don't know," he replied dubiously. "I can imagine

quite a lot."

"Not this. I have solved your problem — the problem with painting, with the gloss. With needing to be in multiple places at once."

His eyebrows shot up. "Is that so?" He didn't sound particularly hopeful, but she did have his attention.

Delline gave him the paper. He inspected it with no sign of comprehension. "What is this?"

"It's the answer to your prayers. It is the only copy of a formula that has been lost for hundreds of years. It's a formula for a gloss *that never dries.*"

"What?"

Delline nodded. Of course he would love her for this; how could he not? "It's true. You have to use drying powder to close the painting — the gloss does not dry on its own. It will stay open as long as you want it to."

His eyes tracked rapidly down the page, processing the formula. She could see his face light up, and the smile that broke his countenance was genuine — perhaps the most genuine smile she had ever seen from him.

"My dear Princess, you are indeed a treasure!" Lord Malrec carefully deposited the formula in a pocket hidden inside his cloak, and took Delline's arm, pulling her close to him. "You must come with me to my chambers and tell me all about your discovery of this miracle. I shall have our dinner served there as well, so we shall not be disturbed. I refuse to share your company with the baron or Lord Diabon tonight."

Delline leaned into Lord Malrec and let him lead her up the stairs, basking in his warm, undivided attention, happy for the first time in three days.

♫

It took a longer time than Alannys would have thought possible to make the short walk to her wagon. It seemed like every Singari in the tribe stopped to wish her well, to shake her bandaged hands and let her know how worried they had been. She appreciated every one of them, and yet she had to admit without Chen there holding her up, she would never have made it to her wagon.

By the time the familiar front door was in sight, all she wanted was to get inside and collapse onto her bed. Before she had struggled up half of her front steps, though, she heard a sound from behind her wagon that changed all her plans.

It was the whinny of a horse.

Alannys froze on the step, looking at Chen in surprise. "Is — is that Quicksilver?"

"It is, but —"

"Help me turn around. I have to go see him."

"Alannys, I'm not sure this is the best time..."

She looked at him in disbelief. "What?"

"He's in kind of rough shape. It might upset you to see him."

"I'm in kind of rough shape too. Do you think it will upset him? Chen, I thought he was *dead.* After everything we've been through, I was afraid I had finally killed him. I have to go see him."

Chen helped her hobble back down the steps, and around to the back of the wagon where Quicksilver was tied.

Chen was right; the horse was in rough shape. She could see half-healed cuts, and bare, shiny patches of skin where the hair had been burned away. He nickered at her, though, and nuzzled her hand as if he was relieved to see her as well.

Then she noticed some of the deeper cuts had been stitched carefully closed, and a thin layer of ointment glistened on his many injuries. "Have you been tending to him, Chen?"

"No. That is, not alone. Nashara cleaned him up and stitched him, and showed me how to use the ointments.

She checks in on him a lot."

"Really? Does she usually tend to animals?"

Chen shrugged. "This was a special case."

"I agree." Alannys sighed in sudden exhaustion, and swayed where she stood.

"I think," Chen said, "it's time you went to bed."

She couldn't argue. She wished she had a carrot or a sugar cube for Quicksilver, but she had to settle for scratching his ears before Chen led her back into the wagon.

She didn't think anything had ever felt quite so good as her own bed and her own pillows. She leaned back against them, sighing, closing her eyes, thinking maybe she would never move again.

"Don't get too comfortable," Chen said gruffly. "I'm sure Nashara will be here soon to check you over."

"No worries. I think I could sleep through surgery right now."

"That's what you say now. Wait till she starts poking around at those cuts — I don't care if they are shallow, they are going to hurt."

Alannys opened her eyes again, frowning. She had tried not to think too much about the cuts. She had no idea how they would heal, and she didn't want to worry before she knew anything. She grabbed for the first thing she could think of to change the subject.

"Chen, is Dahlia — did she..."

He looked away, and shook his head. "Dahlia died in the explosion."

Alannys had known that had to be the case. And yet it kind of knocked the wind out of her to hear it said so bluntly. "I'm sorry."

Chen pulled a chair up next to the bed and sat down. His eyes looked red and strained. "We'll all miss her. It was worse, though, thinking that you might be gone as well."

"I am glad to be back," she admitted, and reached out to take his hand. "For a while there I didn't think I would ever see you again, I didn't think I would get a chance to set things right."

For just a moment, his eyes met hers, and the sadness she saw there tore at her heart. Then he looked away, and ran a gentle finger across the royal bracelet on her wrist. "Alannys, it's fine. You don't love me. You love the king. I get it. I'm slow, but even I learn eventually."

Alannys sighed. "No. It's not that simple. I do love you, Chen, and I have for a long time, whether I wanted to see it or not. But the simple truth is that I love Dorramon more."

"Alannys—"

"I have to go back there, Chen. I have to go back to the Great Palace, even if the whole thing is doomed and has been from the beginning. Even if all I can do there is stand in the audience while he pledges his life to a woman he doesn't love—if it helps him, I have to do it. Do you understand?"

"No. Yes." Chen shook his head. "I mean, when I hear you say things like that, it doesn't make sense to me. It just doesn't. You don't owe him anything. You've moved mountains for him, and you're condemning yourself to a life of frustration and unhappiness. But then I look at myself, and I understand. When you disappeared after that explosion, I discovered that there is something I fear more than losing you personally, Alannys, and that is losing you permanently, for once and for all, gone from this world. It would break my heart to see you leave, but if you *died...*" He shook his head. "Anything would be better than that. I would do anything you asked of me—even take you to the Great Palace myself, if that's what it took, and stand by while—" He broke off. "I understand, that's all. I understand."

Alannys didn't know what to say. Tears burned her eyes, but no words came, and all she could do was cling to his hand as he clung to hers, sharing their support through their suffering.

♫

A long, uncomfortable moment passed through the silent wagon before Chen spoke again. "That doesn't mean I give up, do you hear me?" His voice was rough. "I still hold out hope. Things can change."

"Knock, knock!"

The call from the door interrupted what Alannys found to be a very painful conversation. "Come on in, Nashara," she called back.

Chen moved over to stand by the desk, making room for the healer to approach the bed.

"Well, now," Nashara said, looking down at her sternly, "it looks as though you've found more trouble."

Alannys attempted to grin, and was mostly successful. "It seems as though I've got a knack for that, doesn't it?"

Nashara shook her head, but the corners of her mouth were twitching. "Indeed it does. If even half of the tales I have heard this morning are true, I will have my work cut out for me." She settled into the chair at the bedside. "Now lets see what we have under these bandages."

Alannys closed her eyes and tried not to squirm while Nashara removed the bandages from her face. She didn't find it particularly easy to do; removing the coverings was a rather ticklish matter, and the wounds underneath were very tender.

She heard the healer's sharp intake of breath when the first wound was uncovered, and her eyes popped open. "What? What is it?"

"Nothing, dear child. Nothing at all." Nashara's tone was bright, and her smile seemed forced. "Go ahead and rest, I will take care of everything."

Alannys took her at her word, and relaxed against her pillows, closing her eyes. To her surprise, she did manage to doze while Nashara unbound her wounds, cleaned them, and coated them with ointment. Only when the healer stood to go did Alannys speak again. "Well, what's the prognosis?"

Nashara glanced down at the bed; Alannys followed her gaze and realized that the blankets were pulled up under her chin. Hands, feet, everything was hidden from view. This seemed to encourage Nashara, and the false smile re-emerged.

"Oh, I have no doubt you are going to be fine, my Lady. The cuts are shallow, and quite clean. I think they will heal very nicely — they are such fine, narrow cuts I did not need to stitch them. There will be scars, but they will be fine scars. Perhaps some will be visible only in certain light."

Alannys found nothing in this speech to explain the contrast between the healer's manner and her words. "Well...that's good news then, isn't it?"

"Indeed, indeed," Nashara said, moving toward the door. "If you'll excuse me — lots to do today — I'm going to look in on your horse for a moment and then I'll be off. You should rest now."

"Of course," Alannys said, confused. "Thank you."

The door closed, and Alannys frowned. "Chen, what's wrong with me?"

"Nothing," he said immediately. He seemed to have studied Nashara's false smile closely; the imitation was nearly perfect.

"Hmm. Could I see a mirror?"

"Is that really what you want? This all happened so recently, after all — don't you think it might be better to — "

"Chen, please? Something upset Nashara. It isn't going to go away. I may as well start coming to grips with what happened to me right now. The longer I wait, thinking everything is still the same, the harder it will be later."

"Are you sure you are ready for any more unpleasantness? Nashara said you needed rest."

Nashara had not replaced any of the bandages she took off of Alannys. It surprised her to suddenly realize this — it made sense, though; once the corrupted sun-fruit slime was off of her, the bleeding had stopped quickly on its own.

That meant she didn't have to waste any more time waiting on Chen to allow her to see what had been done to her. She had no idea why it had taken her so long to come to this realization — she really must have needed rest.

She pulled her hands out from under the heavy blanket and held them in front of her, fingers splayed, backs facing her. She could feel the color drain from her face as she regarded them, suddenly unfamiliar to her, like a stranger's hands.

"Ach, I wish you hadn't done that," Chen said. "Are you all right?"

She nodded.

"Because you don't look all right."

"I just—" She cleared her throat and tried again. "I just wonder if you might be able to tell me what on earth I am looking at." She thought she sounded very calm, considering. She had realized that Ethal's ritual included some cuts that seemed to form shapes, but she certainly had never imagined anything like this!

Chen sighed. "I can do that much, at least. Those are runes, Alannys. What you see on your hands are runic representations of the names of the Muses."

"The Muses." Her throat was suddenly dry. "I think I need that mirror now, Chen."

He came over to sit next to her, carrying the little mirror she kept in the desk drawer. "Yes. The Muses. The runes are based on their icons, see?" He cupped her left palm in his own, and gently touched the symbol formed by the angry red lines on the back of her hand.

"This is the symbol for Calliope. It's her writing tablet."

"Calliope," Alannys echoed. "And this one on my right hand?"

"Clio," Chen said. "That's Clio's scroll."

"Oh — Clio, the Proclaimer," Alannys said. "I once sang a hymn that had all of the Muses in it — you'd think I would remember. But these runes...it isn't obvious to me what they are supposed to be."

Chen grimaced. "Don't worry. It will be to everyone else in Ravanmark. I doubt you'll find a single person in the country who won't know what these are."

"This — this is likely to get me into trouble, isn't it?"

"Honestly, I don't know, Alannys. If you were anyone else, I would say yes. But you — I don't know if this would cause any more trouble than you usually find on your own." He placed the little mirror in her hands, and she looked at her face with a shiver. "On your temples, I see Erato's arrow, and Euterpe's flute."

"Okay."

"Your cheeks carry Melpomene's tragic mask, and Terpsichore's lyre."

"Okay."

He glanced at her. "On your feet, there are Polyhymnia's veil and Urania's globe."

"Okay."

"Look, are you sure you're all right? I don't know if 'okay' is all I would say, over and over, if this happened to me."

She shrugged, looking with detachment at the scarred reflection in the mirror. Would she always feel that way? She didn't know. Maybe shock insulated her, held off, for the moment, the reaction Chen expected. "So this one on my collarbone must be Thalia's ivy crown, right? I wouldn't forget that one." She remembered the Ivy Crown in Crinn, the owners of which had organized a midnight mob to assassinate her. Raman had stood to defend her, before he suffered that terrible wound at Mirendasith Hall. She had sung then, the same way she sang much later when Chen suffered a terrible wound as well.

Was this good, the way her mind kept flitting around, lighting briefly on some random topic before leaping to another, only tangentially related topic? Was it right, the way her thoughts seemed fuzzy and indistinct in her own head? She didn't think so. And she wasn't even sure if Chen had answered her or not. All she could seem to do was stare at the face that seemed to belong to someone else, reflected in a mirror held by hands that seemed to belong to someone else, too. Was this what shock felt like?

Chen lifted the mirror from her hands as it started to shake, and pulled the blanket back up over her. "I think Nashara was right, Alannys—you really should rest."

She looked at him a moment, but her mind seemed finally to have emptied itself, and she couldn't think of a single word to say. Was this normal, for someone to tell her what to do, and for her to just—do it? She really didn't know. Maybe it would make more sense after a nap.

She closed her eyes, not holding out much hope for that. It didn't feel like things had made much sense for a very long time.

♪

In her dreams, everyone called her the Tattooed Lady. She didn't understand it—she knew she hadn't chosen them, and besides, they were scars, not tattoos. Even if they were runes representing the Muses, she didn't really like having them on her skin, and she didn't get why people kept singing about it. It didn't make a bit of sense.

But then, she'd expected that.

A jumble of these stressful, confusing dreams left her

feeling tired when she awoke.

Then she caught sight of her hands and realized why she had dreamt about her scars, and about singing. "Chen?"

"Not here, sorry." The voice came from a bit behind her; she could hear the creaking of the wooden chair as the speaker stood. But she knew before he stepped into view that the voice belonged to Trago. "He asked me to sit with you until you woke."

"Muse's Fever, right? He sang?"

"He didn't say. If somebody offered me odds, though, I'd take the bet. He was staggering like a man too full of ale, and I wasn't sure he'd make it to his wagon before he collapsed. And you look a far sight better."

She nodded, tilting her hands, watching the changing light play across the fine, light scars that already looked mostly healed. "He shouldn't have done that. It wasn't worth it, these would have healed on their own."

Trago regarded her solemnly. "I imagine he felt it was worth it. From what he said, those scars upset you pretty badly. If he thought he could help minimize them — well, he didn't hesitate, did he?"

"No. I guess he didn't." She didn't really feel comfortable discussing all this with Trago, and she couldn't think of a subtle way to change the subject, so she settled for the blunt approach. "I notice we aren't moving."

"Beg pardon?"

"The wagons. We're still sitting here. I'm guessing they're waiting for me to give the order to get rolling again?"

Trago pulled the wooden chair over, flipped it around backwards, and straddled it. "I was hoping to talk to you about that."

"Really?"

"Yes. Where were you planning to go?"

"Um—" The question stopped her flat. Abruptly she realized that she didn't actually know where they were. "That's a really good question. Now that you mention it, I have only ever come to this place through paintings. I don't really know where we are now, in relation to where we were before."

Trago nodded, as though he had expected as much. "You'll be pleased to know we really aren't that far from where we were—maybe half a day west."

"Oh. So it wouldn't be hard at all to just continue on like we were."

"No. But I came to ask you if you would consider a detour of sorts. I want to ask you to go even further west."

"Further west? Why?"

The muscles in his jaw clenched, as though he was having a hard time getting the words out. "House Orinthal. I want to go to House Orinthal."

"House Orinthal?" Alannys didn't think she could have been more surprised her if Trago had said he wanted to dive to Cilahar and have dinner with Soth. "Why do you want to go there?"

"This has got to stop, Alannys." His face was very hard. "Orinthal can't go on like this. The baron has abdicated. The baroness has relocated to the Great Palace, and if she's smart she'll never come back here. Evil is out of control—Orinthal Holding is running full sail, and no one is at the wheel."

"I don't argue any of that. But how will us going to House Orinthal fix it?"

"I want to stay there. I want to take my father's place as baron, and clean this place up. The longer this goes on, the harder it's going to be to stop it later."

"I don't know, Trago. I think we need to get out of this place as quickly as we can, not tarry longer." She swallowed hard, trying to seem calm. She did not want him to guess that her arguments came from fear. "You left that life behind years ago. The Singari keep to themselves — they owe nothing to society, remember?"

"That may be true," he said grimly, "for them. But I can't look at this and let it be. Can you?"

His eyes bored into her, challenging her, and she couldn't hold them. She looked down, collapsing back against the pillows. "No. I can't argue with what you're saying. Have you considered the king? It could be taken as treasonous to install yourself as ruler of the holding without his approval."

"This is one case where I think it's better to ask forgiveness than permission. We don't have time for trips to the palace, and deliberations, and investiture ceremonies, and Muses know what else. Something must be done now, not a month or six months or a year from now."

"We'll ride west. And I'll see what I can do about your permission problem. If you could take command with the full backing of the king, I think it would only help you."

"If you can arrange that, you really are a miracle-worker."

Alannys laughed. "I don't know about that. Seems like my part is easy. If you can bring order to this place, you'll be the real miracle-worker. Listen, I need you to round up Drigo and Grald. They are used to carrying out whatever crazy thing I come up with; we'll get them to start everybody moving west. The fewer details we give out, the better, I think."

Trago nodded and let himself out.

Alannys watched him go, wondering if she was doing the right thing. Was it even possible for one man to turn all of this around?

Then she had to laugh at herself. Hadn't she set out

from the Great Palace with the express goal of single-handedly changing Ravanmark's views of the Talents? How was Trago's quest any more difficult than that?

It had to be possible. For the people of Ravanmark to have any hope at all, success had to be possible, for both Trago and herself.

And she refused to give up hope. For any of them.

♪

Maybe an hour later, Alannys felt her wagon lurch into motion and knew the Singari were moving again. It gave her an odd turn, feeling the wagon move and knowing that no one was driving the horses.

Of course, it was like that most days — she usually rode Quicksilver up at the front of the train, while the two pulling horses hauled the wagon somewhere in the middle. They were trained to do that, to follow along with the others. She knew that.

It didn't make it feel any less weird.

Alannys laid back against her pillows and tried to put it out of her mind. She needed to concentrate — she needed to have a conversation. And regardless of her confident attitude to others, she wasn't entirely sure that conversation would go well. Kings could be capricious, even at the best of times, and Dorramon — well, now was not one of his best times, for sure. She knew well enough the stress they had both been under, but losing the mindlink for most of a day seemed to have broken him somehow, and she couldn't even guess what he might be capable of now, or how he might react to pretty much anything.

So she lay still for a few moments, taking deep breaths and calming herself as much as possible before she began. Or maybe she was stalling. Finally she reached for that familiar place where her mind opened outward, a connection she could always feel, though it couldn't be seen.

Dorramon?

Alannys! What a pleasant surprise. You're contacting me to tell me where I can come for you, I presume?

Dorramon. She forced herself not to sigh. At least he sounded like he was in a good mood. *You know you can't do that.*

You might be surprised what I can do, when my mind is made up. But I understand you don't want me to, so I'm attempting to restrain myself.

Even his pouting was light and teasing. It lifted her spirits to hear him sound so happy; his good cheer was contagious. *What are you up to this morning?*

Taking a late breakfast, alone, in my chambers. It's the most wonderful thing in the world.

No court this morning?

There was a slight hesitation. *I needed a break. Court is full of – drama these days.*

That didn't sound good, and she didn't like the way his tone darkened when he spoke of court. Time to change the subject. *Dorramon, what do you know of the current situation in Orinthal Holding?*

Orinthal has a situation? The last briefing I had about Orinthal was from Baron Prubard, when the lords were here before my coronation. Usually each holding sends a runner each month with their status reports, but you can imagine that isn't happening with Orinthal and Glennayre Holdings. With everything else that's been going on, I hadn't really worried too much about it. We've had a couple of servants relocate from House Orinthal to serve Baroness Lae here, and they say the Baron's Guard is keeping things in order until her return.

That may be so, Alannys said slowly, *in the immediate vicinity of House Orinthal. But everywhere else, the holding is falling apart. Just falling apart. Chaos is everywhere.*

Really?

Alannys concentrated on the things she had seen: on the burnt-out husk that once was Shadowkeep, on the bands of thugs preying on anyone they could find, on the smoking ruin that Lord Malrec's homemade bomb had made in the countryside. It took some concentration, but she projected each of these images across the mindlink.

She could hear his horrified gasp. *Alannys, where are you right now?*

Somewhere in Orinthal. We're on our way to House Orinthal.

House Orinthal? She had never realized it was possible to sound curious and aghast, both at the same time. *Why?*

Well, that's what I wanted you to talk about. Trago is hoping he can take control of things, and stop what's happening here before it gets any worse. I don't — I don't think the baroness is ever going to rule here.

Trago? Baron Prubard's son? There was a contemplative pause. *You know, I knew that he had joined the Singari, but it never occurred to me that he would be there with you. I see what you're saying — Lae is not a leader, really — she doesn't even want to go back at all, but especially not as baroness. But do you really think it's a good idea to put him in charge? Wasn't he raised to continue on in what Prubard had already done?*

Sure — why do you think he left? I don't think Trago would continue on with the way Prubard did things. He doesn't seem to like his father much at all.

I don't know, Alannys. Something in your voice when you talk about him — it doesn't sound like you're totally confident about this. Are you sure about him?

I am, she said, but she knew it sounded hollow. Dorramon waited silently for an explanation, and she sighed. *Look, it's true he hasn't always been perfect, and we haven't always gotten along. He messed up pretty horribly — I'd just as soon not go into details. But he's come a long way since then, and since we've come to Orinthal — it's like he's found his purpose. He really wants this.*

I don't know, Alannys, he said again. She could practically hear him biting on his lip. *It sounds like Orinthal* is a mess right now. We can't risk putting someone in charge who will make things worse.

Honestly, Dorramon, I don't think things can _get_ worse. Any ruler is better than no ruler at all, and Trago saved my life. I'm willing to vouch for him.

Dorramon thought about it. _Well, you know him better than I do – I never met the man. If you think he is capable, I suppose I have no objection._

Oh, I'm glad to hear you say that. He's really determined to do this – I don't know how I'd talk him out of it if you said no.

The king laughed. _Well, then, it's a good thing I didn't say no, isn't it? I'll send a rider out with the proclamation, medallions, and seals. We can do the official investiture ceremony any time that he wants._

That sounds terrific. I'm going to send your rider back with something I want you to have, Dorramon – a cask of Talent-proofing solution. Paint the walls of any room with it, and it will suppress the use of any Talent in that room.

That sounds interesting, **Dorramon said,** but why would I need it?

Alannys sighed. _Lord Malrec has explosives. He detonated one of them near us in an attempt to capture me. Dahlia was killed._

Merciful Muses!

What if he paints one of those into the Great Hall, or into your chambers? I don't know how much this cask will cover, but maybe you can use it to make your rooms safe.

Thank you, Alannys. **Dorramon paused.** But if I use that, then I can't use the mindlink to talk to you, is that right?

You can't worry about that! These bombs are horrific!

I don't think Malrec is going to do anything that drastic...he's counting on lots of support, after all. What you're describing doesn't sound likely to gain that support. That's probably why he chose to use it in a deserted rural area of a holding that's already crumbling.

Alannys made a conscious effort to calm down and

consider what he had said. *You're right. Still...*

I know. I don't like the sound of it either. Listen, we can treat the Lesser Hall. Then we have a safe room if we need it, and I'm not in there enough to hinder the mindlink when we need it. But what about you? Shouldn't you Talent-proof the places you stay?

I don't think it would help. Malrec isn't going to place an explosive in my wagon; he wants me alive. He would be putting them far enough away, there's no conceivable way I could prevent it.

I don't think I like the sound of that.

Alannys laughed, trying to lighten the mood. *Me, either. Hurry your rider out here so I can send this to you. Besides, I have a feeling it wouldn't hurt to have your support at House Orinthal sooner rather than later.*

I don't know exactly where you are, but I wouldn't guess my rider will be more than a day behind you. A lone man should make much better time than a wagon train – he'll catch up fast.

Thank you so much. You aren't going to regret this.

You know, I think you're right. I can already see Baron Prubard howling with rage – this day just keeps getting better and better.

Alannys laughed, right up until she opened her eyes and found herself alone in her wagon, bumping and lurching along a path that took her almost directly away from the Great Palace, and the one face she wanted more than any other to see.

♪

The Singari stopped earlier than usual that evening. Everyone was still tired from the all-night drive to meet at Ravan's Light. House Orinthal was high in the mountains on Orinthal's seashore, and it didn't seem like a good idea to start that climb late in the day – mountain paths had a way of becoming narrow and unsuitable for a proper camp.

So it was still light when they set up camp, which was

unusual — in their efforts to get through Orinthal as quickly as possible, they had been riding late into the night. The early stop seemed to raise everyone's spirits, and happy conversations and laughter filled the camp as the cook fires started.

Alannys called a meeting of her music students before dinner, in the scrubby woods that surrounded the clearing where they had pitched camp. She wandered among the leafless trees, inspecting the site, looking for inspiration, as the Singari trickled in. She knew what she wanted to do with them — she just wasn't sure how to do it with no risk of hurting anyone.

"Are you sure you're up to this?" The voice at her back was Chen's.

She spun around to face him, surprised. "I am. Are you sure you are?"

"Well, I may not sing, but you just try getting rid of me. I plan to dog your footsteps. I don't think it's wise for you to be alone from here on out." His glance flicked to the shawl over her head.

She turned away self-consciously. She had tucked the ends of the shawl into the shoulders of her riding cloak, and done her best to make it look normal. So far, no one had asked her about it, or even seemed to notice. But to her, it felt like a glowing neon sign announcing to the world that she was afraid.

She didn't like that.

She gestured with the toe of her boot to some little sprouts, growing in groups near the trunks of the scattered trees. "What are these? I don't recognize them."

"Snowflowers," Chen said, kneeling to brush the tiny plants with his fingers. Their stems were covered with a fine fuzz that looked as though it ought to be soft. "They bloom in the cold of the winter. These get a late start, because the breeze from the sea keeps it a bit warmer here than farther inland."

"Hmm. I think we can use that. Thank you."

"Use that? How?" He looked up at her in confusion, the late afternoon sunshine glinting off his hair and eyes, lighting his face with a warm glow. Since her near-death experience, Alannys was finding herself struck by moments when looking at him seemed to stop her heart dead in her chest. To her discomfort, this seemed to be one of those moments.

She looked away. "I want to start teaching them to sing for a purpose."

"I'm not sure that's really a good idea." He stood up, brushing off his knees.

"What? You think I should teach them to sing—teach them to sing together—but not teach them to sing for a purpose? What is even the point of that?"

"I don't know. I don't care. I just..." He glanced around the clearing, then caught her arm and pulled her farther out of it. "I don't know if it's wise to put that kind of power in their hands, Alannys."

She crossed her arms and studied him. "What's all this, then? You've never said anything like that before."

"Yes, well, things feel different now." He heaved a sigh and turned away from her, looking up into the trees that surrounded them. "Do you remember back a million years ago when we first met, I told you that Singari can't even agree on little things?"

"I do. I thought you were being facetious."

"Maybe I was, at the time. But I didn't know anything about anything back then. Bayred called me a worthless layabout, and he had a point. I'd never been a real part of anything before."

"Chen?"

He turned back to her, and there was a darkness in his face she had never seen there before. "I know better now.

The things I've seen since I've been in a leadership position, Alannys—I knew we relished our petty arguments over inconsequential things, but I never dreamed people among us, people I've lived and worked with all my life, could be so mean-spirited and small-minded. Even about really important things."

"Chen, we can't—"

"I don't think we should put power in the hands of people like that," he blurted out in a rush. "How do we know they will use it for the right reasons?"

Alannys frowned, watching him struggle with his questions. "How can you know that about anyone?"

"What?"

"Anyone can go out and buy a sword. How do we know they will use it for defense and not murder?"

"Alannys, I was serious. I'm not asking for riddles."

"I'm not trying to give you riddles." She thought about it and tried again. "Look, we didn't give them power. They were born with it. All we are doing is showing them how to use what they already had."

"Whatever. They could still turn around and use it for something awful."

"That's true. But at some point we have to let them take responsibility for their own actions. We can't control everything they think or do, just because we lead them. Most people want to do the right thing. Do you believe that?"

"Sure, but others—"

"I know, there are always those bent on benefiting themselves at any cost. Our students here may contain many like us. They may also contain the next Lord Malrec."

"Exactly!" He seemed genuinely agitated. "I don't think we should enable that!"

"Ah, but we don't know who the next Lord Malrec is.

The only way not to teach him is not to teach anyone. And evil men always win when good men can't defend themselves."

"But Alannys —"

"It's true. How would Soth have rescued Ravan, without the Singari? How would Ravan have defeated him? Most people want to do right, Chen. And they will defeat evil. But they must be able to defend themselves, to fight."

"You're right," Chen sighed. "We can't decide who has Talent. We'll hurt more people than we'll help if we try to limit who can use it."

"I think so. Are you ready?"

"Sure," he said. She didn't think he sounded like he meant it, but he turned and went back to the clearing. All she could do was follow.

The dozen Singari who showed up regularly for these lessons had arrived, so Alannys turned to face the group and put on her public speaking voice. "I have to tell you all that you have done more faster than I would have ever dreamed possible. You don't need much teaching from me, that's for sure. But there is one more thing I want to show you."

No one spoke, no one fidgeted or cleared their throat. They all regarded her with silent, respectful attention.

"Singing — or playing — for a purpose is the single most important thing you can do with your music. It was the thing that most excited me about Ravanmark when I first came here — knowing that music was important here, that you could *do* things with it. Making music for a purpose is hard. It drains you, and if you do too much you will suffer Muse's Fever, or worse — you've all gotten to see this several times since I joined the Singari."

Her students nodded solemnly — between her bouts of Muse's Fever and Chen's, there wasn't a person in the tribe who didn't know more than they wanted to about the affliction.

"And yet there are many times it is worth it. You've seen that as well. The severity of Muse's Fever also depends upon your purpose—music used aggressively will result in much more severe illness than music used for defense, or music used to heal. Do you understand?"

There were more nods.

"It is also important to understand reach. When you sing for a purpose, you will be focusing on a target. This target will feel your intent most strongly—but you must remember that your music will affect everyone and everything in earshot. Anyone who can hear your music can be affected by it, whether they are your intended target or not. Music is a powerful tool, but also a dangerous one. If you sing to kill someone, for instance, you may kill your target. But you may also kill other people nearby, people you did not intend to kill. Some people are more susceptible than others to song, and you won't be able to tell how susceptible anyone is until they succumb. Above all, music must be used responsibly."

No one moved; it almost seemed as though no one breathed. She had no idea how much of this they already knew, and in a way it didn't matter. She had decided before she began these lessons that the only way to proceed was to assume they knew nothing—it was too important.

She knelt by the snowflower sprouts, and gestured to her students to gather around her. "The most obvious target for music is other people. That's also the most dangerous, and not a good choice for practice. You can change the weather as well, but that's probably not a really good choice for practice either. For our attempt at singing for a purpose, we're going to attempt to influence these plants.

"Now when you sing, it doesn't matter so much what words you use, as long as you hold your intent clearly in mind. I can use music to make this plant do anything it could normally do—I could make it grow, I could make it die. I could not make it uproot itself and walk away, or grow again after it died. And I would suffer far fewer consequences from helping it to grow than from forcing it to die."

She glanced around, ensuring she still held their attention, and focusing on the plant nearest her feet, she began to sing.

"Snowflower, sleeping on the forest floor,
Wake! and reach for the sun above.
Stretch out your leaves
and open your blossom
and show us the clean
white beauty of winter.
Snowflower, sleeping on the forest floor,
Wake! and feel the sun above."

By the time Alannys finished her song, the snowflower she had chosen stood six inches tall, with a full, round bloom of shining white petals that looked like a snowball. All of the other sprouts were closer to four inches tall, with buds that were almost ready to open.

She pushed herself to her feet. "There now, do you see? It's easy to tell which plant was my target, but all of the plants in this group were affected."

Alannys led them over to another patch of snowflower sprouts a few feet away. "Now keep in mind that multiple people singing together is always stronger. I want you all to sing to help these plants to grow. It will take less time than it did when I sang alone. You can use any words you want; mine, or some you make up, or no words at all.

Eleana, you play your flute—the effect is exactly the same, all that matters is your intent. All together now, on the count of three—one, two, three."

Alannys stepped back as she counted. Still, when the music rang forth, she wasn't ready for the power of it. Most of the Singari used the song she had made up, but a few were creating their own songs as they went, and one or two used no words at all, and only hummed. Eleana's flute soared above them all.

The snowflower sprouts burst up out of the ground, shooting eight and ten inches tall, exploding into full bloom, then withering into brown dry husks on the forest floor, all within the span of about fifteen seconds.

The musicians trailed off into an uneasy silence. Alannys stared at the dead flowers in horror—she had known the combined might of the Singari would be powerful, but she had not expected anything like this. She had chosen to work with the plants because the exercise presented no danger to herself, her students, or the camp —but she had never thought it might be dangerous for the plants.

Her students were looking at her now, seeking some reassurance, some clue as to how they should take this turn of events. She cleared her throat, trying not to show how deeply upset she was.

"Well...you seem to have the gist of it, at any rate. You can see how much more powerful you are working as a group. Singing for a purpose doesn't require practice, necessarily—it's important to know how to do it, and it's clear that you know. So...so that's great, then. When we need help with this type of music, I will be asking you."

Nobody hung around long after the lesson. As exciting as it was to learn how to sing for a purpose, and to see their power in action, the whole thing felt depressing. Within moments, Alannys and Chen were totally alone.

"Well," he said, "I'm guessing that's not how you planned that."

Alannys laughed harshly. "You noticed? My general intent was to teach them, not traumatize them."

"Don't be too hard on yourself. We all knew that music is more powerful in groups, but I don't think anyone could have predicted that. It may actually be for the best."

Alannys pulled her cloak tighter around her against the growing chill of the evening, and they started walking back toward camp. "You may be right. It's upsetting, but I think those flowers taught them more than I ever could about the need to handle music responsibly."

"You're right—I think everyone who was here tonight will be more inclined to be careful. All in all, it's a small loss if it keeps everyone from doing anything foolish."

She appreciated Chen's attempt to put a positive spin on things. It seemed to cheer him up, but she couldn't really feel it. In her mind she saw those withered flowers, artificially drained of life, and it didn't feel like a lesson. It didn't even feel like a mistake, or a grievous miscalculation.

It felt like an omen.

♫

No sooner had they set foot back in camp than Kerb appeared as if from nowhere, pale and breathless, and grabbed Alannys by the arm. "Oh, Lady Alannys, I'm so glad I found you! You've got to stop Lorimar!"

"Stop Lorimar?" She glanced at Chen, but he looked as confused as she felt. "From what?"

"He's destroying the instrument he made for you, my Lady—and himself along with it!"

"What? Where is he?"

"Follow me!" The young man took off for the other side of camp. Alannys ran after him, with Chen at her side. "I'm afraid Lorimar always had his doubts about the instrument—he always worried he was going against the will of the Muses. I guess when it was finished, he decided to put those doubts to rest by putting bow to string."

"Oh, no," Alannys groaned.

Kerb glanced back over his shoulder at her, leading them past the firewood stacked for the bonfire. "You can imagine what it sounded like. It was pretty appalling, and it convinced him there was nothing holy about what he'd created."

"But he's not Talented!" Alannys protested. "And even if he was, nobody's even shown him how to play."

"Try telling him that. Actually I wish you would, because he's not listening to me." Kerb skidded to a halt in a clearing on the far side of camp, out behind the woodworking wagon. "Lorimar, stop!"

"Cheeky boy," the old man muttered, pitching another branch on the pile he'd built. "Apprentices these days— think nothing of arguing with their masters, they don't. Listening to you got me in this mess, boy—I'll hear no more!"

"Stop this madness, Lorimar," Alannys said, leaning over with her hands braced on her knees, trying to catch her breath.

"So he's brought you too, has he?" Lorimar tossed a burning torch on the pyre, and Alannys could hear the crackling as the wood begin to burn. "Well, you're wasting your time. Whether the Muses were behind this or not, I've failed. I've heard the thing sing—it's an abomination."

"How can you say that?" Chen demanded. "You don't even know how to play it!"

"Three of you?" Lorimar paused, tilting his head. "Are you planning to take it from me by force?"

"Of course not," Alannys said. "I just don't want you to do something that you'll regret, before you've even had a chance to think it through."

"Think it through? What else do you think I've been

doing?"

"You haven't been doing it right," Chen said, "if you've decided you and your instrument should burn!"

Lorimar didn't appear to be listening. He turned away from them, and came back a moment later carrying the unmistakable form of a violin case.

But it wasn't hers.

"Lorimar, give me a chance," she said. "I can show you that you're wrong, about your instrument and yourself. Let me play it."

"No!" Real fear flashed across his face.

Alannys's eyes flicked from Lorimar to the funeral pyre, and back again. She could see the flames now; the smoke was beginning to curl up from the wood pile, and the crackling was growing louder. They were running out of time. She had to get through to him, but how? "Are you worried that the violin will harm me, Lorimar? Or that I'll harm the world with it?"

"Both."

"Lorimar!" Kerb scolded. "How can you doubt the Redeemer?"

Alannys held up a hand to silence him. "Let's set all that Redeemer business aside for a moment, shall we? It's all circumstance and speculation at this point anyway. Some say I'm the Redeemer, others say I'm Soth reborn— how is a person supposed to know what to believe? Only the Muses know for sure, and they aren't telling."

"Hear, hear," Lorimar muttered.

"That's ridiculous." Chen was visibly offended. "But even if you believe all of that, you're still *kortha*. We should—"

"*Kortha*," Alannys repeated. "So what? *Korthas* are not above reproach. What if Brutagar demanded the power of a musical instrument? Would you give it to him? No, today we are not talking about Redeemers, or *korthas*, or any role. We're talking about me. You've known me quite a while, Lorimar. I've been leading the Singari a long time. Can you trust me? Or have I failed you somehow?"

A long silence fell over the clearing while Lorimar considered the question. The slight breeze wafted the acrid smell of wood smoke in Alannys's face, and she had to resist a strong urge to wrestle the violin away from the old man just to end this *now*.

"You ran off our *kortha*," Lorimar said slowly, "and you led us into Eversnow Pass. It was the worst experience we've ever had. We even lost one of the *zhotha*."

She could practically feel Chen bristling with indignation beside her, and she put a hand on his arm to forestall any defensive outbursts. She couldn't even tell if this was really criticism, or just a recounting of facts.

"But..." Lorimar's dark expression changed slightly. "Brutagar was the worst *kortha* we've ever had, and you saved his wife with what you did. Eversnow Pass was grueling, but you stayed right with us. Even after what Trago did to you, you didn't leave us. I know you've got Talent, but I think you have just as much courage." He heaved a sigh so deep it sounded painful. "Yes. I trust you."

"Then give me the violin." She stepped toward him, reaching out. "Please."

Slowly, as though fighting against every scrap of his better judgment, Lorimar pried his fingers from the case and handed it to her.

Alannys gently placed the case on the ground and flipped it open, revealing a bundle wrapped in silk scarves.

"Now," she said, "let's see what this thing can do."

Alannys found herself holding her breath as she peeled back the linen wrappings. It was a momentous occasion for her — the very first Singari-produced violin. She had high hopes, and yet she worried about how useful this first prototype really would be.

It took her breath away, varnish gleaming in the light. She carefully picked it up and turned it over in her hands, inspecting every detail.

The body of the violin appeared to be crafted from some type of maple, with a tight, curly grain that looked like it belonged in a rich man's parlor. It had been stained a dark, reddish brown, and polished until it shone. Everything about the instrument looked expertly crafted; from the inlaid ebony purfling, to the finely cut f-holes, to the elegantly carved scroll. It had been properly fitted with a chinrest and tuning pegs of a light, highly figured wood, and Lorimar had put on strings. It was even in tune, almost.

But the most breath-taking bit of all was the back. Most of the top half of the back of the violin's body was devoted to a beautiful intaglio carving of Alannys's face, her hair down and flowing, eyes alight, smiling like a saint. She ran her fingers over it, stunned.

"How did you manage this?" she breathed.

"I did that part," Kerb said. She looked over at him in surprise; he was supporting Lorimar, and he appeared to be blushing. "I made the bow, too, while Lorimar worked on the instrument."

She reached back into the case and pulled out a bow, rosined and well-balanced. She shook her head. "I'm awed. Just awed. I can't imagine how you two did this well on your first attempt at this."

Lorimar shrugged. "Don't be awed yet. You haven't heard it sing." His tone was dark and pessimistic.

"I can't imagine any instrument that looks like this sounding anything but wonderful," she said. She stepped back a few steps, shouldered the instrument, and began to play.

It was a moment the three men would tell stories about long afterward. They swore they heard the Muses themselves sing along when Alannys played the new violin, that a ray of sunshine broke through the evening clouds, and beamed right onto her.

Alannys smiled when she heard these stories, but never contradicted them.

Kerb busied himself putting out the fire, and Lorimar disappeared into the woodworking wagon, while Alannys carefully repacked the new violin. When she stood up again, Lorimar was back, and he held out her original instrument in its familiar case. "Thank you for lending it to me," he said, "but I've no further need for it."

She frowned, lifting it out of his hands. "Are you through making violins, then? Were you unhappy with its sound?"

"Only when I played it." A grin split his leathery face. "Don't worry, I've changed my mind. But I've got my templates now—I can make as many as we want."

"Wonderful. How much do I owe you for this one?"

"Not a split copper, Lady Alannys. Think of it as a thank you—for saving my life." He turned suddenly away before she could respond. "Kerb! Come on, lad, can't have you gallivanting out here all day."

They disappeared into the woodworking wagon.

♪

Alannys carried both violins back across camp to her wagon. As soon as they reached the front steps, she turned and presented the new violin to Chen.

"What, me? Alannys, I—I don't think I deserve this."

"Nonsense. Who better? I've never seen such a natural with string instruments as you are. You'll have this thing down in no time, and who better to start teaching others to play, when more become available?"

He looked uncomfortable. "You, for one."

"If I'm here, sure." She met his gaze levelly.

"Look, don't talk like that. I'll protect you—we all will —and you've got your shawl. You—"

"Even if I knew I was staying here forever, I would want you to have this!" Alannys realized she was shouting, and forced herself to lower her voice. "It's nothing to do with me leaving, Chen. I—I just want to give this to you. You do so much for me, and I'm able to give so little of it back. Please, take it."

Chen flinched away. "All right. All right, I'll do it. But only because you asked me."

"Thank you. You can add it to the list of things I owe you for. Like this shawl—I don't know how you've kept people from asking about it, but I do appreciate it—I would feel terribly awkward explaining it to everybody."

"Are you serious?" Chen looked pained. "That wasn't me, Alannys—I didn't do that. You really don't know what they think?"

She stared at him in unfeigned confusion.

"Alannys, they think it's a headscarf. A *braytha*."

"A *braytha*? You mean they think—they think we're married?"

Chen shrugged. "Honestly, I never said a word. It's Singari custom; everyone just assumed..."

"No, it's fine." She laughed, but it sounded a little awkward. "It would be worse to try to explain what it's really for. Isn't it kind of a strange marriage though? Considering we live in separate wagons?"

He looked away and shrugged again. "The Singari have seen stranger. Maybe they figure we fight a lot. Whatever, it keeps them from asking questions."

"I agree," she said. It still felt weird, though. She cleared her throat uncomfortably, and looked away. "You'd better go get some practice before dinner. You may not get many chances, the way things have been going."

He crossed an arm over his chest in a passable imitation of a Ravanmark military salute. "By your command."

She watched him leave, carrying the new violin in its custom case. So the tribe thought they'd secretly married. She shook her head.

Violin practice sounded like a pretty good idea all of the sudden. She decided to go inside and seize the opportunity herself, trying to ignore the stares she suddenly could feel from every direction.

♫

The next morning dawned cold and overcast. Alannys walked through camp as they packed up and prepared to move on, thinking a bit unpleasantly that the dead snowflowers would have found today quite to their liking. Still, it was nice just being outside among the people and the breeze and the bustle. She dreaded closing herself back up in her wagon for the day.

"Riding inside again today?"

She turned to face Chen, walking up behind her. "Man, I wish I didn't have to. There isn't much to do in the wagon but sit in bed—it's too bouncy to practice, or write, or even sing. But I can't see making poor Quicksilver carry me right now, not while he's still healing."

"Why don't you ride one of the other two? I know you've only used them for pulling, but they are actually fine riding animals as well."

"I don't know," Alannys said doubtfully. "Wouldn't the pulling harness hurt more than the saddle and bridle?"

"I don't think so. Have you looked at a pulling harness? It's much lighter and covers much less of the body than a saddle does."

She looked at him in surprise. "Such an easy solution. Why didn't I think of that?"

"Because you like to make everything complicated," Chen grumbled, but he followed her back to her wagon to help rig up the horses.

Quicksilver, it seemed, was as tired of following behind the wagon as she was of riding inside it. He whinnied and nickered at their approach, and practically danced around to the front where Alannys usually put on his saddle. He accepted the pulling harness without seeming to notice it.

He didn't complain until she brought out his blanket and saddle, and started putting them on the roan mare she had taken out of the pulling harness. She stepped over to settle him down, but as soon as she went back to the roan he put up a terrible fuss, biting at the other pulling horse, kicking, snorting, and throwing himself against the harness. Chen held uselessly on to Quicksilver's bridle, struggling vainly to keep him still. "Alannys, I don't think this is going to work. He's not going to let anyone else carry you!"

Alannys pulled the blanket off the roan and stepped back, watching Quicksilver. "You're right," she sighed. "Let's take him out of there. It looks like another day indoors for me."

"No," Chen said. "Why don't you give him a chance? He obviously thinks he's ready."

"You think so?"

"Today should be a fairly short day anyway—we should reach House Orinthal before supper, right? I say let him try."

"If you're sure."

Alannys was surprised to find that most of Quicksilver's injuries were not touched by the saddle and bridle—and then she felt foolish for being surprised. Of course Quicksilver had been wearing his riding gear at the time of the explosion, so of course he wouldn't be hurt in places that had been covered.

The change in plans obviously pleased Quicksilver. He

high-stepped to the front of the wagon train, his head high and his ears up. Alannys laughed. "He's certainly proud of himself."

"He just doesn't like to see anyone else do his job," Chen said. "He's a very strong-minded horse."

"Yes," Alannys said, leaning forward to scratch Quicksilver's ears. "I think I'll keep him."

That made Chen laugh.

The ride was arduous; House Orinthal was built on the top of a craggy, steep mountain, and the only approach was a narrow path cut into the side of the mountain. The backside of the mountain was a sheer cliff down to the jagged seashore below, treacherous with rocks. It was slow, hard riding.

Shortly after noon Alannys looked up the path and saw groups of rough-looking men, blocking the path, watching the Singari approach. Their clothes had patches on top of patches. They carried old weapons that had seen hard use; mostly short swords, with the occasional long sword. One man even had a bow.

She slid off of Quicksilver, turning to Chen beside her. She could see Drigo and Grald riding hard to the front to find out what was going on. "Get the singers! Everyone else — and all the horses — fall back!"

Nobody questioned or argued. They hurried off to follow her instructions, and it was well that they did. She could already see the men ahead moving, forming groups, preparing to launch their attack. She certainly hadn't expected to face attack here, on the approach to House Orinthal, but it seemed that anything could happen in a holding this far gone to the side of chaos.

She grabbed hold of Quicksilver's reins and turned him back toward the wagon train, then swatted his flank to get him moving. In a few moments, this place wouldn't be fit for animals.

It wasn't exactly a conscious choice she had made—she just didn't know what else they could do. There were a only handful of Singari who were really competent with weapons. She and Trago were probably the best fighters they had. And if you took every Singari who could handle a blade and brought them out, the raiding party up the path would outnumber them by three to one or more.

So it had to be the singers. This wasn't like what she had faced in Westmore Forest all those months ago—this wasn't a case of putting an attacking force to sleep so a handful of people could make a quick escape. They were going to have to go for broke here, and she couldn't do it alone. In fact—considering that they had no possible way to know what else might await them farther up the path, or at the castle itself—it seemed wisest if she didn't do much singing at all. All she needed was to be down with Muse's Fever when the next attack came.

She lined up her two dozen musicians in two lines, and the entire rest of the tribe retreated to a safe distance. Drigo and Grald herded everyone inside the wagons, and advised them all to cover their ears. The raiding party came sauntering down the path, confident, and she addressed her assembled choir in a low tone. "Don't be afraid to use all the force you need. These people want to kill us—all of us, even those we protect behind us. We can't let them get too close to us. Keep calm. This is the last thing they'll expect. The hymn you sang before—to Terpsichore—use that melody. Add all of the harmony and countermelody you want—it will only make you more powerful. And remember, the words don't have to be the same—make up anything you want to express your intent."

Alannys turned to face the raiders, and raised her voice to carry. "I am giving you one chance to leave this place peacefully. Turn around and go now, and you will be spared. Continue, and I will unleash my forces."

"Forces?" sneered one of the men. She figured he was the leader. "A dozen Singari, some women, some even children? These are your forces?" He shook his head, and raised his blade in the air. "No mercy, men!"

A war cry rose behind him, and the raiders all drew their weapons.

"Sing!" Alannys cried, and as the music billowed forth around her, she hurried down the front line of singers, offering encouragement to each one.

An arrow skimmed her shoulder as she reached the end of the line where Chen stood. She grabbed his arm. "Focus on that archer! We need to take him down before he hits anyone!" She joined in singing with him, concentrating on the archer as well.

At first they couldn't see anything much happen, except the shock of men who had not expected this sort of defense. Alannys could see one of the younger men towards the back of the raiding party abruptly sheathe his sword. "It's the Redeemer!" he shouted. "You're fools to fight! Run now, while you still can!"

He turned his back on his comrades and scrambled back up the path.

The man Alannys identified as the leader laughed, a nasty chuckle. "Is that so? Well, now, I expect the Redeemer and her Singari 'forces' will die just like anyone else. Right, boys?"

The raiding party raised another war cry, and started to run towards the singers.

At that moment the Singari split into three-part harmony, with Eleana's flute playing a high counter-melody. Alannys had heard this happen before, but at that time she had only been listening.

It was a completely different experience singing with them—like the difference between watching a tornado from miles away, or standing in its center.

Right now, she knew what it felt like to stand in the center. Singing alone was a constant drain; singing with someone else lessened that drain. Singing with the Singari didn't seem to drain her at all, in fact it felt more like a boost. The energy that coursed through them was wild, palpable, and for a crazy fearful moment Alannys didn't think that they would be able to control it. But they did, all of them — she could feel the channeled power flowing straight at the raiding party, like lightning following a conductor rod.

That was the moment when men started to fall. The archer dropped his bow and slumped to the side. Three other men in the front of the assault crumpled suddenly to the ground, and moved no more.

A few of the men at the back of the crowd saw what was happening, and fled back up the mountain. But most did not.

In less than ten minutes, Alannys's Singari singers decimated the raiding party. Chen, Drigo, and Grald cleared their bodies off of the mountain path so that the wagon train could proceed.

Alannys sat astride Quicksilver and watched their efforts, a grim look on her face. Trago walked his horse up beside her, looking a little shaken.

"Would you believe, even with all my years among the Singari, I never knew music was capable of that?" He sounded shaken, too. "I mean, we've all heard stories, but I don't know how many people really believe them."

"Enough do," she said shortly. "It's the reason music is so hated and feared, and it's a good reason. I gave them a chance. I told them they could turn and leave."

Trago nodded. "It's more than they did for you."

"True." She gestured toward the aftermath of the attack. "This is why it's so important that I teach the

Singari—not just how to use their Talent, but how to use it responsibly. Think of this, but multiplied by a hundred, or a thousand, and you start to have an idea of the horror Soth wrought with his armies. We can't have that again."

"Don't worry. The Singari are a people with a strong sense of honor. They aren't going to do anything like that."

"I know that. It isn't only the Singari I'm thinking of— what about all the other Talented people out there— people like the ones I met at Ravan's Light? They must be allowed to live their lives, and use their Talent—but they must not be allowed to ride roughshod over everyone else. How do I manage that?"

Trago shrugged. "Seems to me you can't. You're only *kortha* of these Singari, Alannys, not Queen of the World."

The cleanup efforts finished, and the Singari resumed their slow, hard climb. Alannys didn't think about the mountain, though, or even the battle they had just won.

...not Queen of the World...

No, but she knew someone who was pretty close. She had the ear of the king of the most powerful nation on the planet, after all. There had to be something they could do to help balance the danger of what she was unleashing with the benefits it would bring.

But what *was* it?

♪

At the top of the path, they found a massive stone gatehouse, with turrets on each side and battlements across the top. The massive oaken gate was reinforced with iron bars.

But the battlements were empty, the gatehouse undefended. The gate hung open, and from the precarious angle of the left half, one of the big hinges was broken.

"I don't like the look of this," Alannys said. "We know people must live here—where else would that raiding party have come from? But the place looks abandoned. I think the wagon train should stay here. Trago and I will go inside and see what can be done here."

"I agree," Chen said, "except that I am going with you."

Alannys laughed. "I guess I expected that. Very well, then." She glanced up at the castle rising out of the jagged rock formations around them, overshadowing them all in a way that struck her as ominous. "Still, this castle—I don't know, Trago, this seems very elegant for a man like your father." House Orinthal was tall and statuesque, with towers reaching up like graceful fingers toward the sky. It looked, aside from its current state of utter disrepair, like something out of a fairy tale.

Trago snorted. "You think he has anything to do with the way this place looks? Only its run-down condition. This castle was designed and built centuries ago. Prubard hasn't given it the maintenance and upkeep it deserves." His mouth twisted. "But it was never this bad, even then."

Alannys sighed. "I still don't like it. Nothing we can do but go in, though."

They left their horses with the wagon train, and ventured through the broken gate.

Beyond the gatehouse was an open cobblestone courtyard, with flower beds and trees with flowering bushes planted around their trunks. The whole thing was dominated by a large fountain in the center. It should have been beautiful.

But the flowers in the flower beds were mostly dead, and the survivors were overrun with weeds. The bushes were wilted and even the evergreen trees were starting to turn brown. A couple of inches of scummy, dirty water had frozen in the bottom of the fountain.

Trago cast a grim look around, and waved them on. At the far end of the courtyard, a red brick wall rose up high over their heads, topped by a rail fence that seemed to indicate a second courtyard higher up. Set into the brick wall were a pair of tall, arched wooden doors.

Beyond the doors they found the throne hall. It had the same sad, once-was-elegant feel as the courtyard outside — the ceiling was high and domed, with ornate decorative patterns in gold gilt. The walls were decorated with columns and arches, and under each arch was a tall, narrow window. On either side of the room, granite staircases led up out of sight. At the far end of the hall was an apse with a marble floor and dome. The apse housed the throne, a detailed affair with sculpted gold arms and back, and rich blue velvet upholstery.

But the hall was littered with trash and refuse, and even the magnificent throne was soiled beyond beauty. The sunlight angling in through the dirty windows was muddled and weak. Alannys looked around the room in a kind of shock, thinking House Orinthal was probably the most depressing place she had seen.

Strong hands grabbed her from behind, and before she even had time to cry out her arms were jerked up behind her. Beside her, Chen was in the same predicament. Trago spun around to face them, sword in hand, but with both of them held fast there was not much he could do.

"Well, well, well. What do we have here?" The voice bounced around the room, off the domes and arches, and Alannys couldn't place it at all until the figure stepped out from behind the once-elegant throne.

Trago spun back toward the apse, still holding his sword. "What kind of trickery is this? Does no one in this rat-hole have the decency to greet visitors properly?"

The stranger swaggered down the marble steps in his own time, apparently confident in his handle on the situation. He was wearing the dirty, rather tattered remains of a uniform that looked as though it had once been quite dashing; a black shirt and blousy black pants, with a red vest over it. He even wore a black hat with a bedraggled red feather. "Trickery?" he echoed, and something in his calm, quiet manner put Alannys on guard. A loud, blustery man would have been less fearsome—this man was quite sure of himself and his abilities. "You call it trickery, then, to guard ourselves against uninvited intruders? Trickery, to take precautions against the people who murdered almost all of the Baron's Guard of House Orinthal?" Quite abruptly he was shouting, and Alannys found she didn't like it any better than his ominous restraint.

"Was that the Baron's Guard?" Trago didn't sound overly concerned. "Good, then—that saves me the trouble of releasing the lot of them. The Baron's Guard should be honorable men, not scum who prey on travelers as soon as times get difficult!"

"You will pay for those words."

"I'd like to see you try to make me. Who are you?"

The man swept his hat off his head and gave them all a bow, in one graceful motion. "I am Riss, Captain of the Baron's Guard, leader of the scum who prey on travelers. Singari life is evidently soft enough that you know little of the desperation that has driven us to do what we must to survive. Give me your names, then—it would please me to know who you are before I dispatch you to your unhappy ends."

Trago turned to point at his friends. "This is Chen, of the—"

"We know who he is." Riss's voice had a sharp edge. "He is one of those who struck down our brethren with the power of song. And she—" Riss jerked his chin in Alannys's direction, "she is the Lady Alannys of Gale, the so-called Redeemer of the Realm. And she is the one who led the singers who slew my men. It will be a pleasure to run them both through. But you, my outspoken friend—

you we have no knowledge of. Who are you?"

Trago made himself as tall as he could. "I am Trago, son of Prubard, Baron of Orinthal. I have come here to claim House Orinthal, as is my right, and restore order to this place."

Riss stepped back, visibly pale. "You? The baron's son?" He paused, pulling himself together, and laughed in a manner that sounded forced. "Little good it will do you, I'm afraid — you abdicated any position you had years ago. And as your father still lives, the throne of House Orinthal is not yours to claim. I will dispose of you, and your fraudulent claim — we have quite enough to deal with here without an opportunistic baron's son stirring things up further."

"King Dorramon supports his claim," Alannys said. "He disenfranchised Prubard over a month ago. He no longer recognizes Prubard as baron. A rider from the Great Palace approaches even now with the king's decree."

"The king's decree." This time, Riss's laugh sounded a good deal more genuine. "Do you know how little I care for King Dorramon, or his decree? If he wants Trago on the throne, he can come put him there himself — and then I'll run him through, as well. The only one who rules in House Orinthal now is *me,* do you understand?"

♪

Alannys stood in the dirty, bedraggled throne hall of House Orinthal, her arms wrenched up behind her back, pain coursing through her brain, and cold fear washing over her. She couldn't believe the treasonous things this half-insane man named Riss had just said. The physical pain of hearing someone talk murder toward the man she was mindlinked to was equaled only by her fear. What on earth could any of them do now?

"No!" The voice came from one of the staircases; as Alannys watched, a young man came hopping down the stairs, obviously distraught. She recognized him as the same young man who had called her out as the Redeemer and run away from the ambush earlier; seen up close, he really was little more than a boy, maybe fourteen. "You can't do that! She's the Redeemer, Uncle Riss—the *Redeemer!* You can't dismiss her, and you certainly can't murder her. If she says Trago is supposed to rule here, how can you not even consider his claim?"

"Dass," Riss said between his teeth, "you are out of line. I said you could watch, not interfere."

"No," Dass said. "Sometimes you have to interfere, sometimes you can't just watch. And you aren't being fair. You are Captain of the Baron's Guard, not the baron. And you shouldn't be baron, you shouldn't even *want* to be baron, and now you're saying that you are!"

"Dass—"

"I'll tell the others. I swear I will, unless you want to run me through, too. You'll have either my death or theirs to answer for to every other person in House Orinthal. And without most of the guard to back you up. How do you think that will go?"

There was a long moment of tense silence. Alannys could see the muscles of Riss's jaw working; it was evident he did not like the situation he found himself in now.

"Very well," Riss said finally. "You say that I should not be Baron of Orinthal. I contend that I have earned that right, by leading this place and its people through the last few months. This fellow Trago claims the same right, by dint of the happy accident of his birth. We will settle this dispute in the old way—the contenders will duel to the death. Will that satisfy you, Dass?"

The young man nodded, frowning.

"And you, Trago, are you content with this arrangement?"

"Happy and content. But I think you are a fool, Riss, to

risk your life for nothing more than to go on leading this broken down place and the remnants of its people into continuing decline."

"I could say the same for you, my friend."

"No. No, you couldn't. I am not here simply to call myself Baron of Orinthal—I am not merely a Captain of the Guard who has decided that my real title is not grand enough for me. I am here to restore this place, and to restore order to the entire holding you have been ignoring." He made a grand, sweeping gesture that seemed to encompass the entire castle. "A real ruler would never have allowed House Orinthal to degenerate like this."

Riss's mouth was a tight, hard line. "Are you finished? I am quite ready to dispose of you, and toss your friends off the cliff." He nodded to the men holding Chen and Alannys. "Bring them up."

Riss started up the nearest staircase, and the men holding Alannys and Chen followed, dragging them along. Dass stood aside while they passed and then hopped up the stairs behind them. "Don't worry," he told Alannys quietly. "I won't let him pitch you off the cliff."

For some reason she actually did find that reassuring. This boy shone like a white light in the gloomy darkness that was House Orinthal, and she could only think his influence over his uncle was a good thing, for all of them. Riss seemed like a good man who had soured—she didn't know what exactly had happened, but she would have bet anything he was not always the greedy, power-hungry creature she saw now.

The stairs led up to a second courtyard, paved in dark red brick. From the center of the courtyard rose the castle keep, tall and imposing. The keep was round, but it was just similar enough to the keep at the Great Palace to give Alannys a sharp pain of homesickness.

Riss jerked his chin toward the keep. "Up there," he said. "We want them out of the way." He gave Dass a healthy shove in the same direction. "You too, boy — wouldn't want you to forget the difference between watching and interfering again."

To Alannys's surprise, the boy went without complaint or protest. She and Chen were urged none too gently up a polished stone staircase that seemed as though it might never end, into the sitting room of a suite at the top of the keep. There was no shortage of windows in the tower, affording breathtaking views that they were all presently immune to. The room had a marble floor with soft rugs over it, tapestries and gold gilt on the walls, and handsomely carved furniture. Everything was dusty from long disuse, but this suite had not been abused as the rest of the castle had. Their captors shoved them into the room and left, slamming the door shut behind them, to stand guard in the stairwell.

Alannys picked herself up off the floor, staring around in disbelief. The suite was just as opulent as the rest of the castle, but struck her as far more tasteful. "What is this place?"

"The baron's chambers," Dass said cheerfully. "They're something, aren't they?"

"I don't believe it," Alannys said flatly. "There's no way Prubard dragged himself up all those stairs every day."

Dass laughed. "Well, that's true. These were the chambers of every baron before him, though, and his wives have kept them. These have stood empty since Baroness Lae left."

Alannys offered her hand to help Chen up. Imagining Lae in these chambers was a lot easier than picturing Prubard up here. It was upsetting, too — standing in these rooms, it was painfully clear that Lae had been a prisoner in this tower suite, every bit as much as Alannys herself had been a prisoner in the tower room of Castle Glennayre. And to think Baron Prubard had wanted to trap her here as well! It made it uncomfortable just to be there. "I don't like this setup, Chen," she said. "Trago has to duel against the Captain of the Baron's Guard?"

"It isn't as hopeless as it sounds." Chen wandered along the wall, touching everything he saw. "Trago was the baron's son, remember? He would have been trained in swordsmanship from a young age. He probably sparred with Riss or someone like him every day. Granted, he's probably not practiced much since he left, but he isn't coming into this completely green."

Chen found a heavy silken cord hanging next to the wall and gave it a pull. A set of maroon brocade drapes parted, revealing a balcony that overlooked the courtyard.

"Good work," Alannys said, clapping him on the shoulder. From the balcony, they had an excellent view of the proceedings below. Trago and Riss circled each other cautiously, defensively, each watching for any weaknesses in the other's stance.

"I hope you won't think ill of my uncle," Dass said quietly, "or of me for not supporting him. He wasn't always like this."

"I got that impression," Alannys said, her eyes following the wary fighters below. So far, no one had found an advantage they felt like pressing. Each made tentative feints, attempting to draw the other out, but neither fell for the ruse. "He seems to me like someone who used to be a very good man, someone who used to be a very good Captain of the Guard."

Dass nodded sadly. A stiff, cold breeze blew over them, ruffling his hair, and the way he shivered made him look small and helpless. "But he isn't anymore. He's changed—all Riss cares about now is power. Getting power and using it to get more power. I think he was serious earlier—I think he really would kill anyone who tried to take House Orinthal from him now, even the king himself. I don't think he wants to change back. I don't think he can."

Riss found an opening in Trago's defense and charged in hard, forcing Trago back a few steps. Trago pulled together a hasty counter and sidestepped. Before anyone quite saw what was happening, he turned things around, and Riss was scrambling backwards under an onslaught of merciless attacks.

"What happened to him?" Alannys said.

"It was his sister," Dass said. "My mother. When this—chaos—first started happening in Orinthal, lots of refugees from the towns would come up here, looking for shelter and for help. We took them in. A couple of men showed up seeking refuge, and while my mother was working out where to put them, they attacked her. They beat her, and...and did other things to her, then they stabbed her. They took everything she had, and they fled."

"Good heavens," Alannys said. She saw Chen reach out and give the boy's shoulder a squeeze. "I'm really sorry, Dass."

Dass dragged his sleeve across his eyes. "You fight against things like that, my Lady. That's why it's so important we have to support you—but my uncle is too blind to see it. He turned bitter after that—he doesn't trust anyone anymore, not even me. He closed up the castle and stopped accepting refugees. Now he attacks any travelers that come near here, and uses their supplies for the people inside the castle. He's so obsessed with protecting everyone in House Orinthal, nothing else matters. He really would have murdered all of you, if it meant he could keep the castle. There used to be many who said these things, but over time they have grown silent, and now—it's only me." He shook his head. "Muses forgive me for saying it, but I'm very afraid of what will happen to us all if he wins this fight."

"You're not the only one," Chen said roughly. His eyes were fixed on the duel below.

It wasn't going well. Trago had sustained cuts in several places, but hadn't managed to touch Riss at all. Tired and sore, hurt and bleeding, he was beginning to flag.

Alannys couldn't stand there and watch that. But she was stuck in the top of a guarded tower, far from the action and essentially useless. She was three stories up — even if she wanted to sing, she'd have to shout. And if she tried that, it was probably a safe bet that Riss had archers hidden away somewhere who would dispose of her pretty quickly. She scanned her surroundings, desperate to do something, anything, to help.

The sides of the balcony were lined with flowerboxes; big, deep flowerboxes that were as tall as the balcony railing. One box grew thyme, the other had a variety of roses. The rest of the castle was falling rapidly into disrepair, but it was apparent that someone had been tending daily to the plants — they had been watered, and covered when necessary, so that they were still healthy. One of the smaller rosebushes was actually still blooming.

"Now that's interesting, isn't it, Alannys?" Chen brushed his fingers against the blossoms. "Thyme and roses, carefully tended even when everything else is falling apart — the baroness wasn't the only devout person in House Orinthal."

Alannys looked at him in total confusion. How could that matter now? "Yes, but —"

"Why," he continued, sounding oddly determined, "if someone wanted to offer prayers to the Muses, they would have everything they need."

"Ah. Look, Chen, I don't think —"

He grabbed a sprig of thyme and a rose blossom, then took her arm and dragged her back into the sitting room. "Come on, now. You want to help, don't you? They'll never let you sing. What can it hurt?"

She crossed her arms and watched him prowl around the room, searching for something. "The Muses have never listened to me before. Why should they start now? You're wasting our time, Chen, and we might not have much of it left."

"Always the pessimist. Aha!" He grabbed her by the shoulders and pushed her into the bedroom. "You're the Redeemer. How could they ignore you? Now me, that would be a waste of time. Why don't you try and see?"

He finally let go of her, right in front of a small alcove in the bedroom wall. In the alcove stood an ornately carved pedestal holding an alabaster basin and a pitcher.

"Chen..."

"Come *on*, Alannys. Humor me." He pressed the thyme and the rose petals into her hand.

With a deep, theatrical sigh, she took up the pitcher and trickled water into the basin. "I consecrate this water unto the Sacred Nine, and offer it to you the Muses, holy and high."

When the bottom of the basin was covered with water, she sprinkled rose petals and thyme leaves across the top.

"I consecrate these roses and this thyme unto the Sacred Nine, and offer it to you the Muses, holy and high."

Offerings and libations thus complete, she dipped her fingertips in the water and streaked it across her forehead. "Muses on high, hear my plea: if it can be done, help Trago to triumph in this battle. For the saving of Orinthal Holding, and the healing of us all, I ask you to raise him to victory. So I have said, so you have heard; if it is your will, so shall it be."

If nothing else, the prayer brought her peace; she didn't

think it would be a good idea to tell Chen, but she did feel better. For a long time she stood there, watching the petals and leaves float on the thin layer of water. Somehow it was hard, watching their gentle motion, to imagine anything could ever really go wrong.

A hand fell on her shoulder. "Alannys, are you all right?"

She turned to face Chen. "Yes. I'm sorry, I was—thinking." In truth she felt odd, like waking from a deep sleep before she was ready. "Is it over?"

"It is. Dass ran downstairs just a moment ago. I thought we should probably go as well." His eyes flicked to the basin on the pedestal, but he said nothing.

Alannys nodded, and followed him out of the suite and down the stairs. The guards were gone, but she didn't know whether that was a good sign or a bad one.

Riss lay on the red brick of the courtyard, gasping for breath around a deep gurgling wound in his chest. Dass leaned over him, clasping his hand. Trago stood back, leaning against the keep, a grim look on his face. He nodded to Chen and Alannys, but said nothing. He was bleeding from a few apparently minor wounds.

"Uncle," Dass said, his tears splashing on Riss's pale face, "I'm sorry."

Alannys hurried over and knelt beside them. "If you want me to, I will sing. I'm not sure how well it will work...I don't know how much I can do here...but I'm more than willing to try."

Riss's hand clenched convulsively on his nephew's. "No. No, there's nothing...you can do. Too late. Dass was right. Hear me, boy?" He paused to suck in a painful breath. "You were right. Should've listened." His eyes wandered toward Alannys, but they didn't seem to focus. "You make sure the baron's boy...takes care of this place."

"Of course," Alannys murmured, but he was beyond

hearing.

"This is that witch's doing!" The bellow caught Alannys by surprise; she whipped her head up to see one of the men who had guarded the keep glaring at her. "She did this, she must have!"

Dass shook his head and wiped his eyes. "No. She never sang; she only prayed. It happened as the Muses willed."

"Pathetic excuses," the guard snarled. "These people should never have been permitted in here. You should have listened to Riss."

"Do you want someone to blame? Do you?" Dass stood up and looked around at the gathered crowd, seeming somehow stronger. "Blame yourselves! Riss's path was *wrong*, not just for him but for all of us. And you all knew it, but not a one of you would move to stop him!"

The guard, so belligerent a moment before, now looked only pained. "Dass, you are too young to understand these things."

"Now who is offering pathetic excuses? I've heard them all—how I'm too young, how adults understand that they must sometimes do what is necessary, even if it is unpleasant. Do you know what I think? Adults are very good at using their so-called wisdom to rationalize away their principles when it's convenient for them—or when they are scared!" The look he cast around the group was damning. "Baron Prubard's son has come to us with the king's support to take his father's place. Riss challenged him to a duel to the death to prove his worth. He has proven it. I give you now the new Baron Trago of Orinthal. Let any man, woman, or child who cannot accept this leave House Orinthal now."

No one spoke. No one moved.

Chen cried out, "Hail the Baron of Orinthal!"

Alannys went down on one knee and bowed her head.

When she looked up, she saw that every person in the courtyard had done the same. Trago stood in front of her, offering his hand to help her up, and he said something that she would have sworn he'd never say, something that brought tears to her eyes.

"The Redeemer of the Realm should never kneel in my presence."

♪

They spent the rest of the afternoon cleaning in the throne hall. The Singari left their camp outside the gatehouse and helped. With so many hands helping, they had the hall clean by dinnertime.

Alannys could not believe the change in the room. The gold glistened, and the bright walls gleamed in the low light of the torches. The hall was the only really clean room in the castle, but it was breathtakingly beautiful.

They brought in long wooden tables, and everyone ate dinner in the throne hall together. It was probably the most informal dinner that place had ever seen; everyone served themselves and carried their plates back to the tables. But spirits were high and the occasion felt festive.

Alannys had just sat down between Trago and Chen when the rider from the Great Palace arrived, looking a bit lost in the doorway to the busy room.

Trago stood up from the table, laying a hand on Alannys's shoulder. "I'll handle this. You go ahead and eat."

"Finally," Chen said with satisfaction, watching the new baron's departing back. "First time I've had you to myself all day."

Alannys laughed. "Oh, and what a great honor that is!"

He poked her in the side. "Quiet, you. I'm just a lowly Singari. I'll take my honors where I can get them."

They ate together, watching the proceedings. Trago had the king's decree proclaiming him Baron of Orinthal mounted on the wall above the ornate throne. He seemed glad to have some official confirmation of his post, and read the proclamation proudly aloud to everyone in the hall.

"Full of himself, isn't he?" Chen said under his breath, slugging back ale.

Alannys laughed. "Go easy on him, Chen. It is a pretty big deal." She sipped carefully at her own tankard. The ale was foamy and dark and very, very stout—she couldn't imagine drinking it the way he was.

"I guess." He thumped his ale down on the table and stared into it, and she wondered suddenly exactly how much he had drunk—and how fast. "It certainly beats anything I've done."

"Chen? You all right?"

For a long moment, he didn't answer—she almost wondered if he hadn't heard her, as impossible as that seemed. She heard the rider congratulate Trago, heard Trago invite him to dinner, before Chen spoke. "No." He sighed. "You know, before you came, I thought I had everything down pretty clear. Life was about fun, and fun —obviously—was about me, whatever pleased me, whatever amused me. I don't think I ever in my life did something that wasn't for me or about me."

"Chen?"

"So tell me how I came to be second in command of the tribe, how I came to be the kind of man who'd spend an entire night camped on a woman's doorstep to protect her from harm, the kind of man who'd charge into a magic cavern carrying a sword he hardly knows how to use, to fight a madman?"

She stared at him, stricken. What could she say? She couldn't answer him, but she couldn't turn away.

"Tell me," he said, reaching out to trace the curve of her lower lip with his thumb, "why I would do it all again in a heartbeat?"

"Forgive my intrusion," said a sudden voice behind her, "but are you Lady Alannys?"

Chen jerked his hand away from her, throwing a sharp, irritated glance over her shoulder. "That was a short-lived honor."

Alannys poked him in the side. "Quiet, you." He laughed, and she tried to ignore the dark tinge to the sound. She turned around to find the royal rider standing there, looking a bit confused. "I apologize. Yes, I am Alannys. What can I do for you?"

He hauled his leather pack up onto the table in front of him, and dug around inside it. "Actually, I think the question is what I can do for you. I have a parcel for you."

"Really?" She pushed her plate away, suddenly excited and nervous. "From the Great Palace? For me?"

He placed a paper-wrapped parcel in her hands. The wax seal on top was purple, with a crown and an ornate D.

Beneath the paper was a small wooden box. She lifted the lid, and found a note card. The writing on the card was scripty and elegant.

My Dearest Alannys,
I once asked you to trust me. If you remember, accept the enclosed token of my trust in you. I will count the days until your return. Be safe.
-D

Underneath the card was a pink primrose blossom.

Alannys couldn't breathe. The walls seemed to press in around her, unbearably close. She clutched the card to her chest, scooped up the box and the paper and went out the door as fast as she could.

In the lower courtyard, she sat down on the edge of the

dirty fountain, with her new treasures in her lap. She picked the wax seal off of the paper and put it inside the wooden box, and cupped the flower in her hand.

If you remember...

How could she forget? She had only known then-Prince Dorramon for a few hours that night when he had picked a pink primrose and tucked it into her hair, asking her to trust him. She had said yes, and she had never looked back.

Alannys stroked the delicate petals with her fingertip, fighting back tears.

..symbol of my trust in you...

She gave up. She placed the rose gently back inside the wooden box, buried her face in her hands, and cried.

She felt someone sit down next to her, felt a hand fall on her shoulder. "Oh, Alannys. Are you all right?"

"Yes. No. I don't know. Oh, Chen, what am I going to do? I love him. I love him with every fiber of my being, and I promised him I would go back. I have to go back. But I can't have him—he's going to marry someone else, and he can never be mine. What am I going to do?"

"Shh." Chen pulled her to him and let her cry on his shoulder. "It's all right. It's all going to work out."

She cried until she had no more tears. She dried her face, and she tried to calm down. But she couldn't believe him.

It didn't feel like anything would ever work out for her again.

♫

When Chen and Alannys got back to the throne hall, they found everyone cleaning up. They helped haul dishes back into the kitchen, and helped move the big tables out.

"Baroness Lae's chambers are nice, but too dusty to actually use," Alannys said. "Where will you sleep, Trago?"

"Funny you should ask that. Since this is the only clean

room in the castle right now, I figured I would get some blankets and sleep in here, along with anyone else who needs a place to sleep. I'd be honored if you and Chen would sleep here too."

"I don't know," Chen said. "We have our wagons just outside the gate. That would probably be more comfortable."

"That's fine," Alannys said. "You go on ahead. I think I'll stay in here—it sounds like fun to me." She didn't want to be alone, but she also didn't want to tell them that.

"If you're staying, I'll stay with you," Chen said. His expression as he studied her face was strange, and she wondered how much he guessed.

In the end there were five of them. The Singari went back to camp, and the castle residents retired to their quarters. Alannys, Trago, Chen, Dass, and Josak all slept on makeshift beds out in the middle of the hall. With the torches out and her friends around, it felt like a camp-out. To her surprise, Alannys fell straight to sleep.

She awoke in a sudden panic in the dead of the night, her heart galloping. The hall was dark and quiet. There was nothing around her but the sounds of sleeping people. What could have awoken her? She was bone tired.

Her leg felt hot.

With unspeakable dread, Alannys reached down and touched her pant leg, where her dagger was hidden. The fabric was hot under her fingers.

Oh no, oh no, oh no...

She had to get out of this place. She refused to be responsible for the deaths of all the people sleeping around her.

Alannys untangled herself from her blankets, reaching out on the floor next to her until her fingers found Songstrike. She strapped the belt around her, and tried to remember everyone's position relative to her own. If she was careful, she thought she could make it to the door without waking anyone else.

She made it about four steps before she felt someone's leg under her foot.

"Aag!"

Ah. She knew that bellow. "I'm sorry, Trago," she whispered.

"Alannys? Alannys, what are you playing at, stomping on me in the dark?"

"Shh! Don't wake the others! I'm sorry—I wasn't trying to step on you. I need to get out of here. The cloaked swordsman is coming."

There was no reply.

"Trago?"

A torch flared in the darkness, and she saw him standing in front of her, holding it up over his head. "Chen!" He poked at Chen's sleeping form with his foot. "Up with you, Chen—we have to protect the damsel in distress."

"No!" Alannys said. "That wasn't what I meant!"

"I know," Trago said sourly, prodding Josak and Dass awake. "You'd run off alone and get slaughtered, just so we wouldn't be bothered."

Chen came up out of his bed with his knife in his hand. "What is it? What's after Alannys?"

"It's the cloaked swordsman," Trago said. "She says he's coming. We don't have much time. Get Songstrike out, Alannys. And move over closer to the wall. Dass, get your sword and get in front of her. Chen, get over there too. I've got my sword. Josak, that suit of armor in the corner has a sword. It may only be decorative, but it's better than nothing. He probably won't look close enough to know. Move in close, everybody. Stand together, now! The door is moving!"

The door pushed slowly open, and a figure cloaked

entirely in black edged stealthily into the room. He saw them standing in formation against the wall, all armed, and he sucked in his breath in a hiss.

"Expecting to launch an ambush on a bunch of sleeping people?" Trago said. "Lost cause. I suggest you give up, my friend."

The cloaked swordsman rocked on the balls of his feet, holding his curved blade in front of himself. Before anyone could react, he flew into motion, spinning out around their defensive knot. As he swooped for the stairs he came close to the side that Dass was guarding, and swung out with his blade.

Dass cried out and fell.

"Coward!" Alannys shouted.

The assassin paused at the top of the stairs leading to the upper courtyard. "Little girl, this isn't over yet. Evaluate my bravery when you aren't hiding behind three men and a boy." He disappeared out the door.

Alannys jumped over Dass and charged up the stairs after the swordsman.

"Alannys, no!" She could hear Chen shout behind her, but she didn't slow down. She barreled out into the upper courtyard, Songstrike in her hands.

There was no one there.

She dropped into Ready position, scanning around her. Chen ran out of the door behind her, and together they circled the keep.

They found no one. The entire courtyard was empty.

"Remember, Alannys, I'm coming for you!" The mocking call echoed off of the castle buildings and towers. It was impossible to tell where it had come from. She turned completely around, watching in all directions, but there was nobody to see.

"Get inside, quickly." Chen sounded furious. "The bastard is playing with you."

"*Playing,* my good man? Ah, you wound me. I assure you I am deadly serious. But I am here for the woman. I have no interest in you, or the baron, or the boy."

"Alannys, *get inside!*"

"Yes, little girl — go hide behind people doomed to die trying to save you." The voice, little more than a hiss, seemed to come from everywhere at once. "More blood on your hands, but what do you care?"

"Shut up, you!" Chen's hands were balled into fists. He kept himself in front of her, whichever direction she turned. "What sort of man hunts women, hurts children? How do you live with yourself, knowing you aren't a man at all?"

"A man does what is necessary, even when it is unpleasant." The mocking had gone from his voice — he sounded very serious. "And that woman must die, so I will kill her. I swear this on all I hold sacred: she will not escape me."

The voice sounded distant now. Chen grabbed her arm and hauled her back down the stairs into the throne hall. Josak was lighting the room's torches. Trago knelt by the wall, tending to Dass.

"How is he?" Alannys asked.

Trago wrapped a bandage around the boy's upper arm and pulled it tight. "He'll be fine. It's not bad — he was only trying to stall us, I think." He clapped Dass on the shoulder. "Run and get the guards. We need to do a room-by-room search of the castle, make sure that man is not still hiding here somewhere."

Dass ran out of the room, seeming none the worse for his injury.

Alannys pursed her lips. "I think he's gone."

"For now," Trago said.

She sighed. "For now. I'm sorry I brought him here, Trago. But I should be gone before he returns."

Trago shook his head. "But how do you stop him from returning?"

"I don't think I can," she said. "He's only got one purpose here, and he isn't going to quit until he achieves it." She could hear him swearing to that purpose in her memory, even now.

A man does what is necessary, even when it is unpleasant.

Dass had argued against just that type of sentiment only yesterday, saying that was how adults rationalized away their own principles.

Was the cloaked swordsman rationalizing away his principles? Was it possible that hunting down a woman was a job he personally disliked? She had never considered that she might be under attack by a principled assailant who could actually be quite decent in other respects, and was hunting her over the objections of his own conscience.

It was certainly possible.

Alannys shivered. For some reason, the thought did little to make her feel better.

♫

Alannys and the Singari left House Orinthal as soon as the sun came up. Everything else aside, they all agreed it was not safe to remain where the cloaked swordsman had already attacked once.

Josak stayed behind. He wanted to work for Baron Trago, to help restore Orinthal. Alannys appointed him her Redeemer's Steward for Orinthal Holding, and left him with a silver medallion.

The royal rider departed with them, and soon outpaced them completely. It made Alannys feel better to see him recede into the distance, the cask of Talent-proofing solution strapped behind his saddle. Maybe once Dorramon had the solution, she would be able to relax again.

They rode steadily, hoping to get through Orinthal

Holding as quickly as possible. It felt to Alannys like the place had been nothing but bad since they got there, and it was only getting worse.

It was mid-morning the next day when they rode through the burned up section of countryside where Lord Malrec had detonated Ravanmark's first bomb.

Alannys found herself riding with one hand clutching the ends of her shawl. Everything about the place profoundly upset her, from the scarred landscape, to her vivid flashbacks of the horrible things that had happened to her here, to the chilling knowledge that it was on this spot Dahlia had met her end, triggering Lord Malrec's attack and giving the rest of them the chance to survive.

Chen glanced at her. He looked like someone who was trying hard not to appear that he noticed her discomfort. "Everything all right?"

"Yes." She couldn't meet his gaze. "No. Stop the wagons."

"Whatever you say, *kortha*." He turned a little away from her and raised his voice, holding his arm up in the air. "Stop the wagons!" Drigo and Grald fell out of line, riding back through the wagon train to convey the message. Chen looked around them, frowning, and turned back to her. "Are you sure this is a good place to stop? We know that Malrec has at least two paintings of this area, right? One where he placed the bomb, and one where you fell?"

Alannys slid off of Quicksilver. "I know. Still, I can't just leave it. Look at this. This was pretty before we rode in. We can make it pretty again, don't you think?"

Now he looked alarmed. "I don't know if that's such a good idea. Remember the snowflowers?"

"I've thought about that. You know, I think my mistake was choosing too narrow a target. There were only what, half a dozen sprouts in that cluster?" She made a sweeping gesture that encompassed the countryside around them. "Now with something like this, we should be able to spread out. Everybody can work on something different. We'll get a good exercise, but it shouldn't be strenuous enough that anyone gets sick. And we can go on with clear consciences."

Chen dismounted. "That's actually not a bad idea."

She affected an attitude of great offense. "Well, what did you expect? Round up the singers, Chen, and let's get started."

She would never have said so to Chen, but he was right —it was risky staying anywhere that they knew Malrec already had paintings of. Still, this was important to her, and Malrec was busy. How likely was it that he would happen to open either of those paintings in the time it would take them to heal the area?

She gave her students a few preliminary instructions. "Don't bother with anything that is clearly dead. You can't bring it back, and you can make yourself sick trying. Anything that's barely alive, grab Chen or I to help you. Don't try to save something too near to death by yourself —that's another fine way to land yourself Muse's Fever, or worse." She darted a glance around—for a moment she had thought she felt a painting. But there was nothing there, and she couldn't feel it anymore. The strain had to be getting to her.

She held onto her shawl and turned back to her waiting audience. She spread them out; between the lot of them they covered the damaged area nicely, without any one person taking on too much work. The rest of the Singari worked alongside them, clearing out dead bushes, flowers, and trees. Alannys moved among them, offering direction where it was needed and joining in where she could. Either she was farther out of shape than she'd realized, or the work was harder than she had figured—this felt more like fighting nature than restoring it. But they were making progress—she could see it.

They had worked for fifteen or twenty minutes when Alannys felt the tell-tale prickling sensation of an open painting. For just a moment, she froze, looking frantically around for the focal point. It hung shimmering in the air *right in front of her*. If she had raised her arm, she could have touched that gray misty blur without moving anything else.

She didn't have time to escape, or even to move farther away. She crumpled into a heap on the ground, pulling her shawl tight over her head and murmuring the incantation Nyrin had taught her, as quietly as she could, over and over.

"Where is she, Creft?" The voice was Lord Malrec's, as loud and clear as if he was standing right next to her. She wished she wasn't quite so close to the painting. She could clearly hear the excitement in his tone. "You've seen the Lady Alannys?"

"I called you as soon as I saw her, my Lord. The very minute." This voice was completely unfamiliar. It sounded like a teenaged boy. She forced herself to remain still, to continue whispering the incantation to herself. "I—I don't understand. She was right here."

There was a small silence. When Lord Malrec spoke again, he sounded irritated. "Now look here, Creft. You know I disapprove of apprentices. I agreed to take you on specifically so that you could monitor these paintings for me. If you can't do that competently, this arrangement is not going to last. It's bad enough that I still have to open paintings for you, or that you can't seem to produce a passable gloss. Now you are wasting my time reporting non-existent sightings?"

"But my Lord! The woman was here! I saw her—she had a dark scarf over her head."

"Alannys?" This voice was Chen's. "Alannys, where are you?"

"There now, see?" Lord Malrec demanded, from behind the gray blur. "That young tatterdemalion is calling for her. Would he be doing that, if she were there? Obviously she is not there. These are *Singari*, boy, most of their women wear headscarves. But Alannys does not. Now close that painting—all that singing is giving me a headache. Run out and try making another batch of gloss. Perhaps this time won't be an utter disaster."

Alannys didn't dare stop chanting, didn't dare make a move, until she felt the painting close. She relaxed her death grip on the shawl, and stood up on legs that were suddenly weak.

Chen saw her and hurried over. "Alannys! What happened? I couldn't find you a minute ago."

She drew a shaky breath. "It was Lord Malrec. He has an apprentice now, watching the paintings for him. The boy saw me. I had to hide."

Chen muttered an oath. "We should leave."

"I agree. Round everybody up, and let's get moving." She looked around at the surrounding country. "We've done well—I wouldn't recognize this as the same place."

"Me, either. But I don't think it was worth the risk."

What could she say? Every single thing she did anymore was a risk. She had always assumed that at some point she would get used to it.

Unfortunately it was beginning to look like that would never happen.

♪

"And so, another brilliant plan has left us empty-handed." Lord Diabon's voice could be as rich and thick as honey, when he wished it. Right now, his tone cut like a razor as he followed Lord Malrec from the study.

"This was not a failure in planning." Malrec matched Diabon's words cut for cut. "This was a silly boy making a mistake."

"So you say. You also said that our first attempt to recapture her would be the most likely to succeed—now she has been warned. She will doubtlessly be more careful in the future."

"Careful how, exactly? We can find her any time we choose."

"Then choose to find her now! These delays are insufferable, Lord Malrec!"

Lord Malrec whirled to face him. "I will choose to find her when it suits me, Diabon. Not one *moment* before. Right now she has a force of singers surrounding her. I would prefer to time my attempt so that they will not be a factor." He strode into the dining room, where Baron Prubard was already tearing into the midday meal.

"A force of singers." Diabon's complexion was pasty. "The woman spreads like a disease. Where we had one singer, now we have many."

Malrec waved a dismissive hand. "The others don't matter. There is no one there with one-tenth of her power."

"If a large force of singers is the problem," Prubard said around a mouthful of roasted chicken, "it seems to me that one of Malrec's miracle explosives is the answer."

Lord Malrec surveyed the baron's stained, matted robes with distaste. Since coming to Glennayre the man had only grown sloppier and, if it were possible, bigger. "What an astoundingly ignorant suggestion. I can't keep creating multiple paintings of the same locations like that —the Herb of Sight will kill me, if the stress of the work doesn't. An attack like that must be carefully calculated. She's no use to us splattered across the countryside."

Prubard shrugged. "Then send the explosive to the Great Palace. You already have paintings. Splatter the king across the countryside, and our job is done."

Diabon buried his face in his hands.

"Just when I thought your ideas couldn't get any worse!" Malrec exploded. "Do you think the princess would continue to support us, if we attacked her brother in that manner? I succeeded in assassinating King Caleb only because it was done in a manner that appeared natural, and was untraceable. She expects Dorramon to meet an honorable end on the field of battle. If we fail her in that, we lose her. And an attack of that nature would only have one conceivable source, do you think she won't see that? We need her support, gentlemen—she is what validates us. I don't think that would be a good way to gain public acceptance, either. A horrific attack like that would alienate everyone we seek to rule."

Prubard's eyes narrowed. "You are full of excuses today, Lord Malrec. The easiest, most direct way we have to dispose of the king is off the table. And even after the considerable time and expense we have put into our preparations for the capture of the music mage, you tell us she is out of reach as well?"

Lord Malrec closed his eyes and counted to ten. It was tempting to place the bomb in the guest chambers of his own castle. He opened his eyes and forced a smile. "Patience, my dear Baron. Everything is proceeding according to plan. We shall have the music mage, and soon."

♫

Two days of riding brought Alannys and the Singari to the border of Danningham Holding, where they found something she had never seen anywhere else in Ravanmark—a border patrol station.

"Is this normal?" she asked as they approached.

Chen shook his head. "This has never been here before."

The border was protected by a hastily-built wooden wall, with a gate where the road crossed through. Riding up to it reminded her of riding into Crinn, and she shivered.

"Hallo travelers," called a man in uniform, stepping out of the gatehouse. A younger man followed respectfully behind him. "How are you this fine day?"

"We're just fine," Alannys said, "Mister...?"

"Mar," he said. "Lieutenant Mar."

"We're just fine, Lieutenant. And we'll be even better once we get out of this holding."

"Ah," the lieutenant said, glancing down the wagon train. "About that..."

She stared at him in disbelief. "You aren't going to let us in?"

"Please understand, it isn't you. But as you've apparently noticed, Orinthal Holding is falling into chaos. We're overrun with people fleeing. Normally I'd welcome you. We could really use the entertainment. But right now —well, right now we can't have any more troublemakers around."

Alannys could feel her face harden. "Troublemakers?" Chen laid a restraining hand on her arm, but she shook him off.

The lieutenant couldn't meet her gaze. "I did say I was sorry, my Lady. If it was any other time..."

"Begging pardon, Lieutenant," the younger man said stiffly, "but I think you should let them through."

"Cadet?" The lieutenant was shocked; whether at the cadet's suggestion or his insolence in speaking out of turn, Alannys couldn't tell.

"Begging the lieutenant's pardon," the cadet repeated, "but this is the Lady Alannys, sir."

"So?"

"So," the cadet said, "haven't you heard how they freed House Orinthal? She and her singing army decimated a force of two hundred marauders to take the castle!"

Alannys goggled at him.

The lieutenant looked impressed in spite of himself. He turned back to her. "Is this true?"

She tried to clear her expression. "Well—ah, um—we did defeat a raiding party on the mountain pass to House Orinthal, so that we could deliver the new baron safely to the castle."

"Well, in that case, come right in. We can use all the help we can get maintaining order in Danningham right now." He nodded to the cadet. "Open the gate."

They waited in awkward silence until the heavy wooden gate stood open before them. The lieutenant saluted her and went back into the gatehouse. Alannys rode into Danningham Holding, with Chen beside her and the Singari train following behind.

"What just happened?" she demanded.

Chen laughed out loud. "It sounds like we are gaining quite a reputation. Singing army, indeed."

Alannys frowned. "I'm not so sure that's a good thing. It sounds like the stories going around are wildly exaggerated."

"I'm not so sure that's a bad thing," Chen countered. "It changed their minds, didn't it?"

"That doesn't mean it's good. If people just go from hating you to fearing you, you haven't gained anything. People who wouldn't attack something they hate will often attack something they fear."

"If we don't want to be hated, and we don't want to be feared, what's left for us?"

"Respect," Alannys said without hesitation. "The same thing I came seeking when I left the Great Palace. The only thing missing from every single interaction I've seen anybody have with you. I don't care if the whole world hates you or fears you—as long as they respect you, too."

Chen thought about that. "You don't ask for much, do you?"

His tone indicated that he was joking, but she answered him seriously. "No. No more than I ask for myself, or anyone else. Why shouldn't you get at least that much?"

He couldn't seem to look at her. They rode on in an uncomfortable silence.

He couldn't seem to answer her, either.

♫

They camped outside of the town of Newstark that night. The next morning, Alannys and Chen rode into town for supplies.

Newstark was a fair-sized town, sprawled at the foot of the hill that held Danningham Manor. A river ran through on its way out to the sea, and Newstark appeared to be a major stop for the boats. It looked like a town that would be bustling later, when the sun got higher and people started moving. Right now, a fog shrouded the cobblestone streets. Most people were still abed.

And yet, some did move. Like ghosts in the mist, people began to emerge from behind or inside decrepit abandoned homes, out of the trash piles at the end of deserted alleys, and a hundred other hiding places no one would ever use under normal circumstances.

But of course these weren't normal circumstances, not for these people. These were refugees from Orinthal, hiding in the crevices of Newstark, scrabbling in the rubble to survive. Alannys shook her head; she should have expected this. Newstark—indeed, all of Danningham Holding—was a fully formed, complete society. There weren't masses of vacant housing and unclaimed jobs waiting for these people to claim. There was nowhere to put them, and no way for them to earn their keep. What else could happen?

Still, there was something creepy and almost

threatening about the way those vague forms floated around in the fog at the edges of her vision. She shivered. Suddenly the border guard's attitude made a lot more sense.

Chen glanced over at her. "They didn't ask for this," he said under his breath, "any more than the townspeople asked to have them here."

"I know." Still, she couldn't stop whipping her head around to regard every ghost in the mists; it felt like they were getting too close.

They found what they needed on the town's central square—a general goods store where they could work on replenishing the tribe's badly depleted stocks.

But when they tied the horses out front and went to the door, they found it locked. Alannys turned away, frowning. "Do you suppose we're too early?"

Before Chen could respond, they heard the lock turn over, and the door creaked open just a crack—enough for one eye to regard them through the opening.

"Hmph," came a reedy voice from the other side of the door. "You don't look entirely destitute. Still, a body has to be sure. Show me your coin, and I'll let you in."

Alannys flashed a look of disbelief at Chen, but she jerked open her beltpouch, brimming with the coins Chira had given her for the trip, and held it up to the door so the eye could see inside. "Will that do?"

"Aye," the voice said shortly, unrepentant. The door jerked open. "Get in, then. Haven't got all day, you know."

She felt worse about this shopping trip all the time. Judging from Chen's expression, he had similar reservations, but he followed her into the shop without comment.

The shopkeep was a thin, stooped fellow, with a mouth that looked permanently turned down. He glanced left and right out the door, then closed it behind them, and jammed the sliding lock shut. "A body can't be too careful. Crazy times."

Alannys didn't know what to say to that, so she busied herself helping Chen find all the things they needed. They shopped, paid for their purchases, and left in an uneasy silence, punctuated by the sharp click of the lock sliding home behind them. They stowed the parcels that they could in their saddlebags, and secured the rest behind their saddles. "Crazy times, all right," Alannys muttered. "*Something* was certainly crazy about that."

Chen laughed.

"Well, now, look who has ventured out of the wagon on this fine day."

The sarcastic cut of the voice whipped her like a lash, and she felt Chen's hand tighten on her arm before she even knew who had spoken.

With an awful sense of deja vu, she swung around to find a wiry middle-aged man in tattered clothes surveying her and Chen with active dislike. "Easy now," she said. "We don't want any trouble."

He laughed, a harsh, barking sound. "I bet you don't." To her horror, she could see other dilapidated people materializing out of the fog behind him—lots of others. "What do you all think of this?" he called, and his voice suddenly burned with fire. "When do you suppose it became acceptable for honest, rightful citizens of Ravanmark to starve in the streets while the king's whore and her Singari lapdog walk right in and come away with food and every kind of supply?"

Alannys knew what she should do. If there was ever a situation that needed her knack for speech, this was it. She needed to step forward and cool this flaming rhetoric. She'd done it before, at other times, in other places.

But she couldn't do it now. Everything about this

situation sent alarm screaming down her spine — it was all too similar to her first, nearly fatal, encounter with Trago. Her fear paralyzed her, and she couldn't force out a single word. She took a hesitant step backward.

It was the wrong thing to do. She could see the homeless man's nostrils flare, like an animal scenting fear.

"You do wrong to malign the Lady Alannys," Chen said quietly. "She has not caused the problems you face."

"Faugh! The dog thinks he has teeth!" The man took a step closer to her. "Are you afraid of us, woman? I think you should be! What have them such as us ever wanted but an honest living for honest work? Now thanks to you and your precious king, we ain't got either!"

Chen stepped in front of Alannys. "Leave her alone! None of this is her fault!"

Before Alannys could react, the man's giant fist swung wide, crashing toward Chen's face.

Chen's hand closed around his wrist, stopping the blow before it could land.

"Finor!" gasped a woman's voice from behind the man. "Come away from there! Don't you think you have done enough?"

"No!" Finor bellowed, wrenching his arm away from Chen. "Did you see how many supplies they brought out of that shop — how much food? I mean to have it! Who's with me?"

Alannys heard a roar from the crowd in the square. She heard a scream from the woman.

The next thing she knew, there were fists flying in every direction. Refugees were fighting with Chen, fighting with her, and fighting amongst themselves. Something had blown the lid off of Newstark.

The sad thing was, it looked like it was probably her.

♪

Looking back on it from the jail cell, Alannys thought that if you had to be sucked into a brawl, Newstark was probably a good place to do it. The guards had the whole thing broken up before anyone had worse than a black eye.

Unfortunately, the shiner was hers.

The guards didn't wait around to ask questions. They grabbed anyone who didn't scatter fast enough and hauled them off to the stone jail where she sat now. There were four of them in that particular cell—she and Chen, Finor, and the woman who had chastised him, apparently his wife.

The cell had only one iron bench. Alannys had marched over to it and parked herself. Anyone who called her the king's whore could jolly well sit on the floor.

So now they sat, hours after the altercation in the town square, all together in a stone cell. Finor studiously ignored all of them, even his wife. Chen laid down across the bench with his head in Alannys's lap, dozing or giving a really good impression. She stroked his hair back from his forehead, wondering if he was really just tired. She had the black eye, but perhaps he'd gotten hurt in ways that weren't visible.

Footsteps in the corridor outside the iron gate distracted her from her brooding. She looked up to see Duke Morryn regarding her through the gate, with three guards behind him. She pushed Chen's head gently off of her lap and stood.

The duke's eyes narrowed, watching.

"Duke Morryn!" She went to the gate. "It is good to see you. I am sorry for the trouble."

It took him a moment to shift his gaze from Chen to her. "Don't apologize, my Lady, that wasn't your fault. Get them out of there," he told the guards, standing back while they unlocked the gate.

Alannys and Chen were each escorted from the cell by a guard, while the third watched over Finor and his wife.

When they were out, Duke Morryn started back down the corridor, with a curt gesture that indicated they should follow.

Alannys couldn't figure why he was acting so oddly. She shrugged at Chen, and followed.

"This isn't the first violent outbreak we've had," the duke said over his shoulder. "Honestly, I think with all the stress and the lack of anything constructive to do, those people just welcome the chance to pick a fight. If it hadn't been you, it would have been someone else."

"I'm sorry," Alannys said again. "I wish there was something I could do. Things should be improving in Orinthal soon, though."

"Yes," Duke Morryn said musingly, "I've heard that you helped the baron's son take over. That was well done. Something had to change, and fast."

He led them outside, where they found Quicksilver and Nightfire tied next to a palomino that Alannys thought must have been his, judging from the grooming and the fine tack the horse wore. Their supplies were miraculously intact.

"I would like to invite you to Danningham Manor." Morryn swung up into the palomino's saddle, and looked down at them as he spoke. "Dinner will not be for some time, but I can offer you a room while you wait. It should at least be more comfortable than that cell." He smiled then, and Alannys thought that he finally looked like the Morryn she remembered. The stress here was telling on him as well.

"That sounds wonderful," she said. "I'd love to accept, but I'm not sure Chen and I should be away from the wagon train that long."

"Yes." Duke Morryn sounded as though she had reminded him of something. "It's probably best that you don't leave them where they are. I can't promise you they won't end up attacked in the night."

"What do you suggest?"

"Send a rider out to them after we get to the manor. Bring them up as well. They can camp inside the curtain wall; it should be safe there."

"Thank you. I think we'll take you up on that. It's a very practical suggestion."

Duke Morryn laughed out loud. "Flattery will get you everywhere, my Lady." He waited while they mounted up, then led them out of town and up the gently winding road to Danningham Manor.

Danningham Manor sat at the top of a low hill, surrounded by a stone curtain wall with an iron gate. Inside the curtain wall, they crossed a large rectangular courtyard, planted with fruit orchards on the left side of the gate, and grassland on the right.

The manor itself was surrounded by a moat, and a drawbridge led into the house. It cut an imposing figure, silhouetted against the sky; a tall, square central tower with wings on the left and right.

Stableboys greeted them in the courtyard and took their horses. Duke Morryn showed them into the vaulted vestibule that was the first floor of the tower, and into the right wing.

"I only had one room prepared before I came to get you. It's no problem to have a second room prepared. Would you prefer that?"

"One room is fine." Alannys registered the sharp look Morryn aimed in her direction, and suddenly understood his intent in asking the question to begin with. She felt her face turn red. She and Chen had lived in each other's faces for so long, she no longer gave any thought to how they appeared to outsiders.

Chen followed behind them, apparently oblivious.

"Hmm." Duke Morryn kept his eyes straight ahead.

His tone revealed nothing.

"There is nothing improper going on, your Grace." Alannys struggled to keep her tone as flat as his.

"I don't doubt it," he said, in a tone that implied a great deal of doubt. "But I wonder if you are aware of how much attention your situation has generated."

"My situation? Do you mean leading these Singari?"

"No. I mean that you travel with a man who is known specifically as your consort."

"What?"

His gaze flicked across her astounded face, then away. "The rumor mill has been busy, my Lady. I don't value rumors much, myself. But I still have to admit it gave me pause to see how casually close you are to this man. Three months ago, at the Great Palace, watching you with our new king—I would not have thought this possible."

"My Lord Duke! Chen is my deputy. And a close friend, it is true. But there is nothing more than that. He is not my consort, nor will he ever be. I understand the Singari gossiping among themselves, but how could this interest the country as a whole? Who could possibly benefit from this?"

They stopped in front of a varnished wooden door, devoid of ornamentation. "Can you think of no one? My Lady, all the land knows of your attachment to the king, of the risks he has taken and the mountains he has moved on your behalf. How great would be his embarrassment, then, to hear of you traveling the land this way, taking another to fill his place?"

Alannys could feel her ears burning. "Duke Morryn, it isn't like that."

He inclined his head. "I believe you. But it does not matter—these rumors that are spreading are not targeted at me. Can you think of no one who would benefit from driving a wedge between you and the king?"

"Lord Malrec." She said the name with vehemence, the way someone else might say a curse word.

"Just so. I doubt the average citizen of Ravanmark knows or cares about the meaning of *markortha*. How fortunate that Lord Malrec is there to explain it to the masses, and to make certain that every nuance is fully understood."

This conversation was putting a bad taste in her mouth. "I have to admit I was unaware of this. Thank you, your Grace, you've given me much to think about."

Duke Morryn crossed his arms and took a step back from them. "I'll leave you to rest, then. I'll send someone for you when it is time for dinner. And Alannys, one request, if I may?"

She looked at him, surprised. "Of course. Anything."

"Please dispense with these silly formalities. I think Morryn suits me better than your Grace, or my Lord Duke. You'll feel better saying it, and I'll feel much less silly hearing it."

He turned and strode away before she could respond.

She stood staring down the corridor after him, mouth agape. Everything he had just told her seemed small, but she was sure there were bigger implications to this that she was missing.

Chen caught her by the shoulders and guided her into the room. "You've talked all the way up here about your first real bath in months. Did you forget?"

She sighed. "No, Chen, I just—"

"The bath chamber is right over there. I think I'll just have a nap while you do that. It's hard work, pretending not to know when you're being talked about."

She laughed, but there wasn't any real humor in the sound. The conversation in the hallway had put a serious damper on her mood, and she didn't feel like doing much of anything right then. Even the prospect of a hot bath couldn't seem to lift her spirits.

She hadn't seen a single servant in Danningham Manor, but wherever they were, they were very efficient. The tub brimmed with steaming water when she walked into the room.

The room was chilly; the stone floor was so cold it hurt her feet to stand on it. By the time she finished undressing, she was shivering. But sinking into that hot tub felt better than anything she'd done in ages. She soaked until the water cooled off too much to be comfortable.

Alannys came out of the bath chamber with her damp hair wrapped up in a towel, expecting to find Chen napping. Instead she found him sitting in a straight-backed chair, staring out the window at the view of Newstark sprawling below.

"Chen? Are you all right? I thought you were tired."

"Oh, I am tired of a great many things." He didn't look at her. "But I'm not sleepy."

She sat down on the bed. It was a simple design of square-cut pine logs, with a woolen blanket over the top. In all honesty, it was probably one of the most uncomfortable beds she had seen since coming to Ravanmark, but at that moment she could have slept in it easily. Coming to Danningham Manor seemed to have drained her. "People continually surprise me," she said, coming at the subject sideways, trying to lighten the mood. "Just when I start taking for granted that they have no interest in the Singari, you become a hot gossip topic."

Chen shook his head. "It isn't us. It's you. Even Lord Malrec couldn't stir up rumors about a bunch of Singari. People only care because you're involved."

"Well...that's good then, isn't it? People aren't out nosing into your affairs. They aren't talking about you with any mean spirit toward you."

"But that's just it! They're using us to drag you down.

To them, it only makes it worse." He turned to face her, running a hand through his hair. "We're Singari, Alannys. We live apart from the country, outside the influence of the monarchy. Always have, always will. And that's fine with me. So why does it bother me that they're using us to embarrass the king?"

"Maybe you're more civic-minded than you think."

"Maybe." He didn't sound convinced. "They're smearing your honor, and I don't like that. But look at it as an outsider — all they know is that they saw you with the king, and now they see you with me. What can they think, except that the king is a fool or you are a whore?"

"Or both. That's the point, don't you see? Like it or not, Ravanmark is going to war. They have to have confidence in their king. Lord Malrec knows this. It's the whole reason he's doing this."

"Sure. But what can we do about it?"

Alannys sighed. "You aren't going to like the answer to that. I have to go back."

"What?"

"Look, Dorramon can't get away from this on his own. Like you said, everybody saw me with him — everybody knows how much he's done for me. No matter what he says, he ends up looking bad. I have to go back. If I'm there, then there are ways out of this for him. He can spin it that everything I did was at the direction of the Great Palace. Or he can even make a public show of washing his hands of me and turning me out into the street to live in disgrace. But if I'm not there, he has no way out. If I'm not there, this is a stain on him, forever."

"You're right. I don't like it." He turned back to the window. "But at least if he turns you out into the streets, you don't have to live in disgrace alone. You'll have a whole tribe of disgraced Singari you can live with."

"Thank you." Her eyes teared up; she didn't know

what else to say. She flopped back on the bed, thinking about taking a nap, or even just pretending to take one. She didn't like this any better than Chen. She had imagined herself as enduring great hardships, suffering many trials in her mission to help Dorramon. She had certainly never realized the humiliation he had suffered! And in all their conversations, he had never said a word about it.

It was humbling. She lay on the uncomfortably hard bed and stared at the ceiling, wondering how many more unpleasant surprises awaited her.

♫

By the time a servant came to fetch them for dinner, Alannys really had fallen asleep. She and Chen took a moment to make themselves as presentable as they could, and followed the servant to Duke Morryn's dining room.

The duke and duchess stood waiting for them by a long, polished, wooden table surrounded by tall-backed chairs. Duke Morryn looked the same as earlier, with his long-sleeved white shirt and blue velvet vest. Duchess Sheeana — Alannys had to look away. It wasn't the same gown she had worn at the Great Palace; if it was possible, this one was even worse. Flaming red silk wrapped her so tightly it might have been painted on. It plunged low in the front and high up the side. Anyone looking at Sheeana saw more than they bargained for, she made sure of that.

"Good evening, my Lord Duke, my Lady Duchess," Alannys said.

"Good evening, my Lord Duke, my Lady Duchess," Chen echoed.

She looked at him sidelong as they took their seats. Was he being facetious? He didn't look much like joking; his face was set with a grim tension she had never seen there before.

She spread her cloth napkin across her lap. Chen, with a furtive glance at her, did the same thing.

Alannys suddenly understood. Chen had probably never even *seen* most of Ravanmark's nobility, much less sat at their tables. How could he possibly know what to do? The best thing for him to do was — whatever she did.

"Lady Alannys," Sheeana said, with an appraising glance at Chen, "Morryn said that you ran into some trouble in Newstark today. It must have been *so* exciting — why, I positively die of boredom here at the manor. But getting into a fistfight with a handsome man by your side — why, I shudder just to think of it."

There was a moment of awkward silence while Alannys tried to come up with an appropriate response to that. Who started a polite conversation with, *so I heard you went to jail today?*

"Yes," she finally said, stumbling over her words, "this morning was...interesting."

"Sheeana," Duke Morryn said, in something that sounded remarkably similar to a growl, "use your thick head. Lady Alannys does not wish to talk about that."

"But why ever not?" Sheeana exclaimed. "It must be so...exciting to travel with Singari." She glanced at Chen again. "One hears such stories, you know. And your guest is quite handsome, if you don't mind me saying so."

Alannys stared at her. Duke Morryn sighed and covered his face with his hand. Surely she couldn't be implying what she seemed to be implying...

"Oh, come, don't be shy." Sheeana was beginning to sound irritated. "There must be so much you can tell us. Are Singari really as...able as they say?"

Alannys felt her face flush.

"I can only imagine what you must have heard," Chen said quietly. "I'm sorry to disappoint you."

"Oh," Sheeana chuckled, "don't misunderstand me. I'm certain you could never disappoint me. In fact, if you are free after dinner, I would — "

"Great Muses, woman!" Duke Morryn exploded. "Have you no civility at all? Must you solicit a clearly uninterested man at my very dinner table?"

Sheeana sniffed. "I don't see what difference it can make. You are as clearly uninterested as they come. And Lady Alannys is not attached to him — the entire kingdom knows her real target is the king!"

"Target?" Alannys took the word the way she might have taken a slap in the face.

"I mean you no disrespect," the duchess said. "I was never bold enough to try for the Crown Prince myself — with a lifelong betrothal, and now that he is king, well...I admire your confidence, I really do."

Alannys gaped at her. She just didn't know what to say to that.

"Oh, come now, Alannys, this is really unnecessary. We're both women of the world, you and I. It's clear that you understand what it takes to get ahead, even if your current state tends to hide that. There should be no quibbles between women such as ourselves, especially over men. You can't seriously imagine I would hold any hard feelings for anything you did with Morryn, can you?"

Alannys had never in her life felt so awkward. Tension settled around them like a shroud. Nobody seemed to know what to say, and the duchess seemed completely unaware of — or unconcerned with — the discomfort she had caused.

"Sheeana," Duke Morryn finally said. "You should go."

"I'd be delighted to!" Sheeana stood up and threw her napkin into her plate. "Not a single one of you is willing to be sociable. If this deadly dull affair is meant to pass for an entertaining dinner, I shall be glad to take mine in more appreciative company!"

"Please do." The duke spoke so quietly Alannys could

barely hear him.

The duchess flounced from the room.

Alannys released a breath she had not realized she was holding. "I'm sorry."

"You're sorry?" Duke Morryn looked as though he might have wanted to curse. "By the very Muses, that woman will be the death of me. No sense. None at all! I apologize, Lady Alannys, and to you as well, Chen. I invited you here as my guests. It was not my intent to see you embarrassed."

"Please, think nothing of it," Alannys said. "Chen and I have survived worse than a little embarrassment, haven't we, Chen?"

Chen laughed, and after a moment, so did the duke.

"Still, you have my apologies." Morryn sounded more like himself now. "The woman is most unsuitable — really, I never should have married her. But I was young, and stupid, and who could tell me anything?" He shook his head. "Perhaps we may enjoy the remainder of our meal in peace. I have something for you, Alannys."

"For me?"

Duke Morryn reached into a pocket on his vest, pulled out a heavy linen paper envelope, and slid it across the table to her.

The envelope had a bright red wax seal, embossed with a large, script L.

Alannys broke the seal with fingers that felt suddenly cold.

My Dear Lady Alannys,

By the time you read this letter, I will already be dead.

I hope it does not shock you to hear this. You must understand—I knew this was coming. There was no other way out of this for me—helping Kalyn escape the castle meant that Lord Malrec necessarily must figure out what I was. If I had run, if I had tried to escape my fate, he would have turned on Princess Delline instead. And I could not allow a member of the royal family to come to harm, if it was in my power to prevent it. I could not strike Lord Malrec down myself—as strange as it may sound he is a limiting influence in the Dark Alliance. Without him, Diabon and Prubard would destroy Ravanmark to a degree that Malrec would never allow. He needs something left to be king of. The other two have no such concern; they wish only to destroy. They would turn easily against Lord Malrec, should he succeed.

Please understand, I do not tell you these things to sadden you. The time is soon coming when you must face Lord Malrec again. I would not have him use my death to hurt you, so I had to make sure you knew before you meet him.

Hold fast, Lady Alannys. The endgame is approaching with frightening speed; I can feel it even as I write this. You must not fear to take a stand, and you must not fear to hurt those who would do you harm. There are things before you now which will make all you have endured thus far pale in comparison, things that will make you question your own strength, things that will make you wish to cast aside the truth and take the path that is easiest. Hold fast to what is right, and you will prevail.

I am past caring about Lord Malrec's evil, about Princess Delline's betrayal, or about the million minor wrongs that seem constantly to plague each of us. But our new King Dorramon is just and wise, and committed to doing his best for his kingdom. And you are brave and resourceful, and never shy away from problems that seem too big to solve. As for the rest, please remember...no one's future is carved in stone. There is always hope. Whatever I have done or have suffered in my life, if it has *aided either of you at all, I do not regret it. It is not my wish that either of you should feel guilty or sorry for me. Remember that, when you see me again.*

I remain,

Your Servant,

Larric

Alannys sat staring at the signature scrawled at the bottom of the letter, unable to think coherently. She supposed she should have fainted, or cried, or had some other dramatic reaction, but all she felt was a dull sort of shock. Everyone had tried to tell her that Dahlia's tortured ravings were just a product of brain fever, but Alannys had known. All this time, she had always known.

"Alannys?" Chen sounded tentative. "Is everything all right?"

"Larric is dead." She couldn't quite accept how final it sounded.

"You have lost a friend?" Duke Morryn said. "I am sorry to hear it."

"I've known Larric longer than almost anyone else I know in Ravanmark. It's hard to believe I'll never see him again." She frowned, looking at the letter again. "But this is odd. His last line says, 'Remember that, when you see me again.' Why would he write that, when he knew that he would be gone before I got this letter?"

Chen shook his head. "Don't spend a lot of time worrying about that, Alannys. There's a reason the Singari say a male Seer is an abomination. Their Sight is spotty, and often unreliable. I'm sure he didn't mean to mislead you, but there's no reason to think that statement is grounded in any kind of reality."

She couldn't argue. Larric had told her himself that his Second Sight was inconsistent, sometimes delivering impressions, sometimes not. Still, she had never known him to be wrong. Dorramon and Raman both placed great faith in him. She frowned. There had to be a meaning. Something...

"It appears your friends have arrived," Duke Morryn said, standing up from the table.

Alannys followed his gaze to the window. The Singari wagon train rolled through the arch in the stone curtain wall, into the courtyard. She could see the camp circle beginning to form on the far side of the yard, across from the orchard. It seemed late—she would have expected to see them sooner—but it was a relief to see them at all. She had never realized how much the Singari weighed on her mind when she was away from them.

"I think that's our cue, Chen," she said. "It's been wonderful, but I think we had better go help set up camp."

"Camp?" Morryn sounded surprised. "But aren't you staying here tonight?"

"I do appreciate the invitation," Alannys said. "But I think the Singari might take it badly."

"Without a doubt," Chen said. "They are only here at all because Alannys commanded it—I imagine the reason they are so late is that there was some serious resistance to spending the night inside anyone's walls, even yours, your Grace. If she was to stay in here—I think they would turn around and leave again."

"That would be a bad idea," Morryn said. "It isn't safe out there right now."

"Don't we know it," Alannys said. "And the worst of it is, there are musical instruments in that camp. The Singari have an ancient lute, but there is also my violin, and at least one copy of it, and several other partially completed copies. I hate to think what would happen if those fell into the wrong hands."

"Copies? They are making new instruments, modeled after yours?"

Alannys nodded. In retrospect, it might not have been a wise idea to mention that, given the high level of resistance she had encountered to music in general, and instruments in particular.

"Well, now." Duke Morryn stroked his chin, considering. "That is amazing. That knowledge has been lost to us for ages — and may have remained lost forever. If we are to study these Talents, we should have access to the necessary tools. This is wise, I think."

"I have to admit, you surprised me. I didn't expect anyone to approve of the instruments."

The duke waved a dismissive hand. "People are too willing to let fear do their thinking for them. It makes no sense. I am glad you came to Newstark, Alannys. It's been very nice seeing you again. And Chen, thank you for coming to dinner with us. I know this isn't your usual fashion."

Chen grinned. "I'm Singari. I don't have a usual fashion."

Morryn smiled, but he shook his head. "People have treated the Singari poorly for too long, and for little cause. I am pleased to see Alannys changing this as well." He glanced out the window. "Good evening, my friends."

Alannys and Chen crossed the grassy courtyard in the low light of two crescent moons. She was glad she'd seen Duke Morryn again, but she was also glad to be leaving. She couldn't remember a more uncomfortable dinner — she hadn't eaten a bite. "That was something else," Alannys said. "Before I came to Ravanmark, I never in my wildest dreams would have believed a duke would call me friend."

Chen laughed. "And that goes double for me."

She knew the remark was lighthearted, but for some reason it left her feeling down. She watched a long, dark, cloud move in front of one of the slivers of moon. It was going to be a long night. She could feel it.

♪

The clashing of swords woke Alannys only a couple of hours after she had gone to sleep. She rolled out of bed, grabbed her shawl, and hurried to the door.

She could see four of Duke Morryn's guards, a few yards from her wagon, fighting a swordsman cloaked in black. Back closer to the manor three archers stood at the ready, waiting for a clean shot.

Duke Morryn ran from the manor, rumpled with sleep but carrying his sword. "He isn't after the castle! Protect the wagons! Don't let him reach the Lady Alannys!"

"Merciful Muses," Chen said. She hadn't even realized he was standing there, but he had his short sword in his hands. "Will he ever give up?"

Alannys shook her head.

"Don't worry. The duke's men can handle him."

Alannys wasn't convinced. She had seen this man defeat the Royal Guard at the Great Palace, and the guards at Mirendasith Hall, Brookeshire Castle, and House Orinthal. He had even escaped an avalanche. Why should she believe this fight would turn out differently?

Even as she watched, the tide of battle was turning; the cloaked swordsman had incapacitated two of the guards, and edged closer to the wagons, using the other two guards as protection from the archers.

All at once the hair stood straight up on the back of her neck.

Someone was watching.

"Look out!" she cried into the chaos. "Lord Malrec paints!" She clutched her shawl down tight over her head, chanting the invocation Nyrin had taught her.

The telltale gray blur hovered just above the ground, off to her left. The cloaked swordsman took one look at it and immediately disengaged, fleeing into the night, leaving the confused guards looking to Morryn for their next command.

Duke Morryn uttered a curse that carried clearly through the courtyard. "After him! Don't let him get away!" He turned to his archers. "Quickly now! Loose your arrows—into the painting!"

Morryn drew his sword and swung it out in front of him, pointing directly toward the misty blur. The archers followed his command, and almost before Alannys could blink, half a dozen arrows shot through the night, and disappeared into the gray blur.

The painting abruptly closed.

Alannys couldn't get over to the duke fast enough. "That was amazing! That was the first time I have seen them forced to close a painting."

Morryn sheathed his sword. "Bah. It would have been amazing if an arrow had flown straight through Malrec's chest and dropped him on the spot. We probably didn't even nick him." He looked around, and saw the guards filing raggedly back into the courtyard, empty-handed. "So your attacker got away after all. Lady Alannys, you aren't safe here."

"I know. Chen is already giving the commands—we're moving out immediately."

Duke Morryn nodded. "That's wise. You can't stay where this assassin knows where to find you. And it looks like Lord Malrec has a painting, as well. How will you know when you are out of the painting's view?"

"We won't. But that portal was very close—I would guess this painting is focused pretty tightly on the courtyard. I don't think we'll have to go far." She sighed. "But it doesn't really matter. We have to go as far as we can, and hope for the best. I'm afraid I haven't done much to improve Newstark, your Grace."

"Newstark's problems are beyond any of us right now. We need Orinthal back on its feet soon. Then you can come back to Newstark, and you'll get a totally different welcome, I assure you."

Chen rode up on Nightfire, leading Quicksilver. She mounted up, surprised how much harder it seemed when she was tired.

"Duke Morryn, thank you for everything. I am sorry about all the trouble. I hope brighter days are ahead for all of us."

But as she and Chen led the wagon train out of the courtyard, she couldn't help remembering Larric's mysterious letter.

Brighter days, it seemed, were not soon to be forthcoming.

♫

Alannys worried about riding out of Newstark, in a way she had not worried about riding in. The riot in the square had left her anxious, wondering whether they would face similar attacks as they departed.

She felt bad about it. Those hadn't been people looking for trouble—they had been people looking for a means to survive. Duke Morryn was right; Orinthal's recovery couldn't come soon enough. In the meantime, what they needed were jobs, money, food—the means to provide for themselves. And she couldn't give that to them.

The sun was high in the sky when they passed a dusty, tired group of people, some on horseback, some on foot. Leading in front and following behind were men in the uniform of the Royal Guard. They reined up when they saw Alannys and the Singari approaching, forcing the exhausted people and horses behind them to lumber to a halt.

"Well, now, what have we here? More volunteers for the king's army?" The lieutenant in charge draped his arm across his saddlehorn, speaking to them in a tone too friendly to be genuine.

"Alas, no," Alannys said. "We are fighting the king's

battles on a different front."

"So I've heard." The lieutenant pulled off his hat and ran a hand through his hair, glancing back at the dusty crowd behind him. "But then, I've also heard that you're the one responsible for all of this, one way or another. Wouldn't kill you to come take your part in the trouble you've started."

"Me? I'm responsible for all of this? How do you figure that?"

"Lord Malrec and our king, Muses preserve him, are fighting over you. Aren't they? You're too powerful a weapon for either of them to ignore." Behind him, she could hear the uncomfortable shifting of the feet of men who didn't seem to think this confrontation with her was wise.

"No. I mean, I can see how it must seem that way, but Lord Malrec had this war planned long before I ever came to Ravanmark. Malrec wants to be king, simple as that."

"I'll give you that much. But what about Cadenda? Sure as Muse's song, we wouldn't be going to war with them if you hadn't come here."

She stared at him, stricken. Going to war? Was it that bad now? No—surely Dorramon would have told her. "King Dorramon doesn't want to marry Princess Varilyn. That really doesn't have anything to do with me."

"Doesn't it, though? Seems strange, doesn't it, that he's been engaged to her since practically forever, and it only became a problem when you showed up?"

"I can't deny that—I have no idea what things were like before I got here. But I'm not at the Great Palace. I'm out here, traveling, and I have been for months. If I was out to thwart the king's wedding, why would I be here? Why wouldn't I have just stayed at the palace, the better to cause trouble?"

"You got me there. Still... Look, you seem remarkably

well-informed about all of this. If you understand all of that, then you understand that between the Dark Alliance and Cadenda, we're fighting not just for King Dorramon — we're fighting for the survival of Ravanmark. And we don't have enough men to defend against all of that."

"I understand that." Alannys kept her tone even, pretty sure she didn't like where this was going.

The lieutenant crushed his cap in his hands. "Then you must also understand how wrong it is for you to blithely ride by with a whole tribe of Singari, full of young, healthy men who could fight for their country just as well as the rest of us."

"So we're discussing right and wrong, are we?" Her temper flared in her voice. "Have you considered how wrong it is to treat the Singari like they aren't really welcome in towns or shops, like they are thieves, or worse? Have you thought about your ideas that they are dirty, that they are untrustworthy? Do you understand how wrong it is that you act like they have no right to live at all, until you are looking for someone to fight for you?"

"Seven Hells! They live here too!"

"Indeed they do. And other under circumstances, they would fight alongside you. They have before, whether you realize it or not. But until Ravanmark in general is willing to treat them like people, I don't think they should be obligated to fight for you." She sighed. "Look, what incentive is the king offering these men?"

"Ten golds on signing." The lieutenant couldn't meet her eyes.

"That's quite a sum. You seem to be headed back to the Great Palace. Why don't you ride by Newstark on the way? I'm sure you've had quite a few refugees from Orinthal enlist already. Newstark is swimming in them — if you go through there, you'll probably double your numbers. And it will be willing men, nobody you've had to force."

He jammed his crumpled cap back on his head. "I wish you good day, then. Smooth travels."

Alannys watched the dusty group stagger on by them, and shook her head. She knew the lieutenant—probably all of them—thought she was taking the easy way out. But her travels hadn't been smooth for a long time.

And judging by her night at Danningham Manor, it would be a long time before anything was smooth again.

♫

Alannys and the Singari pitched camp earlier than usual that evening. Everyone was already tired from their interrupted sleep the night before, and Alannys didn't think it wise to push too hard.

"We need to be on our toes, Chen." The few steps into her wagon seemed longer than ever. She tossed her riding cloak over the hook by the door, and dropped herself on the edge of her bed. She should have been ravenous—she hadn't eaten anything since riding out for Newstark two days before—but she'd been too busy running, and she was too tired to care. "We all have to be alert, but especially you. You could be taking over this operation any day. I don't think I'm going to make it to Weatherby Holding."

"I wish you wouldn't talk like that." Chen flung himself into the wooden chair by the desk, crossing his arms.

"I'm sorry, but it's true. Can't you feel it hanging in the air? It's like it's waiting to swallow us all."

Chen nodded grudgingly. "Oh, I feel it, all right. But nothing is set in stone. We could still evade him. You talk like it's already happened."

"You certainly have been grumbly lately."

He shrugged, slumping lower in the chair. "I'm tired. We all are."

"I don't know...this seems like more than that. You

haven't been the same since...since Dahlia died, I guess. Are you all right?"

"Dahlia." He shook his head. "When Dahlia died, I lost one of my oldest friends. But I could have lost you as well; for a while I thought I *had* lost you as well. I don't think it ever clicked before then—that Lord Malrec was willing to kill you, to further his purposes. I could wake up one day and find that you were dead, gone forever, because of someone else's crazy war that shouldn't affect us at all."

"Chen..." She didn't know what to say.

"But I was wrong. It does affect us. It affects *you,* because it affects him. The king. I always thought I could fight that, you know? I always thought—eventually, with enough time—you would come around. There was no hope for anything else, right? He was engaged, as good as married, and had been since he was born. No hope at all."

Alannys shook her head.

He waved a hand at her, frustrated. "Of course you see hope. You always see it. But me..." He fell silent for so long she wondered if he was done. When he spoke again, his voice was so quiet she had to strain to hear him, even in the small space of the wagon. "It was the rose that did it. Until that moment, I was sure of things. But when he sent you that rose, and that note...he turned everything upside-down. Everything changed that night. He means to marry you, Alannys."

She stared at him. She fought to squeeze words past the sudden pressure in her chest; she couldn't even seem to breathe. "That's not possible."

He watched her with sadness in his eyes, as though she was receding into the distance before him. "It shouldn't be possible. But I think he's past caring about what ought to be possible. I think he's prepared to fight Lord Malrec and the Dark Alliance and Cadenda and every man in this country, if he must. He's just stringing things out so that he doesn't have to fight them all at the same time. But he's decided, mark my words. That package—he would never have risked sending it otherwise, not in the position he's in. You told me before about the rose. We both know what it means."

For a moment Alannys felt like the entire world stood still, frozen with her in the impossibility of what she had heard. Finally the world started spinning again.

Her head spun with it.

"We have to go!" She jumped up from the bed, grabbing her cloak. "If what you say is true, we are headed entirely the wrong direction. We have to turn around—we're going back to the Great Palace!" She stomped back over to his chair and looked at him sharply. "Why are you still sitting there?"

"I don't think we should go anywhere tonight. We're all still just as worn out as we were twenty minutes ago."

Her shoulders slumped. "Yes, but—"

The hair suddenly stood up on the back of her neck. All at once, she knew she was being watched.

Alannys clutched at her shawl, but before she even got her hands on it she knew it wasn't going to help her this time. The gray blur hovered in front of the door; she couldn't even run to escape.

Lord Malrec stepped out of the mist into the room, looking around as though everything he saw displeased him immensely. His black velvet cloak billowed behind him as he came through the portal, making him look especially menacing.

Alannys screamed.

"Yes, my dear, it's lovely to see you again as well." Lord Malrec's skeletal hand shot out and clamped tight around her arm, jerking her toward him. With his other hand, he reached up and snapped a stiff, leathery collar around her neck.

"Let her go!" Chen had produced his knife from somewhere.

"Now, now, boy, don't do anything hasty." Malrec held her in front of him, blocking any attempt Chen might have made to free her. "This shawl is perfectly hideous. Where did you—" He touched it, and recoiled. "Ah! So this is how you have been avoiding me."

Alannys yanked on her arm, but she couldn't break free. "Let go of me!"

Malrec's chuckle was positively nasty. He swept the shawl from her head, and tossed it at Chen. "Keep this, boy, to remember her by. She won't need it where she's going." He hauled her back toward the door. When he spoke again, his voice was low, and so close to her she could feel his lips brushing her ear. "Now, my dear, you are *mine.*"

Lord Malrec stepped into the hovering gray blur, dragging her into the cold, timeless void behind the painting.

Sandra Miller

Chapter Three

IMPRISONED

Alannys hated traveling through paintings. She would never get used to passing through that icy, formless place where time didn't exist and light was but a memory. It made her feel stretched, spread out in a layer too thin to see over a distance too far to imagine, then squeezed through the other side. She couldn't breathe.

She knew that passing through the portal could only take a fraction of a second. And yet it always felt much, much longer. She always remembered many more thoughts than could have been possible in that tiny sliver of time.

The whole experience was horrible. The only comfort was its familiarity.

In fact, the same could be said for her situation in general. The only comfort she had right now was the familiarity—she knew with certainty what awaited her in Castle Glennayre, from the tower room with its barred window, to Lord Malrec's false charm and excessive demands. The only thing missing would be Kalyn, bringing her meals and being her friend.

And Larric.

She stumbled into Lord Malrec's study, thrown

completely off-balance by the transition through the void. If it hadn't been for his vise-like grip on her arm, she would have fallen on her face.

The room was as she remembered it, right down to the chair with the gray velvet upholstery, presently occupied by Lord Diabon. He jumped to his feet as they entered the room. "Merciful Muses! You've actually done it!"

Malrec chose not to respond to that. "The key, Prubard, quickly!"

Baron Prubard stepped forward, holding an ornate brass key. "I told you it was foolish to doubt him. The woman is clever, but no one can stand against Lord Malrec for long."

Malrec snatched the key and jammed it into the mechanism on Alannys's collar, locking it tight. "Now, Diabon! Hurry!"

Lord Diabon moved in front of her and pulled a burlap bag over her head. "Hide the abomination from our sight," he chanted.

"Yes, yes," Malrec said impatiently, "but she can't stay here. Creft! Creft, get that painting ready!"

"Yes, my Lord." The voice, familiar from her near-miss in Orinthal, sounded like it was coming from the art room.

Whatever was going on here was so far out of her experience she couldn't even frame it properly. But she knew she didn't like it. She struggled to free herself from Malrec's grasp, reaching for the sack and for Songstrike.

"Prubard! Stop her!"

The greasy, soft hands that caught hold of hers could only have belonged to the ex-baron. His grip was surprisingly strong. "I still say she is a fine specimen. This is a poor way to treat such a creature, Lord Malrec—the place is falling down! There has been no one there in so long—"

"Shut your mouth, you fool! Don't give her any clues!"

Malrec's tone was cutting. "Creft! By Soth's demented song, boy, what is taking you so long?"

"Whatever you are planning, it isn't going to work." Alannys heard more confidence in her voice than she actually felt. "I will never help you, you must know that."

Malrec laughed, a low and threatening sound. "Isn't that charming. It appears you are operating under the delusion that we require your assistance." His voice was suddenly quiet and right next to her ear. "We don't need your help, Alannys. I admit it would have been better that way, but we are perfectly prepared to proceed without you. We just need you out of the way so you can't help anyone else."

He may as well have dashed cold water in her face. Never, not even once, had she considered the possibility that Lord Malrec could go ahead with his plans, without using her as a weapon. Against her every assumption, they didn't need her help.

They just wanted to be sure she couldn't defend the king.

Her knees crumpled. Malrec and Prubard jerked her to her feet.

"My Lord! The painting is ready!"

"Finally," Malrec muttered. He scooped her up off of her feet and hurried into the art room.

"Where are you taking me?" For the first time since this began, Alannys recognized the quaver of fear in her voice.

Lord Malrec recognized it, too. She heard his chuckle, close to her ear. It made her skin crawl. "You must know I have no intention of telling you that. All I can tell you is that you have brought this upon yourself. I did try to make things nice for you, I did try to keep you here — but alas, you have proven more than once that you will not do things the easy way."

There was a pause — he didn't speak, he didn't move.

Silence and stillness were worse than the noise and activity; she could feel herself edging closer to panic, desperate to know what was happening to her.

"I'm done playing nice with you, Alannys."

He took a sudden step forward, and Alannys felt her breath sucked from her in the icy, timeless void she would always recognize, whether she could see it or not.

When he stepped back out, she could feel herself trembling in his arms. A painting! They could be anywhere in Ravanmark now, anywhere in the world.

They could even be on another world entirely.

"Well, now, Lord Malrec, what do you got for us today?" The voice was female, saucy, and entirely unfamiliar.

Malrec walked toward the woman. Alannys could hear his boots moving against stone—they were probably inside, then. He dumped her unceremoniously onto her feet, and jerked the bag off of her head. Before he had even finished, she could feel the woman fumbling at her waist, and her belt was taken away, with Songstrike still on it.

"I've brought you the woman I told you about," he said, and stepped back, folding his arms.

Alannys faced a middle-aged, plump woman with brassy red hair piled on top of her head. She clearly was not of the nobility, and yet the clothes she wore were of expensive materials, tailored to show more flesh than any fine lady would permit. She wore makeup in gaudy, bright colors. She stood holding Alannys's belt over her arms, peering into her face with evident dislike.

"This is the woman? This is the one what gave you such trouble?"

Lord Malrec lifted his shoulders in an elegant shrug. "Alas, yes. I have done my best for her, Helva. But she will not be swayed." He put his hand on the woman's shoulder, making the gesture somehow intimate. "I know

I can count on you."

Helva laughed, and edged closer to him. "Of course, Lord Malrec. Will I see you tonight?"

He hooked a finger under her chin. "At the usual time, my dear." He kissed her, then turned and disappeared into the gray blur hovering behind him.

Helva dropped Alannys's belt on the ground and immediately began patting her down, searching for concealed weapons.

"Who are you?" Alannys demanded. "Where am I?"

Helva came up holding the enchanted dagger in its leather sheath. "That tone won't do you no good here, woman. I am Helva. And this—this is your own little piece of the Seven Hells." She suddenly raised her voice to an ear-blistering shriek. "Jeisha! Carrow!"

Two other women ran into the room. One was tall, with frizzy black hair, and black eyes that glittered maliciously in the light. The other was shorter and fairer, with blonde hair and sky blue eyes. She looked like a renaissance angel.

"This is Lord Malrec's bitch?" the blonde girl said, and the angelic impression shattered.

Helva laughed. "Such a delicate flower, ain't you, Carrow? Aye. This is her."

The tall woman—Alannys figured she must be Jeisha— moved a little closer, keeping a wary eye on her. "I suppose we had better get her to her room, then."

"I give the orders around here," Helva bristled. "Follow me, woman." She started to walk away.

Alannys glanced quickly around the big room—it was entirely stone, and it looked like it had once been an audience hall. There were only two exits. She turned in the opposite direction Helva had taken—it was pretty clear that whatever these people wanted her to do should be the last thing she actually did.

Jeisha reached out and grabbed her arm, quick as a wink and with a grip that was surprisingly strong. "This way," she said, jerking Alannys back.

Alannys swung her elbow viciously into Jeisha's stomach. The taller woman clearly wasn't expecting that kind of resistance, and the blow doubled her over.

Something crashed into Alannys's back, knocking her onto the floor, and a crushing grip locked around her neck. She heard a non-stop stream of angry swearing, and realized with a shock that it was Carrow.

She couldn't shake her off, and she couldn't get up. She dragged herself across the floor in a slow, painful crawl toward her weapons, lying in a heap where Helva had dumped them. Just as her fingers brushed against Songstrike's grip, Jeisha darted around in front of her and clamped a damp cloth over her face.

Alannys didn't know what the cloth had been soaked in, but it smelled sweet and cloying. She fought to hold her breath, to get Songstrike into her hand, but her vision went fuzzy and gray, and her hand went limp on the floor.

♪

Alannys woke up sore and cold, crumpled in a heap on a bare stone floor. Everything hurt. Her ears rang, and her mouth tasted bad. Her head was absolutely pounding. She put her hands to her temples. Was she hung over? It must have been a heck of a party. She wished she could remember it.

She pushed herself up to sort of sit, leaning on the wall behind her. She was in a very small room—more like a closet, or a cell. The walls and floor were plain gray stone, covered in moss in some places, and scorched black in other places. The ceiling above her was wood—at least, the parts that were left. There were gaping holes, singed black around the edges. The little room had only one door; a big, heavy, wooden door that looked much newer that anything else around it.

And standing in front of that door were three women she recognized, though she suddenly wished she didn't. They stood with their arms folded, regarding her calmly, waiting for her to regain her wits. Songstrike and her dagger were nowhere to be seen.

"What are you going to do to me?" Her mouth was dry and her voice sounded like the rustle of dead leaves.

Helva smiled. It wasn't a pleasant smile. "We're going to teach you your place. Get up."

Alannys just stared at her. The words meant nothing to her; her brain was still fighting off whatever they had used on her in the hall.

"You defiant, or just stupid?" Helva made a sound of impatience. "Girls, get her up."

Jeisha and Carrow grabbed her arms and hauled her to her feet. Alannys stood there wobbling between them, trying to get her head around what was happening, when every hair on the back of her neck stood up at once.

"Painting!" she gasped, and reached reflexively for her shawl. But of course it wasn't there.

Helva laughed, a sound Alannys liked about as much as her smile. "Get used to it, woman, Lord Malrec keeps a close eye on this place." She waggled her fingers at the gray blur hovering on a side wall, and blew a kiss to it.

Alannys shuddered.

"Now Lord Malrec is a right kind man," Helva said, fixing Alannys with a stern gaze. "He's told me to make you this offer. Waste of time, says I. But what Lord Malrec says, I do. And if you was of any account, you'd do the same. So here's your offer. Be a good girl, and you can leave."

"What?"

"It's simple. You been all kinds of trouble to Lord Malrec. No more. Stay by his side, help him, do what he tells you, and you can leave here. You can go to Castle

Glennayre, right now." She gestured at the hovering gray blur. "He's waiting right there to take your apology."

Alannys looked from Helva to the portal, and back again. "Is this a joke? No! No, I'll never help him attack King Dorramon. You're all out of your minds!"

She thought she could hear Malrec's nasty chuckle.

Helva shrugged, as if she had expected as much. "You heard her, girls. Time for the mighty Redeemer to learn her place here." She reached out and lifted the Seeing Stone over Alannys's head, and held it in front of her. "You won't be needing this anymore. Ain't nothing in this stone can help you now." She stepped back.

Jeisha and Carrow didn't hesitate. They dropped her arms and reached for her. Alannys couldn't imagine what they intended to do, but she shrank back against the wall, pushing them away and swatting at their hands.

Her efforts seemed to amuse them. With a truly disturbing smile, Jeisha swung out with one long leg and swept Alannys's feet out from under her. Alannys knocked her head against the wall and slid to the floor, dazed, still wondering what was going on.

Jeisha grabbed Alannys's feet and yanked her boots off. Carrow hauled off the linen workshirt.

And Alannys finally understood their intent. "Stop it! Stop—I won't let you do this!" She fought in earnest, kicking and gouging, punching and biting.

They overpowered her without even seeming to try. In less time than she would have believed, she stood shivering between them, naked and utterly humiliated. She had never in her life felt so completely defenseless.

Jeisha gathered Alannys's hair into one hand, and used her knife to lop it off, short and jagged and uneven. They put her in a garment they had fashioned from burlap sacks —it was sort of like a dress, but it had no sleeves, and it was too short to cover her decently.

"We'd better take this, too," said Carrow, reaching for her wrist. "Too pretty a trinket for a prisoner, don't you think?"

"No!" Alannys jerked her wrist away, folding her arms against herself in an effort to protect her bracelet. "You can't have that—you'll have to kill me. I'll never let you take it!"

"Hold on, Carrow," Helva said, with a cruel, cackling laugh. "Them's royal crests—wouldn't do to commit treason, would it?"

Alannys stared at her, hardly daring to believe she would get to keep her bracelet so easily.

"Don't get too cozy, woman," Helva said shortly. "Soon enough there'll be a new king in Ravanmark, and then—well, then I expect we'll have all the permission we need."

The words left Alannys suddenly cold, but there was nothing she could do.

Helva gathered up all of Alannys's things, and stood watching her for a moment, as she stood wobbling and shivering, with one hand on the dirty wall to steady herself. Alannys stared back, saying nothing. This was easily the most absolutely humiliating thing she had ever experienced. But there was no way she was going to give these three horrible, hateful women the satisfaction of seeing her break.

Without a word, Helva turned and left the room. The other two followed, leaving Alannys alone in the stone cell with the blurry gray portal on the wall.

Alannys sank down onto the floor, struggling to cover herself with the itchy burlap robe. Her shoulders slumped in defeat she could feel, but not quite accept. She had not come this far to lose to Lord Malrec in the end. This wasn't over.

It couldn't be.

Lord Malrec stepped gingerly into the room, looking around with evident distaste. "Charming. You needn't look so woebegone, my dear. I did offer you a chance."

She stared at him.

He reached out and brushed the ragged ends of her hair. "Still, it is difficult for me to see you treated this way. I implore you to reconsider. Come with me, take your place at Castle Glennayre, at my side." He smiled warmly, offering his hand to help her up.

Alannys looked at his handsome face, brimming with sympathy. She looked at the tattered remains of her hair scattered on the stone floor, at the burlap robe that barely kept her decent. She looked at the holes in the ceiling, at the moss and dirt on the walls. Then she looked back at the well-manicured hand he offered her.

She spat into his palm.

Lord Malrec's face knotted in sudden anger. He raised his hand for a backhanded strike across her face.

She flinched against the wall behind her.

Malrec checked himself, and slowly lowered his hand, wiping it clean on his cloak. "My offer stands," he said stiffly. "Your situation grieves me. Simply say the word, and you can come home." He stepped back into the painting, and the portal closed behind him.

She was finally completely alone, for the first time since Lord Malrec had appeared in her wagon. She had been told enough about this collar to guess how it worked, but she had to try. She took a deep breath, and began to sing.

"Oh Muses, most holy and high,
Bring a wind to smite these walls..."

She never made it past those two lines. At the first note, the collar began constricting, slowly at first. But the more she sang, the faster it clamped down on her, until she couldn't squeeze the notes past it.

She sank back against the wall, gasping.

That had been her last chance at freeing herself, and it had failed. She had been disarmed in every possible way. It stung, and bitterly.

The only thing left to do was to tell the king how badly she had failed him.

Dorramon?

Alannys? Where are you? He had responded immediately, which was good—to her horror, the collar began to constrict as soon as she opened the mindlink.

She jammed her fingers in between the collar and her neck and pulled, trying to buy herself a few extra seconds. *I'm sorry, Dorramon, I don't know—I'm sorry—I can't talk. Malrec put a collar on me, it chokes me when I sing or use the mindlink. I'm sorry...*

Alannys closed the mindlink. The collar had clamped down so tightly that she couldn't pull her fingers back out. Her vision was splotched with black, and she saw strange sparkly spots. She sucked in air raggedly, and slowly the collar relaxed.

That was it, then. She was trapped here, in this run-down ruin of a place, with those three horrible women, completely at the mercy of Lord Malrec's whims. She couldn't fight her way out, she couldn't sing her way out, and she couldn't even tell her friends where she was so they could help her out.

There *was* no way out.

Alannys watched her sole remaining possession glimmer in the evening light, a tangible reminder of the one she loved more than anything—and now might never see again. She dropped her face into her hands and cried.

♪

Dorramon swept into the royal dining room like an angry wind. Arch-Prince Raman and Kalyn jumped awkwardly from their seats—the king had been moving so fast there hadn't even been time for the heralds to announce him.

"Raman," he said without preamble, "we need a raiding party. Not too large—say a dozen men—we have to be able to move fast. Supplies for four days. Fastest horses we have. Ready for immediate departure."

Raman picked his jaw up off of the floor. "I—I'll see to it, of course. Where will I be taking this party?"

"Nowhere. I shall lead them myself. We will be going to Castle Glennayre."

"Castle Glennayre." Raman sat down with a thump. He should have guessed—Lady Alannys had to be involved in this somehow. There was nothing else in the world that could make the king so irrational. He glanced sidelong at Kalyn, but she seemed as lost as he was.

"Your Highness," Kalyn said, "why don't you sit down? Eat dinner, and tell us all about what has happened."

Dorramon shook his head. "No time. I have to leave as soon as possible. You can eat after I'm gone."

Raman picked his words carefully. "I'm coming with you, you know that. And we'll leave as soon as we can. But Dorramon, we need to know what we're getting into before we can prepare the party. You have to take a few minutes to tell us what you know."

The king sighed, and sank into a chair like a puppet with its strings cut. "Very well. Lord Malrec has Alannys."

"I gathered that much," Raman said. "But can't she just free herself, the way she did before?"

"No. No, he's got a collar on her that won't let her sing. She can't even use the mindlink—it chokes her."

"The Collar of Silence." Kalyn was suddenly very pale.

Raman whipped around to look at her. "You've heard of this thing?"

Kalyn nodded. She couldn't seem to look at either of

them. "They were...they were still working on it when I left. It was something Princess Delline discovered in her research. It sounded positively beastly."

Dorramon put his open hands out in her direction. "Just so. We can't leave her there, Raman. When can we start?"

"Grayble will have to pull men from the Royal Guard. We'll need the horses selected and prepared. Supplies will have to be requisitioned and packed." Raman shook his head. "It will take until nightfall, at least."

"My Lords," Kalyn said hesitantly, "I fear a raid on Castle Glennayre will do you little good. Lady Alannys is not there."

Raman looked at her in surprise. "You are certain of this?"

"Yes. Please understand, I was not privy to all of the Dark Alliance's plans. But I was told enough, and overheard enough, to know that they did not intend to keep Lady Alannys at the castle."

Dorramon rubbed at his forehead. "Of course. I should have realized—when I asked her where she was, she said she didn't know. If she was at Castle Glennayre, she would have known. She would have said so. Do you know where they were planning to keep her?"

"I'm sorry, your Highness. They never said, at least not where I could hear. I—I don't think it was meant to be very nice, though. They were planning to starve her, and worse."

The king stood up from the table.

"Dorr? Where are you going?" Raman feared he already knew.

"Castle Glennayre," Dorramon said. "I don't have any other choice. To rescue Alannys, we have to know where she is. There are three men in that castle who have the answer. I'm going to take some Royal Guards with me, and we are going to force it out of one of them. I am not going to let them kill her."

Raman stood too. "Wait — you can't do that! Dorr, you know their ultimate goal is assassinating you. Have you considered that this might be a trap?"

"Of course! But what else can I do? I can't ask you to risk your life for this. But I can't abandon her, either. I have to do this myself. I have to find out where she is. I don't have any choice."

"Yes." Raman heard the heavy sound of defeat in his own voice. "Yes, you do. I can find her for you."

"What?"

"Dorr, I — I have a box. In my chambers. It belonged to my father...I brought it with me to the Great Palace, after my parents died, but before the fire at Archford...and I hid it."

Dorramon sat back down. "I don't understand. How is your father's box going to help us find Alannys?"

Raman sighed. "I learned something about my father when I found that box. Something even my mother never suspected. He was a painter. The box — it's full of painting supplies. Brushes, paints — there's even a few leaves of the Herb of Sight in there."

Dorramon stared at him like he couldn't quite believe him. "You've had that all these years — and you never used it? Not once?"

"Not once. You have to understand, I was brought up with such a negative view of the Talents..." He shook his head. "They didn't even know I was Talented — I didn't even know. It would have been like a personal failing."

"I understand," Dorramon said. "It's the same way I was brought up with singing."

Raman nodded. "When I opened that box, and saw those things...Dorr, I was ashamed of my father. I felt like it was a stain on his honor, like I should burn it. I probably would have, but it was all I had left of him. So I kept it, but I hid it away, and I made myself a promise I would never, ever try to use those things."

He trailed off, remembering. He'd never been more serious in his life than when he'd made that vow. And though he had kept the box, he had never in all the intervening years so much as opened it.

He pulled himself from his dismal reverie, and found the others watching him. "But I'm going to break it now," he said. He was trying to be flippant, but his voice cracked in a way that made him sound fearful instead.

"Are you sure?" Dorramon asked, regarding him solemnly.

Kalyn reached out and covered his hand on the table with her own. Raman smiled at her, but it felt like a shaky smile.

"I'm sure. You can't go to Castle Glennayre, Dorramon —they would like nothing better than to see you dead. If you go there, you won't come back. And from what you two have said, it's pretty clear she isn't going to be able to get herself out of this. I can find her. And if we can figure out how to make the gloss, we can bring her back. But you're going to have to be patient—I've never done this before. It's going to take some time."

"I have every confidence in you," Dorramon said.

But somehow that didn't relieve the terrible urgency all of them felt. No one knew how long the rescue might take...

...and no one knew how much time Alannys had left.

♫

The women roasted chickens on a spit over a fire that evening. Alannys could smell the meat, could hear the fat sizzling when it dripped into the flames. But her door was barred from the outside, so she couldn't leave.

She thought she might go mad. She hadn't eaten anything since...she couldn't even remember. She hadn't eaten during the dinner at Duke Morryn's the night before, and she'd been too busy running to eat after that. It had been at least two days, maybe three, since her last meal. The smell of roasting chicken made her light-headed with hunger, made her stomach growl and knot up painfully.

She hadn't had anything to drink since Danningham Manor, either. It was hard to tell which was worse: the hunger, or the thirst.

Surely they would bring her something soon. She knew the women weren't fond of her. But she wasn't any use to anybody dead—she couldn't believe they would let her starve to death. They had to intend to feed her.

One of the moons was high in the sky, peeking past gray clouds to cast its spotty light in her cell, before she admitted that perhaps they did not intend to feed her. She could hear wolves howling in the distance, and she shivered. The temperature was dropping fast in her little cell.

She could smell rain on the air. Lightning flashed way off in the distance. She heard the far-off rumbling of thunder, and it reminded her of the first thunderstorm she ever experienced in Ravanmark, so long ago it seemed like another lifetime, with Dorramon. She had been so scared that night, in her oilcloth tent, all alone in the storm. Dorramon had come to comfort her. She smiled, stroking her bracelet and remembering.

Only now she was all alone without any kind of proper roof over her head, even an oilcloth one. No one could comfort her here—she couldn't even talk to Dorramon, not even through the mindlink.

Alannys wished the bar was on her side of the door, so she could lock those women out. At least she would have some warning if they decided to come in—the bar was rough and crude and made a lot of noise when it was moved. She leaned her head back against the stone wall, watching the heavy gray clouds move across the night sky.

When she woke up maybe an hour later, she was shivering. Big, heavy raindrops were splattering down on her.

She moved over into one of the dark corners, huddling against the walls. What remained of the wooden ceiling was so old and rotted, she couldn't get completely out of the rain. She tucked her feet up under her, trying to retain body warmth. But the cold was unrelenting.

Alannys cupped her hands and held them out, hoping to catch enough rain to collect herself a sip of water. It was a wasted effort—the drops were too widely spaced and too infrequent. Thinking of water made her throat ache.

Even when she was scrunched up in a knot against the walls, the rain managed to splatter on her. It was maddening—how could so much water find her, when she couldn't find herself a few drops for a sip? She didn't know how long she sat there and shivered, damp and cold.

But eventually, she got so tired that even the cold and the wet couldn't keep her awake. Her head drooped toward her chest, and she started to doze.

All at once her hair stood on end, and she felt the presence of unseen eyes. Tears of frustration stung the backs of her eyes—she was so *tired*—and something interfered every single time she started to sleep.

She scrubbed at her eyes with the heels of her hands, and looked around for the tell-tale gray mist. It was off to her right, and high above her. Too high for her to dive into and escape, and certainly too high for anyone to use to come into the cell.

Fine, then. She turned her back on the painting, facing the wall, and curled up to try to sleep again. Lord Malrec was going to have to do better than that if he seriously intended to keep her awake.

She was so full of anger and helpless frustration, it took her a long time to settle down enough to even think about sleeping again. Her eyelids finally got too heavy to fight, and she slipped into the welcoming oblivion of sleep.

The loud, obtrusive sound of the big wooden bar unlatching shattered the quiet. Alannys smothered a curse, trying as hard as she could not to let any of these people know they were getting to her. She turned around, putting her back into the corner, and waited to see what came through the door.

Carrow pushed into the room, bundled in a woolen nightgown with a matching robe. She had velvet slippers on her feet. She had evidently been sleeping; her hair was rumpled into a blonde cloud around her head. She wore her sweetest smile, and she looked angelic again.

"I hope I didn't disturb you," she said.

Alannys wanted to scream. "Not at all."

"I wanted to bring you a blanket. It's a bit chilly out." She leaned forward, and held out a cloth. It was wadded up and ratty looking, but it did appear to be a blanket.

Alannys took it in real surprise. "Thank you." Maybe— maybe there was hope for her situation after all.

Carrow smiled again. "Is there anything else you need?"

She had to be aware that Alannys had a list of needs at this point as long as her arm. It felt like Carrow was baiting her. Still, she had brought the blanket... "Water," Alannys said, trying to ignore the way just saying the word made her throat burn. "I really need some water."

Something in Carrow's expression shifted subtly, as though perhaps she had expected that response. "Hmm," she said, appearing to consider it, "I think they are going to bring you some water in the morning. Things are a bit hectic right now. We spoke to Lord Malrec a few hours ago—he was preparing to launch the attack on the Great Palace. It's well underway by now. I thought you would want to know."

Alannys stared at her, stricken. "They are attacking the palace—in the middle of the night?"

Carrow shrugged. "I don't pretend to be expert in these things, but it seems to me that's the best time. You would catch them off-guard."

Alannys could feel her heart pounding double-time. Sudden cold sweat slicked her palms. For a crazy moment she considered using the mindlink, letting the collar choke her, so that she could warn Dorramon—but then she remembered Carrow's words. The attack was already underway—it was already too late. Anything could have happened!

Carrow watched her with an odd expression. "You aren't going to faint, are you? Honestly, I thought they were teasing me when they told me how attached you are to the king. What woman in her right mind could even look at him when Lord Malrec is around?"

"Me. I could."

"Well—I don't mean to be unkind, but," Carrow wrinkled her nose, "that really just proves my point. You really should reconsider. If Lord Malrec would have you, you would be much better off." She turned for the door. "Sleep well."

Alannys heard the grating scrape and heavy thump of the bar falling into place. She was shivering, but whether from cold or from panic was more than she could tell. She shook out the wad of cloth Carrow had given her, eager for any warmth it could provide.

The thing in her hands had obviously been a blanket, once. But that was before moths had eaten away large holes in the fabric, and fire had evidently burned away even more. The ragged, tattered scraps that remained would not have covered even her feet in any satisfactory fashion.

She should have known. She should have *known*. She thought she could hear Carrow's laughter floating back to her even now. This horrible place, these horrible *people* — they were making her lose her mind, she could feel it. Her own thoughts didn't seem to make much sense anymore.

And now they were attacking the palace!

Alannys cringed against the wall, too cold to sleep, and too worried to care. She had to admit they had done it — they had found a way to keep her awake.

♫

By morning Alannys had no white left on her fingernails at all. She had bitten them down to nothing — even bitten her cuticles. Her fingertips were swollen and bloody, and still she couldn't rest. Anxiety drove her and she paced her little cell like a caged animal. The painting up above her was open, as always, but she was beyond caring who watched or what they saw.

Jeisha came to see her. Alannys had no idea what time it might have been — she could only tell it was morning because the sun had come up. The day was cloudless and bright, a stark contrast to her mood.

"I've brought you some breakfast," Jeisha said. She held out a plate of bread crusts and dried cheese ends — it looked like the remains of someone else's meal.

Or maybe three someone elses.

Alannys looked at it and turned away. She couldn't imagine eating anyway. The very thought turned her stomach.

"Come on, now. You have to eat."

Alannys shook her head. She wouldn't eat a bite until she knew that Dorramon was safe. She couldn't.

Jeisha sighed. "Ah, well. I suppose you'll want to know how last night's raid on the Great Palace turned out. It was amazing—it succeeded beyond anyone's wildest expectations. Both the arch-prince and the king are dead."

The room lurched sideways. Alannys put a hand on the wall to steady herself.

"Of course that means the only heir left to the throne is Princess Delline, which will make Lord Malrec the next king." She brought out a leather waterskin. "I have water for you. You need to recover yourself. They will be having the coronation this evening."

Alannys stared at her in sickly shock. "That can't be true." Her voice was a hoarse echo of its usual self; crying and thirst had ravaged her.

Jeisha laughed. "Oh, it's true, all right. We've all been invited to the ceremony—even you could go if you cleaned up your attitude."

"No."

"I don't know why Lord Malrec extended the invitation, honestly—you've been so ungrateful. Maybe he thinks that it would help smooth the transition, since you were at Dorramon's coronation as well." She shook her head. "I suppose we'll have to round up something presentable for you to wear."

"I won't go."

"What?" Jeisha's tone carried the first white-hot flickers of anger. "You can't really mean that."

Alannys swayed where she stood, but said nothing.

"Lord Malrec is twice the man Dorramon was—twice the man Dorramon ever could have been! How dare you refuse him! You'll go, Alannys, if I have to dress you and drag you there myself!"

"I tell you I will not!" Alannys's voice was black with rage. "No force on this earth could make me. I would see Lord Malrec dead before I would go to his coronation. I would die myself before I would go!"

"And you just might." Jeisha jerked the water bottle

back and backhanded Alannys, knocking her into the wall. "You'll get nothing from us until you're ready to behave reasonably. You brought this on yourself, just you remember that."

Jeisha slammed the door when she left.

Alannys fell onto her knees, wracked with dry heaves. She lay down and pressed her hot face against the cold stone floor, wishing it would open up and swallow her.

Anything seemed better than facing what was ahead of her right now.

♫

Her captors didn't leave her to suffer long alone. Helva came in just a few minutes after Jeisha left. If she was surprised to find Alannys lying with her face in the moss on the floor, she didn't show it.

"Follow me, woman. There's work to do today."

Alannys didn't respond, didn't even move. Why should she? Dorramon was...was...

Helva pulled back and dealt her a vicious kick to the stomach. Pain tore through her like lightning, so intense it was nauseating. Alannys curled up, her arms around her middle, not even able to breathe.

"Get *up*, woman." Helva's voice was low and threatening. "Ain't gonna tell you again."

Alannys dragged herself painfully to her feet, and limped out after the older woman, one hand pressed to her side. She felt like her guts might fall out.

Her little cell was part of a big stone structure. It was something like a villa, laid out in a big square that opened onto a central courtyard.

Or rather, it had been something like a villa. Now it was a crumbling ruin. Towards the front, where she had first come in through the long hall, the building was still fairly solid, though it had obviously been ravaged by fire long ago. But her cell was toward the back of the complex, where the building was falling down around itself. Once there had been a tower on the back corner, a match for the ones that still stood on the other three corners. Now it was a hollowed-out, ragged wreck, with a few jagged walls that barely managed to clear the ground. The whole area was piled with the rubble from the tower.

Helva led Alannys over to the wall of burnt debris. "Lord Malrec tested some sort of thing he called a bomb here," she said, as if she couldn't conceive of a grander thing. "Worked pretty well, as I understand it. Made a mess, though. That's where you come in. Me and the girls got to get ready for the coronation this evening. You can work on clearing this trash while we do."

Alannys was beyond complaint. She hauled rocks out of the rubble, and piled them together. Wood scraps went into another pile, and everything else she found into a third. She staggered between her piles and the wall of debris for hours.

The sun was high and the day was unseasonably hot. The work was back-breaking, and it made her light-headed. But all in all she was better off; taken as a whole, working in the sun and the heat through an exhaustion that made her muscles quiver was better than sitting all day trapped in her cell with nothing but her fear and sadness to occupy her.

She had just finished telling herself that when she fainted.

♫

Alannys woke up slowly. Nothing seemed to make much sense. She remembered all too well the conditions she'd suffered; she remembered with depressing accuracy where she was and why. She still wore the little burlap sack, after all, and her hair was still gone.

But now she was lying on a featherbed, in a room that was cool and quiet and dark. There were no holes in the ceiling here, and no moss growing among the stones that made up the floor and walls.

For a moment all she could do was lie there and soak up the cool softness of the bed beneath her. She could feel it down to her bones. If only she could have stopped the burning thirst, it would almost have been comfortable. It was easy to imagine lying there and never moving again.

But before she had gotten her bearings, warm lips found hers, overwhelming her with the scent of cinnamon.

She jerked her face away, gasping.

"Still you spurn me, even now?" Lord Malrec's dark eyes were unfathomable in the low light. He knelt beside the bed, looking cleaner and fresher than anything she had seen in forever.

"Malrec." Her voice was a croak, a thin, pathetic sound she didn't recognize. "Malrec, please, let me out of here. I don't want to die here, like this."

He shifted slightly, and the weak light played across his cloak, flaring up hints of royal purple. "You must see my difficulty, Alannys. After everything that has happened, how can I trust you? You've not been exactly sympathetic to my interests. And now the girls tell me you are rejecting reality—refusing to accept truth when it is laid in front of you. I love you, Alannys, it kills me to see you like this."

"Then let me out.'

"I can't, don't you see that? You're too unstable. Dorramon is dead, Alannys. You have to accept that."

Her eyes slipped from his and she shook her head.

"Listen to me! He is dead and you are hurting yourself for nothing. You have to move on. I am the king now, and if you want to help Ravanmark, you have to do it through me."

"No."

"You still refuse to believe?"

"I won't help you. It doesn't matter if you are the last man alive in Ravanmark, Malrec—I will never help you."

Tears burned her eyes. She wanted more than anything to tell him what he wanted to hear, to say whatever it took to get out of there, but she couldn't bring herself to betray Dorramon.

Quick as a striking snake, Malrec backhanded her, crushing her brittle lips against her teeth, filling her mouth with the metallic taste of blood. He leaned down over her, his angry face filling her vision. "You miserable whore! You will never see Dorramon again. Do you hear me? Never! He is dead! Your only way out of here is through *me,* Alannys. And I advise you to accept that as quickly as possible. Or you may very well die in this place."

He swept out of the little room, slamming the door behind him. It was quiet, cool, and dark again. Alannys could see a wooden chest across the room. She wondered for a moment what it was for, until she recognized her own leather riding cloak tossed casually across the top of it.

Even in her half-dead state, Alannys realized that the rest of her things were probably inside the chest. She dragged herself out of the bed and across the room.

The chest was locked, and there was no sign of a key anywhere. Disappointment washed over her like a physical force.

The door swung open again, and Helva came in, followed closely by the other two women. Her face was very stern, and Alannys wondered fleetingly if she was about to be punished for snooping.

"You upset Lord Malrec," Helva said. "Don't rightly know why he bothers with you. Or why you're so ungrateful."

"Ungrateful?" Alannys swayed on her feet; she didn't think she had the strength to carry this on for very long. "I can't think of any reason why I should be grateful to him."

"You're still here, ain't you? Would have been easy

enough to kill you outright, if that's what Lord Malrec wanted. Instead, he gives you a chance, and this is how you repay him."

Alannys stared at Helva. One of them obviously had a very skewed view of this situation, and she hoped it wasn't her.

Helva pointed suddenly at Jeisha. "You see her? Jeisha was a whore. Wasn't you, Jeisha?"

Jeisha laughed harshly. "Among other things, yes. I've been a prostitute. I've also been a bouncer at the brothel, tossing out the riff-raff and the troublemakers. I've been a thief for hire, even an assassin, if the price was right. Lord Malrec lifted me out of all that. He provides for me now."

"Flat right." Helva nodded decisively. "Think your precious Dorramon woulda troubled hisself on account of a whore? Not likely." She pointed at Carrow. "And as for Little Miss Angel Face here, think her story is much better?"

"I was born dirt-poor," Carrow said, tossing her blonde hair, "but very pretty. So I've used my obvious gifts to advance my position over the years. I overstepped my bounds when I let the Captain of Glennayre's Guard take me to his bed. His wife pitched quite a fit. I was in a cell in Glennayre's jail. Lord Malrec rescued me that night, just before the jealous woman set the place on fire."

"Saved her life." Helva made each word short and distinct. "Your so-called king wouldn't bestir himself to help Carrow, I'd reckon. And me? I was tied to a gambling, debtor husband. Had two little kids to raise and no money to provide for them. Lord Malrec freed me of Petras, and provided me a right smart sum to boot." She folded her arms. "Dorramon never cared about the problems of a debtor's widow. We'd be fools to turn our backs on a generous man like Lord Malrec. Same as you."

"You're wrong." Alannys wanted the words to sound

bold and defiant, but her voice cracked and they came out pleading and desperate. "You're all wrong. You've pledged your loyalty to a monster!"

"The only monster in this kingdom was Dorramon," Helva said, "and the best thing Lord Malrec ever did was strangle the life out of him!" Helva clenched her hands into angry fists, and only then did Alannys see the glimmer of gold on her wrist.

Only then did she realize her bracelet was gone.

"You..." Alannys staggered, clutching at her own wrist as if to confirm her loss. "What have you done?"

"Only what our new king told me to." Helva sounded satisfied, turning her arm and watching the light play across her stolen bracelet.

"No. Lord Malrec isn't king. There is only one King of Ravanmark, and that's Dorramon."

"Still with this." Helva rolled her eyes toward the ceiling. "King Malrec said this'd happen. He sent a token, just for you." She nodded to Jeisha. "Give the woman the token."

Jeisha stepped toward Alannys and held out a scrap of blue fabric. Slowly, with trembling hands, Alannys took it.

It was precisely the same color and weave as the fabric of the blue riding cloak Dorramon had worn most of the time she had been with him.

It was too much to bear. She clutched the sad scrap of cloth to her chest, sank to her knees, and sobbed as though she would never be able to stop.

♬

Her jailers dragged her back to her cell and left her there without another word. Alannys couldn't have said how long she spent curled up on the cold, mossy floor, crying into her scrap of fabric.

The women swept back into the room, wearing formal gowns made of heavy velvet in jewel tones. They had their hair put up, and Helva even wore extra rouge.

Belatedly, she remembered. The coronation.

"The ceremony starts soon," Helva said. "There's still time, you could still go. All you got to do is swear your loyalty to Lord Malrec."

Her hands tightened convulsively on the scrap of fabric. "No."

"You sure? You're missing out."

"I won't do it."

Helva shrugged. "Fine. Makes no difference to me. But you must be thirsty."

Alannys couldn't look at her. She'd had no water since the dinner at Danningham Manor, forever ago. She nodded.

"Well, then. The girls'll bring you water. All you got to do is own up to what's true."

"What do you mean?"

"The king is dead."

Alannys stared at her.

"Dorramon's dead. Say it. Out loud. And you can have water."

"Dorramon..." Her throat closed up around the words. Alannys shook her head and swallowed thickly. "I can't do it."

Carrow came close to Alannys, smelling of rose water and wearing her sweetest smile. "Come now, Alannys. You've got to have water — you can't keep up like this. Is it that hard, really?"

All at once Alannys was crying again, her face dripping with tears that burned from too much salt. She shook her head.

"Fine." Helva's voice was hard. "We'll leave her to mull it over then, eh?"

With a burst of loud, unkind laughter, the dressed-up women left the room.

Left to her own devices for the first time all day,

Alannys sat down in the corner and huddled close to the wall, clutching the blue scrap against her. Against her every expectation, she fell asleep.

She really didn't know how much later it was when her door opened again. She heard high voices and giggling laughter and guessed that the women had returned, but it was difficult to open her eyes to be sure. They seemed to be stuck shut—they were so dry that just prying them open hurt.

"King Malrec sends his regards," Helva said haughtily. "We wasn't going to bother with you again tonight, but the king took me to the side and asked me to give you one more chance at the water." She shook her head. "I don't know why he worries after you, that's honest as Muse's song. So here it is."

Carrow stepped up next to Helva, holding a battered tin cup with a few swallows of brackish water in it. Under normal circumstances, they couldn't have paid Alannys to drink it. But now—well, her lips were dry and split, and her tongue had cracks in it. She needed water more than anything else in the world at that moment.

"I can see you're interested," Helva said. She smiled, but it was a cruel smile. "You know what to do, then, don't you, woman?"

"Dorramon...Dorramon is..." She looked away and shook her head. She just couldn't make the words come out.

Alannys. The voice was gentle and loving, and it was only in her mind.

"Dorramon!" She hadn't meant to answer out loud, but it didn't matter. The women were all looking at her as though her sanity was suspect, but that didn't matter, either. "Dorramon, I knew it couldn't be true!"

Alannys, you can't go on like this. You have to tell them what they want to hear. You're going to die here if you don't.

For a moment the words didn't even register; it was just such a relief to hear him through the mindlink again, and know that everything was all right.

Alannys! You have to say it!

For one brief, shining moment she soared. And then she realized — the collar was not constricting. Her face paled, and panic closed around her heart like a vise. Either she was hallucinating...

Or Dorramon really was dead.

She was choking with great ripping sobs, but she had no tears. Dorramon's phantom voice was right; if she didn't get some water, she would die here, and soon.

"Dorramon...is...d-dead," she choked out.

Helva leaned closer. "What was that, woman? I couldn't make out what you said."

"Dorramon...is dead. He's dead!"

Helva smiled maliciously. "Too right he is. Give the woman her water, Carrow, she's finally learning. King Malrec will be pleased."

Carrow pressed the cup into Alannys's hands, and all three women filed out of the little cell, closing the door behind them.

Alannys slid down the wall to sit on the floor, clutching the cup. She sipped the rank, stale water until it was gone. It turned her stomach, but she knew that was just because she'd gone so long with nothing.

She wrapped her arms around herself and leaned back against the wall, shuddering. "I'm sorry, Dorramon. Oh, Muses forgive me, I'm so sorry."

She cried herself to sleep, crumbling under the crushing weight of her betrayal.

♪

Alannys woke up disoriented, in the middle of the night, with the stiff feeling of dried tears on her face.

There was a head on the floor, regarding her with an expression of frozen horror.

The head had once belonged to Larric.

Alannys screamed and jumped to her feet. The sudden motion left her instantly light-headed, and she stumbled, catching herself with a hand against the wall. She shut her eyes tight and sucked in air, trying to calm herself. She thought she might never recover.

Remember that, when you see me again.

Good heavens, was *that* what he had meant? Had he known Lord Malrec would desecrate his corpse in this way?

It was too awful to consider. She draped her little piece of blue fabric over him, so she wouldn't have to see that horrified gaze.

Somehow she wound up stretched out flat on the floor, in front of the grisly remains of one of her oldest friends. She wondered how that had happened, until she tried to sit up and found that she simply couldn't move. She no longer had the energy required to hold herself upright.

So she was lying on the mossy stone floor, unable to lift a finger, when the door creaked open and Lord Malrec swept into the room. He wore a royal purple cloak over a black doublet, and an ostentatious gold crown.

"Malrec," she croaked. "Have you come to watch me die?"

He frowned. "You know that would not please me. Do you doubt me still?"

She sighed. "You win, Malrec. I give up."

His eyebrows shot up. "Is that so? I have your solemn vow that you will not use your Talents against me?"

"Yes."

He stepped farther into the room, pushing the door closed behind him with a foot, warming up to the conversation. "And you will stay at Castle Glennayre, and accommodate me in whatever manner I ask of you?"

She couldn't look at him. "I—I suppose so. I don't want

to die here, Lord Malrec."

"*King* Malrec."

"As you say."

He tapped his chin with one long finger, considering. "And will you use your Talents to aid me in clearing out the last of the resistance from the Great Palace?"

"What?" She had not been prepared for that one. "I can't do that, Malrec."

He grabbed her by the shoulders and hauled her to her feet, pushing her back against the wall. "Use my title, damn you!"

"I'm sorry. Your Highness. But I can't do that—I can't betray Dorramon that way."

He shook her till her teeth rattled. "You've already betrayed him, you ignorant woman! You've failed him in every single thing. The songs he trusted you to find have been in my library this entire time, did you know that? You failed him utterly. Every single thing you have done since I left you with Helva has been a betrayal! How could this possibly make it any worse?"

Tears rolled down her cheeks, and she was dizzy from the shaking. But she managed somehow to shake her head. "It would. I'm sorry. I can't. I can't fight against those who remain faithful to him."

He hit her then; twice, three times. She wondered if he would kill her, but she thought about it vaguely, the way she might think about the death of a bug. Her nose bled, and her lips were split and bleeding.

"If you won't help me," he shouted into her face, "then you will die here. Do you hear me, Alannys? You will *die!*"

"I'm sorry." The words were almost unintelligible through her swollen lips, but she did her best. "But I won't help you."

He tossed her to the floor and stormed out of the room.

He slammed the door behind him, but she could still hear his voice, blasting through the courtyard. "No one is to go into that room. None of you! She'll do my bidding or I swear by the Muses she'll meet her fate here!"

The words brushed by her without leaving a mark, meaningless, as though they were meant for someone else.

She really didn't have much concept of time. It was still dark; it could have been a minute or an hour later when she felt a painting open. She could see the misty gray blur coalesce low on the wall opposite her, and she knew that Lord Malrec had come to berate her some more.

She wondered if she would survive it this time.

But it wasn't Lord Malrec who burst into the room, rushing frantically to her side and falling to his knees next to her.

"Alannys—great Muses, Alannys! What has he done to you?" Warm hands reached for her clammy ones, and piercing blue eyes gazed into her own with alarm.

"Dorramon." She breathed the name like a benediction. She had never seen anything more wonderful than the sight of him in that moment. "Am I dead, then? Are you an angel?"

"Dead?" He pushed her matted hair back from her face. The more he looked at her, the more upset he seemed. "No, no, of course not. You're not dead, love, and neither am I."

"Not...dead." She sighed; an enormous weight had just lifted from her. She smiled.

"Is that what they've told you?" His voice shook with anger. "Oh, Alannys, we have got to get you out of here. Where are your things? What happened to your clothes, to Songstrike?"

"I could show you," she said, "if I could move."

Dorramon looked at her, and his face softened. He cradled her head in his lap, and reached into a pouch on his belt. "Here. I've got water, and wine, and dried fruit. We need to get you on your feet. I can't believe that bastard Malrec did this to you."

He closed her hands around a leather water bottle, and she fumbled it to her mouth, doing her best to drink slowly. "I can," she finally said. "He told me early on that I would either serve him or die. I'm beginning to think he meant it."

"It's hard to doubt it, seeing you like this. Here, have some perapple. What? Why are you looking at me like that?"

She pushed herself up on shaky arms, and sat back against the wall. "Oh, I don't know how you could understand. They told me you were dead. Over and over —they wouldn't give me any water unless I said it too. They even had a fake coronation—Malrec showed up earlier wearing a crown. I couldn't even use the mindlink to find out if it was true."

"Merciful Muses. I'm so sorry, Alannys."

She shook her head. "Pass me the wine. Maybe it'll get me up and moving."

Dorramon leaned over to hand her the leather bottle, and frowned. "What's wrong with your leg?"

She followed his gaze to her calf. "Oh, that." She tipped her head back and swallowed more of the sweet wine than probably was wise. "That happened some time ago, actually—it's what's left of a pretty bad burn. That dagger Raman gave me at the palace is enchanted. Whenever the cloaked swordsman gets near me, the dagger gets hot. That particular time...well, he was very close indeed." She slugged back more wine.

The king watched her, shaking his head. "I swear I don't see how you're still alive."

"Me, either. But now that you're here, I'd like to stay that way a bit longer. Can you help me up? I don't think I can stand on my own, and we've got to get moving."

She could see his doubts on his face, but he didn't argue. It was true; they didn't have much time. Lord Malrec or his three harpies could be back at any moment. Dorramon offered her his hand and pulled her gently to her feet.

She swayed, and put her hand against the wall.

"Are you sure you're going to be able to do this?" He peered into her face with concern.

"No. But I'm not leaving Songstrike here, and I'm not leaving you here alone to get it."

"Stubborn as always, I see," he said. But his voice was kind, and he looked at her with such tenderness she could have cried.

Instead she threaded her arm through his and hung on tight. "We've got to go outside," she said. "Helva's room is across the courtyard."

Dorramon squared his shoulders and opened the big door. They stepped out into the moonlit courtyard. He glanced around them, and gasped. "What happened to the East Tower?"

"Malrec tested a bomb here. Looks like it worked. You know this place?"

He forced himself to look away from the rubble of the destroyed tower. "This is Archford Estate. Well, it was. It was destroyed by fire years ago, but this—this is beyond anything the fire could have done. I should have known Malrec would be behind it as well."

Archford Estate. She supposed she should have felt something, realizing that her prison was Raman's ancestral home, but she didn't. She pointed with a trembling finger to the door across the courtyard that led to the room where she had rested when she fainted. "There. Helva has all of my things in there. I don't know how we'll get them out, though—she keeps them in a locked chest, and I couldn't find the key."

He patted her arm. "Don't worry."

They had to move slowly because of her, but they finally made it to the door. Dorramon threw the door open and stomped inside, and Alannys wobbled in behind him.

Helva had been asleep, that much was obvious. She rolled out of her bed, rumpled and confused, and grabbed a robe to throw over her nightgown. "What goes on here?" she demanded. Alannys saw her blink several times, evidently trying to focus on them in the doorway.

"The Lady Alannys," Dorramon said in a voice like the crack of doom, "has come to reclaim her things."

Helva jumped, and smiled at them in a manner she evidently considered quite becoming. "Your Highness! How nice of you to take the time to see us." She glanced quickly around the room.

Alannys thought she was probably looking for any sign of a painting. "She thinks Lord Malrec is coming."

Helva snarled at her, then smiled at Dorramon again. "That's silly. The heat today must have went to the woman's head. Who could look at someone like Lord Malrec when a fine man like you is around?"

Alannys snorted. "Funny, you were saying that the other way around yesterday."

Helva ignored her, oozing her own curious brand of charm at Dorramon. "Why, Lord Malrec is like half a man next to you, your Highness!"

"I am out of patience," Dorramon snapped. He drew his sword.

Helva laughed, a grating and false sound. "Your Highness, do you really figure to run me through?"

"I don't need to. You think having a collar on Alannys makes you safe, but haven't you heard that I can sing too?"

The color drained abruptly from her face. "No. No —

you wouldn't."

"Believe me, I would. After all that you have done to Alannys, it is my opinion that you deserve it. Produce her things now, or I will sing your death and retrieve her belongings myself."

Helva hesitated, weighing the threat against his ability to carry it through.

Dorramon shrugged, and drew a deep breath.

"No!" Helva flung her hands out to him in a desperate gesture. "No, I'll do it, just don't sing!"

She was wearing a ribbon around her neck. She pulled it off—a heavy brass key hung at the end. She unlocked the chest and moved back against the wall, as far away from them as she could get. "There. There's her things. Take them and get, and I hope never to see you all again."

"Trust me, the sentiment is entirely mutual," Dorramon said. "Now take off her bracelet before I cut off your hand and take it myself."

With shaking fingers, Helva did, and tossed the bracelet to Dorramon. He fastened it on Alannys's arm, and for the first time she began to feel like things might really be okay after all.

They scooped up her things and hurried back to her cell. She didn't even dare pause to dress. Dorramon took her hand in his, and they plunged together into the icy void of the painting.

♫

The light hurt Alannys's eyes and she stumbled. Strong hands caught her and held her up. Her eyes started to adjust, and she looked up and saw a familiar face.

"I swear, Alannys, you are a magnet for trouble. I leave you alone for a couple of days, and this is how you come back?"

"Raman," she said. "It's wonderful to see you, too." Her eyes teared up, and she scrubbed at them with her dirty hands.

"Let me guess," Dorramon said. "He was dead, too."

She couldn't look at him. She nodded.

Raman swore, and turned to scatter drying powder on the painting behind her.

She looked around her for the first time. They were in a large room, with two levels of balconies surrounding them. Beautiful archways extended deep into the walls, creating innumerable hiding spots and secret passages.

"The Lesser Hall?" she blurted in surprise. "Raman's been painting in the Lesser Hall?"

"I know," Dorramon said. He looked suddenly guilty. "We were supposed to treat it with the solution you sent. But Raman needed a place to work where he wouldn't be disturbed. And his chambers would have been the first place Lord Malrec looked, if he decided to look."

"My Lady!" A blur of velvet gown and red hair streaked toward her. "My Lady, I am so glad to see you! Let me take your things."

"Kalyn? Kalyn!" Alannys was caught completely off-guard. Kalyn wore a fine gown, and her hair was meticulously coiffed. She had a diamond engagement ring on her left hand.

Alannys sneaked a glance at Raman, who reddened.

"I am sorry I was not here when you arrived," Kalyn said. "I went to fetch the baroness. I thought she would want to be here."

"The baroness?"

Baroness Lae stepped in behind Kalyn, looking bemused at the girl's enthusiasm. "I am here, my Lady. I am glad to see you back."

"The baroness saved the day," Raman said. "She found the formula for gloss in Delline's notes in her chambers. We couldn't have rescued you without it."

"Thank you," Alannys said with feeling.

Lae blushed. "You needn't thank me, my Lady. I'm

afraid I have failed you. I have searched during your absence, but I did not locate either of the songs you need."

Alannys's shoulders slumped. "That's not your fault, my Lady. I was looking in the wrong place all along. The songs are in the library at Castle Glennayre."

Raman looked at her sharply. "Lord Malrec told you this?"

She shrugged. "He mocked me with it." She swayed on her feet. Wine and dried perapples could only keep a person going for so long.

Dorramon looked at her in sudden concern. "Kalyn, would you ring a servant to take Alannys's things to her room? I think we've kept her long enough."

"Of course, your Highness, but—would you like me to take her to her rooms?"

Dorramon shook his head. "Thank you. But I just got her back, I'm not turning loose of her yet." He guided Alannys's arm through his own and grinned at her mischievously. "Besides, I have a promise to keep."

She stared at him, totally lost. "What do you mean?"

"Oh, you'll see," he said. "But not yet."

"Dorramon, are you sure this is the best time for that?" Raman's tone was odd—it was too loud, somehow, too forceful.

Dorramon's expression closed up. "I don't know what you could mean."

Raman sighed, and crossed his arms. "Don't you? Look at her, Dorr. She's dirty, bruised, bloodied, half-dressed, exhausted, starved, dehydrated, and sleep-deprived. The only sensible place for her to go is bed, not off to—"

"Not another word." Dorramon's tone was pretty forceful too, and Alannys had to wonder what was really going on here.

"You're not even going to tell her where you're taking her?"

Dorramon met his gaze evenly, but said nothing.

"Well, then. Allow me to suggest that this is only appropriate if you intend to leave her there permanently." He turned on his heel and left the room before anyone could respond.

Dorramon looked stricken, but didn't say a word as he watched Raman leave the room. He smoothed over his expression, and looked back to Alannys. "Shall we go?"

She considered pushing for more information, but she didn't really have the energy for an argument, and she knew he didn't want to talk about it. So she just tightened her grip on his arm and walked with him out of the room, and didn't ask a thing about where they were going.

But she had to admit she worried about it, just a little.

♫

"And so our courageous leader fails us once again." Lord Diabon's tone was blistering, echoing through Castle Glennayre's cavernous library.

Lord Malrec turned away from him, back to the vast shelves that stretched from floor to domed ceiling, crammed with books. "How so?" His tone was mild. It was possible, Lord Diabon realized with growing anger, that he had not been listening at all.

"The woman is gone," he sneered. "Months spent in the preparation of the collar. Weeks in preparing Archford Estate to serve as a prison. All for the express purpose of breaking her down, of bending her to our will. All wasted."

Malrec thumbed through a leather-bound book, scanning a page here and there. He raised an eyebrow, but Diabon couldn't tell if it was in response to the conversation, or to something he had read. "Wasted?"

"What would you call it? The woman is gone, and with her our last chance of settling this with no risk to ourselves."

Lord Malrec slapped the book shut, and turned his

back to Diabon. "Well, that is certainly one view of the situation. I disagree, for what it is worth."

Diabon felt like his head might explode. "Would you care, then, to share your view of the situation?"

"Tell me, Diabon, have you ever considered the concept of a plan within a plan?"

Diabon's anger fizzled abruptly. At times like this he was never certain whether Lord Malrec was being forthright, or whether he was bluffing, attempting to extricate himself from the consequences of his continued failures. "A plan—within a plan?"

Lord Malrec chuckled. It made the hair stand up on the back of Diabon's neck. "Perhaps you should consider that there is a reason why I am the strategist of this alliance. I admit, it would have been very nice if she had broken. And we were closer even than you realize. If the young duke had taken but a few hours longer to complete his work..." He shook his head, but did not turn back around. "But I digress." He pulled a vellum folder off of the shelf, and turned to proffer it to Diabon. "Do you know what this is, my friend?"

Diabon looked distastefully down his nose at the folder, declining to touch it. "I am afraid that I do not."

"Oh, but you should! This is our guarantee, Diabon. This is our assurance that we will win. That we have won; our dear friends at the Great Palace just have not realized it yet." He peeled back the top sheet, and Diabon saw the unmistakable shapes of musical notes.

"This—this is music?"

"Not just any music. In this folder are the Song of Joining and the Song of Raising. Alannys knows this—she thinks she discovered it accidentally because my temper got the better of me. Now do you see?"

"The woman thinks herself the Redeemer," Diabon said slowly.

"Just so. And so do her friends. They need these songs, Diabon. They will risk anything to acquire them.

"Then — they will come here."

"Yes. It will be soon. If we can't get Alannys to fight this battle for us, the next best thing is to decapitate their forces. I would bet that when Alannys comes here to recover these songs, she will bring with her the exact people we need to dispose of in order to win this. Would you care to bet against me?"

Diabon shook his head. "It seems to me that only a fool would bet against you, Lord Malrec."

Malrec smiled a thin-lipped smile. "It is certainly past time that you realized that, my friend."

Diabon couldn't help noticing that Lord Malrec's smile did not reach his eyes.

♫

Dorramon led Alannys out of the Lesser Hall, and down the arcade-lined corridor.

"Are you sure this is a good idea?" Alannys asked, looking around them with trepidation. "I mean, I'm not what you'd call presentable." That was probably an understatement. She hadn't bathed since Danningham Manor, she was wearing a short, sleeveless garment constructed from burlap sacks, she didn't have any shoes, and her hair was lopped off in a jagged, uneven mess above her shoulders.

Dorramon stopped suddenly, looking into her face. "You are always presentable here," he said seriously. "I'll have the head of anyone who dares to say otherwise."

She stared at him. Maybe it was her profound exhaustion, but his speech touched her. She reached up and brushed his face with her fingertips. "Thank you. But..."

He caught her hand in his and held it tight. "I know. You're dead on your feet. And we'll get you to your room just as soon as we can, I swear it. But I do have a promise to keep. You'll understand soon, and I hope you'll forgive me."

To her relief, Dorramon didn't take her to the vestibule that led outside the keep. He opened the ornate, carved door to the Palace Chapel, and held it for her. She stepped inside, wondering why on earth he had promised to bring her here.

The chapel was just as she remembered it, light and airy with smooth white marble and gold gilt. The altar, the chairs, the tapestries...everything was just as she remembered it. Except—

"Chen!"

He had his back to her, making his offerings at the altar, and he barely managed to turn around in time to catch her when she flew across the room to him, flinging her arms around his neck.

"Alannys!" He wrapped his arms around her, squeezing her so tight it was painful. "Alannys, thank the Muses you are safe. I was so *worried...*" He held her suddenly back at arm's length. "Alannys, you look terrible."

"I know."

"No, I mean, you look really terrible. What did he do to you?"

She shook her head. "I'd rather not talk about it. How did you find me?"

"You had just given the order to head back toward the Great Palace when you were taken. Don't you remember? I knew if you could get yourself away from Malrec, this is where you would come. So we came here immediately, as fast as we could. We're camped outside the palace walls right now." He shrugged uncomfortably. "I'm afraid I've been living in your wagon. It made me feel better, like maybe things were going to be all right. I hope you don't mind."

"Chen, you practically lived there anyway."

"This is true," he said.

She glanced behind her, hoping to find a chair she could fall into, and found Dorramon watching them. "Dorramon! I—he—this..." She couldn't think of a single thing to say, of any way to explain.

Dorramon laughed. It was a familiar, comforting sound, but she couldn't help thinking it sounded strangely distant now. Was she worrying over nothing? "Calm down. Chen told me everything."

"Everything?" She looked at Chen, and her eyes narrowed. "What everything is that? I'm afraid sometimes my everything and your everything are different."

Chen held up his hands defensively. "I told him the truth. I told him I'm crazy in love with you, and I've done everything in my power to steal you away, and you weren't having any of it. Does that assessment suit you?"

She could feel her cheeks burning. "I'm sorry, Chen. I'm—I'm not myself."

"I can see that."

She ignored that, and turned back to the king. "I'm sorry to you, too, Dorramon. I never realized how many problems I would cause for you, out there."

Dorramon shook his head and took her arm, supporting her. "Hush that kind of talk. You've got nothing to apologize for." He sighed. "The Singari arrived yesterday. I'm afraid they caught me at a bad time—I was stuck with nothing I could do to help you, waiting on Raman to finish his painting. And so as soon as I heard they were camped, I rode out to them."

"Really?" Alannys had a hard time imagining that. She figured it was probably the first time in history a King of Ravanmark had visited a Singari tribe.

"Naturally. I wanted to see if they could tell me anything more about what happened to you. I'm afraid I imposed on Chen for rather a long time. When he heard there was a rescue effort underway, he insisted on helping."

"I only left to come talk to the Muses," Chen said. "The more I heard about it—and the more we saw in the painting..." He shook his head. "I was afraid we had finally lost you."

Dorramon's hand tightened convulsively on her arm, and then he carefully released her. "We all were. Thank the Muses we didn't."

"I already have." Chen laughed, a stilted and uncomfortable sound, and looked away. "It's pretty clear I'm keeping you up, when what you need more than anything is rest. I'll let you go. But thank you for coming to see me. I really can't tell you how relieved I am to see that you're going to be all right."

"Thank you, Chen." She wasn't sure she had the energy to smile, but she tried anyway.

Before she knew what was going to happen, Chen leaned forward and kissed her forehead softly. "Goodbye, Alannys," he said, right next to her ear. "I hope you find everything you're looking for here."

She looked up in surprise, blinking fast to hide her tears. Everything he said and did tore at her heart. Goodbye—that meant no more days riding side-by-side through the country, no more nights eating together at bonfires, no more mornings waking up with him in her wagon—didn't it? She couldn't imagine it, it hurt too much. "Chen, I—" She cleared her throat and tried again. "I'm sorry."

"Don't apologize. I know you won't believe me, but I am happy for you." Even his familiar smile was painful, as he reached out to ruffle her hair. She tried to smile back, but it felt too shaky to be convincing. Chen turned and let himself out of the chapel, closing the door behind him.

For a long moment nobody spoke.

"Are you all right?" Dorramon finally asked. He looked concerned, he *sounded* concerned, but he made no move toward her, holding himself a few steps away.

"I—I think so."

"Are you sure? That sounded...final."

"Yes." Alannys laughed, but it was a harsh laugh, with no humor in it. "Yes, I think it was. He wasn't kidding about what he told you. He's tried everything he could think of. I'm afraid I must seem very cruel."

"No. At least, I can tell you he doesn't see you that way." He was talking to her normally, but it didn't *feel* normal at all. Why was he keeping such distance from her? "What about you, Alannys? Is that what you wanted?"

"I beg your pardon?"

He nodded at the door. "There's still time. You look upset."

"I *am* upset. He's a very good friend."

"I see." He appeared to consider that, studying her. "Do you think you will still be able to be friends?"

"I certainly hope so. I'm afraid we'll have to get along, if I get my way. What would you say if I made Chen my Redeemer's Steward to the Singari?"

"Redeemer's Steward...to the Singari?" Dorramon looked at her for a moment, thinking it through. "Your other stewards have been to holdings. Making a steward to the Singari would be like...separating them."

"Yes. It would be recognizing them as the distinct part of Ravanmark that they are. It wouldn't bring them under your control, like the holdings are. But it would give them a legitimate right to be here, in the eyes of the rest of the people. It might even start to get them some respect."

"Then it sounds like a good idea to me."

"Thank you, Dorramon."

"You're welcome. Now let's get you back to your rooms." He finally came over to her, taking her arm and leading her to the door.

She never would have made it back without his support. The walk back to her chambers seemed like the longest walk she had ever taken, and she almost wondered if it wasn't worth it. Sleeping in the courtyard might not be so bad, if it meant that she could sleep *now*.

But when she stood in her own sitting room again, she found it was worth it after all. Everything was as she remembered it, from the sofa and armchair on the area rug, to the tapestry hanging on the wall. The only thing missing was the sheet music she'd left covering every available surface.

That was probably an improvement.

She teared up. She had honestly believed she would never see this place again.

"I should let you rest," Dorramon said, but he didn't sound sure, and he didn't move any closer to the door. "Are you sure you will be all right?"

She looked at him, at the concern written plainly on his handsome face, and finally managed a real smile. "I don't know how you can look at me like that, with me as dirty and wretched as I am. If I felt better, I would ask you to stay."

Dorramon chuckled. He pulled her into his arms and kissed her. "If you felt better," he said, low and close to her ear, "you wouldn't have to ask."

A tap at the door startled her. She jumped, and then she was embarrassed for jumping.

Dorramon smiled. "Come in," he called, but he didn't release her.

Tralice exploded into the room with more energy than Alannys could imagine having ever again. "My Lord King! I've just heard, I—" She gasped, her eyes bulging. "My

Lady—you're already here! I'm so happy to see you, I— you look terrible!" She finally stopped for breath. "I'm glad you're back, my Lady, but we can't have you looking like that! I'll just fill the tub, then." She bustled through the arch into the bedroom, clucking disapprovingly.

Dorramon laughed. "I would say that's probably my cue to leave."

"Probably." But she didn't let go of him. "Thank you, Dorramon. You and Raman saved my life. He would have let me die there, just to be sure that if I wouldn't help him, I couldn't help anyone else."

Dorramon sighed. "At some point, we're going to have to talk about what happened. But tonight, it's enough just to have you home."

"More than enough," she said.

"I'll see you in the morning, then. Sleep well."

Dorramon kissed her once more, then left the room, closing the door as quietly as if she were already asleep.

Sleep was tempting. The giant bed waited just through the archway, practically calling her name. But she couldn't ignore Tralice working in the bathroom, and a hot bath was even more tempting.

After a long soak, with freshly scrubbed, trimmed hair and a clean nightgown, Tralice brought her a fruit and cheese tray and a pitcher of berry juice in the sitting room. She ate until hunger no longer cramped her stomach, and drank until her mouth was no longer painfully dry.

Then she dragged herself into the bedroom and collapsed into a black, dreamless sleep. It suited her fine— just being back at the Great Palace was a dream come true.

She just hoped she wouldn't wake up in the morning and find the dream was over.

♫

Unfortunately, her sleep did not remain dreamless all night. Perhaps it was only normal after all she had been through; perhaps she should have expected nightmares.

After a few hours of sleep, her dreams turned to twisting mazes fraught with severed heads, with endless labor and blistering, burning thirst. She was surrounded by paintings that never closed, by watching eyes that never slept. And through it all the crowds kept chanting "The king is dead. Long live the king!"

But it wasn't until Lord Malrec reached through one of the paintings and grabbed her that she screamed.

She sat straight up in the dark, panicked and disoriented, trying to figure out where she was.

"Everything is all right. You are safe." The voice was soothing; washing over her ears like healing balm. She could feel a warm hand wrap around hers.

Even before she registered his silhouette sitting on the edge of her bed, she recognized the voice as Dorramon's. It calmed her, and slowly things started making sense again.

"I'm sorry." Her voice was raspy from sleep or from screaming. "I didn't mean to wake you."

"Don't apologize. I think I'd worry about you if you didn't have nightmares, after what you've been through."

"Maybe so," she said, "but you'd think I could have them without waking you, too."

He laughed. "I'm just glad you're here to wake me."

"Me, too." She could remember only too well a time when she had thought she would never hear his voice again—which reminded her of something else. "You know," she began, trying hard to sound casual.

Dorramon's hand tightened suddenly around hers. "What?" He sounded as though he was on his guard.

So much for casual. "Nothing important. I was just thinking...back at Archford Estate, you threatened to sing against Helva. It occurred to me that I have never actually heard you sing."

It was hard to be sure in the darkness, but his face

seemed to be red. "Yes. Well...if it makes you feel any better, I can tell you that very few people have. You know I was raised to hide my Talent. And then, when Tryn was executed — my parents told me I had caused his death. Because I had sung. So you can imagine I don't do it often. That's why I asked you to sing in Westmore Forest — when we were attacked — rather than do it myself. I was so far out of practice, I don't think I could have saved us then. I literally had not sung a note in years."

"That's too bad."

"Why?"

"I've listened to that way you speak-sing, Dorramon — when you want to use your Talent but you don't dare sing. Like you did when I woke up just now. It never fails you. I think you would be a very good singer."

"Is that so?" It wasn't really a question. He sounded amused.

"Yes, that's so." She wanted to sound offended, but she was too tired. She fell back against her pillows with a sigh she couldn't suppress. "And if I could keep my eyes open, I'd argue with you until you admitted it."

Dorramon didn't say anything. But she felt his fingers stroke the back of her hand, and as her eyes fell shut of their own volition, she heard him begin to softly sing, a lullaby just for her.

She smiled. She had time to reflect that he was, indeed, a very good singer, before the music swept her off to sleep.

♫

When Alannys woke up the next morning in her own soft bed, with sunlight streaming in through the window and casting a cheery light through her chambers, she finally began to accept that maybe this was real after all. Maybe she really had seen the last of the prison that the ruins of Archford Estate had become. Maybe they really had foiled Lord Malrec's plans. And maybe Dorramon really had sung her to sleep after her nightmare last night.

She blushed, remembering that. It seemed intimate, somehow. She had sung for Chen, and with Chen, and Chen had sung to her, more than once. Why was this so different?

She felt like she had been lying in the same position for hours, and she was stiff all over. She stretched, and pushed herself to sit up against the pillows.

The sound of movement out in the sitting room startled her, and she froze. She had thought she was alone here.

Kalyn peeked in through the archway at her. "Lady Alannys, you're awake!"

Alannys relaxed. "Apparently so." She frowned at the sunlight scattering across the floor. "Although it seems I've overslept."

"Tommyrot," Kalyn said. "You're not on any schedule here. You sit right there, and I'll bring you your breakfast."

She disappeared, and came back in shortly with a covered platter on a tray that she propped up on the bed, over Alannys's knees.

"Thank you," Alannys said. "But you shouldn't be waiting on me, Kalyn. You aren't a servant here."

"More's the pity! I certainly would have done a better job of this. His Highness thought you might want your rest this morning, and ordered that you should not be disturbed with breakfast. He ordered your breakfast brought into your rooms instead. So the silly girl puts it on the table in the sitting room and leaves!"

"Is that wrong?"

Kalyn shook her head impatiently. "Not under normal circumstances, no. But after what you've been through, it's clear you need your rest. I decided I would wait here so I could bring this to you, so you wouldn't have to go hunting for it."

"Thank you, Kalyn. I really do appreciate it."

Kalyn smiled. "Don't give it another thought. I can't do the things you can do, Alannys, or the things Raman and the king do. I try to help by doing the things I know how to do. A smoothly running household isn't grand or important, but it is difficult to do grand or important things without one."

"I'll second that." Alannys peeked under the cover on her breakfast dish, and found poached eggs, with toasted bread and fried potatoes. All at once she was ravenously hungry.

"I'm going to go now so you can eat," Kalyn said. "I'll let Raman and the king know you are awake and well—they were asking after you this morning. And I'll send your silly maid in to check on you. Rest well."

"I will. Thank you, Kalyn."

Kalyn curtsied and let herself out of the room.

Everything on the breakfast tray tasted as good as it smelled, and it didn't take her long to finish it all. She was just considering taking her dirty dishes to the sitting room, when she heard a knock at the door. "Come in," she called.

Tralice hurried into the room, out of breath and clutching a bundle of fabric to her chest. Her curly black hair was disheveled, and her dress was rumpled. Alannys wondered how long she'd been running, and why. "Ach, my Lady, I'm sorry I wasn't here when you woke up! I meant to bring you your breakfast, really I did, but it took forever to find this and—"

"Tralice! Breathe!" Alannys cut her off, trying not to laugh. "It sounds like Kalyn must have said something to you."

Tralice drew herself up to her full height; while it wasn't much, it did show pretty clearly that she was offended. "Indeed she did! And I might be excused for saying that Lady Kalyn is fearsome when she's angry!"

Alannys couldn't imagine it, not really. But she tried not to let on. "I'm sorry, Tralice. I didn't put her up to that. I'm afraid Kalyn just has strong ideas about how things should be done."

"Oh, I wasn't trying to say—that is, I never for one moment suspected—" She stopped, and forced herself to laugh. "I know you better than that, my Lady. And I don't blame Lady Kalyn—not at all. If I was about to become an arch-prince's wife, you can bet nobody could do this job well enough to suit me. But I had a good reason!"

"Good...reason?"

"Just so! I was looking for this!" Tralice raised the fabric bundle as if she was brandishing it at her. "Took nigh on to forever to find it, too."

She sounded proud of herself. Alannys knew she had to be missing something, but she couldn't even guess what. "It...did? What *is* it, exactly?"

"It's a dress, my Lady." She shook out the bundle, revealing a white linen dress with a bright blue overdress. Glittering silver embroidery adorned the bodice and the edge of the skirt. The particular shade of blue reminded her of Dorramon's cloak. She shied away from the other associations the blue fabric brought to mind. "Princess Delline wore it once, years ago," Tralice said. "I thought...with your hair...it would be adorable." She glanced at Alannys, and it wasn't hard to see the worry in her dark eyes. "Not that there's anything *wrong* with your hair, my Lady—I know it wasn't your choice, and I did trim it up the best I could. But still...ladies just don't wear their hair that short. It will take some care to make it look good, and save you as much embarrassment as we can. I thought this dress would help."

"I—I see."

"I *was* thinking of you, my Lady, just as much as Lady Kalyn, in my own way."

"You certainly were." The realization touched her—it felt good to be among friends again. "Thank you, Tralice."

"Don't bother thanking me. Just hand me those dishes, and we'll get you dressed. Then we'll know whether all that searching amounted to anything."

The dress fit well, which was encouraging. Tralice seemed pleased, if the bounce in her step and her constant chatter were any indications. "I was sure enough right, my Lady—sure enough! Why, you're as cute as a ceramic poppet, and that's honest as Muse's song."

No sooner had Tralice fastened the last hook than they heard a quiet tap at the door. Tralice hurried to answer it, and Alannys followed her out into the sitting room.

Raman came in. "Good morning, Alannys." He glanced around the sitting room in surprise. "No stacks of music this morning?"

"No. They had cleared it out before I even came in last night. I'm glad—I think looking at it now would feel like failure."

Tralice brought the dirty dishes out of the bedroom. "I'll leave you two to catch up." She closed the door behind her.

Alannys settled into the chair, pleased to be able to sit in it again. "Have a seat, Raman, and let's hear what's on your mind."

Raman perched himself on the edge of the sofa. He looked uncomfortable. "I just wanted to talk to you. I haven't been able to thank you properly for saving my life."

"You know that's not necessary. Besides, you saved mine first. How are you doing with that?"

Raman shrugged. "A little stiff. I get winded easily. But I'm not complaining—I'm lucky just to be here. I'm sorry I didn't ride back out to join you as soon as I was able. Dorramon practically forbade it. He said he needed my help here, if you can imagine."

"Hmm." Alannys could remember more than once when Raman had talked about how unnecessary he was at court. "That does seem strange. Tell me, Raman, how have things been? I've only heard what Dorramon has chosen to tell me, and I'm afraid he may not have presented a...balanced view."

Raman laughed out loud. "I swear you should be a diplomat. You'd be a natural. No, I'll wager 'balanced' doesn't even begin to describe it. I've never seen him so stubborn. And I've never seen him so set on a path so sure to lead to trouble."

"So he still isn't receiving envoys from Cadenda."

"No. There's talk that a delegation is on their way right now. Dorramon has already said he won't receive them, even though it is rumored a member of the Cadendan royal family accompanies them."

"You don't think it's Varilyn?" Alannys said in sudden alarm.

Raman smiled at her, but it was a knowing smile. "No. I don't think it's the princess—I doubt wild horses could drag her to Ravanmark right now. Her embarrassment is too acute. No, someone else has come to speak on her behalf. Some have even said King Rathmar of Cadenda himself travels with the delegation."

"The King of Cadenda," Alannys echoed, her mind racing. "And yet he's already said he won't receive them. What does he hope to accomplish?"

Raman threw his hands up in utter frustration. "How should I know? He won't talk to me! If I try to discuss any of this with him, he leaves. He won't explain anything."

Alannys couldn't make sense of it. If Dorramon was willing to marry Varilyn to prevent war, this was the time to say so. And yet he did not, steadfastly refusing to speak to Cadenda at all. If, on the other hand, he had decided to marry her, then where was the sense in allowing this dangerous stalemate to continue?

She had to admit it was all speculation, with little fact to support it. Dorramon had not explained anything to Raman, and he certainly had not explained anything to her. How could either of them hope to make sense of his actions?

Alannys shook her head. "It doesn't really matter, I suppose. Dorramon is the king, and he's going to do what he thinks he needs to do, regardless of what either of us says about it."

"Regardless of what *I* say about it, in any event," Raman said. "I don't think he would dismiss you so readily."

"What are you suggesting?"

"Merely that you should discuss this with him. I think he would listen to you. He might even talk to you."

"Okay," she said, but even she could hear the reluctance in her tone. She could probably imagine a more awkward conversation she could have with Dorramon, if she tried. She just couldn't do it right now.

Alannys stood up suddenly, eager to leave that train of thought behind.

Raman looked up at her in surprise. "Are you leaving?"

"Not exactly. I need to go out to the Singari camp. There are some things I need to do."

"Are you sure that's wise? I'm not sure you should be out of bed at all today, let alone out of the palace."

She shook her head. "I don't think I have much choice. I don't know how long they are going to stay."

Raman sat back and crossed his arms. He looked serious—was it her imagination, or was there a mischievous twinkle in his eye? "From what I hear, they aren't going to be in any hurry to leave without you."

Alannys could feel her cheeks burning. "Well, be that as it may," she said airily, "I prefer not to make them wait on me."

He stood up, laughing. "I'm only teasing you. I can see I'm not going to talk you out of this. I don't think you should go alone, though. Will you at least wait while I go tell Dorramon what you're up to?"

"What? Why?"

"I imagine he'll want to come with you. I will, if he doesn't. I'm serious, I don't think you should wander around alone, especially in your state."

She frowned. "But doesn't the king have more important things to do than escort me around the grounds?"

"Yes." He sighed. "But honestly, he's past the point of caring, Alannys. Just wait, will you?"

"No. No, I think I'll come with you instead. I haven't got my fill of being back yet—I don't want to be left here alone. Is it all right with you if I tag along?"

"It's more than all right, it's terrific. Life gets pretty boring around here without you causing a stir every couple of hours." He offered his arm, and his smile was genuine.

She had to laugh as she took his arm and they left the room. At the same time though, she couldn't help but think a laugh had been the only purpose of his remark.

It didn't sound like things had been boring at the Great Palace for a long time.

♫

Alannys had never seen the cavernous Great Hall quite so empty. A few courtiers dotted the long room, carrying on quiet conversations with strained expressions. None of the rulers of the holdings were in attendance, and no foreign ambassadors jockeyed for position near the throne. The hall was oppressively quiet.

She couldn't hide her surprise. "How long has it been

like this?" The words were barely a murmur; even a normal speaking voice would have been obtrusive in the tomblike atmosphere.

Raman shook his head. "Not long. When Lord Malrec abducted you, word spread like wildfire. People scattered from the Great Palace like rats from a sinking ship—everyone knew that if the Dark Alliance had you, if they'd been bold enough to make a move like that against you, an attack on the king directly couldn't be far behind."

"So they left."

His eyes cut to her, but he did not turn his head. "Don't sound so bitter. Everyone knows the king is Malrec's real target—it isn't the job of the courtiers or the people to be human shields for him."

Alannys said nothing, but she could feel her face tighten, looking up the long hall at Dorramon, sitting leaned to one side in his throne, deep in conversation with Captain Grayble. He seemed so vulnerable, and there was so little she could do to protect him. She remembered all the school children she had seen playing kings and queens —even herself—and she shook her head. It seemed to her right now the height of folly to aspire to a throne, any throne. Too much responsibility, too little fun, and no way to please everyone who relied on you—who would want that? The sense of duty Dorramon carried like an albatross around his neck would have crushed a lesser man years ago.

Still, she relished the sight, happy just to be there to see him. She would have gladly stood there unnoticed until he finished his business with the captain, but a page stepped solemnly to the edge of the dais to receive them. She and Raman knelt.

"The Crown recognizes Raman, Arch-Prince of Ravanmark, and Alannys, Redeemer of the Realm. His Majesty bids you approach."

Raman stood, and helped her to her feet.

"What a pleasant surprise," Dorramon said. "I didn't expect to see you out and about today." He studied her intensely, and she felt her color rise.

His attention unsettled her, and she tried to smile. "I hate sitting. I can recuperate just as well on my feet, right?"

"Perhaps." He didn't sound convinced. He stood up and approached her, looking critically at her face. "I don't know what happened to you, but I don't think it's going to be as easy as that to shake."

Captain Grayble frowned at her. "My Lady, what is that around your neck?"

"The Collar of Silence," she said sourly. "It suppresses any use of Talent. Or rather, I can use it, but the collar chokes me until I stop."

"What a horrible device." Captain Grayble looked alarmed—it was the first time Alannys had ever seen a look like that on his craggy face. "Can't you remove it?"

She shook her head. "It has a lock on it. I assume Lord Malrec still has the key."

Grayble glowered like a thundercloud. "You can't sing, and you aren't carrying Songstrike. You are completely, totally unarmed. Do you imagine the cloaked assassin has conceded defeat?"

She couldn't meet his eyes. "No. I—I don't know what I was thinking. I'll wear Songstrike from now on."

Dorramon reached out and ran a finger gently along the front of the collar. "We do need to figure out how to get that off of you, though."

"That ought to be easy," Alannys said sarcastically. "I imagine Lord Malrec will gladly give me the key if I just say please."

"No," Raman said, "but maybe we don't need the key. What is this thing made of, some kind of treated eel skin?"

He reached into his belt and pulled out a dagger.

"I don't know if that's such a good idea." Dorramon sounded alarmed. "I think that eel skin has been treated with more than just tannin."

"Hold still," Raman told her, slipping the fingers of his left hand between the collar and her throat. He raised the dagger, and sawed against the surface of the collar.

The collar clamped down instantly, stronger than Alannys had ever felt it. She collapsed to her knees, completely unable to breathe. Raman fell with her, dropping the dagger.

Slowly the collar relaxed, and Alannys sucked in ragged, panting gasps of air. Raman freed his hand and sat back on his heels, rubbing his fingers and staring at her in shock.

"Perhaps it would work better if the blade was inserted under the collar." Grayble sounded shaken. "The collar would damage itself when it constricted."

Dorramon and Raman were shaking their heads before the captain even finished speaking.

"We'd kill her," Raman said. "It's too tight—I couldn't even get my fingers out. And her neck is going to be softer than that collar. The dagger would jam into her throat before it even marked the collar."

"It appears," Alannys said hoarsely, "I'm going to have to live with the collar for the time being."

Dorramon offered his hand to help her to her feet. "I am sorry. I wish there was something we could do."

Alannys knew that she was holding onto his hand longer than was strictly necessary, but she couldn't seem to help it. "I suppose I'll survive. I actually didn't come to pester you about the collar."

"No? What can I help you with?"

"You can talk some sense into her," Raman said. "Tell her she is in no shape to go traipsing out to the Singari."

Dorramon seemed amused at Raman's outburst, but at the last word he looked back at her sharply. "You're going all the way out there?"

She could feel her face redden. "I need to. All of my things are out there. And I need to talk to Chen before he leaves."

Everyone looked at Dorramon for some reaction to this.

He gave none. He watched her thoughtfully for a moment, rubbing his chin. "Raman, take over for me."

"What?" Raman sounded like that was not the response he had expected.

"I'm going with her. I need you to watch things here. It's not as if the Great Hall is swarmed with people. Besides," he said cryptically, "you're going to have to get used to being in charge at some point."

Raman's face colored. "Look, Dorramon, I don't know if—"

"Oh, so you're giving up, then? I suppose that's probably for the best; the place was awfully rough, after all. I'll just—"

"All right, damn you." Raman stomped over and stood next to the throne, arms crossed and glowering. "Go on, get. I'll handle anything that comes up."

Alannys thought that was a peculiar exchange. Clearly there was more going on here than she understood. She would have asked them about it, but Dorramon immediately turned and summoned the page who had greeted her.

"I need the carriage," he said.

The page didn't question or hesitate. He dropped a quick bow and ran out of the Great Hall, moving nearly soundlessly on the stone floor in his soft slippers.

"It's good to be king," Alannys said.

Dorramon laughed. He took her arm and they started after the page, leaving Grayble and Raman on the dais.

"Sometimes."

By the time they left the hall, Alannys could feel her legs wobbling with every step she took. Her knees were jelly, and she clung to Dorramon's arm tighter than should have been necessary. She was doing her best to control her breathing, to hide how hard she was working just to stay upright.

"Are you all right?" Dorramon's tone was light, but the look he gave her was very sharp and focused. "Are you sure this is a good idea?"

"No." She didn't indicate which question she was answering. Maybe she was answering both. "It doesn't really matter. I have to go. Everything I have is out there."

He searched her face for a long moment. "Not everything, I think." His gaze slid away, out over the unusually thin crowds milling in the Inner Ward. "You don't have to go yourself. We could send a servant to collect your things."

"I know. But it wouldn't be right. I've been with them for months, Dorramon, through things I can't even describe properly. They deserve more than that. I can't take my leave of them by proxy."

He looked into her eyes, thinking thoughts she couldn't read. "Very well," he said finally. "You know I will help you however I can."

The royal carriage arrived in a clatter of hoofbeats, precluding any further conversation for the moment. The carriage gleamed in the morning sun, white and polished, sunlight glinting off of windows so clean and clear they sparkled. Gold trim accented the wheels and the ornamental curls and swirls that adorned the carriage frame and top. Lanterns were mounted to each of the four corners of the passenger cabin, and purple flags bearing the red and blue royal crest fluttered above. A uniformed footman rode on the back, and a pair of well-matched white horses pulled the whole affair.

Alannys swallowed hard. Would she ever get used to the pomp and circumstance that surrounded Ravanmark's royalty?

The footman hopped down from his perch and held the door open for them, revealing a comfortable-looking interior completely upholstered in light blue silk. Alannys couldn't have afforded a scarf made of that silk before she came to Ravanmark, and now she was going to sit on it? She surveyed the inside of the carriage doubtfully, trying to get her mind around it.

Dorramon smiled at her. Of course he couldn't have had any idea what she was thinking, but his eyes danced with what appeared to be amusement. "Is everything all right?"

"All right." She looked from the opulent carriage to him, and back again. "Everything is more than all right. Everything is fabulous. Especially this. Do you realize that this carriage is worth more than the apartment I used to live in? I've never seen anything so nice."

"Is that so? You can't have been traveling with the right sort of people, then."

She drew herself up in mock-indignation. "The last carriage I was in belonged to Lord Arik. Perhaps you'd like to tell him he's the wrong sort of person?"

Dorramon laughed. "Peace! You win. I was only teasing you."

"Hmm." She looked at the few people in the Inner Ward, trying to go about their business while sneaking glances at the royal carriage, and at the footman, rigidly holding the door and pretending to hear none of their exchange. "It's possible I was exaggerating just a little. I never actually rode in the carriage, I only helped Raman in."

"Well, then." Dorramon offered his hand. "Allow me to

return the favor for him."

He helped her up into the carriage. Inside, the rich blue silk covered two facing bench-style seats, cushioned and comfortable. Alannys sat down on the rear bench, fighting a sense of unreality. It all seemed worlds away from anywhere she had been, anything she had done, for months.

Dorramon stepped up into the carriage behind her, and settled himself on the seat opposite her. That seemed strange to her — wouldn't he normally sit with her?

"My Lord King!" The footman spoke for the first time, and he sounded positively scandalized. "You mustn't— she shouldn't..." He trailed off, swallowing hard under Dorramon's grim stare.

"Everything in this carriage is fine," Dorramon said, in a voice that was quiet but very, very firm. "I've chosen my seat. Let's get moving, please."

"Your Highness..." The footman watched him for a moment longer, then frowned at Alannys. "At least put the window curtains down," he snapped, "so no one will see your insolence." He shut the door.

Alannys frowned out the window, watching the footman walk stiffly to his post on the back of the carriage. "Dorramon, why —"

"It's nothing," Dorramon said, smiling. "He was out of line, nothing for you to worry about. Next time we take out the carriage, there will be a new footman. I'll see to that."

Evidently that was supposed to make her feel better. It didn't, really — how could she say whether the footman deserved that or not, when she didn't even understand his complaint? Dorramon clearly wasn't going to explain, though. At least, she figured it couldn't hurt to follow the footman's advice.

But as soon as she reached for the curtain, Dorramon

leaned forward and grabbed her hand. "No, leave it. What's the point of a carriage ride on a pretty day if it's closed up and dark, and you can't even see where you're going?"

"Dorramon..."

The carriage lurched into motion. "There, see, we're off. Look out, enjoy the views. Do you make it a general habit to argue with kings? It seems ill-advised."

She laughed, letting him win this one, and turned toward the window. "I suppose it does, at that."

The Inner Ward had seemed desolate, as all the nobles and courtiers who frequented it took themselves back to their affluent homelands, as far as they could get from the epicenter of the coming war. But in the Outer Ward, things could not have been more different. The Outer Ward was not home to the wealthy or the influential. These people worked hard for their livings, and by and large they were poor. They had their families and their livelihoods, and not much else.

And yet, Alannys realized, as scenes of the crowded ward moved past the window, they had *stayed*. They did not have the means of the nobles at their disposal, but even the poorest among these people could have left, even if it meant walking out through the main gate carrying their possessions on their backs. But they had not. The Outer Ward seemed even more crowded than the last time she had seen it, as everyone who lived here pulled in tight and buckled down for war.

Even now she could see children tossing flower petals towards the carriage. Where had they managed to come up with flower petals? She had no idea, but the gesture moved her. Men doffed their caps and saluted as they passed; women paused in their labors to wave at the passing royal carriage. "Long live the king!" she heard more than once. "Long live King Dorramon!"

"Dark indeed must be the thoughts behind a frown as deep as that," Dorramon said.

She turned away from the window, and found him watching her. She couldn't smile and feel right about it, but she did try not to frown. "I'm sorry. I guess I'm not very good company. I just—I never realized, I suppose, how great the differences are between the nobility and the commoners. It seems like all of the nobles have abandoned you, running to safety where they can wait and see who comes out on top. But these people, they still support you."

"Yes." He looked out the window, as though he might find the words he sought in the crammed, colorful Outer Ward. "I have urged them all to leave, you know. Yet they remain. There are those who mutter against me, but..." He shrugged. "I don't know if I can explain that so it makes sense, not really. Politics...well, it's almost like a game for some nobles. They spend their entire life jockeying for position, scrambling for more than whatever they already have. A civil war like this isn't about what is best for the country—to them, it's about what looks most likely to advance their position. Do you think either Lord Diabon or Baron Prubard honestly believe Ravanmark—or even their own holdings—would be better served with Lord Malrec as king? It's all about whose coattails they can ride to the greatest success. These people around us now, I don't believe they look at things that way. I'm king, Lord Malrec is king—but their lot is very much the same. Things would be worse under Malrec, certainly—but it's mainly a matter of degree. The kingdom is prosperous now, and lives are the best they've ever been, perhaps. But there is still a gulf that separates common and noble, and no king can bridge that. Do you see? To these people, I *am* Ravanmark. And they love what Ravanmark is now. They don't want to hand that over to Lord Malrec or anyone like him."

She nodded. "Of course not. I understand that. What I can't understand are the people who do support Malrec—not just Diabon and Prubard, but all of the others, the peasants and merchants and aristocrats and all of them. What are *they* thinking?"

"How could I know?" Dorramon shrugged. "Maybe they don't realize how evil he really is—Lord Malrec can be quite charismatic when he decides to. Or maybe they think like the nobles do—maybe they really believe their lot would be better. I don't suppose it matters, in the end."

"No," Alannys said with dry humor, "I don't suppose it does."

♫

Before Dorramon and Alannys reached the drawbridge, half a dozen Royal Guardsmen on horses took up positions around the royal carriage. This surprised Alannys, then she felt foolish for her surprise. They were on the brink of war, after all. There was no such thing as being too careful.

War. She had known it was coming for months, had seen it building in the places she traveled. Hadn't she and the Singari she led been accosted only recently by those looking to recruit them to fight? Hadn't she only just escaped from Lord Malrec's most desperate, most brutal attempt yet to secure the one weapon he felt would win the war in one stroke—her?

And yet none of that seemed real, it didn't drive the sharp edge of reality into her being the way it did to see the troops encamped on the gentle slope of the hill, encircling the Great Palace. She could see soldiers practicing training exercises, and runners carrying messages across the camps. Men sharpened blades, and waxed bowstrings. Farther out, she could see scouts mounted on horseback, patrolling the edges of Westmore Forest. They all expected attack any time, and they all knew it would come from Castle Glennayre.

She frowned. She couldn't argue their logic, but it seemed wrong somehow.

Before she could sort out what was bothering her, the carriage had left the military encampment behind, and she could see the familiar sprawl of the Singari camp at the foot of the low hill they had descended.

Her breath caught in her throat—it felt strange and *wrong* to be approaching this particular camp on anything but her own horse, doing anything but heading to her own wagon. She leaned closer to the window, taking in every detail her eyes could capture. How could it seem so much the same, when everything was so *different*?

The carriage pulled to a smooth stop a respectful distance away from the camp. Alannys turned away from the window, ready to get out, but Dorramon wasn't moving. He sat biting his lip, watching her with an expression she wasn't sure she liked.

"Dorramon? Are you all right?"

She could feel the slight jostle as the footman dismounted. The door with its heavy glass window swung open.

"Dorramon?"

He shook himself, and gave her a smile that looked as though it had been carefully arranged on his face. "I'm fine, of course. Now, then, we had better be getting on with this business of yours."

He stepped out of the carriage, then turned and offered his hand to help her out.

She smoothed her dress and took it, placing her foot with exaggerated care on the footstep. In her mind she had a clear vision of herself landing flat on her face in the dirt and the grass—which was not exactly the picture of herself she hoped to leave with the Singari.

They were watching, of course. The stately approach of

the royal carriage could hardly have been missed. They stood in groups and alone, men with tools still in their hands, women with children hiding in their skirts. The king helped her from the carriage and took her arm, and they watched as though she was a stranger to them all.

She *felt* like a stranger.

Chen stepped in front of the camp to meet them. "Good morrow, your Highness, my Lady." He wore the same white shirt, tucked into the same black pants, with the same red sash around his waist. His black hair shone in the sun, brushing against his shoulders. He looked entirely the same as always.

Alannys knew this, and yet she couldn't help thinking he looked completely different. She took a closer look at him, and realized it wasn't so much how he looked, it was how he acted. Calm and cool—careful, even—as though Alannys had come to be part of that dangerous and capricious royalty he had warned her against so often. As though the months they had spent in each other's close company had never happened.

Her heart sank. But what could she do? It had to be this way, even she saw that. She'd had to make a choice. Everyone knew that.

What Chen had not realized was only that she had made that choice before she ever met him.

The silence was becoming awkward. Chen looked at her, eyebrows raised, and she realized all at once what was missing—the spark of playfulness, of joy, that had colored all of her interactions with him. He regarded her now with eyes that were flat, that did not dance. He had finally, she realized, given up hope on her.

Was that it, then? Did being Chen's friend—and only his friend--mean giving up the fun? She floundered for a moment, considering it.

Dorramon watched her, his face impassive. She

couldn't tell what he was thinking, but she wondered if he might be questioning her sanity. Had she dragged them both all the way out here so she could stare at Chen?

She held tighter to Dorramon's arm, smothering an urge to giggle that was probably insane. "Good morrow," she said, choosing to deal with the awkward pause by ignoring it entirely. "I hope we find you well this day. I wonder if I might come into camp? I need to gather my things."

"Of course." Chen stood back, holding his arms out beside him, inviting them to pass.

"Thank you." Still clutching Dorramon's arm, she started into the camp.

As she passed, Chen leaned close to her. "When did you get so formal?"

She laughed, but it was a tense laugh, with no real joy in the sound. "Sorry about that. I was just following your lead there."

"Well," he said, falling into step beside her, "that's a first."

This time she laughed out loud in genuine amusement. Dorramon glanced at her and smiled, and even Chen's eyes held some of the same mischievous laughter she was accustomed to seeing there. "Yeah," she said, "sorry about that, too."

The large brass lock hanging from the door of her wagon surprised her. Chen stepped up with a key and removed it.

"A lock?" She frowned. "I've never had to lock my door before."

Chen opened the door. He seemed grateful for the excuse not to look at her. "Well," he said uncomfortably, "Singari don't generally steal from their own. But an outsider...well, that could be a different story."

She crossed her arms and gave him her best stern glare.

"What, so you're telling me now there's some truth to this idea of Singari as thieves?"

"I didn't say anything like that! You know we—" He saw her laughing at him, and abruptly relaxed. "No. You know that. But this situation is—unique."

"I see." She walked past him into the wagon, and he followed. Dorramon came inside as well, and lingered by the door, as if he was not certain what he should do there. "So now that I am living inside the Great Palace, that changes me? I'm someone fundamentally different now?"

Chen regarded her thoughtfully. "I've never seen you wear a dress before."

"What?" She looked down at her white shift and blue overdress, and felt her face color. "No, my usual clothes are having a much-needed trip to the laundry. I still feel weird without them, to be honest. But when I'm planning extended trips across the countryside, I don't generally bring many day dresses along. I don't understand your point, Chen. Is that all I am to you, to all of the Singari—surface appearances? If I don't wear work clothes and carry a sword, I'm not to be trusted?"

Chen shook his head. "No, of course not. I never said anything like that. You always were good at putting words in my mouth. No ruler is ever beloved by every single one of their subjects, Alannys. That's all I'm saying. Now that you are absent, we thought your unguarded possessions might present too convenient an opportunity for those who would like to strike a parting blow at you."

"Oh." She didn't know what else to say.

He gave her a crooked smile. "Speechless? Today is a day for firsts, I guess. I told you that you will always have a place here, Alannys, and I meant it."

"I—thank you." She looked around the little room where she had spent so much time. All of the sudden she didn't even know where to begin in vacating it. She couldn't quite believe she would never see it again.

She pulled open the drawer on the writing desk, and started lifting things out of it. Quills, ink, paper—the wooden box full of tiles she found was Chen's, so she left that—her Redeemer's Steward medals, the map Lord Arik had given her...the drawer had more things in it than she had even remembered. She scooped everything out of it and laid it on the desktop so she wouldn't forget any of it. She hauled her violin out and laid it on top of the bed.

Chen handed her the shawl Nyrin gave her. "Don't forget this. You won't want to be without it."

She ran her fingers over the heavy weave, savoring the familiar feel of its texture under her fingers. "Oh, I couldn't. Lord Malrec gave it to you, remember?"

Chen snorted. "Ha, ha. I wish that had gone differently, Alannys. I would have loved to separate that bastard from his head for you. Take the shawl. You know you're going to need it."

"What is this?" Dorramon asked. He touched a finger to the dark material in Alannys's hands, then pulled it back. "This thing is from Lord Malrec?"

"No," Alannys said. "I was only teasing Chen. This shawl was a gift from a friend in a group called Ravan's Light. It's the same place the Talent-proofing solution came from. She gave this to me because it can be used to hide from paintings."

"Hide from paintings? And Malrec left it here?"

She shrugged, folding the shawl and laying it on top of her violin case. "I don't think he expected me to ever be in a position to use it again. He could have taken it to Archford, I suppose, but then there was always the chance I would manage to retrieve it. Thank you for keeping it safe for me, Chen."

Chen shrugged uncomfortably.

Alannys glanced around her room one last time. "I

think, if it's all right with you and the *zhotha*, that this wagon should go to Grald. His family doesn't have much. And he does a lot, in his deputy position."

Chen nodded. "I'll make it happen."

She slung her violin case over her shoulder, pulled the shawl over her head, and gathered her pile of assorted possessions into her arms. Both men offered to carry her things for her, but for reasons she couldn't articulate clearly even to herself, she refused. This was her leave-taking, after all, and she was going to move all of her things herself. It was symbolic to her, somehow.

She carried her things around to the back of the wagon, where Quicksilver was tied. The horse nickered at her and nuzzled his nose into her neck.

"I know," she said. "I'm glad to see you, too."

She piled all of her things except the shawl into Quicksilver's saddlebags, and strapped her violin case behind his saddle.

Then she realized what she had forgotten.

"Oh no!" she cried, and ran back into the wagon.

Alannys tossed the pillow aside and found it right where she had left it—the little wooden box the royal runner had brought her in House Orinthal. She scooped it up in both hands.

Dorramon and Chen were waiting for her outside.

"Are you all right?" Chen asked.

"Yes. I—I just forgot my box." Her fingers tightened around it convulsively.

Dorramon ran his fingers over the wood. "You kept this?"

"Of course! I pressed the flower. I even kept the wax seal. It's all in there."

He smiled brilliantly at her, as though she had answered a question he hadn't even asked, and put his arm around her shoulders. "Well, then, we had better get it packed with everything else. It wouldn't do to forget that."

"I should say not." She stowed the little box in the saddlebags with everything else, and dug around until she found a Redeemer's Steward medal. She pulled it out, and turned to Chen.

He looked from the satin ribbon dangling from her fingers to her face with an expression she couldn't identify. "Alannys, what are you up to?"

"Up to?" She tried to sound innocent, but she didn't think she had pulled it off. "I can't imagine what you could mean. When am I ever up to anything?"

He watched her warily, unconvinced.

"I've named a Redeemer's Steward in every province I've visited, Chen. But the Singari don't have one. I think it should be you."

"Me?" Chen said. She knew exactly what to make of his expression right then—he looked cornered. She might have guessed as much; Chen hated any kind of responsibility. "I'm already *kortha*. Don't you think you've done enough?"

She laughed. "I don't think so. The Redeemer's Steward is a role I kind of made up; you know that. In most places it's just an official permission for people to continue using their Talent without persecution. But for the Singari..." She hesitated, looking at the silver medallion turning slowly on its ribbon. "It's even more important for the Singari. You've seen what I've started here. You've been involved from the beginning. The Redeemer's Steward here needs to carry that on, and continue teaching. That has to be you, Chen. There's no one else who can do it."

"All right." He looked away. "You know I can't say no to you. Whatever you need, I'll do it."

"Thank you, Chen." She lowered the medal over his

head, and arranged the ribbon over his shoulders.

"Don't thank me yet. I may make a terrible mess out of all of this."

"No. You'll see, you'll be brilliant."

"Brilliant." Chen shook his head. "If you say so."

Alannys turned back to Quicksilver, and frowned. "I do have a problem, though. I have to admit I hadn't thought this far in advance. How am I going to ride Quicksilver back up to the Great Palace in this dress?"

"Perhaps you could tie him behind the carriage," Dorramon suggested.

"No," Chen said. "I think that would only upset him. Quicksilver has shown before he can be — difficult if Alannys is going somewhere and he isn't carrying her. How about if I ride him up for you?"

"You would do that for me? That would be great, Chen — you'd really get me out of a fix. Thank you so much."

Chen took Quicksilver's reins in his hands and stood back a little. He looked at her oddly, almost as though she had done something rude.

"What? What's the matter?"

Chen shook his head. "I don't know how to take you sometimes, Alannys. You've traveled the country for months with people by your side who would gladly die for you. The arch-prince very nearly did die, the way I hear it. And me...well, I can't even count the sticky situations I've gotten into with you, or the ones I've just barely gotten you out of. That doesn't seem to bother you, sometimes it seems like you don't even notice. But somebody offers you a minor favor, and it's like the biggest thing in the world to you."

Alannys could feel her face turn red. Her throat seemed suddenly dry. "Chen, that's — you know that's not true. You know I value everything you've done for me — and Dorramon, and Raman, and everyone else who has been put in harm's way for me. But what can I say? 'Gee, thanks, you really got me out of a fix' works fine for someone who just offered to take my horse home for me. But can I say that to Dorramon, who risked everything he had to free me from Castle Glennayre? Who stood in the royal catacombs between me and the man meant to assassinate me, without flinching? Who shielded me with his position, over and over again, increasing his own peril each time? Dorramon, who risked everything just to *know* me? Can I say it to Raman, who raced into my chambers in the middle of the night and nearly met his own death trying to save me from the cloaked swordsman? Who defended me to a mob demanding my blood not once, but twice? And what about you, Chen? Can I say that to someone who just barreled into a Talent-draining cavern to rescue me from the middle of a blood-sacrifice ritual?"

"Alannys, stop." Dorramon laid a hand on her shoulder, but she shook it off. She couldn't stop, not now.

"Can I say that to someone who just spent eighteen hours to dig me out of an avalanche? Eighteen hours digging in the snow, with every reason to believe I was dead at the bottom of it? Can I say that to someone who stood silent, someone who took a sword through the gut just to give me the chance to escape?" Alannys knew tears ran freely down her face, but she couldn't spare the time to wipe them away. She threw her hands up in a gesture of helpless frustration. "I owe debts bigger than I can pay all over Ravanmark. What would you have me do?"

Chen stepped forward and swept her into a crushing hug. "Stop. Stop—I'm sorry. I'm sorry, I never meant to cause this. You're right, of course you're right."

"No." She scrubbed at her eyes with the heels of her hands. "You're right, it's not enough. It could never be enough." She drew a shuddering breath and forced herself to look him in the eyes. "I'm sorry, Chen. I'm sorry I can't give you what you want from me. Even that wouldn't be enough to repay all that you've done for me. But I can't. I can't change how I feel. I know it doesn't make sense. But I just can't do it."

Chen kissed the top of her head. "I know. You don't have anything to apologize for." He stepped back from her and ran his hands through his hair. "Muses, I've got you in a state now. Look, everything is going to work out. You'll see. You two go on ahead. I'll bring Quicksilver along behind you."

"Are you sure?" She looked at him anxiously, suddenly nervous about going back to the palace. "I could—"

"No. Go now, quickly. It's better if he doesn't see you leaving."

She nodded and turned away. It took her a moment to realize that he may not have been talking about the horse at all.

♫

Dorramon put his arm around Alannys's waist and clamped her tightly to his side, as though he feared she might fall.

She could understand that. She thought the same thing herself. She wore her shawl over her head, more to hide her face from those around her than because she felt she might need it.

"I'm sorry." He handed her a linen handkerchief. "That had to be hard for you."

"I had not planned things quite that way, no." She dabbed at her eyes. "I shouldn't have dragged you out to see that. It seems like I've done nothing but cause you trouble today. What did I do wrong in the carriage?"

"Nothing. And you didn't drag me anywhere, if you'll permit me to take issue with your wording."

"My wording? Look, that isn't important. Your footman didn't seem to think whatever I did was nothing."

"So what? I've already told you, he'll be replaced. It seems to me that what just happened wasn't your fault. It wasn't a fair question."

"No, he had a point. Everyone has done so much for me, and what have I done to repay that? What *can* I do to repay that?"

The footman waited by the open carriage door, rigid and impassive. She gave him a smile she was pretty sure he didn't even see, and stepped inside, slumping down onto the seat like she might never get up again.

Dorramon sat down next to her, and regarded her thoughtfully. "Why do you feel any payment is necessary?"

"What?"

"Do you think these people—Chen, Raman, myself, anybody—did these things for you because they hoped to gain something from you in return?"

"Dorramon—I don't see why we're talking about this, to tell you the truth. It doesn't matter. But if I'm doing something wrong, I need to know, or I won't be able to fix it."

"No, I think it is important," he said, exactly as if he hadn't heard anything else she'd said. "You know this is going to bother you, right? You won't have any peace of mind until you settle this. So tell me, is that what you think?"

"No." She sighed, defeated. It sounded pretty awful when he put it that way. "No, of course not."

"Well, then, it seems clear that any debt that exists, exists entirely in your mind. No one else seems to expect that."

"It isn't that easy. I haven't done anything to deserve the sacrifices people make for me. They have to be acknowledged, somehow."

"Hmm." Dorramon looked out of the window for a

moment. "There exists, in Ravanmark, a class of people that I think embody the principles you are talking about. People who benefit constantly from the sacrifices others make for them. You wouldn't believe what people do for this class—they give them money, food, they build fantastic places for them to live. Because of the efforts and the sacrifices of everyone else, this class of people never knows hunger, or physical labor, or has to do without. People swear everything they have to this class. People even die protecting them. Do you know who I am talking about?"

"You're talking about yourself." The words were flat. "But Dorramon, that's different. You are a *king*. You are important. You—"

He held up a hand, and she fell silent. "Hear me out. You say I am important? What makes me so? Only the will of these people, only their willingness to have a king at all, and to have me as that king. How can I repay them for that, for all that they do?"

Alannys sighed impatiently. "I don't know." This still felt like distraction, like Dorramon avoiding subjects he didn't want to discuss.

"By *serving*, Alannys. Do you see? These people serve me, but I serve them as well. I serve the country, and that is how I repay the country's trust in me and sacrifice for me. Any wise ruler remembers that, any good ruler knows that they are the true servant, not the people they rule. They do everything for me. In return, everything I do must be for them."

"But..." She struggled with the concept, trying to get her head around what he was telling her, how it could possibly apply to her. "But I'm not a king, Dorramon. I'm nobody. How can my service be worth anything to anybody?"

He shook his head. "You have always said that. You've

always maintained you have no particular importance here. It isn't true, you must see that now. You are the Redeemer. And everything you have done in that role has been a repayment of everything Ravanmark has done for you. Do you see? All these months, all of the travel and the hardship and the danger and the sacrifice—that was the Redeemer serving Ravanmark. And you bear the scars to prove it." He took her hand in his, running his finger along the fine lines in the back of it.

"I had hoped you wouldn't notice those," she said, looking away.

"I didn't, until I saw you out in the sunlight. They really aren't very noticeable. Chen told me what had happened, he told me about the scars, but even so I didn't see them at all inside. Even outside in the sun..." He shook his head. "I don't think I would have seen them if I hadn't already known they were there."

"Oh." She didn't know what else to say.

The carriage rumbled over the big drawbridge. The shopping and socializing were in full swing out in the fair, so they veered left.

"He certainly seems to care for you," Dorramon said hesitantly. "I think...I got the impression he would be very happy if you stayed with the Singari."

She whipped her head around to look at him. "Is that what was the matter with you on the way out? Did you think I was going back out to stay?"

He looked uncomfortable. He glanced out the window next to him, and the image of him seemed to freeze in Alannys's mind; his strong profile outlined by the sunlight in the window next to him, his blue eyes sparkling with reflected light.

A deafening sound ripped through the carriage. The world tipped sideways, and heat washed over her like a physical force. Everything was motion, and sound, and a jumble of mixed-up sights and feelings that didn't make any sense.

She didn't even have time to panic. Before she could form a coherent thought, the world settled into darkness and silence, and she sank to the bottom of it, fell out of consciousness like a stone descending to the bottom of a murky lake.

♪

Alannys woke up coughing. It was hard to breathe. The air hung heavy around her, and everything smelled burnt. She hurt all over.

The last thing she remembered was riding in the royal carriage with Dorramon through the Outer Ward of the Great Palace. Why did she hurt all over?

She cracked an eye open. Everything looked as wrong as it smelled. She recognized the blue silk interior of the carriage, but it was turned funny. The bench seats rose on either side of her like plush blue columns, and she was lying flat on her back on the ground, in the spot where the door that she had used to get inside should have been. The other side of the carriage seemed an unnaturally long way off. Where the other door had hung there now gaped an open hole, surrounded by twisted, blackened metal. The air was gray and hazy.

"Your Highness? Your Highness!" She could hear the footman's voice drifting in from somewhere outside. He sounded frantic. "Your Highness, you must come away from there! The carriage is still unstable, and—great Muses, your Majesty, you must not *climb* on it!"

"If you aren't going to help me, kindly get out of the way." Dorramon sounded grim and determined, with none of the panic of his footman. "Lady Alannys is still in there. Do you hear me? She's still in there!"

"What? But your Highness..."

Alannys coughed again, a painful, convulsing cough that made her wonder how much of the haze in the air was also in her lungs. When she could open her eyes again, she saw Dorramon's face peering down at her through the ruined door frame above her. Soot smeared his face, and a cut above his left eye dripped blood onto his cheek.

"Thank the Muses," he said. "Can you stand?"

"I don't know," she said, but she pushed and struggled and managed to sit up. "What happened?"

"I don't know." He hoisted himself up higher onto the overturned carriage, and leaned farther in. "First things first. We've got to get you out of there. Then we'll worry about what happened."

Alannys braced herself against the scorched bench seats. Climbing out of the carriage was not as easy as she expected; the blue silk was slippery and soft and her slippers could find no purchase there. It seemed to take forever before she could reach up and grasp Dorramon's hand as he strained to reach her.

With the king's help, she scrambled out of the wrecked carriage and slid down the outside. By the time she stood on her feet in the open again, she was gasping for breath and her legs felt like rubber bands. She and Dorramon had both cut their arms on the jagged metal, and her dress was in tatters.

But she didn't even notice. The nightmare surrounding her held her attention entirely.

She knew where she was; it was the back corner of the Outer Ward. This part of the Great Palace was not as affluent as the other side, where the marketplace and inns were. Over here were the food storage facilities, and the run-down houses of those who worked there. Washlines of clothes strung back and forth across the alleys, hung with laundry that was little more than rags. The tanneries and candle makers were back here as well, and the stench of them was inescapable. The enormous curtain wall separated the Outer Ward from the Inner Ward, and on the other side of that wall, in the Inner Ward, was the barracks of the Royal Guard.

At least, that was how this part of the castle appeared under normal circumstances. The present circumstances, however, were anything but normal.

Behind her was the wreckage of the royal carriage, thrown over on its side in a twisted heap, both doors blown off, the royal flags lying limp over the mess like the skins of dead animals. The horses lay dead in a grotesque heap, still in their harnesses, their limbs and their long, graceful necks all protruding at unnatural angles. The driver was not far away, dead as well. It was difficult to look at the carriage and believe that anything living had come out of it.

The curtain wall had been breached. An enormous, gaping hole yawned, charred black around the edges, where the wall's solidity had once stood. Smoke wafted out across the Outer Ward. The shanties that had huddled up against that wall on the Outer Ward side were gone, the debris of them scattered across the ground like litter carelessly dropped from some giant child. The colorful rags that had dangled from the washlines now lay rumpled and knotted on the ground like the bright internal organs of some terrible beast, half burned and suitable only for decay. The barracks themselves had fared little better; the back half of the building was a crumbled, smoldering ruin.

Alannys looked around at that utter devastation, that nightmare so out of place in Ravanmark, and she knew there was only one person on the planet who could be responsible for such an atrocity.

Her hands started to shake, her knees trembled, and her breath came in great tearing gasps. How was such evil possible? An attack on her, alone, she could absorb—but this? Inside the very walls of the Great Palace itself? Her vision went spotty; she thought she might faint.

Dorramon grabbed her hand, and peered into her face. "Pull yourself together, Alannys. I know it's horrible. But there are people trapped in this, and they need our help."

Alannys nodded, and swallowed hard. "You're right. I'm sorry. I'm all right."

Dorramon summoned up a smile from somewhere for her. "No, you're not. But you will be." He patted her shoulder and turned toward the site of the blast.

Privately Alannys couldn't imagine that anything could be living in that massive, jumbled pile of crumbled stone and splintered wood. But she remembered her own miraculous survival in Eversnow Pass, and the Singari who dug her out despite all the evidence their eyes could offer that she must have been dead. She took a deep, steadying breath, and started to follow Dorramon. It wasn't easy—debris littered the ground and footing was uncertain.

"Steady there, my Lady." As if from nowhere, the footman appeared at her side, holding her elbow to support her. His uniform was torn and stained and even singed in places, and his face was bruised and bloodied, but he walked stalwartly alongside her into the rubble.

"Thank you," she said. She glanced sidelong at his face, alert for any lingering traces of anger or hostility in his expression. There were none—the man seemed to have put the whole incident behind him entirely.

For herself, it wasn't that easy. She didn't know what she had done, but she had obviously stepped out of line. And if she didn't know how she had messed up, what was to stop her from doing it again?

"While I've got you," she said hesitantly, "do you think...could you tell me what I did to upset you when I got in the carriage, when we left the palace?"

The footman looked at her, then looked at her again. "Are you serious? You really don't know?"

"I wouldn't ask if I wasn't serious. I asked Dorramon, but he wouldn't tell me."

"I see." The footman stopped walking, keeping them well out of earshot of the king. "I should probably not tell you either, then, but I would hate to see this happen again. I'm afraid his Majesty does not always place proper importance on these things." He crossed his arms. "Lady Alannys, in any carriage, the most important passenger sits in the back, facing forward."

"Then..." She gasped, and her hand flew to her mouth. "Then I placed myself *above the king* by sitting where I did?"

The footman nodded grimly. "And he did the same thing, by sitting across from you. He could have sat beside you, as he did on the way back, but he chose not to. On the way out, during the parade through the busiest part of the palace, he gave everyone who looked at the royal carriage the clear message that you are more important than him."

She should have known. She should have *known*. This was Dorramon, after all, who had made his own coronation as much about her as himself. She shook her head. "I'm sorry. It won't happen again."

The footman nodded. "I'm glad. I don't like to see—" His gaze drifted over her shoulder, and his eyes widened. "Your Highness, no! You must not move that alone—let me help you!" He ran off into the wreckage.

Alannys heard the footsteps running behind her before she registered the voice frantically calling her name and realized that it was Chen. He grabbed her by the shoulders and turned her to face him. "Great Muses! Alannys, are you all right?"

She nodded. "More shaken up than anything, I think."

He cast a critical eye over her. "If you say so. You're all

over blood and dirt. *Why* do these things always happen to you?"

Alannys shook her head. "I wish I knew. But this time, it isn't just me." She gestured helplessly at the destruction surrounding them. "Just look at this. I've never seen anything like it. What can we possibly do against something like this?"

Chen pulled his hands from her shoulders and sighed. "You aren't going to like the answer to that. But all we can do is what we can do, Alannys, no matter how little it might seem. All that we can do right now is what you and the king are already doing. And for what it's worth, I'll help."

"Thanks, Chen." She smiled, but it was a tired smile; she wasn't sure how long she would last at this. It seemed like her whole life lately was just recovering from the latest bad thing that had happened to her. The thought didn't make her feel any better.

Chen turned from her and pushed up his sleeves, helping the royal footman heft some heavy rocks. Alannys pushed her hair out of her face and looked around for Dorramon. She found him, not too far away, up to his knees in dirt and rubble.

Before she made it to him, she heard hard, fast footsteps and raised voices, coming at them from the opposite direction Chen had come. She recognized the voices before she could make out the faces: Raman and Grayble.

"Merciful Muses!" Raman's hand clamped around the grip of his sword; the tendons stood out like cords under his skin, though he must have known no sword could defend against what had happened here. "What devilry is this?"

"This was one of Lord Malrec's bombs." Alannys's tone was sour, but her voice shook. Dorramon glanced at her and waded over to her, supporting her with his hand under her elbow.

"Seven Hells!" Captain Grayble surveyed the Outer Ward as though everything he saw displeased him. "He has weapons capable of this?"

"It would appear that he does," Dorramon said. Alannys didn't see how he could be so calm. She'd been through a smaller bomb attack once before, and she still had to battle down panic, standing there looking at that. "But this is not the time to strategize. People need our help."

"Of course." Raman finally convinced his hand to part from his sword, and he and Captain Grayble joined the efforts to clear the rubble.

"Wagons!" Dorramon called. A page ran by them; he reached out and hooked the boy by the vest before he could pass. "Whatever errand you are on, I must ask it to wait. I need you to find every man you can with a wagon, and send him over here. Can you do that?"

The page nodded, his eyes wide. "Y—yes, your Highness."

"Thank you. Go quickly!"

The boy didn't wait to be told twice.

"Over here!" Chen shouted from deep in the debris, near the curtain wall. "There's someone alive over here!"

"Over there?" Dorramon echoed doubtfully. Alannys understood—she didn't know whether the bomb had been placed on the Inner Ward or Outer Ward side of the curtain wall, but either way the area was awfully close to ground zero. It was hard to imagine anything living in the scattered wreckage of the blast. But they both hurried over there, as fast as they could clamber through the rubble.

"Did I hear you right?" Alannys said. "You found someone alive in this?"

Chen nodded grimly. "Alive, but just barely."

They had found the mangled remains of a little shack, half buried under rock blasted from the curtain wall. Even as she approached, Alannys saw that Chen and the footman were hauling the survivor out of the debris.

When she got a clear look at the bright red underbust overdress and long black curls, Alannys stumbled and nearly fell down.

The survivor was Tralice.

♫

Alannys arranged some of the rags and half-burnt clothes and blankets they had found into a makeshift bed where they could put Tralice for the moment. She stood back, shaking her head, while Chen and the footman laid Tralice on the pile of dirty cloth scraps.

"I don't understand," she said. "Why was Tralice even out here?"

"I believe she lives here," Dorramon said, and then he frowned, too. "But it is an odd time for her to be out here —usually she would be working."

Chen looked at them in surprise. "You know her?"

Alannys nodded miserably. "She's my maid."

Chen looked from Tralice to Alannys with that expression she had seen so often lately—the one that reminded her how much things had changed. "She needs help, and there are no healers about. And I need to get back into the house to see if there are more survivors."

"I would gladly sing for her," Alannys said, touching the Collar of Silence on her throat, "if I could. Maybe I should go in while you sing."

"It's too dangerous in there," Chen said immediately. "The place is literally falling down. I won't let you get squished."

"I'll do it," Dorramon said quietly. "I'll sing."

Alannys looked at him in surprise, ready to object. She didn't doubt his abilities, but she didn't want to expose him to the risk.

But before she could say anything, Chen stood up, nodding to the king as he turned to leave. "Good luck, your Majesty. I'll keep you informed of our progress."

Chen walked away, and Dorramon sat down near Tralice, reaching for her limp hand, preparing to sing.

"Wait," Alannys said, and before she knew quite what she was going to do she had plunked herself down between Dorramon and Tralice.

"What do you plan to do now?" Dorramon sounded amused.

Alannys shook her head. "I'm not exactly sure how to explain it—it's something I noticed during my travels. Physical contact seems to play a role in the effects of singing."

"Does it?" He sounded interested, and his gaze was penetrating. "Did you have much opportunity, then, for singing with physical contact?"

She wanted to pretend she hadn't noticed his teasing, but her bright red face gave her away, so she slugged his arm instead. "I'm trying to help you! I can't pretend to understand how it all works, but I wonder, even though I can't sing, if I might help shoulder some of the cost. I don't know if it will work, but it's worth a try, isn't it?"

"I don't know..."

"Please, Dorramon. Let me at least try to help."

"All right," he sighed. "What is it you want to do?"

"Not much. I'm going to try to insert myself into this— maybe we can still use my energy for this even though I can't sing. But don't sing until I tell you." She grabbed Tralice's cold hand in one of hers, and Dorramon's warm hand in the other, sending tendrils of electricity up to her elbow. She closed her eyes, and whispered under her breath, "Oh, Muses, please let this work."

"Okay," she said out loud, eyes still closed. "Go ahead."

She could hear him take a deep breath, and then he sang.

"Oh, Muses, most holy and high,
Look down and grant Tralice strength,
Help her to fight to go on and to heal,
Bring her back to us to live."

Alannys learned a few things in the opening lines of the song. Any bare skin contact between her and Dorramon generated that familiar electric tingle, but singing intensified it to a crackling current that seemed to envelop them both.

Also, something about singing together, even when she sang only in her mind, turned the mindlink into a floodgate — wide-open, uncontrolled, and immersive, like swimming in each other's minds. The collar never twitched — they weren't *using* the mindlink, it was more like they *were* the mindlink. She couldn't have said whether the words they sang came from him or from her, or some magical fusion of both. She wasn't singing, but she could hear her own voice exactly as if she was. And she could hear Dorramon's voice inside her head, feel it resonating in the bones of her face.

She was dimly aware that Chen came back out and sat down to join them, taking Tralice's other hand, but she couldn't spare much attention for it, letting it register on the fringes of her consciousness, then fade away.

She didn't recall making any conscious decision to end the song, either — there was just a sudden awareness that it was no longer necessary, and her little group brought the music to a seemingly natural end, as if by mutual accord.

Music in a group of people was like a force of nature, beautiful and powerful, and scarier the more she learned about it.

Alannys sat back and released everyone, feeling sort of like resurfacing after a deep dive, or waking from a long dream.

Tralice's eyes fluttered open, and she pushed herself to sit up. "Where am I?" she asked thickly. "What happened?"

Alannys leaned forward, helping to support her. "It's all right. We're in the Outer Ward. There's been a bit of trouble."

"My — my Lady?" Tralice craned slowly around to look at her. "Ach, my Lady, you look a fright." The maid's eyes wandered down her own frame. "I look a fright! Lady Alannys, what happened here?"

Alannys hesitated, unsure how much to tell her. "What do you remember? There's been an explosion."

"Explosion?" Tralice's voice rose in alarm, and her face went suddenly pale. "I remember! The noise, and the shaking — Jard!" She grabbed Alannys by the arm. "Where is Jard?"

"I'm sorry," Alannys said. "But who is Jard?"

"My husband, my Lady! He was in the house with me — and my sister's two boys."

Alannys glanced at Chen. He met her eyes and shook his head.

"Tralice, I'm so sorry," she said. "But they didn't find any other survivors."

"What?" The single word was a despairing wail. "But — but — "

"I'm sorry," Alannys said again. "This was a bomb attack — it was Lord Malrec. There was nothing we could do."

Tralice's eyes, usually so saucy and full of laughter, seemed hollow and bleak. "Lord Malrec did this thing? With his Talent?"

Alannys nodded.

Tralice looked out across the devastation that surrounded them, at the charred and broken remains of what had been her home. Her face never changed. "You should not have saved me."

"What?"

Tralice shook her head, but she didn't even seem to see Alannys. "I don't want to live in a world where Talented people wreak this kind of destruction on normal folk. I don't want to live in a world without Jard." Her voice broke on the name.

"I understand," Dorramon said, his voice lilting, washing calm over them all. "But everything will be all right, you'll see. Just try to—"

"Stop!" Tralice shrieked, pushing herself to her feet. She swayed unsteadily, but glared at them all as if she dared any of them to intervene. "Don't you *dare* use your damned Talent on me! I won't stand for it, do you hear me? People with Talent think they can do anything they want, even this!" She flung her arms out in a gesture that encompassed all of the blast debris around them. "I won't stand for it! You should have let me *die!*"

She tottered off through the wreckage, gasping and staggering, refusing to slow down or look back.

Alannys stared after her in shock. "What do we do now?"

Chen shook his head. "I think you'd better leave her alone."

"But—"

Dorramon reached out and took her hand. "He's right, Alannys. She needs some time alone. She's taken a big blow today. Give her some time to adjust. She'll be fine."

Alannys wished she could believe him. But she thought of the Tralice she knew, who loved Dorramon, and would never have dreamed of speaking that way to him. The Tralice she knew so admired the Talents that she had ruined her voice trying to force it to sing. The way this Tralice had acted and spoken was so far out of her experience she didn't even know how to frame it properly. When would her friend Tralice be back?

And she wondered, what if it wasn't just the shock and the grief talking? What if this was a real change in Tralice?

Was that the kind of change a person *could* come back from?

♫

"What do you two imagine you are doing?" Chen's voice rang across the ruined Outer Ward with uncharacteristic sternness, and he stood with his hands on his hips.

Alannys glanced at Dorramon, then back at Chen, wondering what on earth they could be in trouble for. "Following you back to the dig. We're going to help."

"Are you always insane, or just when I'm around?" Chen ran his hand through his hair in evident exasperation. "Alannys, neither of you are in any shape to help. I only sang a few notes, but—has it occurred to you that both of you are probably headed for Muse's Fever?"

Alannys stared at him. "But I didn't even sing!"

"Do you think that matters?" Chen shot back. "Muse's Fever comes from being a channel for the power of the Muses. You may not have sung, Alannys, but you were damn sure a channel. Your Talent was mixed up in all that one way or another. I could feel it."

She wanted to protest, but the words stuck in her throat. As glad as she was to have found a loophole around the Collar of Silence, there was something deeply unnerving about the whole experience, and Chen's words only made that worse.

"He's right," Dorramon said heavily. "We aren't going to be good for anything for much longer."

"But..." Alannys looked out at the chaos and devastation surrounding them. "There's still so much to do!"

"And it will get done, don't you worry," Chen told her. "I've already had a runner from camp; they are gathering tools and wagons and people to help with the clean up as we speak."

"They would do that?" Alannys heard surprise in her own voice.

Chen looked pained. "Alannys, when are you going to believe me? I told you that you are one of us. Always. You may choose not to be involved with the tribe every day, but you are still the Redeemer. Any of us would do anything we could for you."

Alannys knew Chen was overstating his case — sentiment inside the tribe was never that homogenous, not about anything. But she could hardly point that out right now, as she supposed he knew well enough.

She also supposed that it wasn't an appropriate time to point out how casually the man with a self-professed dislike of royalty was interacting with members of that same royalty now.

Raman and Grayble were not too far away, both dusty and gray. They stopped working in the rubble when they saw Chen approaching with Dorramon and herself behind him.

"Are these two giving you trouble, Chen?" Raman dragged his sleeve across his forehead, smearing more dirt and sweat than he cleared.

Chen threw an unreadable glance at Alannys. "Only because they refuse to leave. Apparently they think collapsing here in the middle of the rescue effort would be somehow helpful."

"Oh, so you're saying they're *stubborn*." Raman grinned at them. Alannys didn't see how he managed to stay so positive. "Those two have stubborn down to an art."

"You'll get no argument from me," Chen said. "Do you think one of you might take them back to the keep? The Singari will arrive soon, and I need to be here to put them to work."

"Half of this rubble is from the barracks," Captain Grayble said. "Some of my men are buried—more than I want to know. Unless my Lady or my Lord King has urgent need of me, I would prefer to stay and work to recover what can be recovered from this." He couldn't seem to look any of them in the eye. "A decent burial is the least I owe them, I think."

"Please stay," Alannys said quickly. "This is anything but urgent. We just wanted to stay and help. Dorramon and I are perfectly capable of finding our own rooms."

"We have been to the keep a time or two," the king said wryly. "I'm well acquainted with Alannys's room, as she is with mine." The look that crossed Chen's face wasn't entirely pleasant, and Alannys turned to go, ready to leave immediately to avoid seeing it any longer.

"No, wait, I'll go with you," Raman said, beating the dust from his clothes as he stepped toward them. "Chen is right. Neither of you should be wandering around alone— who knows how long you have before the fever sets in." He fell in step between them, and they made their way toward the back of the Outer Ward. "Besides, this attack seemed very carefully targeted. Lord Malrec may have more up his sleeve."

"Targeted?" Dorramon sounded surprised; Alannys had to wonder where he got the energy for it. She had all she could do just to stay upright, to keep trudging toward the Inner Ward. "I disagree. I think he targeted exactly what he destroyed—the curtain wall and the guard barracks. Alannys and I were just collateral damage."

The look Raman gave him was not convinced. "That seems like suspiciously convenient collateral damage to me. Either way, I think we have to assume this attack was targeted at you or Alannys, or both."

Dorramon shook his head. "It seems curious for a bomb targeting us to be placed in the back of the barracks, don't you think? If Captain Grayble had been in his quarters, we would have lost him. We did lose dozens of guards who were ill, or who were sleeping after the night shift. Don't you think that was more likely his goal— reducing our forces and spreading panic? Without significant observation, he wouldn't have even known the royal carriage was going to be there, and no paintings have followed Alannys and I this morning."

Raman grunted in what may or may not have been agreement.

Dorramon sighed. "But of course you're right. We have to assume that this attack was a deliberate attempt to decapitate the government. We've put it off as long as we can—now that we have Alannys back, we have to use the Talent-proofing solution."

"Wonderful." Raman's voice echoed in the vaulted vestibule of the keep. "I think we should—"

The king shook his head. "But I can't make any decisions about it right now. I'm too tired, and I'm not thinking straight. Why don't you draw up a list of potential locations? We'll discuss it when I wake up."

"All right." Raman ran his hand through his hair, looking away in a manner that suggested he was not unfamiliar with the king ducking important decisions. "I'm going to go organize the cleanup effort. You won't be able to, and I'm afraid Captain Grayble is too distracted. And I don't think many of the palace folk will listen to Chen."

"All right. Thank you, Raman." Dorramon's tone sounded easy and pleasant; only the whiteness and lines in his face revealed how hard he was working just to stay conscious.

Alannys understood. She watched Raman turn to leave, aware that her own rooms were only a few steps away.

But she still wondered if she would make it that far.

♪

Alannys staggered into her chambers, dizzy, with sparkling black spots in her vision. She knew it wasn't objectively very far from the blast site to her rooms, but she couldn't help feeling proud of herself for making it under her own steam. In her state it felt like a herculean accomplishment.

It was decidedly strange to drag herself into the familiar rooms knowing Tralice wouldn't be there. She wondered if anything would ever feel normal again.

Then she looked up and saw someone standing in her sitting room, and realized the answer was no.

It wasn't Tralice, of course. Kalyn stood next to the coffee table, wearing an elegant silk gown, her hair swept up on top of her head. She looked so completely like a woman who should have been engaged to an arch-prince that for a split second Alannys didn't even recognize her.

Kalyn's eyes widened, and she turned to the little table, fussing with a silver tea service. "Please let me stay, my Lady. I know it isn't usual, but—I believe you are in need of a maid at the moment."

"News sure travels fast. But I can't imagine why you would want to do that."

Kalyn inclined her head. "You are my friend, Lady Alannys. It would be my honor to help you." She spooned crushed dried leaves of different colors into a teacup, and poured in steaming water. "To tell the truth of it, my Lady, I've felt so *useless* since coming to the Great Palace—you would be doing me a favor, really."

"How can I argue?" Alannys said. "I'm about to drop. Thank you, Kalyn." She stifled a yawn, dragged her hand across her forehead, and turned for the bedroom.

"Wait!" Alannys heard Kalyn say, and before she could get herself turned around, her new maid was right there in front of her, holding the silver teacup in her face. "You must drink this!"

The scent of tea wafted up at her, and her stomach lurched sideways. "I'm sorry, Kalyn—I really don't like tea."

"And this isn't likely to change that," Kalyn said, but she didn't budge. "It smells perfectly foul. But you must drink it, my Lady—Baroness Lae gave me the recipe. She asked me to make it for you."

"The baroness?" Alannys sniffed experimentally at the cup, and wrinkled her nose. "Why does she want to torture me?"

Kalyn laughed, and pushed the teacup into Alannys's hands. "*Hurry,* my Lady! This tea will help lessen Muse's Fever!"

"What?" Alannys grabbed the cup and slugged back half of the scalding liquid. It brought tears to her eyes, but she couldn't tell whether it was the heat or the taste that made her cry. The tea tasted about like it smelled; like it had been brewed with dirty water and old socks. "Good heavens, that's awful," she choked. "What's *in* this stuff?"

Kalyn shrugged, somehow making the gesture seem apologetic. "Lots of things, my Lady—far too many for a proper tea. Laurel, chamomile, nutmeg, fennel, horseradish—even more that I don't remember right now."

"Horseradish!" Alannys choked down another swallow of tea. "Egads, no wonder it tastes so terrible!" Another gagging mouthful of tea. "He won't thank you for it, but you need to get some of this to Dorramon, too."

"It's already done, my Lady. The king's valet has a tray ready for him as well."

"Terrific. At least I'm not suffering alone." Alannys smiled, right up until she took another drink of Muse's Tea. She might have opened the mindlink and teased him about it, if she hadn't been wearing the collar, and if they hadn't both felt so awful.

"I know, my Lady," Kalyn said sympathetically. She took the empty teacup and set it aside, then threaded Alannys's arm through her own. "Let's get you to bed." She shook her head. "To think that such a thing could happen in the Great Palace!"

"It's Lord Malrec," Alannys said sourly, letting Kalyn help her into her bedroom. "He means to rule the world, and he'll destroy any part of it he can't control."

"I know," Kalyn said, and something in her tone made Alannys look at her in sudden consternation. There was a sadness she had never heard there before.

"I'm sorry," Alannys said.

Kalyn helped her out of her ruined dress. "Don't be. I should have seen it myself, years ago—it should have been obvious what kind of man he was. At least I am working for the right side now. I am grateful for that."

"Me, too," Alannys said.

Kalyn looked at her doubtfully. "My Lady needs a bath, but you really need to be in bed—I'm not sure you would make it through a bath right now. What do you think?"

Alannys's brain felt fuzzy. She tried to consider her possible responses to that question. She could have said a bath would be fine. She could have said she would prefer to go to bed now and bathe later. She could even have said that she didn't care either way and would do whatever Kalyn thought best. Any of those would have been reasonable answers to the question at hand.

Instead, she crumpled to the floor in a dirty heap, unconscious and burning with fever.

♪

Alannys woke up feeling completely spent. It was a struggle just to open her eyes, and when she did the first thing she saw was Chen, sitting on the edge of her bed.

It felt so familiar, it was painful, and for a moment she couldn't seem to convince her voice to make words. It might have been any day of her life from the last three months.

Only this wasn't a little bed built into a Singari wagon —they were inside the keep of the Great Palace, and that one fact changed everything.

"Hello, sleepyhead," Chen said, and smiled at her.

Well, maybe not *everything* had changed.

"Hello yourself. Aren't you a little...dirty to be on the bed?" It seemed like a fair question. Everything from his black hair to his black boots was gray and dirty from the excavation. Even his caramel-colored skin was a crusty, powdery gray.

Chen rolled his eyes toward the ceiling. "Oh, sure, bring out the dirty Singari bit. I figured you wouldn't mind." He nodded at the bed.

Alannys glanced at the bedding around her and realized he was right—she had forgotten that she'd collapsed before she could bathe. The bed was already so dirty nothing he could do would make much difference.

She laughed, and stretched. "How long have I been out?"

"About two hours, or so Kalyn tells me."

"Two hours! That tea must really work. The way I felt, I shouldn't have woken up until tomorrow, at least." She frowned. "You know Kalyn?"

"I do now. I don't know what she expected—it sounds like her old master told her all sort of horrible things about Singari. But she seems very nice, and I think she likes me fine." Chen shook his head. "I've never seen anything like it, Alannys. I don't think there are two people in the entire world with less in common than a king and a Singari. And people like Kalyn, the arch-prince, the baroness—someone like me should never have occasion to exchange a single word with people like that. But everyone pulled together to save you. And now that you're back, somehow we're all of us acting like old friends. How do you *do* that?"

"Hey, don't blame me," Alannys objected. "All I did was nearly die in the remains of Archford Estate. You guys did the rest all by yourselves."

Chen laughed. "You're the same as ever, I suppose. Turn the entire world on its ear, then act like it's no big deal, really. I just came in to bring your things. Quicksilver is safe in the stables, and all of your things are out in the sitting room."

"Thank you," she said. "I really do appreciate it. But...which part of that means you needed to sit on my bed till I woke up?"

She had expected that question to get a laugh, but Chen didn't even crack a smile. "Nothing. You're right. I just...I'm procrastinating. It's pretty awful out there."

"I'm sorry," she said, struggling to sit up. "I wish I could have helped. Maybe now that I'm awake, I can—"

He held out a hand to stop her. "No. No, you're not in any shape to go out there. And honestly, Alannys, even if you were I would encourage you not to. It's like something straight out of a nightmare. There's so many of us out there, and we're all doing so much, but it doesn't seem to be making much difference."

"I should be out there! Even a single pair of hands might help you get survivors out more quickly!"

She broke off abruptly, alarmed by the somber expression on Chen's face. "Chen...there are survivors, aren't there?"

He couldn't seem to meet her gaze. To her horror, he shook his head. "I'm sorry, Alannys. I didn't come here to upset you. I just wanted a few minutes away from the dig, because it's bad. Very, very bad—we've probably found twenty or thirty people. But your maid was the only one we found alive."

"Oh, Chen. I'm so sorry." She couldn't imagine what it must be like out there, digging in that.

"Don't be." He still couldn't quite seem to look at her. "You need to stay here and rest up, give us all something to keep fighting for." He stood up. "I'd better get back out there. I meant what I said earlier, Alannys. I don't know how you do it, but you're the mortar holding this group of people together. And the more people you meet, the bigger that group gets. All of this...I don't think it could happen without you."

"Wow," she said. "Thank you, Chen."

"Don't thank me." He reached out hesitantly and stroked her hair with a dirty hand. "Just...don't die or anything, all right? Please, just don't die."

He turned and left, and a cold wind seemed to blow through the room behind him. ♫

Kalyn came into the bedroom after Chen left, and helped Alannys into the bath chamber to bathe. "I hope it was all right that I let Chen sit with you, my Lady. He looked terrible. I think just being around you helps him somehow."

"It was fine," Alannys said, lowering herself onto the wooden chair while Kalyn dumped hot water into the tub. "I'm glad to help Chen any way I can. I don't think I was very good company, though."

Kalyn smiled. The steam rising up into her face made her hair cling to her cheeks and forehead in damp tendrils. "I don't think he minded, my Lady."

Alannys didn't have a response that she cared to utter aloud, so she said nothing and concentrated on getting into the tub without breaking her neck. She lowered herself gingerly into the steaming water. Every muscle she had screamed in protest. It was probably a good thing she didn't remember much about the explosion — it must have been a rough ride.

Kalyn dumped a bucket of water over Alannys, dousing her hair. "The king is also awake and about. I thought you would like to know."

"Thank you, Kalyn." She was glad to hear that. They had both gotten off easy, it seemed. "That tea of yours is some pretty potent stuff."

"Thank you, but it isn't mine," Kalyn said. "Baroness Lae found the recipe in Princess Delline's notes."

Alannys stared at her. All of the sudden, she didn't even feel the bathwater — water that had seemed scalding hot only a moment before. "Delline's notes? This tea was in Delline's notes?"

"Well, yes. That is — the king said the baroness could stay in Princess Delline's old room, of course, and she was searching for a gloss formula so that Raman could rescue you, and she found the tea — she wasn't snooping, my Lady, or intending any disrespect."

Alannys waved that aside. "No — no, of course not. But if this was in her notes — then she's known about it. All this time, every single Muse's Fever I've had since leaving Castle Glennayre, Delline could have prevented all of them." She floundered around in the water, scrambling for enough leverage to stand up.

"No, my Lady — you aren't done yet." Kalyn held her down. "Calm down and let me finish your hair."

"I can't calm down! Do you realize the very first day I met her I got Muse's Fever? I sang to save us all — her included — from Malrec's assassins. And she let me suffer, even though she could have stopped it, even though she didn't know a thing about me, even though I had just saved her *life!*"

"My Lady, this is all past. You must let go of it—calm yourself!"

"All this *time*," Alannys said again, fighting the urge to tear her hair out. She clambered out of the tub and threw on her robe. "And not just me—she's let her own brother suffer Muse's Fever, for years, when she could have helped him! What kind of person could be so heartless, so *evil?*"

"Well," Kalyn said slowly, "I suppose she's a good match for Lord Malrec."

Alannys blinked at her. "You're right." She couldn't help it; she laughed out loud. "Hang it all, you're *right*. The joke's on me, I suppose, for being surprised."

A knock at the door interrupted her. Kalyn looked as surprised as she was, so she tromped out through the sitting room in her bathrobe to answer it, damp and dripping on the floor.

Tralice stood there, wrapped in a shapeless black dress that looked too big for her. It cut a sharp contrast to the washed-out white of her face, with deep hollows under eyes that no longer danced with laughter.

"Tralice! Come in, come in. You don't have to knock; you practically live here yourself."

Tralice shook her head. "Not anymore." She stepped past Alannys and sat down on the sofa, wrapping her arms tight around herself. "I'm sorry—of course I will be back, I'm not fit to do anything else, and I've still got to eat. But right now...well, I'm not ready yet."

"I'm so sorry," Alannys said. "Is there anything I can do?"

Tralice didn't even look at her, just kept on shaking her head. "I just came to apologize for the way I acted earlier. That was no way to treat the people who had just saved my life. If I can ask a favor, would you convey my apologies to the king? I—I don't think I can face him right now."

"Of course. But you really don't have to apologize. I can't even imagine what you're going through right now. I hope you can forgive me, Tralice—I didn't even know you were married."

Tralice shrugged, but she seemed to draw in on herself. The sofa made her look small and lost somehow, sitting alone in its expanse of cushions. "How could you know? I never told you. Jard and I have been married since we were fourteen. He's my anchor—everything that I am in my life, I'm free to be because of him."

"He sounds wonderful," Alannys said.

"Aye, he certainly is. Was. I was never able to have children myself, but a month ago my sister passed on and we took in her two boys. One was just a baby." She wiped a tear from her sunken cheek. "It was like we were a real family at last—not that I was glad to lose Helva, Muses bless her."

"Helva?" The name felt like an electric shock. "Your sister's name was Helva?"

Tralice watched her warily. "Yes, that's right."

"Short lady, kind of plump? Red hair, all piled up on top of her head? Lots of rouge? Had a husband named Petras?"

"Yes, that was her. But how could you have known her?"

Alannys buried her face in her hands. "Oh, Tralice, I am sorry. But your sister is not dead. She is alive and well in Glennayre Holding. She abandoned everything to do Lord Malrec's bidding."

Tralice sat very still. For a long moment nobody spoke. "My sister...is not dead?"

"That's right."

"She left everything—abandoned her own children to me—so that she could serve Lord Malrec."

"Basically," Alannys said, "yes. I am sorry, Tralice. Maybe I shouldn't have said anything."

"No. I needed to know." Tralice took a deep breath and stood up from the couch. "It's just another Talented person turning ordinary lives upside down on their whim, I suppose."

"No," Alannys said, alarmed at her tone. "It's an *evil* person turning lives upside down."

"If you say so. It seems suspicious to me that Talent is always involved. It hardly seems fair, does it?"

Alannys stared at her, stricken.

"Please convey my apologies to the king. I should go."

And she left, without another word or a backward glance. Alannys sat heavily down in the chair, thinking about Tralice's dark new attitude about the Talents she had once envied. And that was when it hit her — the whole time they had talked, Tralice had not called her Lady. Not once.

Alannys shivered in a sudden chill that had nothing to do with the temperature of the room around her.

♪

Alannys paced her sitting room the next morning, wearing a dark burgundy dress and a frown. It didn't feel right somehow to wear black, and yet it didn't feel right wearing burgundy either. The only thing that sounded tempting to her at all was going back to bed and forgetting the whole thing. But that would *certainly* be wrong, so she did the best she could, which was to pace around her room in a dress that was dark, but not black.

A knock at the door interrupted her spiral of thoughts. She put her dress out of her mind and went to answer it.

Chen stood fidgeting in the corridor, looking immensely uncomfortable in a red velvet doublet. She looked at him and then looked at him again, flabbergasted. She'd always known Chen was handsome, of course — but not until she saw him cleaned up and regally dressed did she really realize *how* handsome. The realization took her breath away, made her mouth feel dry. She swallowed hard, trying to regain her composure.

Chen's face lit up when he saw her. "Oh, thank the Muses! I was afraid you had left already."

"No," she said, stepping aside to let him in. "Dorramon should be coming soon — we're going together."

"Oh, good! Can I come along? I have no idea where I'm going. I get lost as soon as I step out of the keep. All these buildings make me nervous."

She tried not to let her amusement show, but she could feel her mouth quirk in spite of herself. "Of course. But Chen, your room is closer to Dorramon's than mine. Why didn't you just ask him?"

Chen stared at her. "You're joking, right? Right?"

Alannys laughed out loud. "Yes. It was nice of him to put you in a room in the keep, though. Especially with all the work you've done in the cleanup — you deserve it."

"I suppose so," he said grudgingly. "But the *zhotha* aren't happy about it, I can tell you that. And I feel like someone's pet monkey, dressed up in these clothes."

"I don't know," she said, feeling her face burn, "you clean up pretty nice. I think you look quite dashing."

"Really?"

"Really." She looked away, acutely uncomfortable.

"Well, that's all right, then." Chen sounded a lot brighter.

Another knock at the door saved her from making any response to that. She said a silent thank you as she moved to answer it, wondering if Chen would ever get tired of yanking her chain.

Dorramon waited at the door this time; if she hadn't been so distracted she would have realized that sooner. He looked uncertainly from her red face to Chen, standing in the middle of the room. "Is this a bad time?"

"No. No, your timing is perfect as usual, your Highness," Alannys said. She grabbed his arm and pulled him inside, leaving the door open for the two Royal Guards following him.

"Thank you for inviting me to attend the funeral from the parapets, your Majesty," Chen said primly.

The king looked from Alannys to Chen, as though he was pretty sure he was missing something. "Of course. Think nothing of it. Any friend of Lady Alannys's is a friend of mine. Besides, I think it will be good for her to have friends up there. I'm going to have to deliver a speech, so I won't be there."

"You won't?" Alannys tried not to sound alarmed. "Why do you have to speak?"

Dorramon shook his head. "Alannys, regardless of what Raman believes, I don't think that explosion was a direct attack on you or me. That bomb was carefully placed exactly where it was."

"He seems to have a very fine amount of control with them," Alannys admitted. "When Ravan's Light rescued me, he wanted me incapacitated but alive—and that's exactly how I was. I could easily have been killed, or left able to walk away, but he knew just how to place it."

Chen snorted. "You're giving him too much credit. Dahlia was there, riding stubbornly out ahead of us, remember? She triggered the explosion before you were close. It wasn't any brilliance on Lord Malrec's part."

"It was deliberate," Alannys insisted.

"Just so," Dorramon said. "Twenty-five Royal Guardsmen died in that explosion, which has to be a good thing for Lord Malrec. But he could easily have killed twice that number if he had destroyed the entire barracks, and more if he had done it at night. Why didn't he?"

"Crippling the Royal Guard wasn't his only goal," Alannys said, realizing it for the first time. "Maybe not even his primary goal. He blew up part of the inner wall and destroyed a bunch of peasant homes — because that was his target, too."

"But why?" Chen said. "Why would someone like Lord Malrec spend his time and effort — and powerful weapons — just to terrorize peasants?"

Alannys shook her head. "It isn't about the people themselves, if that's what you're saying. Malrec doesn't care about them. They're just a means to an end for him."

"And what is that end?" Dorramon said. "Look at the court, at the Inner Ward. You've said yourself how deserted they are. The Outer Ward is about the only place where I still have strong support. If Malrec can frighten enough people into leaving..."

"Then you're alone, unsupported. It makes his job that much easier." Alannys sank into the chair. "It's the same reason he wanted me out of the way at Archford."

"Yes." Dorramon couldn't quite seem to look at her, but then, neither could Chen. He looked at the tapestry on the far wall, inspected it as if it might have some insight to offer. "That's why I'm giving a speech today. I can't stop him from spreading fear. But people should know who they have to thank for this attack. They should consider this type of violence before deciding they would support him as king."

"I agree," Chen said. "But Lord Malrec doesn't seem likely to give anyone a choice."

"There's always a choice," Alannys said. "Always. Don't you ever forget that. If Malrec succeeds, he can make himself king. But he can't make the people support him, and they'll work against him. He can't make them love him."

"But why should he care?" Chen said. "That's the part of this I don't understand — why should it matter if they love King Dorramon? How does Lord Malrec benefit from attacking peasants?"

"It isn't that simple." Alannys stood up out of her chair and went to stare out of the window, as though the view could make these subjects easier to discuss. "Lord Malrec is a very jealous man by nature. Whether he will admit it or not, a big part of the reason Malrec wants to rule is because he craves that kind of love and admiration for himself."

"Logic doesn't guide his every move," Dorramon said, and something about the way he said it made her turn around to look at him. "It isn't all about winning — it isn't enough just to win. He wants to destroy everything I ever cared about, and leave me completely devastated and humiliated first."

He sounded unmoved as he said it, as though he might have been discussing someone else entirely. But his blue eyes looked haunted and unfathomably sad, and Alannys knew he felt the reality of what he said all too well.

She threw herself into his arms, wrapping her arms around his neck and burying her face in his chest. "Don't you worry. He's never going to succeed. You're never going to be alone, do you hear me? I won't let you be."

She had caught him off guard with her spontaneous gesture, she knew that. But almost immediately she felt his arms around her, squeezing her tight. "I can't believe you still feel that way," he said hoarsely, "after what you went through at Archford. And all because he wanted to make sure you couldn't help me, and use you against me if he could." He leaned back from her and traced his finger along the Collar of Silence. "You're still not over it."

"No," she said, recognizing the futility of denying it. "But it doesn't change anything. I'm staying here. I'm not running from Lord Malrec, or the King of Cadenda, or anyone else who cares to take a stand. I'm staying here beside you and fighting. Till the bitter end."

Dorramon stared at her, stricken. She could see his throat working, but he couldn't seem to make any sound. Nobody moved. Alannys hardly dared breathe.

"Alannys," Dorramon finally managed, and then stopped. For a long, aching pause that left her oddly nervous, Alannys hung there in a silence that suddenly felt somehow momentous. "Alannys, I—"

Chen loudly cleared his throat, shattering the moment and utterly derailing whatever had been about to happen. "I hate to interrupt, but if we don't hurry, we're going to be late."

Alannys couldn't help but think that he didn't *sound* like he hated interrupting. His face, when she spun around to regard him, was placid—perhaps, she thought suspiciously, *too* placid.

"He's right," Dorramon said. "We do need to go." He offered his arm, and led her out of the room.

Alannys walked down the corridor of the keep with the king, her mind racing in frustration. *Something* had almost happened back there, but she couldn't for the life of her figure out what, and that bugged her more than she could say.

She could hear the slight sounds of Chen walking behind them, seemingly oblivious to the distress he had caused. Was that—was he actually *humming?*

Perhaps he wasn't as oblivious as she had thought. In fact, she suddenly wondered if he didn't understand a lot more about what had happened back there than she did.

♫

High in the parapets of the outer wall, directly over the great drawbridge, Alannys stood sandwiched between Raman and Chen, shivering so hard her teeth chattered. The whipping wind never really subsided in the parapets anyway, but today it was a cold wind, laced with the promise of an unseasonably late snow. The blistering heat she remembered from Archford Estate was but a distant memory now, a false start to the spring that now seemed to be receding into the distance before her.

Alannys hadn't been up in the parapets since King Caleb's funeral, and to be honest, she would have been just as happy never to go up there again. Nothing good ever brought her to the parapets, and just being there was enough to depress her.

Today, though, she looked down on seventy-eight wooden coffins, arranged in neat rows in the palace anteyard. There were Royal Guardsmen, peasants, and even children in those coffins. Every woodworker in the Great Palace had stayed up all night working on the coffins. Almost everybody knew somebody who was now being laid to rest in one.

They knew her, too, and some of the looks she was getting right now were not very friendly at all. She could see people below shifting, straining their necks to turn around and glare at her.

"Should've stayed gone, woman." The derisive shout was not addressed to her by name, but it carried clearly, even over the tempestuous wind. "The king's whore brought this trouble here!"

The muscles of Chen's jaw twitched, as if he had a thing or two he would have liked to shout back. Raman checked his sword in its scabbard, and Alannys swallowed hard. This was all she needed—another riot at another funeral, because of her.

But there was nothing she could say to them, nothing in the world that might convince them this would have happened even without her. So she watched Dorramon step solemnly out onto the hastily constructed dais below, in silence. She stood with Raman's arm around her back, clinging to Chen's arm as though she might fall without the support, and did her best to listen.

"Today we gather together to bid a final farewell to

peasants and to Royal Guards, to mothers and fathers, sons and daughters, to valued friends and neighbors." Dorramon's somber voice carried effortlessly to each of them, from the weeping families at the front of the dais to the resolutely stoic faces up on the parapets. "Today we stand with broken hearts and determined hands, ready to do for our departed loved ones the very best that we can. What we must do is made for us all the harder by the knowledge that no act of the Muses has taken our fallen friends away — they were stolen away, torn away from us by a craven attack, a cowardly act of horrible violence whose only purpose was to scare and demoralize us, to make us run."

The king held the undivided attention of every person in the Outer Ward. Someone coughed, but most people regarded Dorramon with silent, rapt attention. Up in the parapets, Alannys couldn't feel her fingers wrapped around Chen's arm. The cold, angry wind was getting to her more than she had anticipated, but she would not have dreamed of leaving. She would have sworn he was not using his Talent, and yet the spell he wove there in the cold, quiet Outer Ward felt almost magical. She wondered if anything she had done, leading the Singari, had come close to what Dorramon was doing here, now, surrounded by his bereaved subjects.

"And yet I assure you that I will not run!" Dorramon's voice rose now, weaving among them in a dramatic crescendo that rang with righteous anger. "I will not abandon the Great Palace, and the Redeemer will not abandon the Great Palace. Together we will stand and fight! We fight for ourselves, and we fight for you, and we fight for all of those we honor on this black day. This I promise you: the fates of all who live in Ravanmark will never be handed to the monster who wrought this evil!"

Alannys never knew who started it — she heard a man

down in the crowd shout "Hear, hear!" and then a woman yelled "All hail his Majesty!" and the next thing anybody knew the entire crowd was cheering and clapping, stomping and shouting for their king.

Alannys disentangled herself from her friends and clapped along with them, adding her sounds of support to the throng surrounding them. He had done a wonderful thing here, almost miraculous in light of the circumstances.

But as he looked up to meet her gaze, Alannys could see the grimness of his expression. The same thought rang in two minds.

What he had done here was incredible.

But would it be enough?

♫

Delline erupted into Castle Glennayre's study, sending the polished wood door crashing into the stone wall behind it.

Lord Malrec didn't move, hunched over some papers spread across the top of his desk. "Something amiss, my dear?" His tone was mild, but irritation flashed like lightning in the eyes that flicked her direction. Knowing him, he was even now congratulating himself on concealing his emotions so well. Insufferable as always.

"I should say so," she shot back, "and I'm surprised you care to feign ignorance! Didn't I specifically forbid any of your foul bomb attacks on the Great Palace?"

He sat back in his chair, abandoning his papers, no longer bothering to hide his anger. "No, actually, what you raised such a fuss about was the use of the weapon against your brother. This particular bomb was not employed against him, so I really fail to see your complaint."

"It's rather convenient, don't you think, that it very nearly killed him anyway!"

Malrec shrugged. "Mere coincidence, I assure you. The

location for the bomb had been chosen days before — we were unaware his Majesty was in the vicinity when we placed it."

"That still sounds awfully convenient," Delline said. "Suspiciously convenient, in fact."

"How dare you question me!" Malrec exploded, coming out of his chair in sudden fury. "If I say the king's involvement was accidental, then it *was* accidental, and you are not at liberty to be skeptical. My honesty is above reproach!"

Delline stared at him. "How can you say that with a straight face? Do you expect me to believe that just because you say it, it's true?"

Malrec's eyes narrowed, twin glinting flints, and she took a reflexive step back. "As a matter of fact, my dear, I do. It is the minimum respect you owe to the Lord of Glennayre." He advanced on her and she backed away from him, startled to find her back suddenly against the cold, bare wall. Perhaps it had not been such a good idea to confront him about this after all. "Which reminds me, my dear, these recent episodes have brought certain...doubts to my mind. I have begun to wonder, in light of recent events, if you can be trusted at all. Your loyalty seems questionable at best."

"My Lord! Surely you cannot think that of your wife, the one who brought you the extended gloss recipe, who voluntarily undertook the focus bond! How can you question the devotion of the woman who did these things for you?"

"It would seem so, wouldn't it?" Malrec mused. Everything about him emanated danger, and Delline desperately wanted to sidle away from him and flee the study. But as if he could sense her desire, Malrec planted his palms against the wall on either side of her shoulders, blocking any escape. "And yet I wonder...as we have finally begun to make real progress toward our goals, you've become more of a hindrance than a help. You allowed a palace spy to operate undetected in the castle. No sooner did I develop a weapon capable of ending this thing than you *forbade* its use on the one person we need to eliminate. And *now* you have the audacity, the sheer unmitigated *gall* to scold me for attacking the Great Palace *at all?* I wonder, dear lady, what you *want* me to think!"

Delline swallowed thickly. Danger surrounded her, a palpable thing. "I don't know what you mean. I only wish to see this transition happen with as little bloodshed as possible. Surely you cannot fault that."

"No." He seemed suddenly contemplative. Delline was grateful for his distraction, but he didn't step back or move his arms. "No, that is a fine concern. I do hope you realize, though, that in order for our coup to succeed, there is one person whose royal blood absolutely must be shed."

Delline felt cold. Her stomach dropped. "Yes. Yes, of course. I understand that."

"Do you? Because I wonder, my dear, in light of your recent behavior, if you might prove to be more of a liability than an asset to us when it is time to make our final move. How do you suggest I eliminate that doubt?"

"My Lord! You know you can trust me absolutely!"

"Do I? I would certainly like to. Baron Prubard calls it sentimental rot."

"Prubard! My Lord knows better than to take advice from that fat, incompetent, disgusting—"

"Yes," Malrec said, "he is easy to discount, isn't he? And yet Lord Diabon has worries as well. He tells me I should lock you up somewhere remote until this is all over."

"Does he now?" Delline seethed with anger she didn't dare express—she was also very, very worried. Why was he even telling her these things? "I should think you know your wife better than either of those men, and I hope you did not hesitate to tell them so."

"Ah, but how can I?" Malrec cried dramatically. "You have given us so little support of late, how can I argue? I am trapped, my dear, in a most untenable position."

"I don't understand." Her palms slicked with sweat. *Why was he telling her this?* "What do you want me to do?"

"Now there is the question." Malrec smiled at her, one of those warm smiles that seemed to make her head go fuzzy. "I am so pleased to find you amenable to redeeming yourself! It is most encouraging. And I have a task for you, perfect for the purpose."

Dread clenched her stomach like a vise. "Anything. You know I will do anything you ask of me."

He positively beamed at her. "I knew we could depend on you. I defended you to the others—I wouldn't hear a word against you. And to show their support, and their sincere regret for doubting you, our friends have given you a great honor. You are to strike the crowning blow, so to speak, that will bring all of our plans to fruition."

"Wh-what?"

Lord Malrec reached inside his dark velvet cloak and withdrew a dagger in a black leather sheath. Without a word, he laid it solemnly across her hands.

"I see." The dagger was small, with a viciously pointed, rippled blade. A metal snake wound around the grip, with his tail at the tip of the handle and his head in the center of the hilt, jaws open and fangs extended. Set in the open mouth, behind the fangs, was a single smooth, round ruby, glowing a deep black-red in the torchlight. It looked like blood. Delline shivered. "So the great honor I have been given is the murder of my brother."

"Now, now, my dear, you mustn't think of it that way. The assassination of an unjust king is the responsibility of any true patriot."

"Even if I agreed with that, this is my brother we are talking about here. My *brother*. Don't you think the position you're putting me in is just a bit cruel?"

Malrec folded his arms. His dark eyes glinted in the low light. "Not half as cruel as the position you shall find yourself in should you betray me. It's very simple, my dear — you are either with us or against us. Which will it be?"

Delline's throat tightened up, and her hands started to shake. For a moment she feared she might drop the dagger, then she thought that might actually be for the best.

Lord Malrec's manner finally softened. He reached out and closed her fingers around the sheath. "Look, it really isn't so bad. Let me tell you something which may help soothe your fevered conscience — that is no ordinary dagger you hold."

"It isn't?"

"No, my dear. The blade of that weapon has been treated with a very special poison. The smallest scratch from that dagger will prove fatal, but it will be a singularly gentle death, like — like falling asleep."

"A gentle death," she echoed. "Like falling asleep?"

"Just so. I can assure you he will meet no such end from any of the rest of us. You'd be doing him a kindness. Now you really must give me an answer, my dear. We have plans to finish, and we must be prepared to dispose of him ourselves if you will not." His eyes said he might dispose of a good deal more than just her brother. "I must know right now, if I can trust you. If you undertake this thing for me, I give you my solemn word there will be no more explosions."

"Yes." She swallowed hard, trying to bury the feeling she was doing something unconscionable. "Of course you can trust me completely, Lord Malrec, you must know that."

"Wonderful. Then you must be prepared to demonstrate your loyalty. You will assassinate your brother?"

"I will assassinate my brother."

"Most excellent." He kissed her then, the kind of kiss that always took her breath away and made her knees weak.

She didn't even feel it.

Delline staggered from the room, clutching the poisoned dagger with numb hands.

A gentle death...like falling asleep.

She could do that, couldn't she? Even to the brother who had never given her any real reason for her animosity?

She stumbled on the stairs. She would be doing him a kindness. She *would*. She could have let Lord Malrec blast him limb from limb in a raging ball of fire and debris. Instead, he would fall gently to sleep.

I can do this, Delline told herself. *I'm strong enough for this.*

I have to be.

♪

On the west side of the Great Palace, the ridge descended sharply and steeply to a big flat field that was too rocky for proper farming. It was this field that the people of the palace used for their cemetery, and it was here that the rows of plain wooden coffins were brought after the funeral.

A large white tent had been pitched halfway up the ridge, with the royal crest fluttering outside. Chen had gone to assess the progress of the cleanup at the blast site, and Raman had gone with him. Dorramon and Alannys sat in tall-backed chairs inside the sprawling tent, looking out over the cemetery where men dug rows of graves, and bereaved families lingered near coffins. It was chilly and windy on the hillside, but they both thought it was important to be there.

"To think that such a thing could come to pass within the palace walls," Dorramon said. "I never thought I would live to witness such a horror. I really never believed my sister would allow it."

"There are two possibilities then," Alannys said hesitantly. "Either the princess has turned completely to Lord Malrec, or he has gone completely past caring what she will allow."

"I don't like either of those," Dorramon sighed.

"Neither do I," Alannys admitted. "But I can't think of any other way it might have happened."

"It doesn't matter anyway," Dorramon said. He seemed impervious to the brisk wind that swept through the royal tent, but Alannys burrowed down in her chair, pulling her leather riding cloak tight around her against the chill. "It's clear that we're going to have to use your Talent-proofing solution. I just can't justify *not* using it, not after this."

"It makes sense to me to use it," Alannys said. "If I'm honest, I really don't understand why you've waited so long."

Dorramon shook his head. "I don't see why you should understand—I can't pretend it makes any sort of rational sense. But I don't feel right about Talent-proofing. It's like...admitting defeat, somehow."

"Admitting defeat?"

"Well, yes, in a way. We're both Talented, you and I. Everything you've done since you got here has been about making a place for the Talents in Ravanmark. Talent-proofing...it's like hiding. It's like saying we really can't handle this stuff after all. It reminds me of every nasty thing Delline and my mother ever said about my Talent, and it makes me wonder if they were right."

"Like admitting defeat," Alannys murmured. "I suppose I can see where you could feel that way. For what it's worth, I don't agree. I do believe there is a place here for the Talents, obviously, but that doesn't mean everyone with Talent can be counted on to use it wisely. We should be able to defend against bad Talent, so to speak, without forfeiting our right to use good Talent. You can't lump us all together."

"I suppose," Dorramon said. "It still doesn't feel right. But the danger is too great. We have to use the solution— the only question is where."

"I never thought about that," Alannys said. Down in the cemetery, she could see the gravediggers hard at work, men who didn't have the luxury of feeling cold. "I don't suppose there is enough of it to do the whole Great Hall."

"No. But honestly, even if there was, I don't know that it would really protect us, even if we stayed in the Great Hall all the time. Talent-proofing the hall won't stop Lord Malrec from transporting one of his bombs onto the roof, or even into the antechamber."

"Good heavens—I never thought of that," Alannys said. "Can we make any room truly safe, then? As long as he can get above it, or below it, or next to it, it's still in danger."

"You can see my difficulty," Dorramon said. "It isn't just my misgivings that have kept us from using the solution. If you remember, I tasked Raman with the creation of a list of potential locations. He did create the list, and they all suffered from that same inherent flaw. It is a thorny problem."

"Indeed it is." Alannys thought about it, and for a few moments silence filled the tent. Two Royal Guards stood at the entrance, watching impassively everything that happened in the cemetery below. She watched them watching, and shivered in the breeze, and tried to concentrate. "What if the walls and ceiling were very thick —really thick, like a chamber below ground...like a cave? What if we put you in the catacombs, and Talent-proofed the cavern?"

Now Dorramon shivered. "Muses preserve me—I think I would almost rather suffer the explosion. Buried alive in the catacombs—leave it to you to think of something like that. Even Raman didn't go that far."

Alannys gave him a sympathetic glance. "I'm sorry. I know you don't like the catacombs. But it was the only place I could think of where you would be safe."

"It *would* be safer," Dorramon said grudgingly. "But I don't think it would be the absolute answer you desire. There would be constant traffic in and out of the caves. It wouldn't take much effort to find me. And once he did— well, I should think a few well-placed bombs would be enough to seal me inside permanently."

"Oh, my," Alannys gasped. "Oh, no." She reached out and clutched his hand in hers, horrified by the mental picture he had painted. "No, we certainly can't have that. I'm sorry, Dorramon, I guess I really don't have any good answers for you."

Dorramon patted the back of her hand. "Don't feel bad. We've all struggled with it—I'm beginning to think there *are* no good answers. The Grand Chancellor tells me there is nothing we can do but wait for Lord Malrec to launch his attack. We know that he has amassed quite a force of men."

"Wait for him to attack," Alannys murmured. She remembered the newly-mustered palace army, camped out in front of Westmore Forest awaiting that same attack —and she suddenly understood. It was wrong, all of it, *wrong,* even the Grand Chancellor. "No. No, we mustn't wait for his attack! We *cannot* do that!"

Dorramon looked at her in surprise. "I know it seems

counter-intuitive, but it would not behoove us to scatter our forces into Westmore Forest and possibly miss his approach. Sometimes you just have to wait. It's how wars are fought."

"No! No, Dorramon, you aren't fighting a war — you're fighting a *painter!* Whether he has men or not, the only rules he will follow are his own. Just because he has an army doesn't mean he will fight with it. Look, properly placed, that bomb could have taken out quite a chunk of your army. Why didn't he do it?"

"The army isn't his target," Dorramon said. His face looked strained, and his hand around hers was suddenly cold.

"Right! They don't matter to him. Why waste time with them when he can nip in and dispose of us one by one — and disappear immediately if he gets into a tight spot? Armies are just distractions, because he knows you've been trained to think like that."

"Muses, you're right." Dorramon left his chair and paced the length of the tent, snapping off short strides in apparent agitation. "Even if he does launch an attack, it's liable to be a distraction — a cover for the more covert business of attacking by stealth through paintings."

She watched him prowl like a caged animal, feeling her own nerves jangle. "What do we do?"

"A trap," Dorramon muttered. "We know he's planning to attack...we can be ready for him. We can turn it around on him."

"Perhaps," Alannys said doubtfully. "But he has allies who might well be watching, ready to dive in if he runs into trouble. And I am not at all confident that we can anticipate his attack — it will be designed to surprise. The risk is too great."

Dorramon stopped, and turned to look at her.

"There's only one thing we can do," Alannys said.

"And you aren't going to like it. But we have to attack first. We have to do a stealth strike on Castle Glennayre, exactly the same as what he's planning to do here. We have to do it right away, before he can move against us."

"A preemptive strike," Dorramon said. "I think you're right. I think that is the best option." He stood motionless, and he didn't take his eyes off of her. "But why do you keep saying 'we?'"

She tried to smile at him, but his face never flickered. "Oh, Dorramon, you must see what I'm getting at."

"I see no such thing." He folded his arms. "If it's the collar you're worried about, we can take care of that when this is over. Leave the fighting to the fighters."

"I can't! Dorramon, you can't move the army. They have to stay where they are, because I'm sure Lord Malrec does intend to use that army of his. He wants your forces too busy to come to your defense." She left her chair and approached him hesitantly—his dark expression was unreadable. "And the Royal Guard have to stay at the Great Palace, and be extra vigilant, because there's a good chance he expects us to come to this conclusion. If we leave the palace undefended, he will move in behind us as soon as we leave. This has to be someone who can go and not be missed at all. Don't you see?" She took a deep breath for courage, knowing what her next words would cost her.

"It has to be me."

♫

Dorramon stared at Alannys through the heavy silence that filled the tent. His face never changed; he never spoke.

He just shook his head.

"Dorramon, it has to be me. It has to. You see that, don't you?" She reached out and touched his arm. It might have been her imagination, but he almost seemed to flinch. "Dorramon?"

For a long moment, no one spoke, no one moved. Then all at once Dorramon seemed to explode into action, grabbing her arm and hauling her up against him into a crushing embrace. "No," he growled into her ear, "I don't see that. I will never see that. There is nothing you can say that will convince me you should be the one to take this risk. I've nearly lost you so many times, Alannys...I can't take that chance again. I just *can't*."

Tendons stood out like cords in his neck and his hands. The arms around her trembled, and Alannys held very still, suddenly afraid of pushing him over the edge.

"Dorramon." Her voice was soft, and she wrapped her arms around him, willing him to relax. "Dorramon, I—"

"Hallo, my friends, we're back!" Chen bellowed cheerfully from behind her.

"Damn him," Alannys muttered under her breath.

Dorramon looked down at her and forced a smile, visibly pulling himself together. He carefully released her, and together they turned to face their visitors. "What news from the cleanup?" the king asked, and his voice was completely controlled.

"It goes well," Raman said, but he was frowning at them. "Is everything all right here?"

"It is," Dorramon said evenly, just as Alannys said, "No, actually I—"

Raman looked back and forth between them, and his frown deepened.

"I don't understand," Chen said. "What goes on here?"

Dorramon caught Alannys by the arm and pulled her next to him, wrapping his arm tightly around her shoulders, as if he could keep her quiet by keeping her close. The false smile plastered on his face alarmed her. "Nothing. Nothing at all, Lady Alannys and I were just talking."

Alannys frowned. "No," she said, "I—"

Dorramon's fingers dug into her shoulder and she stopped, gasping more from surprise than pain.

"Dorr, stop it," Raman snapped. "Can't you see you're hurting her?"

Alannys lifted Dorramon's arm from her shoulders, and held his hand tightly in hers. "It's all right," she said. "He's just upset. You'll understand, when you hear about it yourself. We've figured out that Lord Malrec is relying on his army as a distraction so that he can attack the king directly by stealth, using paintings. We've decided that the only chance we have is to attack Lord Malrec directly, by stealth, right away."

"I...see," Raman said. "But why does that upset Dorr?"

Chen buried his face into his hand, rubbing at his temples. "Because Alannys thinks she needs to be the one to carry out this stealth attack."

"What?" Raman looked around at all of them as though he'd just discovered he was surrounded by lunatics. "How do you know that?"

"Spend a few months traveling the country with her," Chen said, gesturing her direction. "You'll understand. She's completely insane that way."

Raman looked at her levelly. "So that's what's got Dorramon so wound up. Is that true, Alannys? You think you need to be the one to sneak in and murder Lord Malrec?"

Alannys was beginning to feel unfairly cornered, and the stealth mission sounded a lot less appealing phrased that way. But she swallowed her reservations and nodded, trying to put into her voice confidence that she did not feel. "Yes. It has to be me, Raman. It's the only way that makes sense."

Dorramon suddenly released her hand and turned away, stomping toward the back of the tent.

"I see," Raman said. He grabbed the nearest chair,

flipped it backwards and straddled it, folding his arms over the back. "I assume you won't mind answering some questions."

"Of course not." It was amazing how much more uncomfortable it was to stand in the middle of the tent, when she stood alone.

"Very well. How do you intend to get to Lord Malrec?"

"That's easy," she said. "You'll paint me there."

Raman laughed sharply. "Will I? You'll have to find a way to convince the king not to forbid it first. It doesn't look like your chances are good."

"Dorramon is reasonable," she said. "You'll see. If you and Chen see the necessity of this, he will too."

"Leave me out of this," Chen said darkly. "I've had about all I can stand of you riding off into danger."

"Hear, hear," Dorramon muttered from the back of the tent.

Raman looked at her significantly, then continued. "You know there's more to the Dark Alliance than just Lord Malrec. Why are you focusing on eliminating him?"

"Because Lord Malrec is the one driving this thing." Alannys folded her arms behind her back and began to pace — it made her feel a bit less like she was being interrogated. "I have no objection to removing Prubard and Diabon as well, in fact that is probably a good goal for us to aim for. But Lord Malrec is paramount. Baron Prubard lacks the motivation or the ability to carry out this kind of attack. Lord Diabon is certainly cunning, but he is fundamentally a follower. I question whether he could ever lead something like that. Neither of them are driven to rule the way Malrec is. And neither of them can paint. Remove Lord Malrec, and you remove the biggest threat."

"I see." Raman considered for a moment. "And why do you think you must do this? Why can't Captain Grayble take a contingent of Royal Guards?"

"Because Captain Grayble must stay here. I think Lord Malrec may be expecting something like this, and if he is, he'll have an invasion force ready to move in immediately if we leave the Great Palace without adequate defense. All of the Royal Guard must be here, and Captain Grayble must be here to command them. If my guess is correct, he'll also launch his ground force attack at the same time, so we need to leave the army in place to repel that. On top of all that, there's the Song of Raising and the Song of Joining. Lord Malrec has them. If Baron Prubard and Lord Diabon survive, no one may be able to get into Castle Glennayre for a long time. I need to look for the songs while I am there, and I am the one best equipped to recognize them."

Raman looked surprised. "That...makes sense."

It took all of her self-control not to say 'I told you so.'

"I'll go with you," Chen said immediately.

She couldn't help but smile. "I do appreciate the offer, Chen. But you can't do that. Like I said, the Royal Guard are going to have all they can do to guard the Great Palace. We can't be sure where Lord Malrec might choose to enter, and they are already short-handed because of the explosion. I may be speaking out of turn, but I have a hunch Captain Grayble could use you and the Talented Singari to help defend the Great Hall. I'd bet dollars to doughnuts that's where Malrec will end up."

"Dollars to doughnuts," Chen muttered. "Who can argue with logic like that? Alannys, you need me."

"They need you more," she insisted. "Do you think the Singari would listen to Captain Grayble? Or Arch-Prince Raman? Or even the king?"

Chen turned away from her and ran his hand through his hair. The Royal Guards hastily averted their eyes— Alannys supposed she could forgive them for staring; it probably wasn't every day that Singari visited the royal tent. "They won't listen to anyone who isn't me," Chen finally admitted. "But you can't go alone."

"She won't go alone." Dorramon's voice was forceful and determined, and it was right in her ear. She jumped — she hadn't realized he was that close behind her. "I'm going with her."

"You can't!" she gasped, spinning to face him. "The whole point of this is to protect you!"

"She's right," Raman said. "It doesn't make sense."

"It makes as much sense as letting her go," Dorramon shot back. "She's the Redeemer, have you forgotten? Absolutely irreplaceable, and the one person Lord Malrec desires most in the world. The whole thing is insanity, but if she's going, so am I."

"But—" Alannys began.

"You may as well save your breath," Raman cut in. "You aren't going to change his mind. Let him go. I'll go, too. We'll make a regular party of it."

"You, too?" Alannys said. "How many lives do we have to risk here?"

"You won't change my mind, either," Raman said. "I have unfinished business with Lord Malrec, and people to avenge. Besides, Kalyn and I are getting married tomorrow. I would just as soon not have Lord Malrec hanging over our heads."

"Tomorrow?" Alannys echoed with sudden dread. "You mean we are going to attack..."

"Tonight," Raman affirmed, and stood up. "I'm going to go back to the palace and get started right now on the painting we'll need. We know Lord Malrec has paintings of the Great Palace. We'll use one of those to get back." He turned and left the tent without another word, focused on the work ahead. Chen shook his head and followed the arch-prince out.

Alannys heaved a shaky sigh. That was not what she

had expected — while she recognized the importance of time, she had never even considered moving as soon as this very evening! But she couldn't argue against it — the sooner, the safer. She knew that.

Dorramon's hand fell heavily on her shoulder. "I am begging you to reconsider this. Raman and I will take care of this. There is no reason for you to risk yourself."

She spun around to face him in surprise. "Are you kidding me? Sit here at the Great Palace while you two go out and risk your lives? Not happening. Besides, what makes you think the palace is going to be any safer? Come tonight, I think Castle Glennayre and the Great Palace are going to be the two most dangerous places in all of Ravanmark."

"Then we'll send you somewhere else." Dorramon's gaze never flickered, and she realized with some shock that he was serious. "We have a painter, we can make it happen. We can send you anywhere else you care to go to hide. Danningham Manor, maybe. Duke Morryn would be glad to have you. Mirendasith Hall — Lord Arik loves you. Anywhere, just so long as you aren't part of whatever happens tonight."

"No." She shook her head, trying to imagine actually leaving here, having a pleasant dinner in someone else's castle, and spending the night in someone else's bed, pretending all the while that Dorramon wasn't out risking his life on a mission she had dreamed up to begin with. "No, that's crazy. I'm not leaving, Dorramon. I'm going with you. I'm not going to stand helplessly by while you live or die without me. If we die tonight, we'll die together."

He turned away from her, into the relative darkness of the back of the tent. "I could order you to stay, you know. I could have the Royal Guard lock you in your chambers until all of this is over."

"You wouldn't!"

"But something tells me it would be wasted effort. You would find some way around anything I could do. And I'm afraid you'd get yourself into even more trouble alone. So just promise me you'll stay with us tonight, and don't do anything rash."

"Of course," she said. "I promise."

"Very well, then." He didn't sound pleased with the assurances he'd extracted from her. He sounded defeated. "It's going to be a long night. You'd better go back to the keep and get some rest."

Alannys recognized a dismissal when she heard it. But she didn't like leaving, not like this. She put her hand on his shoulder, hoping to soften his reserve, to lessen the distance she suddenly felt between them. But he didn't turn around; he didn't react at all.

"I'll see you later, then," she said. "I love you."

And she turned and left the royal tent, feeling distinctly unsettled. Even the mindlink was closed tight against her, not that she could have used it anyway.

Chen waited outside, watching her with sad eyes.

"What?" she demanded, startled. How had she not seen this coming?

Chen fell into step beside her, walking back up the ridge toward the Great Palace. "Nothing. I know you too well to expect that you'd listen to me. I did hope that you might listen to him, though."

"You were *eavesdropping*?"

"Of course not. I didn't need a mindlink to know he was going to try to talk you out of it. And I can tell by your expression that you got your way."

Something about the way he said that made her feel defensive. "I can't believe you're going to seriously argue that I shouldn't take up my part in all this. Go hide in the corner and let others face the danger that is as much mine as anyone else's." Her foot came down wrong on a stone, and she stumbled.

Chen caught her arm and pulled her up, shaking his head. "I told you I already know you won't listen to me. You've heard a million times how I feel about things, and it's never slowed you down before. Just...be careful, will you? I have a bad feeling about all of this. Did you see the red glow of the moons this morning? My grandmother would have said it's an omen."

"An omen?" she said, interested in spite of herself. "What does it mean?"

"Blood," he said shortly. He didn't look at her. "Much blood will be spilled this night. Try to make sure none of it is yours."

He released her arm and left her, turning away to walk towards the Singari camp.

Chapter Four

ENDGAME

"**T**onight's the night!" Lord Malrec crowed, rubbing his hands together gleefully. "Everything we have worked for these past months has led up to this attack. And you, my friend—you have the most important role!"

Lord Diabon smiled broadly on the other side of the desk in Castle Glennayre's study, like a cat contemplating a particularly nice bowl of cream. "The most important role? Is this true?"

"Of course, of course! Nothing less for my right-hand man, the linchpin of the Dark Alliance." Malrec beamed at Diabon exactly as if the charismatic fool *was* his right-hand man. "Clearing the palace forces is the most essential part of our plans, the single most necessary thing that must be done to give us access to the king."

Diabon frowned. "Is this so? I thought you said—"

"There's been a change of plans, my friend," Malrec said, waving a hand negligently. "Apparently our royal do-gooders are not as set on doing good as I believed. My observations indicate they have no intention of coming here after the songs. Such dereliction of duty! Ah, well, I suppose it shouldn't surprise me. No, we're going to have to do this the hard way. Just think—the commander of the victorious invading forces—you'll be legend, my friend! Legend!"

Lord Diabon smiled faintly, considering it. "But my Lord, I have heard that Prubard will be leading the ambush on the Great Hall itself. Isn't this a much more prestigious role? Shouldn't it be *me* leading that ambush?"

Malrec snorted derisively. "Boasting, is he? Don't you worry, my friend—don't you give it another thought. This is a nighttime attack. Do you really think the king and all his supporters will be rallied in the Great Hall waiting for us? No, this mission fell to the baron because our fat friend is too dim to handle anything more important. Launching an assault on an empty hall is about the most I can trust him with."

Diabon's smile was as pointy as his carefully trimmed beard, and his chuckle was mean-spirited. "True enough, my Lord, true enough."

Lord Malrec stood up from his chair behind the desk. "Let me show you what awaits you, my friend. I think you will agree you can handle this challenge quite easily." He turned toward the art room and raised his voice. "Creft! Bring in the painting for Lord Diabon, lad!"

Lord Diabon looked distinctly unsettled. "Painting? You have a painting of this place?"

Malrec stifled a brief but intense flare of irritation. "Naturally, my friend, naturally. How else would we keep apprised of their preparation? Unless you prefer the grueling two and a half day march your army has endured, this is the only way we can get you there in time."

"Has endured? Do you mean to say you have deployed *my* army without me?"

"Honestly, I expected you to thank me," Malrec snapped, glancing impatiently at the art room. Where *was* that damned boy? "Any group of fools can handle marching east through the woods. I saved you for the important matters that need a commander. I thought you would appreciate that. Besides, I know how much you value your 'civilized necessities.'"

Lord Diabon took a step back. At that angle, the flickering torchlight lent a menacing aspect to his face, with its sharply pointed chin and carefully groomed black beard and mustache—but the effect was completely ruined by his startled, fearful expression. Apparently Malrec had not hidden his anger well enough. "Of course, my Lord. I—I thank you for your consideration."

Creft emerged at last from the art room, squeezing sideways through the door, struggling with an oversized canvas he could barely see over. "I have the painting, my Lord."

"And about time, too," Lord Malrec muttered under his breath. To the others, though, he smiled benignly, waving his apprentice toward the empty easel waiting in the middle of the room. "Don't keep us waiting, lad. Show Lord Diabon the size of the mighty force the Great Palace has mustered against us."

He watched with satisfaction as Lord Diabon swallowed in visible trepidation. Creft wrangled the canvas up onto the easel and stepped back, and Diabon moved in for a closer look.

"Is this a jest? There's nothing here. It's just an empty field."

Lord Malrec's smile broadened. He absolutely loved being in command of every situation, having more information than those around him. "Of course, my friend. You should know by now that when I paint a portal, I only paint the landscape. The people in that landscape will not appear until we open the portal."

"Of course," Lord Diabon replied, in a tone that suggested he didn't find that clear at all. Creft handed

Lord Malrec the jar of gloss and brush, and Diabon stood back while it was applied. He seemed impatient, though, leaning over Malrec's shoulder to see better. It annoyed Malrec to no end, but he said nothing and took much satisfaction from Diabon's surprised gasp when the encamped army shimmered into view.

"Is...is that all?" Diabon erupted into cackling, derisive laughter. "Ravanmark's most beloved king, hero of all he surveys...and *this* is the best his country could do for him? Why, I'd be shocked if that's more than three hundred men!"

"Exactly," Lord Malrec said. He nodded to Creft to begin scattering the drying powder. "I'm sending you to this battle with a force of one thousand men."

"It isn't going to be a battle," Diabon crowed, "it's going to be a massacre!"

"Right again." Malrec clapped Lord Diabon on the back as though they were the best of friends. "It will be a glorious defeat, the stuff of legends. And the man in those legends, my friend, will be you."

"Thank you," Diabon said sincerely. "Thank you, Lord Malrec. I shall be honored to lead this charge."

"Wonderful. You had better go and get some rest while you can...I will send someone for you when it is time to join your forces."

Lord Diabon inclined his head and swept from the room in long, purposeful strides, glowing with anticipation for the bloodshed to come.

♫

"Thank you, Creft." Lord Malrec turned back to his apprentice when Diabon's footsteps had receded. "That went better than I could have hoped. You did a wonderful job with this painting."

"Don't mention it." Creft's wide grin revealed several broken teeth. The young man's low class origins were a source of constant annoyance for Lord Malrec, and his training had gotten off to a bit of a rough start, but there was no denying the boy could paint. "I'm a dab hand at showing only what I want people to see."

"You certainly are. And now, it's time to get you in position—I meant what I told that imbecile; it won't be long at all before we are ready to move. Everything will be over this very night."

"I see. So if Lord Diabon'll be entertaining the palace troops, and Baron Prubard'll be assaulting the empty Great Hall—you'll be attacking King Dorramon yourself, I guess? Don't you want some soldiers here?"

Lord Malrec frowned, heading for the art room with his apprentice in tow. "It does not do to be too inquisitive about matters that do not concern you, Creft. But no, I do not wish any soldiers in Castle Glennayre. Our royal friends must believe they have caught us unawares. I have no intention of fighting the king myself if I can avoid it—it would be far too dangerous. Regardless of his other shortcomings, the boy is very good with a sword. No, that particular honor shall fall to my dear wife."

"The princess?" Creft was behind Malrec, so he couldn't see the boy's face, but he could hear the frown in the words. "Is it really a good idea to make her do that?"

"One of my very best ideas, I should say," Malrec said archly. "She will be in far less danger from him than any of the rest of us would face."

"I see, my Lord, but that ain't really my point. Don't you think it's kind of cruel?"

"You are my apprentice, boy," Malrec snapped. "That doesn't give you any right to question my decisions."

"Decisions? I figured this was just—just a bit of business you didn't put much thought in. If you made this decision, well, that makes it worse! She's a princess, and you treat her just awful. You should—"

"*You* should do yourself the favor of holding your

tongue!" Malrec stopped in front of a painting in the art room and turned on his apprentice. "How dare you question me, and how *dare* you criticize me! How I plan my affairs, and how I handle my marriage are *none of your business!*"

For a moment longer, Creft stood glaring, fists balled at his sides, face screwed up in anger, and Malrec thought he would have to fight the young fool. Great Muses, what if he killed the boy? No one else could take his place in the coming battle—it would cause no end of headaches if they had to fight without him.

But then Creft stepped back, pulling a deep breath and exerting visible effort to calm himself. "I am sorry, Master. You are right."

"In this as in all things," Malrec said airily. "I am glad you have the sense to see it. Now come with me—we need to get you settled and we don't have a lot of time."

Creft nodded. Lord Malrec turned his back on him and spread a thin coat of gloss over the painting in front of him. He couldn't say it was anywhere he particularly wanted to go, but it was worth it to have Creft in place.

He stepped through, landing with practiced grace in the long, empty, rundown stone hall of Archford Estate. A quick glance around assured him he was alone, so he turned to the hovering mist behind him. "I hope you understand what an important role you are playing in our plans. We are all relying on you."

Creft stumbled from the gray blur into the room, nearly running into Lord Malrec. "Aye, Master."

"Keep your voice down!" Malrec looked around the room again—so far, so good. "I have no wish to see Helva or any of her companions. If the Muses are merciful, I'll never see them again! Look boy, I have arranged your paintings over here. I even brought you a stool."

"How thoughtful." The words had an edge to them

that seemed almost like sarcasm. Creft stood next to the little stool and surveyed his small circle of paintings, each propped on its own easel. Malrec's eyes followed him, from the fields in front of the Great Palace, where the king's army was encamped, to the Great Hall itself. Several paintings depicted locations within Castle Glennayre.

"We're counting on you, boy. Should any of us run into trouble, you are to extract us immediately and bring us here."

"Of course, sir."

"On the other side of this room you'll find food for your wait. There is also a stockpile of weapons and armor for any of us you may have to rescue. We can rearm ourselves and travel back to a more opportune location."

"Aye, Master."

Lord Malrec looked around the room one last time. He saw nothing else that needed explanation, and he thought he could hear voices outside. "I'd best be getting back to the castle. There is much left to do."

He turned and went back into the cold mist, pleased with how well things were progressing. By morning, he would be King of Ravanmark.

He could feel it.

♫

"This is crazy," Alannys fretted, pacing around her sitting room in her familiar leather pants and linen workshirt. "We're crazy for doing this. *I'm* crazy for ever suggesting it."

"No, my Lady." Kalyn watched her pace, biting her lip. The light of the setting sun through the window behind her gave her red hair a vibrant orange glow. "It is the right thing to do. Could you have convinced the king himself, if the idea was bad?"

"I don't know," Alannys said. "He puts too much weight in what I say. This can't possibly work. We're all going to our deaths."

"No." Kalyn put her hands on Alannys's shoulders, putting an abrupt halt to her worried pacing. "Listen to me. You are going to face this evil, and you are going to do fine. You have the king and the arch-prince with you. You have been through so much—you won't fail now."

Alannys looked into Kalyn's face and realized these weren't just words to make her feel better. Kalyn truly believed what she said. That probably should have lifted her spirits, inspired her—but instead it left her with a feeling of pressure, of expectations yet unmet. "You're right," she said, looking away. "I've just—got cold feet, I guess."

A sudden knock at the door startled them both. Kalyn hurried to answer it, and a moment later Raman strode into the room. An unfamiliar man followed behind him, short and rather squat, with a ring of hair around the edge of his head that did nothing to cover the top. Raman quietly greeted Kalyn, then turned back to Alannys's brooding form.

"Good evening, my Lady," he said, with more cheer than she felt she could bear right then. "Are you ready to undertake our glorious quest?"

She couldn't find any sarcasm in his tone, only humor. "As ready as I'll ever be, I suppose."

"Actually I'm here to make you a bit readier. Or rather, this gentleman is. Lady Alannys, I'd like to present Perth. He is a locksmith, one of the finest in the Great Palace."

"It's a pleasure to meet you, Perth," she said, trying not to show her confusion. "What brings you here this evening?"

"You, my Lady," Perth said. "Leastways, that collar of yours." He stepped in front of her, peering up at the eel skin band around her neck. "I'm here to have a crack at unlocking it, if that suits you."

"Oh. Oh! Of course!" Alannys plopped herself down on the sofa and held still, putting the collar and its formidable lock in easy reach of the locksmith.

"Good, good," he muttered. "Now let's see here..."

He was still poking at the lock and examining it from different angles when a knock sounded at the door, and Kalyn ushered King Dorramon into the room.

Dorramon took in the scene at a quick glance. "Why is there a locksmith in here?"

"To unlock the Collar of Silence, obviously," Raman said. "Do you think it's wise for her to go to Castle Glennayre with her biggest weapon locked away?"

"Of course not. But I do think messing with that collar is risky. We've seen before how dangerous it can be."

"That was different," Raman said, watching with interest as Perth opened his leather bag and started laying out lock-picking tools on the sofa next to Alannys. "We were trying to cut it. It's meant to be unlocked, Dorr, or it wouldn't have a lock or a key. We aren't damaging it—just opening it as it's meant to be opened."

"I disagree. If it was meant to be picked, it wouldn't have a key."

Raman made a sound that might have been a laugh, or might have been a snort, and turned to watch Perth make his attempt at the lock.

"This is a bad idea," Dorramon muttered.

Alannys did her best to ignore him and hold still. She couldn't deny it made her nervous to have anyone poking around at the collar. But Raman did have a point—the collar was meant to be unlocked. They had to try.

Perth selected two long, slender metal picks and slid them inside the keyhole in the collar, carefully probing the lock.

The collar reacted instantly, clamping down with such speed and ferocity that Alannys didn't even have time to make a sound before her air supply was completely cut off. She jerked in sudden fright, but couldn't make a sound.

"That's enough!" Dorramon's voice cut through the fog of panic shrouding her brain. "You'll kill her if you keep going — get away!"

Perth glanced at her face and paled. His lock-picks clattered to the floor and he shrank back from her. "My Lady! I am sorry!"

The collar began to relax and Alannys sucked in ragged, gasping breaths, one hand against her throat as if it could somehow relieve the burning pain. "Not...your fault," she croaked.

Raman's hand fell on her shoulder. She hadn't even realized he had moved behind the sofa. "No, it's mine. I'm sorry. Dorramon was right — I should have figured something like this might happen. I should have been more careful."

"Indeed," Dorramon said. "Everything we do tonight must be done with an overabundance of caution. Let this be our only mistake. If not, I fear this entire undertaking must end very badly."

No one spoke. No one moved. No one could even look at anyone else.

Alannys shivered. She understood. The words didn't feel much like a warning.

They felt like an omen.

♪

After the ill-fated attempt to remove the Collar of Silence, the locksmith left Alannys's room in a hurry without another word. The silence he left behind felt heavy and awkward.

"I'd like to offer one last chance for reconsideration." Dorramon's voice was low and somber. "No one in this room will be forced to do this thing."

The corner of Raman's mouth quirked into a sardonic

expression he probably couldn't suppress. "No, but by the Muses we'll all be forced to live with the consequences, if we stand by and do nothing. I'll go."

"I expected as much." Dorramon turned to Alannys with something that looked a lot like dread. "And you, my Lady? Will you not be dissuaded from this thing?"

"No." She couldn't hold his gaze. "I'm sorry; I know you don't want me to go. But I can't sit back and watch everyone else do this. It's—it's personal, do you understand? Lord Malrec didn't bring just anyone here to be his weapon of mass destruction. He brought *me*. It's me he's tried to manipulate, use, and abuse ever since I got here. It was me that he spent days torturing, me that he's locked up in this damned collar, me that he wanted so badly he detonated the first bomb in the history of Ravanmark. And why is he holding the Song of Raising and the Song of Joining in his library? Because *I* need them." Alannys shook her head. "I know he's after you, Dorramon. I know he intends to be king. But I can't forget everything he's done to me, and I can't renounce my stake in this. This ends, and it ends tonight, and I'm going to do my part."

Dorramon nodded, and turned away from her, leading them into the corridor and out of the keep.

Alannys hurried to catch up. "But you, Dorramon—you don't have to do this. And frankly, I wish you wouldn't. It's too dangerous, especially for the king. What good will it do us to eliminate Lord Malrec if we lose you, too?"

Dorramon didn't answer. He crossed the Inner Ward so fast that Alannys was winded by the time they walked into the Great Hall.

There was none of the fanfare she would usually have expected to herald the entrance of the king. No courtiers littered the hall this night; instead the large room rang with the shouts of men preparing for battle.

"No, no, no!" Captain Grayble sounded more frustrated than she had heard him in a good long time. "Archers in the *front*, singers in the *back!* Look, it isn't confusing. I want you men shooting from the front of the balcony. The singers will be behind you. What is so complicated about that?"

"It ain't complicated," one of the archers shouted back, "it's just daft! Why should they be behind us?"

"So you don't shoot them!" Grayble roared, his face bright red. "I refuse to believe any man in my command is too stupid to understand this! No man can sing with an arrow in his back!"

"You say that like it's a bad thing," the archer countered. "What makes you think we want Singari singing at our backs? That ain't just daft, it's dangerous!"

"You are an idiot," Grayble said distinctly. "The Singari are on your side. They won't be targeting you, unless you continue to make derogatory remarks about them. We've given you earwraps to protect you from any unintended effects. I fail to see your complaint."

The archer buckled down for another angry response.

"No," a quiet voice interrupted. It sounded so firm and confident that it took Alannys a moment to recognize the voice as Chen's. "There is a simple solution to this. Put your archers on the left side of the room. My singers will cover the right."

Captain Grayble shook his head, but the argumentative archer looked pleased. "See there," he said, "the Singari can see reason about it."

"And after this is all over," Chen continued pleasantly, as if the archer had not spoken, "we'll count up which side has the most casualties. I'm willing to bet dollars to doughnuts, as Lady Alannys says, that it will be your archers."

"I'd back that bet," Alannys said.

"Well, then," Captain Grayble said, his scowl replaced with a broad grin, "it seems we have reached a consensus. Any man who is not happy fighting with the Singari can come down here, and we'll arrange for you to fight alone. Don't be shy, now—come right down."

Feet shuffled awkwardly in the balconies, throats cleared loudly in the sudden silence, but no man moved to take the captain up on his offer.

"Ah, so we *have* reached a consensus," Grayble said. "A wise decision. You will not regret it." He turned away from the archers and approached Dorramon, Raman, and Alannys. "Your Majesty, what is this madness I have heard of you accompanying the strike force to Castle Glennayre?"

Dorramon mustered a smile from somewhere. "Always one for bluntness, Captain Grayble."

"When the occasion warrants it." Grayble didn't back down. "Your Highness can't possibly be serious. This is madness. What if some harm should befall you? The King of Ravanmark can't be gallivanting about like a knight errant."

"Exactly what I tried to tell him," Alannys muttered.

"Stay here, your Highness," Grayble pressed. "Let me take your place on the mission. I assure you that the Lady Alannys can have no more dedicated guard."

"Peace, Captain." Dorramon's smile looked a bit more genuine now. "I appreciate your concern. But I'm going to have to overrule it. Your place is here, with your men. You must keep the Great Palace safe so that I have something to return to."

"But your Majesty—"

"My decision is final, Captain. I'll hear no more about it."

Chen watched them all with eyes that seemed sad, and

older somehow than last time she had seen him. "You all have made up your minds, then?"

Her smile felt as false as Dorramon's had looked. "I'm afraid so. It has to be done, and it has to be done now." She glanced around the room, at the archers waxing bowstrings, the guards honing blades, the Singari in the balconies quietly planning songs and lyrics. Even Eleana stood up there, clutching her flute with white knuckles and listening to the plans, her face pinched. Alannys had more friends at stake than she could count, and the thought brought a cold lump to her stomach. "Be careful, Chen."

"Me?" Chen raked a hand through his hair. "I don't think it's me you have to worry about. Just don't do anything crazy, all right?"

"Chen, I'm surprised at you. When have I ever done anything crazy?"

He grunted and turned away, scrubbing at his face with his hands.

"We should go," Raman said. "It looks like things are well in hand here."

"Indeed." Dorramon looked around the Great Hall, then at his friends standing with him. "They probably have things more in control than we do."

They turned as a group and left the Great Hall, heading back across the Inner Ward toward the Lesser Hall in grim silence.

Halfway to the keep, a running, gasping, cloaked figure caught up with them. "Your Highness! Your Highness, please...wait!"

Alannys glimpsed the curve of a sharply hooked nose under the hood of the cloak, and recognized Grand Chancellor Ebrad. Dorramon looked at him, but didn't slow down. "What is it, Ebrad?"

"Your Majesty, please," Ebrad said raggedly. "You

must reconsider!"

"We've been through this," Dorramon warned.

"But your Majesty! Please, heed your duty. Wars are not for kings to fight—not *personally!* Heed your duty, my Lord King, and stay here. Let those more expendable do your battles."

Dorramon did stop then, and turned on the chancellor with a glare that nailed him to the spot. "Don't ever let me hear you say that again. Our Redeemer is many things, but *expendable* will never be one of them. And I imagine we would all feel the loss of the arch-prince."

"Of—of course, Sire," Ebrad stammered, glancing nervously between them all. "I—I meant no offense, of course. I only intended—your Highness, *please* don't do this."

The king turned away, back on his original course to the keep. "Calm down, Ebrad. This isn't for you to worry about. I know you won't believe me, but the palace won't be safe tonight either. We must all do what we can to secure the future of the kingdom. We will take care of Lord Malrec. You concentrate on making sure you're here to run the Great Palace when I get back."

"Yes, your Majesty," the chancellor gulped, and fell behind.

"Stubborn as ever," Raman said. "Does it matter how many people try to tell you the same thing?"

"No," Dorramon said shortly, holding the vestibule door open for his friends. "I'm sorry. Nothing will convince me to stay here while you two do this." He fell in beside them as they moved through the corridor. "Besides, I meant what I told the chancellor. We're assuming the Dark Alliance will target the Great Hall—and that is where I expect they will end up. But I don't expect that will be their only angle of attack, and I don't think they will very much care who or what they destroy trying to get in. No place in the Great Palace will be safe tonight."

He said the words with flat conviction, and hearing them, Alannys couldn't deny that they were true. It gave her a cold shiver she couldn't suppress, and a feeling of foreboding she wished she could shake.

♪

The Lesser Hall did nothing to ease Alannys's jangling nerves. The towering room no longer looked even remotely appropriate for royal audiences, with armored archers high in the recessed balconies, and three Royal Guardsmen on duty — one stationed on the imposing dais, and two patrolling the audience hall. A long wooden table held armor and weapons for the strike party, and an easel dominated the room, holding a big painting of the kitchen in Castle Glennayre a foot or so off the ground.

"The kitchen?" Alannys blurted in surprise. "We're going to the kitchen?"

Raman shrugged. "Kalyn said it would most likely be empty this time of night. I thought we might not like an audience when we arrive — we'll need a minute to get our bearings."

Alannys nodded. She couldn't deny it made sense, and yet she couldn't seem to look away from the painting. The kitchen looked so familiar — even after all she had been through, it felt as though she might have just seen those gleaming copper countertops yesterday. And that feeling brought home to her the one fact she had been pushing aside all day — against every bit of rational sense she had, *she was going back there.* Back to the place she had almost died in Archford Estate to avoid, back to the one place in Ravanmark she felt sure she would never leave alive again. She swallowed hard, and tried to tell herself that she wasn't afraid to see Lord Malrec again, that the thought of facing him with the intent to kill didn't make her hands and feet icy cold.

"Alannys?" Dorramon frowned at her, frozen in the

middle of pulling a heavy leather gauntlet onto his arm. "Are you all right?"

She nodded and turned quickly away, scanning the table for anything that might fit her. She knew it was useless to lie to Dorramon, but she refused to admit, now that it came to it, how much this mission scared her.

She knew she hadn't fooled him, but he let it drop, watching her closely as he finished suiting up. Kalyn appeared as if from nowhere beside her, holding what appeared to be an armload of tiny steel rings. "Let me help you, my Lady."

Alannys looked dubiously at the tangle of bright metal. "Help me what? Am I supposed to — wear that?"

Kalyn held her hands up, and the rings rolled down toward the floor, forming the unmistakable shape of a tall, narrow shirt with long sleeves. "Certainly, my Lady. It is a mail shirt. With this and a steel cuirass, you'll have the best protection we can offer."

Alannys didn't doubt that, but she couldn't pretend to be enthusiastic about the mail shirt...she couldn't remember when she'd ever seen anything that looked so uncomfortable to wear. But a quick glance to her right showed Raman fastening a cuirass over the same type of mail, so she held out her arms and let Kalyn help her into it. Immediately she wished she hadn't — the thing hung off her shoulders like thirty pounds of lead, pushing her toward the floor like the hand of a giant. She staggered under the weight.

"Oof," she grunted. "Kalyn, I don't think I can do this. I have to wear something else *over* this?"

Kalyn frowned, watching her. "Yes. But I think you are right, my Lady. I don't see how you can defend yourself like that."

"I can't," Alannys said. "You'll have to throw a black cloak over me and I'll cower in a lump on the floor and hope Lord Malrec doesn't trip over me."

"You'll forgive me," Dorramon said from behind her, with wry humor, "if I say that's a lousy plan."

She turned to face him, ready with a snappy rejoinder, but the words died unspoken. Dorramon wore hardened leather armor, dark brown, reinforced with steel plating depicting the royal crest—two large stags on their hind legs, antlers locked in battle. His gauntlets and greaves matched, each with one metal stag glimmering on their surface. Chain mail covered the gaps, although he looked rather more used to bearing its weight. He looked dashing and commanding, ready to march in and win any battle.

Alannys swallowed hard, struggling to think clearly. "I...don't suppose you have a better one?"

The king grinned at her, as if he was perfectly well aware of the source of her discomfort and found it amusing. "It just so happens I do. Kalyn, grab that brigandine." He helped Alannys pull the mail shirt back over her head, and tossed it onto the table.

Kalyn returned carrying a quilted leather jacket with no sleeves, and flared flaps that looked like they were meant to hang over her hips. She helped Alannys into it, and buckled up the front. "Is that better, my Lady?"

"Much," Alannys said, surprised to realize it. She swung her arms, and twisted around. It was a little stiff, but nothing like as heavy as the chain mail had been.

"I'm afraid it won't protect you as well," Kalyn fretted.

"But at least you'll be able to move," Dorramon said. He held out her swordbelt and she buckled it on, then pulled on a smaller pair of gauntlets.

"Now look," Raman said suddenly. They all turned to face him, and found him regarding them sternly, chain and plate metal protecting his entire torso. "Before we take another step I want to be sure we all understand our parts in this."

"What do you mean?" Alannys asked, immediately on her guard.

Raman leveled one big finger at her. "You are here to find the songs. That's it. We arrive at Castle Glennayre, you're going straight to the library. Dorramon will go with you. I will go find Lord Malrec and any of his men that are in the castle. I'll find you in the library when I'm done."

"Now, wait—" Alannys began.

"No, I'm serious. This keeps the two most important people in the kingdom out of direct danger. I'm not going to open that painting until you both agree."

"All right," Dorramon said at once. He put his arm around her and squeezed her shoulders, as if encouraging her to agree as well. She heard his whisper, though she was pretty sure Raman could not. "But if we just so happen to get lost and go help him, I don't think we'll be breaking our word."

Alannys felt the corners of her mouth twitch, and tried mightily not to smile. "Okay," she said aloud. "We'll find the songs. You hunt the Dark Alliance."

Raman regarded them both through narrowed eyes. "That was easy," he muttered.

"Only because you're right," Dorramon said. "It makes sense."

Raman inspected them both a moment longer, but evidently found nothing he could take issue with, and turned to the easel. The gloss and the paintbrush were laid out on the tray in front of the painting, and with graceful curving gestures, he covered the surface of the painting.

The change was disturbing, even though Alannys knew it was coming. The painting instantly went dark—all the shining copper on the counters, the brick oven with its warm earth tones, the dark stone floor, everything disappeared into unrelenting blackness. Of course she had expected the room to be dark; it was the middle of the night. But knowing in an abstract way that the castle would be dark was somehow not the same as facing the gaping black abyss of the painting, knowing she would soon be stepping through. It didn't feel like the normal, flat black she would expect from a painted canvas—this blackness felt deep somehow, *alive*, like a yawning maw waiting to swallow them all.

It felt malevolent.

Perhaps the others felt it, too. Perhaps that was why for a long moment no one moved, or spoke.

Kalyn rushed by Alannys and threw herself into Raman's arms. "Please be careful," she said, her voice muffled in his chest. "*Please.*"

Alannys turned away, deliberately not hearing whatever Raman might have said in return, and found Dorramon watching her steadily. "Are you still sure you want to do this?" he said.

"No," she said. "Stepping into that painting is about the last thing I want to do right now. But if we don't do this, it won't get done. And he's got to be stopped, Dorramon. We can't let him win. We just can't."

Dorramon nodded and took her hand in his. It felt strange, holding hands in their heavy leather coverings, with no electricity. Before either of them could change their mind, they stepped together into the blackness.

♫

The icy void took her breath away. She didn't exist, yet she was freezing; she couldn't breathe, and yet her lungs burned with cold. Alannys hated traveling through paintings. She didn't think she would ever get used to it.

Dorramon caught her arm when she stumbled, and steadied her. The blackness was only slightly less intense on this side of the painting; staring into the darkness around them, Alannys could just begin to make out the form of the kitchen around her.

It was enough for her to get her bearings, and she

turned for the door that led to the long, narrow stone corridor through Castle Glennayre's middle.

"Stop right there," hissed a low voice behind her. "Where do you think you are going?"

Alannys nearly jumped out of her skin. She was halfway back around, her hand on Songstrike's grip, when she placed the voice. "Raman! You scared me to death!"

Raman stood glaring at them both with his hands on his hips, unapologetic. "You both know the plan perfectly well. Sneaking out ahead of me doesn't change things."

"Of course not, Raman." Dorramon's voice washed calm over them both. "We weren't trying to leave you behind. Alannys and I are headed straight to the library to search for the songs."

The arch-prince relaxed, mollified. "All right, then. Let's get moving." He moved out in front of them, and led them both out into the darkness of the corridor. Alannys couldn't hear anything but the hammering of her own heart—a sound so loud she was sure the others had to hear it, too.

Raman stepped out into the chilly hallway. He glanced over at the library at the far end, and froze. He could see forms in the library.

Human forms.

Damn it! He couldn't send Dorramon and Alannys in there, but he wasn't comfortable leaving them here, either —he knew they would follow him. The whole situation stank. His hand clenched on the grip of his sword. "Stay here," he hissed, turning to favor each of his companions with a hard glare. "I mean that. Don't follow me—don't move from that spot."

They both nodded immediately, their pale faces strained in the dim light. He could see worry written in every line and shadow of their expressions—but he felt like he couldn't quite trust them, like as soon as he turned his back they would be off, like naughty toddlers, tearing into everything he'd warned them away from.

"I mean it," he growled, and loped away from them on cat's feet, moving like a shadow down the silent corridor, reminding himself that they were both adults and they understood the danger as well as he did.

It didn't matter. He couldn't do it; he paused, halfway down the hallway, to look back, reassuring himself. They hadn't moved. Of course they hadn't; where would they go? He chided himself for a mother hen, and ran on toward Castle Glennayre's library, moving soundlessly on the balls of his feet.

Gathered around a table in the dimly lit library stood three men Raman had recognized at first glance — Lord Malrec, Lord Diabon, and Baron Prubard. A few paces away stood a smaller man facing an easel. Raman could only assume this was the apprentice he had heard about. It didn't matter — the apprentice was of no consequence. But all three leaders of the Dark Alliance, together and *right in front of him...!*

Raman had his sword in his hands before he made it to the end of the hallway, had his attack mapped out in his mind before he charged into the library with a war cry and a mighty swing of the blade that took all of his anger and hate and delivered it in a sweeping blow, separating Malrec's torso from his legs in the process.

Raman's thinking mind knew it wasn't right, could feel with the first bite of the blade that this was no living human body he struck. But he fought from a level far below his thinking mind, where things were more ingrained and animalistic, and his second swing skewered Lord Diabon even as he recognized that the thing regarding him across the table, with Baron Prubard's matted fur cloak draped around it, was some sort of wooden form with a wig, and a leather sack for a torso.

He jammed the sword back in its scabbard and stood, panting raggedly, regarding the destruction he'd wrought. The two dummies he had attacked had spewed and splattered fluid all over each other, all over the table, the floor all the way over to some of the enormous bookshelves — all over him. It was a thin, clear liquid, with the strong smell of pine.

Raman recognized the cloying scent of turpentine in the same moment his head wrenched in sudden pain, and all of his hair stood on end. He'd been watched since they first arrived in the castle, he knew that, but this painting was newly-opened, and it was close.

His hand flew to the grip of his sword and he scrambled, searching wildly for the telltale gray blur of an open portal. He had walked right into a trap — he'd known that since his blade slid too easily through the thing wearing Lord Malrec's dark cloak, but now it was time for the trap to spring, and he wasn't at all sure which direction to run, or if running would only make things worse.

The portal hung in the middle of the round room, yawning open over the round table and its turpentine-soaked maps and music papers. In the same instant Raman finally saw it, the portal winked out of existence, leaving behind a burning torch tumbling end over end toward the table below.

Raman's eyes widened in sudden, gut-cramping fear. He had never seen something move so fast, while seeming to move so slow. There wasn't time to run, not even time to swear. He wrenched himself around and flung himself back toward the corridor, his arms stretched out toward the doorway he couldn't reach, as the torch hit the turpentine and the room exploded into flames around him.

♫

"Dorramon!" The angry shriek assaulted Alannys and

Dorramon as soon as they were alone in the hall, piercing and derisive. "By the Sacred Song—haven't you got any sense at all? What are you *doing* here?"

Alannys spun around to see Dorramon staring down the hall in pole-axed surprise at Princess Delline, the Lady of Glennayre—the one person they had really not planned on seeing this evening. She stood at the far end of the corridor, in front of the spiral staircase to the tower bedroom.

"Delline?" Dorramon sounded as flabbergasted as she felt.

"Dorramon..." Alannys began, hoping to convince him to ignore this unexpected wrinkle in their plans.

Delline made a sound of utter impatience. "I'm serious, Dorramon. This was stupid—*you* were stupid to come here. Leave! Go now, while you still can!"

The princess lifted her skirts up to her knees and ran up the tower steps, faster than Alannys had ever seen her move before. Her footsteps receded quickly, never slowing.

"Dorramon..." Alannys said again, and realized in sudden cold fear that he was no longer beside her. "Dorramon!"

He was already halfway down the corridor, moving fast. He stopped and turned to her when she called, but he still looked over his shoulder at the stairs. "Wait here, Alannys. She's my sister. I have to go after her."

"Dorramon, you can't! She bombed the Great Palace, remember? Sister or not, she's dangerous!"

"I have to try. If she didn't care, she wouldn't have warned me away. Find the songs, Alannys!" He turned and ran for the stairs.

Alannys took a couple of uncertain steps towards his rapidly receding back. A glance behind her showed Raman in the library, attacking Lord Malrec and the Dark

Alliance. Could she just leave him down here alone? She had a bad feeling about all of this. But she knew she would only slow him down, and she knew that, whatever Dorramon believed, Delline had to be leading him into a trap.

"Dorramon, wait!" She ran for the tower stairs, pausing at the bottom to look back toward the library again, guilt gnawing at her conscience. "Forgive me, Raman," she whispered, and before she could even turn back around, the library burst into flames.

Alannys's hands felt suddenly cold, staring into the blazing inferno that had suddenly become of Castle Glennayre's library. Dorramon and Raman—both were in mortal danger, and she could only help one of them. She bit her lip, hesitating. What should she do?

All at once the mindlink disappeared—just popped out of existence as if it had never existed at all. She hadn't been able to use it since Archford, but she could still feel it. Now—it was gone. Blind, unreasoning panic drove her up the stairs. She knew the tower room was Talent-proofed, but still—every fiber of her being screamed that something was wrong when the mindlink disappeared. She hoped again that Raman would forgive her, and ran as fast as her legs would carry her. She had been right in a way—this certainly was a trap.

But it was a trap for all of them.

Alannys ran into the tower bedroom at full tilt and skidded to a halt, her soft soled boots slipping on the stone floor. Delline lay sprawled flat on her back on the little rug, apparently unconscious. Dorramon knelt beside her.

"Dorramon!" she gasped in relief. She stepped over behind him, feeling her pulse finally begin to slow. She had been so sure this was a trick... "Dorramon, we have to go! Raman is—"

The wardrobe doors exploded open behind her, and

before she could even turn completely around, her arms were wrenched up behind her back. "Welcome home, Alannys," hissed a voice in her ear, wafting her with the scent of cinnamon.

Delline scrambled to her feet, whirling on Dorramon and brandishing a dagger.

It took all of the self-control Alannys had not to say "I told you so." She knew she shouldn't even be thinking that, given the utter desperation of their predicament, but she couldn't help it.

The whole thing had been a trap.

And Princess Delline had led them right into it.

♪

"Well, now," Lord Malrec drawled, "isn't this cozy?"

"Dorramon," Alannys said, gritting her teeth against the pain as Malrec jerked her arms up higher behind her, "get out of here. Run!"

Lord Malrec's chuckle was decidedly unpleasant. "Now that wouldn't be very noble, would it? However, one must be prepared for all eventualities..." He dragged Alannys over to the door, using the mass of both of their bodies to block the room's only exit.

Dorramon watched Delline, sadness putting lines in his face that had not been there before. "Do you intend to murder me, then?"

Delline's eyes burned unnaturally bright. Now that Alannys got a good look at her in decent light, she was horrified by what she saw. Delline's skin was wrinkled and thin, stretched across her bones as if it had weathered many more decades than she had been alive. The chestnut of her hair was shot through with gray — if Alannys hadn't known better, she'd have sworn the princess was older than Queen Farrine. She had never seen anything like it, and she could only think of one possible cause: the focus bond Larric had originally told her Lord Malrec shared with Kalyn. The Lord of Glennayre seemed to be at the root of almost every problem Alannys encountered.

Delline held the dagger out in front of herself as though she expected attack, but it wavered uncertainly in her hands. She looked at the dagger, and looked at her brother, but she did not speak a word.

"Delline!" Malrec urged. "Don't just stand there, woman—this is your moment! Victory is within our grasp! *Finish him!*"

"No!" Alannys wailed, lunging forward in a desperate, hopeless attempt to break Lord Malrec's iron grip.

"A gentle death," Delline muttered, quietly but distinctly. "Like falling asleep. A kindness."

"Quit procrastinating!" Malrec snapped. "Kill him!"

"Delline," Alannys cried, "don't do this!"

Dorramon didn't say a word. He watched his sister somberly, silently, never moving.

Delline's feverish eyes flicked from Dorramon to Lord Malrec, and back again. "A princess has a duty," she said clearly, "to do not what is best for herself, but what is best for her kingdom."

Lord Malrec smiled, a broad smile that looked somehow sharp.

Moving faster than Alannys had ever seen her move before, Delline flipped the glittering dagger around. Swiftly, before anyone in the room could intervene, she plunged it into her own breast.

"A gentle death," she murmured, and slumped to the cold stone floor.

"Delline!" Dorramon fell to his knees beside her, pale and strained. He reached uncertainly for the handle of the dagger, then pulled his hands back. "Delline, what have you done?"

"Like falling asleep," she said, though she didn't look much like sleeping. Her face was gray and tight with pain, and her form had a peculiar rigid look to it, sprawled there on the floor.

Delline began to shudder and jerk, seizing uncontrollably. Her back arched, her mouth foamed, and her eyes bulged, but she couldn't seem to make a sound. The princess convulsed painfully to her death, while her brother watched on in helpless horror.

Lord Malrec swore under his breath. This, Alannys realized, was finally a development he had not predicted.

Dorramon sprang to his feet, turning on Malrec in sudden, murderous fury. "You will pay for this," he said, his voice shaking with fury, drawing his sword. "I swear to the Muses you will pay for my sister's life with your own!"

Lord Malrec swore again, keeping Alannys carefully in front of him, dragging her with him as he backed out onto the wooden landing at the top of the spiral stairs. As soon as they left the confines of the tower room, all of the hair on her neck stood on end; someone, somewhere, had this place in a painting—and the painting was open. She couldn't see the misty gray blur, but she knew it was hanging there, somewhere very nearby. "Not today, young man, not today," Malrec said. He sounded almost amused. "Creft! Get me out of here at once!"

He wasn't loosening his hold on Alannys, and she realized with sudden cold fear that he meant to take her with him, wherever Creft was hiding with the painting. She braced herself, tensed every muscle, ready to struggle for all she was worth.

But nothing happened—no portal opened near her or Lord Malrec. They heard a nasty chuckle, and the sensation of watching eyes abruptly vanished.

Malrec's apprentice had closed the painting.

"Creft!" Malrec bellowed, his face purple and mottled. "By the Muses, boy, I'll have your stones on a stick for this!" He pushed Alannys toward the edge of the landing.

She stumbled toward the sheer drop, and as Dorramon lurched forward to catch her, Malrec whirled away from them and ran headlong down the stairs.

Dorramon caught Alannys by the arm and steadied her. "Are you all right?"

"Yes. Yes, I'm fine." She caught a glimpse of Delline's remains, cold and stiff and gray on the floor of the tower room, and flinched away. "He got away, though."

"Yes. He did." Dorramon jammed his sword back into the sheath. "But not for long."

And they both started down the stairs, ready to follow Lord Malrec anywhere he might try to run, to uncover him anyplace he might try to hide. Whatever happened, they would end this thing, for once and for all.

Tonight.

♫

Lord Diabon stumbled on the uneven terrain, but quickly gained his feet, brushing at his cloak as though the journey had dirtied it. Traveling through the painting had been frankly terrifying, but Diabon would have cut off his own hands before admitting it, especially in front of the crass, backward men who made up his army. "Is everything ready?" he demanded, without so much as glancing at the lieutenants scurrying to keep up with him.

"Yes, my Lord," answered a dirty, bedraggled man on his left. Lord Diabon did not know the man's name, nor did he care to. He couldn't wait until this was all over. As the new king's closest advisor, he would never have to associate with people like this again. "The men are ready to move as soon as you give word. Your horse is waiting, just over there."

Diabon was forced to look at the man long over to ascertain the direction he pointed. Following the gesture, he was surprised to find he could see the animal clearly, even at this distance.

"White?" he blurted in displeasure and dismay. "We

launch a midnight attack, and you put me on a white horse? In the moonlight that beast will practically glow! Who is responsible for this?"

"Why, Lord Malrec, my Lord," the lieutenant said meekly. "He sent the horse for you special. Are you – are you refusing?"

A feather of something unpleasant tickled against Lord Diabon's awareness. He frowned. "No, no of course not. Ready the men. We'll move as soon as I mount up."

The lieutenant nodded and ran into the distance, either relieved or giving a very good impression of it. Lord Diabon strode up to his special horse and frowned at it. He didn't like his situation, but he couldn't see any way out of it.

The horse snorted and shook its head, as though the situation didn't look any better from where it stood.

"Quiet, you." Lord Diabon grabbed hold of the pommel and swung himself into the saddle quickly, roughly. His tone and his manner would have spooked almost any horse in Brookeshire Castle's stable, he knew that well enough. Perhaps he hoped to spook this horse into misbehaving as well, so that he would have some grounds to complain to Lord Malrec, something tangible and more significant than the animal's color. He knew it had probably been an oversight – Lord Malrec had clearly assigned the horse based on its excellent behavior – but still, it left him with an uneasy feeling he wished he could ignore.

Diabon pulled on his leather gauntlets. Metal plates reinforced the backs of them, making them safer but also stiffer. He flexed his fingers, and wrapped them around the reins with some difficulty. He *detested* combat. Ah, well, at least he could take comfort in the overwhelming numbers of his forces – the battle would at least be quick.

He rode the white horse out to the front of his lines of

men, all maintaining as much formation as they could in the dense forest. Now was the time for a rousing speech, but any shout that could reach all of these men risked reaching the forces encamped outside the Great Palace as well, and even given their advantage, that was a risk he did not wish to take.

So he raised his arm high over his head and swung it forward, a silent signal to advance. He and his few lieutenants charged out of Westmore Forest on horseback, while the rest of the men thundered along behind them on foot, clutching swords and spears with white knuckles.

Lord Diabon broke out into the open, and reined up sharply. For a long, surreal moment his brain utterly refused to accept the evidence his eyes saw before him, even when his lieutenants stopped next to him in uncertain silence.

The palace army was enormous. There were men encamped *everywhere he looked.* He was outnumbered, badly outnumbered — five to one, maybe more.

Lord Diabon swallowed hard. This was a fool's errand — the painting Creft had shown him had been carefully staged, deliberately angled to show only a tiny fraction of the true force they faced. The white horse on which he now rode was no accident — this was a beacon, to call all eyes to him, to make him an easy target. He finally understood — contrary to all the excuses he had offered, Lord Malrec had sent him here to die.

Lord Diabon was supremely unwilling to die — for Lord Malrec, King Dorramon, or anyone else. The palace forces had already seen them — already their men mounted up, grabbed weapons, and prepared to attack. He squared his shoulders and turned to his lieutenants.

"Two groups," he snapped. "You —" he picked a man at random, " — take half of the men and move around to the south. You over there, take the other half and go straight in from here."

The lieutenants nodded. The whites of their eyes flashed large and frightened in the bright moonlight. "And — and you, my Lord?" one of them asked.

"I will pull half a dozen men and move in stealth to take the anteyard. We will dispose of the gate guards. Once we have done that we will sound a call, and both of you and all of your men must quickly make for the palace. When they must funnel through the gate to attack us, we can defeat this army."

"Yes, my Lord!" With renewed enthusiasm, the lieutenants turned and barked orders to the foot-soldiers. As his forces deployed around him, Lord Diabon sat tall on his white beacon, cutting a brave silhouette against the dark forest, inspiring them all.

Once they had all passed by, he scrambled down off of the accursed beast and slapped its flank, driving it riderless into the fray of combat.

Then he turned and ran along the edge of the forest, keeping low and tearing through the underbrush like a mad thing. He had one chance: he had to get out of here, back to Brookeshire Castle, and he had to smooth everything over with the Crown right away. Unless Lord Malrec managed to win the day. If that happened — he had to be ready to leave Ravanmark. Immediately.

He glanced back over his shoulder. He was still too close to the battle to risk leaving the cover of the forest. Soon, though, he would be far enough away to be safe — and then he was going to cut out across the open country. Straight to Brookeshire, as fast as possible.

♫

It was perhaps twenty minutes into the skirmish when a Royal Guard patrolling the high watchtower saw a single figure out on the far side of the ridge, running northeast as though Soth himself pursued.

He watched the man run a moment, cocking his head

to the side. Who could the runner be? He'd wager it wasn't anyone from the palace army. Must have been one of Diabon's men.

He nocked an arrow on his bowstring and pulled it back. Allowing for the height difference and the wind, he could take the runner down if he aimed right...about...*there*.

A hand fell on his arm, spoiling the shot. "Nah, don't bother. Ain't worth the trouble."

He whipped his head around to find his shift partner standing there next to him, shaking his head, watching the runner disappear. "Nalay! What're you playing at?"

"No point wasting your arrow on an iffy shot at some coward."

He lowered his bow. "I suppose you're right. Still, rubs me the wrong way, letting the enemy escape."

Nalay scoffed. "Enemy. You give him too much credit. That ain't nobody. What difference could one deserter make?"

He watched the man recede into the distance, gnawing on the inside of his lip, and wondering.

What difference *could* one deserter make?

♫

It felt like hours later when Raman reached out with a shaking hand and grabbed hold of the door jamb, pulling himself to a shaky stand. He still couldn't quite believe he had survived. He staggered out into the hallway, pulling a ragged breath, savoring the taste of air that wasn't heavy with the smoke that filled the library tower.

Dorramon and Alannys were nowhere to be seen. In a way it made sense—they never would have left him in there alone if they had been nearby—but where could they possibly have gone? Where were they now?

Raman caught a sudden glimpse of Lord Malrec darting into the study, his dark velvet cloak billowing behind him.

Raman raced after him, down the corridor and into the study, moving as quietly as he could on the smooth stone. Lord Malrec was hefting a painting up onto the wooden easel—it was a large painting, but Raman couldn't tell where exactly it was a painting *of*. All he could see was a mess of flagstones, expertly shaped, now broken and uneven, with grass and weeds growing up between them. Watching Malrec's furtive, hurried manner, though, it didn't take a genius to guess that he was planning on going there, and soon.

"Just where do you think you are going?" Raman demanded, drawing his sword and leveling it at Lord Malrec.

Malrec startled violently, but recovered himself quickly. He turned to face Raman, laughing like the crunching of dead leaves under boots. "If it isn't my dear little brother. So you survived the library. Ah, well, I suppose I shouldn't be surprised. The surest plans, and all that rot."

"The surest plans of mortal men are foiled by the whims of the Muses," Raman quoted. "Are you claiming you had all of this planned, Malrec?"

Lord Malrec snorted derisively, an explosive sound in the quiet that enveloped the study like a shroud. "Obviously not this precise sequence of events. I certainly did not anticipate betrayal from that misbegotten whelp of an apprentice." He faced Raman, seeming absorbed in their conversation, but his hand snaked out as if of its own accord and snatched the jar of gloss off the mantel.

Raman tracked the motion and frowned. "Your apprentice betrayed you?"

"Yes, boy, yes! Creft was supposed to watch tonight and rescue me or my fellow lords, should we need it. He's still watching, but he's done no bloody rescuing. Do you hear me, Creft, you craven son of a goat?" he shouted, shaking his fist at the blur in the back of the room, hovering on the ceiling. "I'm coming for you! You'll answer for this betrayal with blood!"

A nasty chuckle floated out of the misty blur.

"So you find yourself in a rough spot," Raman said, keeping his blade trained on Malrec, "and now you're going to run. Is that it?"

"No." Lord Malrec pulled himself up straighter, apparently stung by the accusation of cowardice. "No, I am going to rid myself of a traitorous apprentice, and then I am going to regroup. Creft guards a trove of weapons, and paintings of every conceivable place I might need to go. This changes nothing. Your friends will not live to see the dawn; I shall make certain of that." He stepped over to the desk and grabbed a paintbrush, emboldened by his speech.

"You must know I have no intention of letting you leave."

Lord Malrec looked at him, contempt burning in his eyes. "You must know your intentions do not concern me at all." He turned his back on Raman, and began to stir the gloss with the brush.

Dorramon and Alannys charged into the study, stopping just inside the door. The king saw Malrec preparing the painting, and frowned. He started forward, his hand on the grip of his sword, but Alannys grabbed his arm and shook her head.

Raman nodded grimly and turned back to the painting. He didn't have much time; Lord Malrec swept gloss over the canvas, and the image shimmered to life.

Paintings were spying all over Castle Glennayre— they'd had Raman's head pounding since he'd first arrived. But the opening of this new one seemed more intense, pushing the pain to a whole new stabbing level of awful. He shoved the pain aside and tried to focus on what had to be done.

"I'm warning you one more time, Lord Malrec, stop where you are," he said.

Lord Malrec didn't even turn around. He laughed — actually *laughed,* and in the sound Raman heard the same withering contempt that had filled his eyes earlier. "I'm in no danger from you, boy. You won't harm me — I'm the last family you have! Run along now, I've got a coup to finish."

Without so much as a glance behind him, he swung one leg into the painting.

Raman charged up behind him. Lord Malrec turned halfway round to face him, disdain in every line of his face, and his eyes widened in disbelief when he saw that Raman's sword was still drawn.

Still leveled at his middle.

Raman ran the sword through Lord Malrec's gut, and right out the other side.

"That," he panted raggedly, "is for the family I haven't got any more."

Lord Malrec grunted, pain clouding his face, as he hung there part in the painting and part out. "It seems I — underestimated you."

Malrec curled inward, unable to stand straight against the pain, and Raman saw a metallic glint at his collar; a twinkle of polished brass that formed a familiar shape.

"I should have known," Raman said. He grabbed the key on its silken cord and hauled it over Malrec's head. "I think this might prove useful, Lady Alannys." He tossed the key back to the doorway where she stood.

Lord Malrec's eyes wandered over and locked on her. He managed a ghastly, sickly smile, disturbing on his pale waxy face. "You can't win," he gasped. "The songs — are gone. You — are no Redeemer. And when — you are shown false — your precious king will fall."

He summoned his remaining strength, and pushed himself into the painting behind him.

They all rushed forward, peering into the painting.

Lord Malrec lay dead, sprawled gracelessly on the broken flagstones, Raman's sword buried in his middle, his velvet cloak fluttering around him in a breeze they could not feel.

♫

For a long moment, nobody moved. Nobody spoke. Nobody breathed. The castle burned around them; smoke laced the air even in the study, and Alannys could hear the distant crackle of flames. But they stood there, grimly regarding what remained of Lord Malrec.

Alannys felt her hands begin to shake. "Is it...is it over?"

Her voice shook, too.

Dorramon slipped his arm around her shoulders. "It is. It's over. The Dark Alliance is through."

"Lord Malrec is through," Raman said, and Alannys couldn't tell if he was agreeing with Dorramon, or correcting him. "But then, so are we. He was right; the songs are gone."

"What?" Alannys felt the blood drain from her face, leaving her dizzy and unsteady on her face. "No. No, there's no way. He was bluffing!"

Raman waved a hand at the corridor. "The library is on fire. You said yourself the songs were there."

"They were, but—surely Lord Malrec would have moved them before setting a trap like that. Surely *someone* would have moved them!"

Raman shook his head. "I saw music on the library table, just before the fire started. That had to be the songs. I'm sorry, Alannys. If only I'd acted quicker—thought it through better—I could have saved them."

She stared at him, uncomprehending. Gone? The songs of the Redeemer were...gone? *Destroyed?*

Alannys never made any conscious decision to move—one minute she was listening to Raman calmly explain that everything she needed to prove her own legitimacy—and save Dorramon—had gone up in smoke in front of him...

...and the next minute she was gone, shaking off Dorramon's arm and running in blind, unreasoning panic out of the study and into the hallway.

The library, down at the end of the hall, was a blazing inferno. Out here, the crackle and hiss of flames were loud, louder than she could have imagined. The ceiling, the wooden supports, the tapestries—everything was burning, and the fire was spreading. She stared into the harsh, dancing light, without really seeing it, registered the heat on her skin without really feeling it.

"Alannys!" The frantic voice belonged to Dorramon, and so, she assumed, did the strong hands that caught her under the arms and hauled her to her feet. When had she fallen on her knees? "Alannys, what are you doing? Have you gone mad?"

Maybe, she thought. Part of her mind actually considered it, objectively, distractedly, as though everything around her wasn't going to hell, in a hell of a hurry.

Going to hell in a hell of a hurry. She liked that. It had a ring to it. And thinking about that right now probably meant that she *was* crazy. She wanted to scream.

What actually came out of her mouth sounded more like a moan, or a long, mourning sob. "The songs..."

"There isn't time to worry about that now." The words were sharp, and they hadn't come from Dorramon. She found Raman on her other side, looking at her as sharply as he'd just spoken. "This place is falling down around us. We have to get out of here."

Alannys nodded, but made to move to leave. She watched the library burn—all of those many thousands of books going up in smoke—and she wondered which of the ashes in the air had come from the songs of the Redeemer. Her songs.

"Seven Hells," Dorramon snapped. "She's gone again. Raman, help me."

They each took hold of one of her arms, and without waiting for any further comment from her, Dorramon and Raman hustled her back out of the hallway, away from the destruction of the legacy that should have been hers.

♫

Alannys staggered back towards the study, propped between her two friends, not quite able to put her feet down and determine her own direction. Maybe the feet below her now were someone else's feet. It certainly would explain why she was so clumsy on them.

The flickering light of the fire in the study spilled cheerfully across the room, but it wasn't enough to raise her mood. It felt like a muted echo of the destruction raging in the library. Alannys felt her spirits dragging, each step coming harder than the last. Despair hung in the air like old smoke. Sure, they had defeated Lord Malrec, but Lord Diabon and Baron Prubard still had the armies of the Dark Alliance, and the Great Palace was still under attack, with the rest of her friends inside. The songs of the Redeemer were gone, and in the end Lord Malrec *was* right—if people decided she was a false Redeemer, neither she nor Dorramon would have any future here. Yes, Lord Malrec was dead, but by destroying the songs, he had destroyed them all.

Alannys stumbled along between the others across the room, and suddenly stopped cold.

"The painting—it's gone. And what's that?" she demanded, breaking free and heading for the big polished desk.

Dorramon and Raman stopped in the doorway to the art room, looking back at her. "What's what?" Dorramon asked. He sounded wary, the way she might have sounded talking to a maniac who'd just run out into a fire.

Alannys picked up the sword laying across the top of the desk. It took both hands to lift it—this sword was nowhere near as light as Songstrike. Dried blood streaked the blade.

"That's my sword," Raman said. "How did that get in here?"

Alannys shook her head. "I'm sure I don't know. Last time I saw it, Lord Malrec was skewered on it. Does this mean Malrec isn't dead? Is he here?"

"No," Dorramon said immediately. "No, there's no way. He was dead, absolutely dead. Someone else brought that back."

"I'm not sure I like that any better, actually," Raman said. He took the sword from Alannys, and hunted around for a cloth to clean the blade. "It feels threatening. How do we know who did this and why?"

Alannys looked back down at the desk. "I think I can answer that," she said. "There are some papers here—the sword was on top of them. There's a note on top of the stack." She picked up the hand-scrawled scrap of paper, and began to read it aloud.

To our Most Esteemed Redeemer and her Royal Companions,

Thank you for giving justice to Lord Malrec. He treated Princess Delline bad, wrong as he could. In the end he gave her a death she didn't deserve.

He deserved his.

As thanks I left you with your lives, and this small token. Use it well, in the time you got left. Winds of change are beginning to blow, and the power of the few shall soon come to the many. And when it does, neither King nor Redeemer shall long last.

—Creft

P.S. Best tell your friends in the hall to watch it—there's men waiting to ambush them from behind.

Alannys frowned, considering the abrupt change in tone at the end of the note. It almost didn't even sound like Creft anymore. It almost sounded like...Elossa.

How was that even possible?

"Small token?" Raman echoed. Alannys looked up and saw that he had managed to find a cloth after all. "Is that my sword?"

"No," she said, pushing aside her unsettling concerns. "Not that it wasn't nice of him to return it, but I think his token of gratitude was this."

She scooped the papers off the desk and held them out for the others to see. Music, written in brightly colored inks, danced across the ancient pages. In contrast to every other piece of written music she had seen, these had titles carefully lettered across the tops.

"The Song of Raising," said one.

"The Song of Joining," said the other.

♪

In the art room, they found a painting of the bedroom in Alannys's chambers. She knew the painting had to exist —she remembered all too well the night Lord Malrec had used it—but it still gave her a turn to see it. The painting waited on the easel just inside the door, with a jar of gloss and a paintbrush conveniently set out beside it.

"This apprentice," Dorramon said, "is awfully helpful, for all his threats."

"Of course," Raman said, taking up the gloss and the brush. "Malrec meant to kill him. We probably saved his life."

"Perhaps," Dorramon said, frowning as the painting shimmered to life in front of them. "Still, he's been helping

Lord Malrec for weeks to try to kill us all. And he doesn't seem to hold any love for us. It seems suspicious. What if this painting is a trap?"

Raman started to set the gloss aside, then corked the jar and pocketed it instead. "I agree he doesn't much like us. But it doesn't matter. The painting is Alannys's room — there's no way he could trap that; a painting has to go where it shows, right? And what choice do we have, anyway? We can use his painting and be back at the Great Palace in less time than it takes to talk about it. Or we can go out to the stables, find some horses and start riding, and get back two days from now, too late to help with whatever is going on there. And he still has two days to take us out before we make it back."

Dorramon sighed. "I suppose you're right. There's nothing for it but to trust the painting. But I can't shake the feeling this fellow is up to something."

Raman, showing none of the reservations that plagued the king, stepped into the sparkling painting and disappeared.

Alannys stepped closer to Dorramon. "Maybe I'm just paranoid," she said. "But I have the exact same feeling."

Winds of change are beginning to blow... She could see the words in her mind, scrawled across the page in Creft's blocky handwriting, the words that seemed a bit too eloquent, somehow, to really be his.

...neither King nor Redeemer shall long last.

Castle Glennayre was burning down around her. She knew that. But Alannys thought of those words, and she shivered.

Dorramon seemed to feel much the same, watching her with worry clouding his blue eyes. "Still, we've come this far. And the battle isn't over yet. We have to keep going; we have to finish."

"You're right." She blew out her cheeks — he was right.

"Onward we go, then."

"Together."

She met his gaze and smiled. "Yes. Together. To the very end."

He took her hand, and together they put their doubts aside, and stepped into the icy void between worlds.

Sandra Miller

Don't miss the exciting continuation of Alannys's story:

The Ravanmark Saga
Book Four

*A*cts of the *R*edeemer

*Wi*th the death of Lord Malrec, Alannys and her friends have turned the tide of civil war in Ravanmark in their favor. And yet, there is no time to relax. The rest of the Dark Alliance continues to fight. Cadenda comes calling, bringing the promise of war to enforce Dorramon's engagement. And from the shadows, an even larger threat emerges. Strange, inflammatory rhetoric sweeps the nation, and even the stalwart Royal Guard can no longer be trusted.

*Bu*t how can Alannys defend against a menace she can't even see?

As the movement to 'take the power of the few to the many' continues to grow, and opposition to her swells stronger than ever, Alannys turns to the one thing that can prove her beyond a doubt—or destroy her beyond any recovery—the Acts of the Redeemer.

*Jo*in Alannys and her friends again as they embark on an epic journey to save Ravanmark--and themselves.

Sandra Miller